THE LET

Marina Warner's fiction includes *Indigo*, *The Lost Father* (winner of a Commonwealth Writers' Prize and shortlisted for the Booker Prize), as well as a collection of stories, *Mermaids in the Basement*. Among her acclaimed studies of myth and fairy tale are *Alone Of All Her Sex*, *Monuments and Maidens*, *From the Beast to the Blonde*, *No Go the Bogeyman* and *Managing Monsters* (the 1994 Reith Lectures on BBC Radio). She has recently been a Getty Scholar, and a Visiting Fellow Commoner at Trinity College, Cambridge. She has also been appointed a Chevalier de l'Ordre des Arts et des Lettres by the French Government.

Marina Warner

THE LETO BUNDLE

V

VINTAGE

Published by Vintage 2002

2 4 6 8 10 9 7 5 3 1

Copyright © Marina Warner 2001

Marina Warner has asserted her right under the Copyright,
Designs and Patents Act 1988 to be identified as the author of
this work

First published in Great Britain by
Chatto & Windus 2001

Vintage
Random House, 20 Vauxhall Bridge Road,
London SW1V 2SA

Random House Australia (Pty) Limited
20 Alfred Street, Milsons Point, Sydney
New South Wales 2061, Australia

Random House New Zealand Limited
18 Poland Road, Glenfield, Auckland 10,
New Zealand

Random House (Pty) Limited
Endulini, 5A Jubilee Road, Parktown 2193,
South Africa

The Random House Group Limited Reg. No. 954009
www.randomhouse.co.uk

A CIP catalogue record for this book
is available from the British Library

ISBN 0 09 928465 0

Papers used by Random House are natural, recyclable
products made from wood grown in sustainable forests.
The manufacturing processes conform to the environ-
mental regulations of the country of origin

Text design by Peter Ward

Printed and bound in Great Britain by
Bookmarque Ltd, Croydon, Surrey

FOR IRÈNE, BELOVED FRIEND

CONTENTS

PROLOGUE

In the customs depot on the airfield in Shiloh, several crates were padlocked behind chainlink fences in a single pen. Bonded goods, perishable and hazardous materials, special interest cargoes to declare, valuables and treasures of all kinds were stored there, randomly, awaiting clearance; although the containers wore precise dockets, labels of provenance and destination, and many warning notices in HAZCHEM liveries of red, black, and yellow, most kept their contents secret. Doctor Hortense Fernly could pick out the bulky, well-buttressed pine crate that she was conducting; she was pleased to see that it had been placed right side up. Near it, through the bars of the small windows on either side of a special airfreight box, the eye of a racehorse could be glimpsed, and a groom was standing close up against the wire: 'There there, my beauty, there there,' he was cooing. 'Don't fret, it won't be long now.' He made soft sounds against his teeth and the mare heaved and stamped in response, but quietly, as if familiar with the wait in her constricted quarters. And in a corner of the shed, a widow keened quietly through the wire over the coffin of her husband.

Hortense Fernly was a museum curator, the deputy keeper of Classical Antiquities at the National Museum of Albion. When she was at work in the building, she kissed an electronic scanner with the special card round her neck to gain access through nuclear-proof steel doors to the vaults where the most precious objects, paintings, sculptures and documents were kept. But treasures were unpredictable these days: no longer dragons' hoards of precious stones, shooting such bright lights they lit up their hiding place, no longer verdigris'd doubloons spilling from crocks of pirates in concealed coves of palm-fringed islands. Hortense had colleagues who exulted over a chipped badge from a failed protest movement or the end of a roll of film in a rusty can; meanwhile the salerooms were full of luxuries and souvenirs – celebrity relics, preferably hauled from the site of a shipwreck, or the bedroom of a suicide. In her field of expertise treasures were usually broken and lustreless: potsherds, moth-casings of papyri, tatters of painted linen. She might find, in a tray of rubble, the single, crooked piece of elbow that solved a shattered marble figure's pose, or the fragment with a speech from one of a great tragedian's lost plays. The vital bit that changed the picture might look, at first, like nothing at all.

In one corner of the depot, the widow was hugging herself, though it wasn't especially cold; now and then, with an impatient movement of her head, she walked up to the fence and stared hard at the coffin.

'That's my husband in there,' she announced to the air, and paced back as far as she could, taking up her post against the wall. 'Keeled over in the hotel shower,' she wailed. 'I was always telling him, Herb, you should cut down on these trips. But he wouldn't listen, and then he has to go and die over there and they put him in this damned ugly box. I can't wait to get him out of it. I want a nice one, white with brass handles. I told them that was what I wanted.'

Nobody responded; they kept their distance from her grief, and this drew the rest of them a little closer. One man, in a slim-cut, light-coloured and crumpled suit, with expensive trainers, took out a pen like a jeweller's punch and began tapping the keypad on a pocket calculator. Another found an empty packing case and sat down: Tom Bampton, also known, on account of his pallor and thinness, as TB, was waiting to clear Gramercy Poule's stacks of electronic equipment for her tour. Taking out a copy of a music magazine, he waved it in the direction of Hortense, who was flexing her knees to get the circulation going after the flight. She was small and neatly made, in a dark maroon skirt cut from a surprising lavishness of soft cloth, over espadrilles she'd worn for the flight but were still pinching her swollen feet. She came over, shook her head at his offer of the magazine; he understood, and offered her the packing case instead with a mock bow; she accepted.

'Are you an old hand at this?' she asked him. Her eyes were sore-rimmed from the dry air inside the plane; she blinked hard to moisten them.

He shrugged. 'This is routine. I've seen volatile medical supplies worth millions – standing out in the heat while some puffed-up arsehole keeps everyone sweating. I've waited next to dodgy doctors who wouldn't say what they were carrying in that special refrigerated cabinet: a liver? An expensive kidney or two?' He was whispering, and eyed the man in the pale suit speculatively. 'No endangered species here today – sometimes there's parrots, caymans, even one time a rhino. Huge great beast. Crossing the world to breed. "Handsome, intelligent, white, successful rhino, likes classical music and Cajun cooking, looking for a long-term relationship with like-minded rhino partner – no beauty, but must be under twenty-five years old." What've you got in there?'

'Art.'

'Oh right – Old Master?'

'Not exactly.' Hortense Fernly looked at TB with surprise – she'd rather expected less animation from the starveling young man. 'I'm a museum curator. In fact I'm also escorting a body – oh my god.' She began to laugh behind her hand, then looked shamefaced at the newly widowed woman hugging the wall. 'Oh, why am I laughing? Stop it, Hetty,' she said to herself. 'It must be the jet lag. Or the bad air. They say they thin the oxygen to save fuel.' She overcame her fit and answered, calm now: 'I'm accompanying a mummy – and she's very very old.'

'Very Gothic,' said TB. 'How old?'

'We don't really know – the tomb was carved around eighteen hundred years ago – but the rest . . . We don't treat it as a corpse, of course, not as a person . . .' She hesitated. There had been difficulties over taking it out of the country for the travelling exhibition. She changed the subject. 'What are you carrying?'

'Electronics.' He gestured at a stack of matt black, chrome-cleated boxes. 'Gramercy Poule's touring. Six cities in a week. Or that's what it'll feel like.'

'Gramercy Poule?' Hortense echoed him.

'You must've heard of her—' he paused. 'It's a three week tour, more like.'

'Pop music isn't exactly my area of expertise.'

'Not pop. Folk rock.'

'Like . . . Joni Mitchell?' At his silence, she hesitated. 'Does that date me?'

TB paused again. 'Naw. Gram wouldn't like it, but you're not so far off the mark. Gramercy Poule was really big ten years ago – she sings high, too.' He warbled, '"Peeeoople like you . . ."' Think Kate Bush. No? Well. I'm her roadie, and it's always toothcomb time for us with customs. They think, Drugs, sex 'n' rock 'n' roll. This airport's especially uptight. Fucking nuisance, they've seen too many hard guys on TV and they like to swagger a bit and push you around. So who's in the box, then?'

Hortense Fernly hadn't spoken to anyone since her special charge was, as it were, smuggled out of the Museum. The man in the seat beside her on the flight had been intent on his special dietary needs, which were elaborate and involved prayers, and she didn't want to talk at all, let alone about the problems.

'Gramercy's a singer-songwriter,' TB went on. 'With an agitprop edge. Not, absolutely not, a pop star. She'd savage you for thinking it. Go on, who's the body?'

Hortense took a breath and answered: 'We've always called her "Helen", because the cartonnage – the face mask – is very beautiful. We don't really know – there are other stories. It's the sarcophagus she's buried in that's the real treasure – and the mask. She's just a bundle of old bandages. But Greek, and very late Greek at that.' She hesitated again, then plunged on. 'We had some trouble taking her out of the country, in fact. There was a protest. A rather noisy protest.'

From TB's saddlebag came a light squeal. He fished inside and answered the phone.

'Monica?'

' . . . '

'Yeah, everything's excellent. We're just waiting for clearance.'

' . . . '

'No, no boa constrictors this time. Just the usual. A racehorse and . . .' He lowered his voice. 'Two corpses. How's Gram doing?'

' . . . '

'Excellent. "The village shop is selling organic tofu." ' He glanced over at Hortense, who looked away, but smiled, too. 'Wow – wish I could be there. Tofu *and* blackberries! Most likely I'll do room service and the mini-bar tonight. But we'll have this lot set up by tomorrow at the latest. And I'll make sure your rooms at the Clairmont are OK as soon as I've checked in.'

4

'. . .'

'No, nothing exciting, no bullet holes, no men in black looking us over. Just a museum curator and her mummy. How's things with you?'

'. . .'

'Yeah?'

'. . .'

'Maybe it is.'

More silence as he listened.

He looked across at Hortense. 'There was a protest, you said?'

She nodded.

'All right, I'll ask her.'

'You're escorting the Leto Bundle?'

'Yes,' said Hortense, with a funny kick inside, of pride and of apprehension. 'People do seem to be calling it that.'

'I'll see if I can find out more,' said TB. 'Cheers.' He switched off and stowed his phone.

PART ONE

Lycania
('The Letoniast Version')

I

A Grainy Blue Egg

[G: Skipwith 673.1841: Misc. Mss. G. Fr. 17, papyrus, c. 325–350 CE, translation in the hand of Hereward Meeks, keeper of Near Eastern Antiquities, 1858–76.]

Leto licked the girl's head, working with her tongue at the flakes of albumen on the scalp, where Phoebe's scant hair, so fine it seemed gossamer, was wadded together. The savour was whey-like, saline, and came at her taste buds in starbursts, as strong as sherbet, and as surprising, so much more powerful than the tiny forms of her twin babies. She swallowed, but her throat was dry; it was difficult to make the saliva flow. Here and there, her tongue discovered a speck of shell, and she crunched it, lightly, hoping the calcium might replenish her sapped forces a little. The twins had been entwined as one and hidden inside her; now there they were, two of them, miraculously entities, separate, different from one another, a boy and a girl, lying beside her. She was not prepared for their neediness. Shell and bone, albumen, lymph and milk: could the three of them survive by exchanges of their substance, their fluids, their flesh?

The pelican might peck her own breast till the blood flowed into the open beaks of her young, or so her own wet nurse had told her, voluptuously, when Leto was a little girl and her nurse was dreaming of founding dynasties. Leto had laughed, but inwardly she thought the pelican sacrificed herself to excess and folly – a weakened or dead mother was no good to anyone. Surely there were sounder strategies for survival – the little sea-mouse lifts the thick eyelashes of the whale so that

9

it can see where it is going, and in return is allowed to ride on the whale's back and share its feeding grounds; the tiny toothpicker fish that swims into the jaws of huge ocean predators and cleans their triple rows of teeth, feeds on parasites swarming in the host's gums and so staves off rottenness and toothache for its host, so the shark or stingray or whatever realises where its best interests lie and does not snap, but lets the small fry prosper. This was how she would adapt, how she would struggle and survive.

When Leto was flying from her lover, and the god, now man, now dove, now fish, now hawk, was pursuing her, they had skimmed and swooped over the surface of the water together in their long, hard duel, and it was when his strong wings had beaten to enfold her and his extended neck had gripped her and his soft silken breast had pressed her to the ground under him that she had opened to him; and conceived. Her children were born of saltwater, of marshland and reedbeds and the tang of the mist hanging in the fringed river where it ran into the sea. Given their origins, they could have taken on the scales and fins of fish, or the claws of raptors; she was glad that they looked like babies and their peculiar hatching could be concealed. Who would know that her twin children had no navels? That no bud of flesh peeped stickily from the infants' taut, chestnut-smooth, domed tummies? That there had been no umbilical cord for her hatchlings?

When she had made a small improvement to the girl's head, she turned to the boy, to loosen the rime on his narrower head, and longer, even more fragile and lighter limbs. She worked her teeth and tongue to make saliva, and succeeded in bringing some spittle to her swollen lips. He had a kink at the apex of his left ear where he'd been bunched up against something inside her; both babies had three crowns on their scalps as if their skulls had been doodled on by a creator dreaming of shells: the usual central whorl, another at the peak of the forehead, and another behind the ear, the left again on the boy's head, the right on the girl's.

The babies' salty natal flesh might give her meagre nourishment but could not quench her, only exacerbate her thirst. Yet the sight, the feel, the smell of the twins made something inside her leap brokenly, the slow legato of her normal breathing had been jolted into a wild rhythm, and she was whirling to it.

Where was she? Under the bent scant tree which, of all the spirits on earth, had agreed to give her shelter, on the stones that had answered her implorations, in a parched wilderness that had accepted her when she begged for an end to her flight; condemned every one to barrenness, they had defied the goddess's vengeance. 'What can your enemy do to me?' asked the tree. 'I've not fruited since the day the seed that bore me caught in the cracks between the stones.'

'What can she do to us now?' cried the rocks. 'We were once girls who talked of men and hoped for love, but she noticed our beauty and she struck us into this shape. She can do us no more harm, and so, Leto, accept us, as your resting place, a temporary mooring.'

'The goddess can do nothing to me,' said the wilderness. 'I shall spite her, and receive you and your offspring. I don't begrudge you their brightness, their juiciness. You have brought me a memory of sap, from long ago.'

After the clandestine closeness of the last months inside her, her own hot, tight secret, their new separateness from her gave her a sense of deep exile, of estrangement from her own self.

That girl, *that* boy, *those* babies. They were dazzling her: silver flashes in her eyes, gold mischief in his.

Setting the boy down in his cotton wrap on the ground, she lifted the scrap of tunic the little girl was wound in, to look at her body; it was smeary and wrinkled, the limbs very thin and purplish-red, with dark down streaked here and there. She bent her head to the infant body again and gently plied her tongue over the parts that still seemed caked in the dried fluids of the albumen sac. Leto felt her daughter squirm with pleasure in response, and all of a sudden, the baby flexed her limbs, her legs and arms working together in a quick, surprisingly gymnastic movement. As she did so, she opened her eyes: the silvery flash again, a moonbow against the newborn's slate black iris, with its blueish bloom.

She'd pushed hard: a grainy blue egg. Huge relief from a load followed, as after a bout of constipation.

Now she was drifting into sleep, but fitfully. The small fists of the baby, kneading at her breast, woke her; the boy beside her was mewling, too small to wail more loudly than a kitten. She sat up, bundling her scraps of clothing under them to support their small bodies, and arranged them in her lap. They were only mites, but she was too weak to bear their weight in her arms while they fed. Her breasts were hard from the milk, and the infants' tiny hard gums closed on her flow, clamped tightly as seashells to rock as the tide rises.

And she was rank as a hyena now; she must find water. Water, food, shelter, but water, above all.

2

Protest in the Museum

The catalogue entry for National Museum of Albion, Accession Number
G: Skipwith 673.1841, reads as follows:

'Cartonnage, gilded and painted, high relief, glass eyes and braided wig.
Mummified body inside wrapped in coffering style of weave. Linen,
papyrus, horsehair, glass, ?human remains, c. 425–475 CE. Found in
sarcophagus with sphinxes rampant at four corners, lotus flowers in bas-
relief on sides, lid with scene of Bacchic frenzy? Nativity scene?
Alabaster. Extensive damage to exterior carving. Probably from a Greek
workshop in ?Alexandria, c. 250–275 CE. [G: Skipwith 674.1841]

'Mummy: 157.5 × 52 × 48 cm (5'2" × 1'10 $\frac{1}{2}$" × 1'7"); sarcophagus:
192 × 109 × 86.5 (6'3" × 3'7" × 2'10").

'Found in niche 153 of columbarium 7, south-west passage, Lycania,
by Sir Giles Skipwith, 26 April 1841.'

Room XIX lay off the main display of classical sculpture, and did not
lead on to another major section of the Museum's collections, so it was
never as crowded as those high-vaulted rooms where the centrepieces
numbered among them original Wonders of the World, and even that
Grecian urn, on which the passions of pursuit are stilled and the rule of
metamorphosis overturned. Just before the doorway of Room XIX, two
maenads were thrashing in ecstasy, tearing a doe limb from limb, their
frenzy defying the chill inertia of the Parian marble from which they had
been carved. Like demon guardians of the threshold, they scared off

visitors to the chamber. Besides, having reached this point in the museum, the visitor would have already walked the length of several ancient civilisations, surveyed carvings on wide entablatures and solid mausolea, and gazed long on giant gods of basalt with smashed noses, and curious creatures of pink granite, endowed with special powers in certain vital areas – book-keeping, midwifery, floods and famine. Listening to the Museum's Acoustiguide, even the keenest might be sated by chronicles of the blood sports of dead kings and thirsty from contact with deserts that had yielded up treasures from their dry and stony wastes. Moreover, Room XIX was positioned at right angles to the new café, where coffee was offered in various pungent combinations of froth and bitterness, with twists of sugar in designer papers and free-to-sprinkle nutmeg, chocolate or cinnamon from casters on the cutlery counter.

So it came as a surprise when the number of visitors to Room XIX began to grow.

The room did not have its own dedicated guard; he or she perambulated from the more frequented adjacent rooms to supervise it, now and then. So it was Pilar, one of the cleaners on the early morning shift, who noticed the change, though she did not feel it necessary at first to report that dustballs were collecting in the corners. This was a familiar sign, instantly legible to her and the troop of women trundling round their laden carts of mops and brooms and bin liners, that human traffic had increased; after a blockbuster show had drawn its daily record-breaking attendance, the crowds would have left behind them – especially in winter when they were wrapped up in woollens and tweeds – a tideline of hair and flakes of skin and lint, making a slut's wool, a mortal rime of leavings, which the cleaners would sweep up as best they could. They weren't allowed to damp it down, because such a procedure would affect the humidity and temperature controls, and they did not use vacuum cleaners but gave the floors a weekly polish with powered revolving brushes that seemed to whirl their handlers about the rooms like dodgems. A fair amount of the human spoor escaped trapping. But Pilar also found, a few days after the dustballs began to gather, offerings of flowers and even a photograph and a message or two tucked under the laminated label on the wall ('Anonymous Female, known as "Helen", c. 425–475 CE; Sarcophagus, c. 250–275 CE'), as well as fastened

– with hairgrips and chewing gum and other means – to the cords around the sarcophagus and its inmate.

Pilar told one of her fellow cleaners in their canteen afterwards, 'Like prayer,' she said. 'In my country, that's what we do when a child is sick . . . ' She took out a snapshot from the pocket of her overalls, with a message on ruled paper torn from a notepad in big letters.

Her team worker, Eileen, who was nearer home in Enoch than Pilar and could read besides, did so: 'HOMELESS LADY YOU KIND GIV ME WERK.' The photograph showed a woman, shadowed by a headscarf.

'Looks religious, mind,' Eileen commented. 'I don't see eye to eye with that stuff, not since what the holy fathers did to my Timmy . . .' She accepted another scrap from Pilar, and read: '"Dear Lady of Scattered People, please find me shelter." That's more like it.'

Pilar's eyes flickered at the words. She handed Eileen another message, this time densely inked in a fluent, tightly controlled script.

Eileen turned it around. 'It's in one of those back-to-front languages.' And she chuckled.

One of the guards, overhearing the two cleaning ladies, came up. He suggested reporting the rise in visitors and their peculiar offerings.

But the gearing of security at the National Museum is very precise and deeply considered, and changes are undertaken with caution. So by the time something was being done, much more than the appointment of a single guard to Room XIX was needed. A rota of the most experienced wardens was appointed to the task of guarding the sarcophagus, which stood free on a dais, and the mummy, which was positioned upright in a glass case beside it. A double cordon to keep the queue orderly was arranged, extending from Skipwith 673 to the maenads and beyond them into the next room, and a notice was put up: 'Please do not touch the exhibits. Even the lightest fingermark can damage works of art.'

In spite of the wardens' new vigilance, someone had managed to deface this sign, and 'LADY' was written in large capitals over 'the exhibits', while other words had been struck out and 'our holy mother' inserted so that the notice now read, 'Please do not touch the lady. Even the lightest mark can damage our holy mother'.

Someone had also added, in lime green highlighter, the word ASYLUM. And the fingermarks on the glass case began to need extra supplies of cleaning spray each morning.

'Helen', as the cartonnage mask of Skipwith 673 had come to be called, was attracting so much public attention to the hitherto neglected Room XIX of the National Museum because she was specially featured on the new CD-ROM issued by the Museum's Department of Outreach: Events and Marketing. The software itself was on sale for a sum far too large for most schools, even after the government's special funds for computer learning, but much of the material it contained could be accessed on the Museum's website at http://www.natmus.enoch.uk. which schoolchildren were encouraged to visit.

There, the first item under 'The Ancient World', 'Helen' appeared, revolving slowly to the softly spoken question, enunciated by a fluent, pleasing voice well known from money-spinning privatisation campaigns of public utilities on the telly:

'Is this the face that launched a thousand ships
And burned the topmost towers of Ilium?'

The full trapezoid head, with a thin gold fillet lightly laid on heavy braids, came to a standstill on the screen, facing forward as the camera approached closer, until the caramel-coloured glass eyes in the gilded and painted face seemed to flicker with light and the vermilion lips to be poised to part. A gold bead necklace encircled the woman's neck; a small tubular capsule of silver was attached by a brooch to lie across to her breast.

'No,' another voice picked up, purposely contemporary, even chilled out, in style. 'But Helen might well have looked like this beautiful woman, who died aged around twenty-eight years old and was buried in a family grave in ancient Lycania.'

The picture flipped over, and a view of an archaeological site replaced 'Helen': not the usual sun-baked boneyard of stony ruins, but the rim of dark wet walls poking through reeds and grasses, as if a hulk lay rotting there. A red arrow floated over the image, and pointed to a position; then, like a smart bomb nosing out its target, the camera dipped under ground, travelled bumpily down a dark passage in the earth and entered a chamber, then rose up into a runnelled, subterranean cavern, where dozens of empty dark ledges were piled one above the other. The arrow reappeared, danced over the image, and pointed again.

'Here lay Helen, in her alabaster tomb, miraculously sealed from light and air and water, for over a millennium, until the Victorian archaeologist, Sir Giles Skipwith, saved her from historical neglect and the ravages of wind and weather.'

'Helen' now reappeared full-length, and began to spin slowly in space. The first voice resumed the commentary, as it now took a scientific turn, itself spinning details of CAT scans and carbon dating and other technical analyses that had been performed on the mummy. As it enumerated them, Helen gradually shed her bandages. Or at least the mummy did. First centrifugal diagrams of bones and blood vessels and nervature radiated from the body and vanished off the edge of the screen, then, as these disincarnate Helens were expelled, she gradually began to cohere in living colour and move towards the viewer. She was dressed in 'a simple linen shift' and her face was 'high cheek-boned, full-lipped, her complexion dark and her real hair, under the elaborate wig, was found to be scanty ... The cause of death was acute vitamin deficiency, probably caused by a succession of failed harvests in the harsh area and by successive childbearing.'

The realised portrait, computer-generated from the data pulled from the effigy by tomography, 'the same methods used today to diagnose tumours', hung on the screen as if in space. It did not look like a photograph of a person. For one thing, the colours were discordant and artificial, forged on the palette of digitalised imagery; for another, 'Helen' was semi-transparent, spectral. But she loomed nonetheless, as if three-dimensional and viewed in the round, and her face, lingering in close up, looked as if it belonged to someone who was there, mute, but breathing.

An advertising company, newly appointed to represent the National Museum at a time of controversy over admission charges, elitism, and relevance, viewed the CD-ROM and then chose this picture of 'Helen' to give the venerable institution a new image. In order to promote thousands of national treasures stewarded by the Museum, 'Helen' floated into households nationwide on the envelopes of a million cold mailings; she appeared on the monitors of computers in schools, universities, cybercafés and on domestic PCs with e-mail. And the numbers of visitors to Room XIX began to grow to see for themselves the 'Anonymous Female, c. 425–475 CE'.

So the day that the customary queue formed at the Museum doors before opening time and, on reaching Room XIX, found that G.

Skipwith 673.1841 was not there, and that a handwritten notice pinned beside the identifying label informed the public that it had been removed for exhibition abroad, there was widespread frustration, and, in pockets, anger.

On the first day, this took the form of a stunned, mournful drifting around the vacated rostrum where the tomb and the glass case had stood; then one woman in a salwar kameez placed her votive offering beside it just the same, and with a little girl, around five years old, who unlike her was wearing jeans and a fleecy zipped-up jacket, squatted down on the floor.

'You can't sit there,' said the guard. The visitor scrambled to her feet, pulling her daughter with her.

'Why not?' A young man pushed his way to her side and taking her by the shoulders pressed the woman down on to the Museum parquet again. He turned to the guard. 'Why has Helen been taken away? Why was there no prior warning? Where is she now?' Kim McQuy dropped down on to the floor. 'I want to see someone. Some of us have taken time off work to come and visit her, some of us have travelled far, we've paid our admission and we want to see what we came to see.' His tone wasn't aggressive, but authoritative; he had a way of hitting certain words with an edgy emphasis that their meaning didn't altogether warrant. The effect was more threatening than he intended, and a general murmur of relief that someone had taken charge greeted his words. Several others in the queue sat down, too; the floor space was filling up.

The two guards retreated to a corner, and, turning their backs on the gathering, began to push buttons on their walkie-talkies and mutter.

Kim McQuy sprang to his feet: 'That's right,' he called out. 'You tell them we're waiting. We're here and we want some action round here.'

Everyone laughed, but it was a chilly, frightened shiver of a sound.

A young woman, with bleached hair, a nose-ring and a stud in her eyebrow, peered closer at the temporary notice of removal by the label. 'It's signed by H—something Fernly.' She spelled out the first name: 'H-O-R-T-E-N-S-E'.

More guards came running into the room.

'Hang on,' called one of them. 'You can't just sit down like that. This is a museum. There is seating elsewhere if you want to sit. You've got to circulate.'

The protestors shifted, but no one rose.

'If you won't come willingly, we'll have to use force.' This guard, clearly a veteran of TV police dramas, caused general mutterings, still a little frightened in temper.

'I'm warning you,' he continued. 'I'll have you arrested.'

One or two of the visitors responded uneasily and sidled out. The guard nodded approval.

'Let's get this Dr Fernly,' one of the sitters-in whispered.

'Doctor Fernly! Doctor Fernly!' The chant went up. 'We want Helen back, we want Our Lady back!' The rhythm of their shouts grew more rapid as the voices gathered in unison, accompanied to beating on their bags and other possessions: 'Helen, Helen. Bring her back! Bring her back!'

The Museum director, informed of the trouble in Room XIX, looked at the surveillance screens in the security room, saw a gaggle of women, children and youths of what appeared to be various nationalities, and decided to come down in person. He was a new appointment, with a background in international trade fairs, and he prided himself on his social skills and person management. He told his staff to keep calm, to chat nicely with the demonstrators.

'No panic. I want no one to panic. This is a flash in the pan. Still, just imagine you're in a hostage scenario,' he said. 'Win their trust. Softly softly – that's the way to defuse the situation.'

So there were no more threats or hard language, though some of the guards, returning to their posts in other rooms, were highly indignant, and told journalists off the record that nothing like it had ever happened in the Museum before and would never have been allowed under the old director. 'He would have had them all out by the ears, no messing.'

The television teams who requested permission to film were not allowed in; as there was a general rule against the use of cameras and camcorders, this did not prove difficult to enforce – on the first and second days.

From the core of the early morning that first day, many left to go back to work, Kim McQuy among them; school was starting again the following week and he had to attend the meeting about the cuts to the music programme versus the library. But the general numbers in Room XIX did not dwindle.

On the third day, the press department issued a short statement about 'Helen', and this move made it impossible for them to continue to refuse access to the media, who were soon greatly swelling the crowd in front of the empty dais in Room XIX.

The press release was left in a dispenser at the entrance, near the maenads in their frenzy. It was soon emptied, and photocopies had to be made to replenish it.

'The beauty of the cartonnage has understandably given rise to the popular name for the exhibit, which is known as "Helen". This is of course merely a nickname, since the mask and the mummy were made around 425–475 CE, at least a thousand years after Troy fell. The alabaster tomb, of earlier manufacture, was reused for "Helen's" burial, according to a long tradition of recycling classical artefacts. Many of the caves in Lycania contain the remains of a religious community, which never fully recovered after the ancient sea wall protecting the sanctuary gave way, in 620 CE, and the temple complex was buried in the landslide that followed.

'Sir Giles Skipwith, an eminent scholar and amateur scientist, finding the site neglected and overgrown, undertook excavations in 1839. Digging also revealed an extensive necropolis and other buildings surviving under the silt deposited by the flood. However, the entire complex was damaged by looting by tomb-robbers as well as locals who carried off the marbles to build their villages, their homes and even byres and sheds for livestock. It was not unusual, Skipwith reported, to find a unique bas-relief in use as a manger. In the case of the sarcophagus, it had become a midden, filled with deposits from over a thousand years of changing settlement in the area.

'The temple to the goddess Leto (pronounced LAY-T-OH, and meaning Lady) was especially rich in sculptures, including the tomb (G: Skipwith 674.1841) which depicts an episode from her story.

'With these violations of our international cultural heritage in mind, the Admiralty authorised Sir Giles Skipwith to negotiate terms with the provincial governor of the region and he was granted permission by the Sultan then in power to transport the results of his excavations to the newly founded Royal Museum in 1841. This remarkable group of remains were known as the Leto Marbles, after the dedication of the principal shrine at the site. Skipwith 673 and 674 are only two of these recovered glories. It is unlikely that any of these treasures would have survived if they had been left *in situ*.'

The curious, peering in at the room across the cordon that had been placed at the entrance, asked for the reasons for the news teams' camcorders; many of these, even when the reply was not intelligible to them, joined the hubbub around the vacant dais.

'It's Helen of Troy.'

'No, it's not. Listen to what the man said. He said she's something else.'

'That'd've been a real turn up for the books, fuckin' Helen of Troy.'

'What's her name then?'

'There's this Leto goddess then. Look, that's what the handout says.'

'What kinda name's that?'

'LAY-T-OH, you pronounce it, that's what it says, see. Means "Lady" in her language.'

'No, that's just the name of the outside of her. Not her name. Not of the name of the lady, not of the lady herself.'

'What's a midden?'

'It's the marble's called that.'

'The tomb what she's buried in.'

'We're here for the person, the person inside. Not here for the tomb. Where's she gone?'

'To Shiloh, it says.'

'She shouldn't be travelling all over the place like that.'

Two women sitting on the floor in bird of paradise silks now added lamentation to the protest:

'I want her back.'

'To make *puja* to her.'

'To bury her properly.'

'Yes, to make a shrine to her.'

The young men standing beside them joined in:

'Not everyone gawking at her like this.'

'Gawping at her.'

Someone objected:

'But she's not here.'

Then others all together:

'She was here.'

21

'She should be here.'

'They're gawping at her over there.'

'At the bundle.'

'It was her body was in there.'

'A real body.'

'Her mortal remains.'

'In a fucking museum.'

'A fucking freak show.'

'In frigging Shiloh.'

'Watch your language.'

'Kids around.'

'Nothing they don't know.'

'You lot—'

'Should show more respect.'

'Am showing respect.'

'It's those put her here like as if she wasn't nothing but a stone.'

'A piece of fucking marble.'

'An art work.'

'That's what's fucking dissing her.'

'Watch it, told you to watch it.'

'But she's not here.'

'We want her back here.'

'Yes.'

'Yes! Then we'll lay her to rest, somewhere decent.'

'Give her a bit of peace and quiet.'

'Been a while.'

'At long last.'

All this was heard and recorded when the newspapermen held out their Dictaphones to the group, and the soundmen angled their boom to catch the burden of the protest.

On the fourth day, the morning crowd of around forty people found another sign beside the notice of Temporary Removal. At 11.00 a.m., Dr Hortense Fernly would be giving an illustrated talk, in the Lecture Hall of the Museum.

It was the director's idea: 'I'll introduce you; I'll say something about this glitch. Then you talk for half an hour to forty minutes maximum, and I'll come on again and wind up. You don't have to do the hard part. I'll do that. I'll address the politics. You give exactly the same talk you would give in the ordinary course of events. The history of the piece, of the accession, of its iconography, its relation to other works of this kind.'

'But I can't stand up in front of that kind of a crowd and spout about Hellenistic antiquities.' Hortense was stuttering, as she struggled to extricate herself. 'They're not the usual crowd, ladies who lunch plus a sprinkling of homeless in off the streets for some comfort. They'll get exasperated. And rightly.'

'A detective's coming along to explain various security aspects to you – so that you need have nothing to worry about, and there'll be plain-clothes men in the audience, on the lookout for any real troublemakers. But they're no-hoper types, honestly. Nothing to be afraid of.'

Doctor Fernly was taken to look at the surveillance tapes. The image was microscopic, as if the assembly on the floor of Room XIX was a sample of live bacteria, compacted tightly of various, separate organisms.

She was shown, at pencil point, one figure after another as the detective passed on what he knew.

'Lots of women,' he was saying. 'Females who're just lost for something to believe in. Some male long-term unemployed and their children. Ex-minicab drivers whose cars have been repossessed. First generation failed economic migrants. Second, third generation immigrants. Some in work, but lots of urban flotsam. Single fathers. Kids. No school parties, though.'

Hortense bridled at his tone; she twisted an earring and tugged at it as she tried to concentrate her energies. She didn't know where to begin, to savage his condescension or wail at the director imperturbably throwing her to the wolves. With Daniel away in Shiloh, working, she knew she was treated with faint contempt – however unconsciously. She was either ordered about, or flirted with lugubriously, as if it were rude not to show gallantry to an unattached woman of her age. Because she was small, and neatly made, she sometimes thought she should wear higher heels and harder suits to avert such moments, but the idea of power-dressing irritated her even more, on balance. Daniel was teaching, for lots of money, in a prestige antebellum private school on the other side of the globe near the city where he was born. They'd married so they could live and work together either here or there, but somehow, not having a complete grip on their destinies, like figures on a double spiral stair who pass again and again but never meet, they were both condemned to homesickness for part of the year – when the Museum sent her to accompany one of its treasures, they'd tryst for a weekend, when they'd tiptoe around each other, anxious not to admit to enjoying their separate lives, but consequently depressed by the string of protestations and complaints with which they reassured each other that life apart was miserable.

'Basically we want to bore them,' the director was saying. 'Sorry, Hetty, you know how much I value your work. But it's wasted on them and that's the point. Bore them till they find something else to distract them. Bore them till they leave off this particular passing fad.'

She kept her eyes trained on the monitor. Even at her old university, in the department where one or two of the longer serving members still shuddered in the presence of women, like anchorites in hagiography when the devil tempts them with visions of cloven-hoofed and scented whores, she hadn't been so nakedly patronised.

The detective was tapping the screen where appeared a young man in a suit, with neat dark hair and eyebrows that were sufficiently defined for Hortense to make them out in the fuzz of pixillated greys.

'He fancies himself as a kind of spokesperson – he'll be at your lecture, Dr Fernly, and one of my men – or women – will be keeping a close eye.'

'So what's eating him?' The director was casting about, Hortense noted, for information that would belittle the demonstrators.

'Schoolteacher in Cantelowes.' The detective tossed his head. 'Just up the road from here.' He paused. 'Wasn't born here, as you can see.' Hetty shifted, annoyed, but he went on, fluently. 'Comes from Tirzah. Bit of a gippo, I'd say – that lot from there, usually lighter-skinned. Almost like us.' Hetty opened her mouth to remonstrate, and the director put his hand on her arm as the policeman continued. 'This McQuy (sounds like McKay, by the way, but it's written –' and he wrote the name on a pad – 'has some loopy notion about a New Albion. Leftish, but right of left, you know. The new patriotism. Got into agitation during the Eighties when there was a fair bit of . . . unrest in the colleges. Went to sixth-form college, became a student leader. Then teacher training. He's in his mid-twenties. Talks about cooking a lot, about sugar and garlic and pepper travelling all over the world and belonging everywhere. How we wouldn't be who we are without them.

Claims he's seen in this . . . mm, mummy . . . some kind of figurehead for his ideas.'

Hortense looked at the tiny figure, standing up now, and clearly addressing the crowd. But the tape was silent, and, in the absence of his words, he appeared oddly kinetic, as if his movements were triggered by outside impulses.

'He started HSWU,' the detective continued, writing the initials down on the pad, 'about five years ago. Grew out of his other political involvements. Known as "Zwu". It's a kind of off-the-wall political movement, active only on the web. Not many members, no programme to speak of. We keep an eye on them, but they're not into direct action, not till now, anyhow. Just flannelling away. Stands for "History Starts With Us".'

Hortense looked at Kim McQuy's audience paying attention to him. There were the women in the iridescent folds of fabric sitting cross-legged on the floor beside padded and frilled pushchairs. Some young blacks, again mostly women, turned out with sharp shoulders and short skirts in urban street executive style; they were standing, flicking fingers as they talked, fast, at one another. Some older men, belonging to that breed of amateur archaeologists and family genealogists who haunted Public Records offices and with whom Hortense had sometimes kept company in archives here and there, who, as she realised, obliged the archival service to the public to continue; one past sell-by date punk with a mohican, another skinny youth in what looked like studded leathers; a round fat man very close in to the vacant exhibition space, scanning the label. A mixture in short, a kind of snapshot of the crowd on the escalators in the centre of town at around 11.00 a.m. any weekday.

'When you say you're winding it up,' Hortense forced herself to speak calmly. 'What are you going to say? I'm not going to mislead them. We've done enough of that already. What, for instance, do you expect me to do about this ridiculous Helen imbroglio?'

'Imbroglio! If you use words like that, they'll be utterly bemused – which is what we want.'

Hortense gave him a look, demanding an answer to her question.

'I'm going to play it by ear. Take the temperature of the hall.'

3

In the She-Wolf's Den

[G. Skipwith 673.1841: Misc. Mss. G. Fr. 18, papyrus, c. 325–350 CE, translation in the hand of Hereward Meeks, keeper of Near Eastern Antiquities, 1858–76.]

Leto and the twins left the byre. The ground of the cemetery was broken; dusty sharp plants, low-lying for want of water and already sere from the springtime sun, had worked stones loose from their matrix of rock; this was lizard and tortoise and snake terrain, and scorpions would already be baking under the hot rocks. She tried to pick out greener patches, where water lay perhaps concealed under the earth. Around her, some tombs stood freely, here and there marked by a pillar of honeyed stone with carved inscriptions; others were niches dug in the rock, empty, riddling the ground at random. She looked down into one: no water, only the pocked colander of the limestone where the rainfall drained away.

But a cleft in the slabs flowed, moist and springing with plants; she tugged up green grasses and sucked their stems as she had done when a child; their dew gave back for a moment's respite the familiar scale and contours to her tongue. So she took heart and followed the damp track of growth; even if there were no surface water, there might be a stream farther on, springing inside the rocks.

The greenery took her down a narrow fissure between two escarpments of the tomb, and the temperature of the air cooled, turned musty; in the interior chamber, a dark green slab of water, flyblown over most of its surface. She knelt to it, splashed the larvae aside and dipped

26

into its silk, then bent her face to the liquid sluicing through her cupped hands and drank.

It was acrid; pungent, too. A watering hole, of course. Fouled by its users.

So she recognised the animal by the gamey odour stirring from the recesses of the den; she knew she was in a cave used by wolves.

Then, from the shadows beyond the pool, she saw a she-wolf ambling towards them, the animal's powerful shoulders moving to her stride and her long narrow head cocked.

Leto stopped drinking, put one hand over the head of the baby girl against her breast, tied with the stole, and the other on the head of her baby son on her back, where it lay against her neck. Though she had felt so dry-mouthed and sere she'd thought there was no fluid left anywhere inside her, a hot dribble spurted from between her legs, the heat of it searing the soreness there from the birth of her twins.

But the wolf did not gather pace and did not collect its limbs to pounce. Instead it came steadily on until Leto could see that the tilt of the animal's head was not menacing; then the she-wolf's narrow jaws parted to greet her instead, speaking from deep within her throat. Leto still clung tightly to the baby at her breast; began picking at the material that held the boy to her back because she wanted to take him into her arms, to shield him, too. For the wolf might be beguiling her.

She could not be sure how she heard the animal talk to her: her thirst and exhaustion made the words vibrate inside her head like the commotion of fever. But her terror began to subside, for it seemed the she-wolf was tossing her thin snout to indicate a higher point in the rocks above the cave, and offering her and her babies shelter. 'I was patrolling the area, keeping a lookout after they abandoned you. In case they came back to do you and the babes further injury.' She stressed the word babes. Her long pink tongue showed itself between her thin jaws, in a smile that was less wolfish than nurse-like, a coaxing look, urging confidence on her patient. She was very close to Leto now, and her breath was hot and rank, but Leto did not recoil, for there was a smiling invitation in her glowing eye, her flossy pale ears, her lithe furry flanks. 'They exposed you on the hillside. They do that. You're lucky they didn't pierce your feet!

'They want you to die by nature's work. I suppose that way they feel less guilty – not dealing the *coup de grâce* but trusting to the elements – or to beasts like us – to do it for them.

'But they don't know the intricacy of our loyalties and our thinking. And besides, our kind can't be done away with so easily.'

Leto began to cry, against her will, with the hunger, the fright, the darkness, the sudden reprieve; the wolf's sympathy.

They would wait until nightfall, the she-wolf decided, and then she would show Leto the water hole in the valley, on the other side of this outcrop, in the direction of the sea. Meanwhile, they would use the pool by the wolf's lair. 'The supply's not the freshest, so if your milk is dry and thin, you and your babes can drink mine – my own cubs are so lively they excite more than enough from their mother. It'd be a relief to me.' She drew Leto deeper into the cave. Leto was trembling. But she began unwinding the sodden bundle of her twins that, by comparison to her host's surroundings, was almost fragrant.

To Leto the fetor in the cave was nothing; for the first time since she'd been discovered with her lover, she was safe.

[Fr. 19]

Lycia the she-wolf sang to Leto and the twins during the days they stayed in her den. She intoned a rasping, sad, tuneless kind of a lullaby, that began in her throat as a rumble and left her jaws as a thin howl, and it spread heaviness through Leto that nevertheless soothed her. As she grasped the song, she added her high quivering voice and then, to the steady intake and exhalation of breath, she and her babies slept quietly.

The cubs played with a tortoise, sniffing inside the shell, trying to coax it to poke out its limbs. It refused, of course, and in its fright, dropped green smears, which the cubs investigated curiously, beating their short, plumed tails on the cave floor in excitement. The wolf also shared food with her: she suckled her, and gave her bones to pick; with a stiff grass blade Leto probed the marrow and drew some renewed strength from it.

'Don't let any of these troubles put you off living—,' the wolf urged her. 'Or put you off sex either, for that matter! There's many more where your lover came from. Forget that one, even if he was a god (animals don't much care for rank, you know). Sometimes you've just got to sit out the evil in your fate. It's got to be cleared from the air, like the weight of a storm before it breaks and lifts and brightens the summer again. You've started young, so there's lots of time. On the human scale, you'll still be a young woman when this lot –' she eyed Leto's twins – 'are giving you trouble with *their* mistakes . . .'

'Why did he let it happen like this?' Leto managed to wail. 'He could have protected me. I didn't have to end up giving birth – in a wilderness. He said he loved me. He promised to take care of me – he said he would always love me.' Leto glanced upwards to the roof of the cave, to where the stars would be, had they been outside under the night sky. 'He said he was miserable with his wife and that she never did anything to give him pleasure . . . That's what he said. The other girls were nothing, he said. He said he didn't care for anyone as much as he cared for me.'

The wolf clicked disapproval. 'Love! You don't have to love someone to enjoy them! You humans justify your actions with grand passions and grander promises. What hypocrisy, in the name of Love! Another god who's full of nothing but excuses. You're a child, Leto, you're still simple as sky after rain. But you'll find the less candid shadows far more kindly and their colours, once you get your eyes used to the dark, so much more interesting.' She batted a cub out the way, as it tried to attract its mother's attention. 'Try not to believe a word men say. They're different, different from us creatures, different from you people, different from women, from mothers, from our kind.

'And part of their power lies in your belief in that power, remember. Don't give them that satisfaction. I forbid you to love, to believe in love, to let that kind of love rule you. Remember what I say when you feel that rush to the head, that heat in the gut, that melting sensation between your thighs, that swoony feeling behind your eyes . . .'

'But I'm cursed,' cried Leto. 'I've given birth to strangers, to children unlike any others in the world. Until someone takes me – not for a stranger, not for an intruder; until someone takes me in, takes me home . . . I'll never rest. That's the curse I bear.'

'That's a heavy burden.' The she-wolf was quiet, reflective. 'If that's your destiny, to wander until you and your babies are no longer taken for strangers.' She paused. 'Then it's even more crucial that you don't throw yourself on the mercy of others without full knowledge of what you're doing. Never make yourself needier than you are, and the love of men does that, believe me. So keep your heart closed, the better to defend yourself. Remember how we survive: we look to our own kind.'

'But *you* came to my rescue.'

'It happens, sometimes, that kindness goes beyond kin.'

4

'A Vanished Mystery Religion'

Five minutes into her talk, Hortense found to her surprise that she was enjoying herself; compared to the usual soporific lecture audience, this one was restive, like a huge unruly classroom of children. She quelled the thought – now *she* was being condescending. But their murmurs and sighs and even grunts at what she was saying and showing made her feel that the audience, as a mass, wanted to find something out, rather than acquire a gloss of culture to preen before their friends.

She was saying, 'So, in spite of the long tradition that the tomb represents a scene of drunken revelry in the cult of Dionysus, the god of wine, everything points to a different story. The site was dedicated to the goddess Leto, who was one of the Titans. The Titans were the rather mysterious giants whose power Zeus and the other Olympians took over – in the case of the Titanesses, usually through rape.' She departed from her prepared notes at this point, lifted her head, and spoke directly into the darkness of the hall where her audience sat, invisible to her. 'This is still going on, of course: in wars everywhere soldiers kill their male enemies and rape the women – leaving them to have their offspring.' She sighed; an echo of her sigh rose back to meet her out of the dark.

Pressing the button on the console, she brought up a slide, a photograph of the site where the tomb had stood. 'Although almost nothing remains of it now, a famous temple stood there.' She changed image, to an artist's reconstruction of the necropolis, as it would have looked, around a thousand and five hundred years ago. It was Skipwith's sketch, from his notebook on the excavations. 'Leto', she went on, 'means "Lady" in Lycanian, the local language there in antiquity – it's like the Virgin Mary being known as Our Lady or Madonna, or even – some of you may have seen the film of Rider Haggard's classic – simply being called "She".

'Leto was a very important goddess in that part of the world: she was the mother of the twins, of the god of the sun Apollo and of the goddess of the moon Artemis, after she was pursued and raped by the father of the gods, Zeus. Like many other objects of Zeus's desires, Leto was then harried across the world by the fury of the queen of the gods, Hera, his wife, and couldn't find anywhere to lay herself down to have her babies – there are various different endings to this story . . .

'The carved relief on the cist – that's the front slab of the tomb – is terribly damaged, as you saw, but the creatures on either end – always taken previously for sphinxes – are more likely to be wolves, who were sacred to the goddess because one helped her when she was fleeing. In the middle you can see her seated on the ground with the two babies playing at her feet – this is the kind of antique composition Leonardo had in mind when he painted the Virgin with Jesus and John the Baptist as infants. Then there are the frogs, carved on the inside of the sarcophagus . . . Leto turned her enemies into frogs.' She paused. 'I expect many of us would enjoy having such powers!'

No laughter greeted this remark, as she would have expected from the usual lunchtime audience, acknowledging that such a hope might exist, in another world, among another people, rather more naïve and less stoic than themselves. But in this company, her words met a kind of high-pressure wave of hope: *as if*, she could almost hear them murmur. *If only*.

She continued, bringing up a view of a papyrus fragment, minutely pecked with script: 'There hasn't been much work done on the huge heap of materials – artefacts, remains, and many, many manuscripts – found inside the tomb, packed around the body. After the middle of the last century, the biblical scholar and palaeographer Hereward Meeks, one of my predecessors here at the Royal Museum (as the National Museum of Albion was called then) – he began cataloguing the deposit made by Sir Giles Skipwith. But, for various reasons, he left this work unfinished.

'Recently, by serendipity, I was looking for something else in the Archives here and I came across Hereward Meeks's editing notes, working papers – and, best of all, the drafts of his translations from the

Skipwith hoard. It was his work on Misc. Mss. that made it possible for me to identify the myth of Leto's persecution and the birth of the twins on the tomb.' Here she returned to a slide of the relief carving of Leto and the twins, hatching at her side. 'The rediscovery of this fragmentary, late Hellenistic romance opens an important and exciting new chapter in the history of the Skipwith deposit. The narrative, with its discordant echoes of the Infancy Gospels – of the Flight into Egypt and the Massacre of the Innocents – throws light on the flourishing syncretism of religious cults in the period.'

There was a stir in the hall; she couldn't decipher it: impatience? excitement?

She began again, moving more rapidly through her technical notes: 'Hereward Meeks's palaeographical expertise can only astonish us today. However his methods betray the characteristic wishfulness of his times. He was able to identify the hand in these strips as belonging to the Circumflex Scribe, so-called from his habit of decorating the end of every other line with a redundant chevron made of two indentations of his reed stylus.' She pressed the button on the console and brought up a close up slide of a line of serried writing, and pointed the red dot of her laser at the mark ∧ at the end of each line.

'According to the conventions of his time, Meeks assumed that the scribe was male; this is likely to be the case, but shouldn't foreclose the possibility that the author might have dictated to a scribe. In which case, the writer could have been a woman. This distant, Hellenistic author, who was most likely working in the mid-fourth century of our era, Meeks called "The Letoniast". His or, as I think, her – narrative braids disparate strands of mythology from the region in order, it would seem, to enhance the status of the sanctuary that Skipwith was excavating. We can make an informed guess that the Letoniast may well have been a priestess of the cult, but the Circumflex Scribe who, before the fifth century CE, wrote down the story of the goddess for her cult followers, may have been taking down dictation from one of her successors in the temple.'

The hall was stirring, impatiently: she was boring them. Hortense pressed the button again and now showed a map. 'In 1841,' she continued, 'Skipwith's archaeological explorations revealed an extensive complex, with capacious storage space for wine and grain, living quarters for pilgrims and temple attendants. Analysis of traces on the three sacrificial altars' – she pointed to A, B, C – 'marked on the map here and here and here indicate abundant libations of red wine and olive oil. The burned offerings did not consist of large or small mammals, but only of the local frogs (*rana silvestris*), still plentiful in the marshland on which the temple stands. This of course helps to clinch the identity of the female figure in the carving. The many tortoise shells also found on site indicate that these were used for divination: the cracks made in the shell by a heated tool were read in augury: like tea leaves or coffee grounds! Or,' she added as an afterthought with regard to her audience, 'cutting open a tomato or an aubergine and finding a sacred message inside.'

There was a light sprinkling of laughter at this. Encouraged that she hadn't been offensive, Hortense Fernly ran on rapidly towards her conclusion: 'The wolf – the region of Lycania is named after its wolves – was the animal familiar of goddesses of childbirth, like Leto herself, and to Artemis, her daughter. This story of Leto is profoundly coloured by the exaltation of pity and suffering in the new religion that supplanted pagan myth.

'Through these surviving fragments of the Letoniast's mythography, in the recension of the Circumflex Scribe and the patient mediation of Hereward Meeks, we can perhaps catch the voice of a woman who presided over a cult of a female deity, featured here not as a Titaness, or a towering mother goddess, but as a young, persecuted fugitive.

'We can perhaps hear, in this story of pagan metamorphosis and survival, the far thunder of a vanished mystery religion.

'Of course it's all a myth,' she added, as she switched the lights back on and the two slides of the tomb, one in close up showing the swirl of figures on the relief, the other a shot of it *in toto*, faded into the weave of the screen.

There was commotion, some cries like the start of questions, sputtering applause as the director left his seat in the auditorium and joined Hortense at the podium. He stilled the hubbub:

'Thank you, Hetty, for this fascinating account of an important item in the National Museum's collections. I think that everyone will agree and want to join me in a show of our appreciation.'

He led more clapping, which he managed to rouse to a greater degree of enthusiasm than before. Hortense took a place to the side of the stage, wishing she could leave it and go back to her office. She loathed this use of first names; the director's new style of common touch made her writhe.

'Some of you . . . ' he stilled the audience with a look and turned up the wattage of the lights to extinguish the slides altogether, 'will have been surprised, perhaps, that Hetty didn't show you the film that many of you have seen on your screens, at home, at school, or elsewhere – the film that so dramatically materialises the body in three dimensions through the latest technological methods of tomography. You will have been disappointed, I sense, not to have seen again the beautiful face and figure behind the mask known as "Helen".'

Shouts and murmurs of agreement followed these words.

'Hetty is a scholar, and she keeps to the strict paths of intellectual enquiry. She knows she must only explore within the limits of what can be verified. Myths, fairy tales aren't to her taste. I too love truth. Of course. But other considerations apply in running a great public institution that is dependent on revenue for its survival.'

He paused, and walked out with the laser beam pointer in his hand.

'First slide, please.'

The lights went down again. The cartonnage of Skipwith 673 reappeared.

'This is one of the most beautiful faces we have in the collection of late antiquities, a face as appealing as Kate Moss or Isabella Rossellini or any of the divas and supermodels whom companies pay to acquire exclusive rights to the use of their features. It was chosen to represent us. For very good reasons.'

He pointed at the projector, and an image of a mummy appeared, with a plain case beside it.

Hortense realised, *He's going to tell them.*

'This is another mummy from the collection, which, as you can see, was buried in a case that possesses none of the glorious, splendid cartonnage casing of the one you know by now so well.'

He paused, and faced the audience.

'I have something to confess. We took this body, which is very well preserved, to make the "Helen".'

The audience stirred, hummed, asked one another what the director was saying and if they'd heard right.

'Yes, you are quite justified in being taken aback. The woman you've seen come to life isn't in fact the same as the woman of the cartonnage and mummy case of Skipwith 673. Do you follow me? We have combined the two in the interests of aesthetic impact.'

He paused; sighed; continued: 'The Museum has withdrawn the publicity material and is in the process of rewriting the accompanying commentary. We did not set out to deceive. We simply wanted to display the kind of body that would, in more usual conditions, have been found under such an exquisite face mask.

'I have also drafted an explanation in a press release that will be available as you leave.'

There was a pause, a silence in the hall, as the audience tried to understand what they'd been told. Kim McQuy leapt to his feet. He wasn't alone in waving excitedly towards the speaker.

'What was in the tomb then?' he called out. 'Where is she? You owe us a full explanation. Whose is the face on the mask? What were the other things you found there? Were they hers? Her treasure? Her hoard?'

More stirring and murmurs of approval accompanied his demand.

The director paused, looked at Hortense, who shook her head and left it to him.

'There was no body,' resumed the director. 'That's why we used another mummy to illustrate the way the mask and case were used to enclose the deceased.'

Kim McQuy was on his feet now, a slim, whippy-bodied young man in a dark suit with a plain tie and a white shirt. 'What do you mean "no body"?' he cried. 'How can a tomb like that contain "no body"?'

The director cast a look at Hortense, but she gestured for him to go on. So he nodded, and continued, 'There was a bundle of stuff, linen strips braided in mummy style. But the X-ray showed, to our very great surprise, that there was no body inside them. There were some traces of human remains, of hair and skin, but no more than you'd find on a hotel carpet. You know the tomb was used as a midden – if you like, it was the equivalent of one of those big wheeled recycling bins the council puts out, and there were lots of odds and ends dumped inside it, of varied interest and value. Then, there were the wrappings themselves. But no one, it seems, was ever buried there, odd as it sounds. It's just like Andy Warhol – he said he wanted for his epitaph, "Here lies a figment". Well, the Helen is a figment, I'm afraid.' The director paused, then, in the reproachful silence that followed, added, with an elegant spreading of his slim fingertips, 'More than a thousand years ago, our post-modern condition was foreshadowed – hah! That's life, we've got to accept it.'

Kim was leaping along the row, too fast for the people sitting near him to move out of his way, and he ran up towards the podium and turned to face the auditorium. A Museum guard tried to restrain him, but he brushed him aside and addressed the room.

'You can't just say one thing and then another. How do we know what to believe if you can mislead us and then just turn around like this?'

Hortense shifted uncomfortably, trying, as she realised later, to put distance between herself and the director, even though she knew it would be appalling cowardice to leave him alone on stage.

'We are doing everything in our power to rectify the . . . ' he began.

But Kim was carrying on, while the audience were getting up, some of them in support but others in embarrassment, looking for their bags and coats, looking away, made shy by his earnestness, his vehemence.

'We want a full analysis of the bundle, we want to see the same tests, the CAT scan and the tomography photographs and the computer-generated 3D model and all the things you've done to the other mummy, we want it all done to the stuff in that tomb, to the Leto Bundle. You've misled the public, and we demand you make reparations.'

Hortense looked at the young man, startled. This young man, in his boring dark suit with his cheap haircut, who had taken in her research and baptised Skipwith 673 just like that, no fuss, no problem, with the name of her highly contested speculations. She found herself almost laughing. His excitement was contagious; his indignation refreshed her after the director's double tongue, after the detective's speeches. There was the light of outrage playing about Kim McQuy, with a vitality that jumped like lightning from him to her to the crowd in the hall, from whom there came shouts of encouragement, assent.

The director attempted to break in: 'Your enthusiasm is admirable,' he said to Kim. 'We might wish dusty old collections caused such excitement all the time.'

Kim spun around; his face was shining with fervour, his eyes dilated into polished mirrors. He pointed at the director, '*You* said there were odds and ends, that there were wrappings – but what are they, what's on the wrappings? *She* said there were documents like the one she was talking about. What are they? What do they say?'

He swivelled so that his finger was stabbing at the air between himself and Hortense.

She found herself nodding. 'Yes,' she said. 'There are more manuscripts, plenty more.'

Kim grew very quiet, and with him the remaining supporters in the hall went silent too. They were all gathered now near the front, guards hovering around them, trying to usher them out.

The director began moving to the steps that led down from the podium.

'What,' asked Kim, 'what do they tell us?'

'Look,' the director cut in, as he jerked his head towards Hortense to follow him out of the hall. 'I've said we're full of admiration for your keen interest and we shall be doing everything we can to deepen our analysis of the Leto Bundle.'

Now he was using the phrase. Hortense leant her head towards the leading troublemaker as she sped in the director's wake out of the lecture room. Conciliatory, she whispered, 'Mummy wrappings often have prayers and charms and magic formulae and those sort of texts written on them. Get in touch with me if you really want to know more—' She took her business card from her wallet and handed it to Kim.

As soon as they reached the offices behind the door marked Private Museum Staff Only, the director commented, 'Wasn't that a little unwise? He's a nutter and clearly an attention-seeker and you'd do well to steer clear.'

Hortense shrugged. 'I'm hardly going to be making an assignation with him in a dark alley. I'm actually pretty intrigued, myself. Nobody's looked at that stuff since forever. It's been lying around in the basement, mouldering. Besides,' she added, almost gaily, 'it'll give a new twist to the notion of Outreach, won't it?'

'I knew it,' Kim McQuy was crying out as he left the Museum, two or three of the faithful still attached to him. 'I knew it! She's here! She's with us! Here, now, everywhere!'

5

'The Angel of the Present'

Voice of the Street, a newspaper hawked by approved beggars on the pavements of Enoch, ran a front page on the unprecedented popular interest in the so-called 'Helen'. This organ showed a familiarity with the circumstances that none of the broadsheets' journalists possessed or were able to acquire, it seemed, as they remained torn between contempt at the credulity of some people and outrage at a public institution's fraud. In the tabloids, the phenomenon was welcomed more warmly: it was seen as another instance of the new loosened-up sense of national identity, the response of a country newly in touch with its feelings. But *Voice* was closer to the bush telegraph on the pavements, the tube, on the escalators, in the bus queues and the Post Office lines, and it ran the first interview with Kim McQuy, the schoolteacher from Cantelowes.

Gramercy Poule, in the country where she was trying to tone herself up before leaving on her two month tour, her first for several – was it really five? – years, was reading that issue of *Voice* one evening, after Monica, her manager, had picked it up for her at the station before leaving the capital, from a stubby teenage girl with schoolgirl bunches and a sniffle hanging in her nose ring.

Fellmoor, where Gramercy Poule had bought land under a toothed ridge of the Nine Maidens, was protected by its status as a National Park: it was still a wilderness, where past attempts to settle or enclose the ground, to till or even, on the higher reaches, to graze, had collapsed in rocky ruins; the stones marched down to reclaim their territory and to trap wanderers, it was said, on moonless nights into dancing till they also turned to stone, like the young revellers who had given their names to the peak, and had been punished for their wantonness. Fellmoor had once been a pious and austere community, where fine gentlemen were lynched for attempting to make changes in the liturgy of local chapels.

On Fellmoor, Gramercy Poule exchanged her red patent stiletto thigh-high boots, her bespoke gold lace shifts, her glitter blusher and violet eyeshadows, her cross-laced camisoles and her luxury hose for waxed weatherproofing and thick socks and walking boots that braced her ankles so that not even the most hostile stone could crack her bones. She never wandered very far up on the moor, as the incline taxed her smoker's lungs, and she did not want to heal them, not even with country air, for her singing was distinguished by her high-pitched emphysemic whisper. But she could also walk out to the bottom of her garden in the night beyond the lights of the house and stand before the slow strong black rise of the moor. Out there, it was solid and implacable, she felt, as a minor chord hanging in space when the amp's been turned right up, and she could let herself fall upwards into the darkroom of the universe, where the sky unfurled like God's photographer's hood and gradually, by the glinting liquid stars, allowed a ghostly picture to reveal itself: in the summer, flaring with comets, in the winter louring with inky clouds chased across out to sea by the wind.

One of her songs included her recordings of the moor's silence in the dark; it only seemed silent. It thrummed and rustled and twitched and moaned, to her ears as she watched and listened in the night, and to the sensors of her machine that quivered and jolted to the pulses of the landscape's consciousness.

What Kim McQuy had to say was crazy. 'Listen to this, Mon,' she called out to her manager. She began to read aloud: 'Kim McQuy is the kind of sharp outer Enochite you'd expect to be thrashing out the latest team changes in his local football club rather than spooking us with *X Files*-type stories. "I'm not a believer, not at all. I'm not a Jesus freak!" Kim told the *Voice* reporter. "This isn't a religious experience, this has nothing to do with God or the Virgin Mary or Princess Diana being in heaven. This is History. *History Starts With US* – that's the message. HSWU – by the way, say 'zwu' to rhyme with 'who' – is the way things are and the way things were. Okay, I got to know about it through unusual experiences, but, you know the stories: Newton's apple, Eureka!, the sudden flash in the night – we've all had that."

'Kim McQuy maintains that he was surfing the web late one Saturday night – he looked at his watch afterwards ("Don't forget, I'm a teacher, I keep time!") and it was 2.20 a.m. He'd been looking at the CNN news and visiting lots of homepages for a laugh. He doesn't do rooms, he says – no weirdos in his hair. His conversation with "Helen" was the very first time he'd had a two-way experience on the net. And no, he wasn't on anything: he claims he doesn't do "any of that stuff". (We'll be watching you, Kim!)

'So "Helen", the auncient baebe of the National Museum, spoke to our Kim at 2.20 a.m. last Sunday morning, and this is what she's supposed to have revealed:

> '"I came from somewhere, but now I'm everywhere –
> My everywhere is your here and now –
> I am the angel of the present time."'

'Hey!' put in Monica. 'That sounds familiar.'

'Doesn't it?' Gramercy Poule chuckled. 'Shall we take him to the cleaners for plagiarism?'

Monica took *Voice* from Gramercy Poule, who put her feet up on her big, deep sofa with the soft crewel bolsters in front of her woodburner and closed her eyes.

'I don't know whether I'm more pissed off or flattered – go on.'

Monica began reading: '"I felt I was going crazy," says Kim. "The face was speaking to me and I was so stunned that I couldn't take down what she was saying. So I asked her to repeat it – actually, I ordered her to, and she smiled back with her eyes, the way they have lights in them, and she did say it again. Only this time she added:

> ' "I am one of the scattered ones,
> The homing doves, the wanderers,
> I am the angel of the present."'

'It's my lost peoples song!' She took the paper back and scanned the words again. 'Not word for word, exactly. But. Close. My phantom ship idea, all over again, except he's left out the Flying Dutchman and the sirens, calling the way.' Gramercy hummed a bluesy bar and then laughed. 'What a nerve.'

Monica resumed: 'Kim McQuy contests that it's a bit – well – incredible – that she was speaking English, but says she was stiff and had an accent, as if it wasn't her first language. "It's the international language – everyone has to speak English now – it's the language of science, air traffic control, doctors, and parliaments all over the world. So it's logical she should speak it. She knows what's going down to be understood – globally.'"

'Fucking annoying *Voice* didn't catch he's taken my words. Honestly. Give them a call, Mon. Tell 'em.'

Monica read on, 'Kim waxes quite emotional, however, about what the message is from the Lady of the Scattered Ones, the Angel of the Present, Lady Homeless (take your pick). This issue, as you all out there know, matters quite a lot to *Voice*. "She's a figure for the way we live now," he says. "That's what she means when she says, 'My everywhere is your here and now . . .' She's like millions of people who make their homes where they can. She's an alternative story, that's not about people springing up here and being rooted – she's about now, she's about the new Albion, the Albion of the planetary diaspora, of the lost peoples."'

'There it is! What did I say? Bloody hell.'

'Outrageous,' Monica continued, 'If Kim McQuy's an opportunist, he hasn't chosen an easy row to hoe: nobody wants more aliens, refugees or immigrants. They don't want the ones who are already here. So is this weirdo in a suit a representative of the people in the making? Is he just a young man in a hurry? Has he got his eye on politics? What's his game?' She paused and put down the paper. 'Listen, Gramercy, if he's putting it out on his website with music, we'll really do him over.'

Gramercy Poule replied, slowly, 'They were impressed by him, a bit against the grain though, don't you think?' She took the paper and turned to the article's continuation. 'They even finish the piece saying, "We were prepared to find an *X Files* crazy, but Kim McQuy may be more interesting than he first sounds. Watch this space."' She leant back, holding the photograph at arm's length and sizing up Kim as he stood, unsmilingly, arms by his sides, on the steps of the Museum.

'He's quite dishy, actually. Sort of pretending to be straight. What d'you think he is? Indian? Half this and half that, no? Needs a bit of restyling – new hair, new clothes, you know. I think, Mon, we should make an approach. See where he's at. See how he reacts when we get on the line.'

So, when Monica rang TB later that evening to check that he and the equipment had arrived safely at Gramercy's first stop on the Shiloh tour, they knew almost instantly what it was that Dr Hortense Fernly was conveying alongside Gramercy Poule's lighting equipment, amplifiers, synthesisers and musical instruments.

6

A Tirzahner Baby

Kim McQuy took the short-term contract teaching post offered at Cantelowes Primary School straight after finishing his training, and then stayed on because he liked the sense of valiant urgency this first job gave him. The school occupied a purpose-built redbrick gabled Edwardian enclave behind a narrow yard and a pair of cast-iron gates that still said Girls on one side and Boys on the other. The gasometers that had fuelled the capital in the last century were visible above the high wall; when Kim first started working there at the turn of the Eighties, he would watch them out of the classroom window: he'd notch a column in his mind's eye, keep his gaze steady and blink hard, then open them again to see how far the drum had lifted under the slow pressure of the gas piped through from the cold sea far away. He'd show the children how the great city of Enoch was powered by invisible essences, flowing near them.

The drums no longer rose within their armature's scarlet and black battledress, but Kim McQuy still felt the stir of air around him, fuelling his energies. He could look out and hear the spirits of the city's past lives jostling in Enoch's clay beneath him; the dead were mutating below, like mulch, like peat, setting will o' the wisps flickering in his head, leaping inside him in methane tongues of fire. These angelic exhalations buoyed him; he was lifted on the blue, cold energy of the spirits rising from the thousands of the nameless stacked under the crust of the world, who were calling out to him.

The school stood in the heart of the heart of Enochite blight, where the railways converged on the metropolis and the crisscrossing bridges sheltered shanties where the surprising yellow smiles of lemon slices lay scattered among the runaways' sodden duvets. The original brick building had been sporadically extended during the last fifty years and accretions of prefabs on concrete rafts filled the space back towards the flats where most of the children lived. Long, low, four-storey developments, they'd been put up in the reaction against tower blocks. Small, boxed-in, tiered terraces for gardens faced south, away from the school; these bloomed mostly with washing, with children's football gear in preternaturally bright fast colours, like spring bulbs in a junk mail garden catalogue. On the other side, outdoor galleries with thick stone parapets linked one neighbour to another, their front doors side by side, lit with storm lanterns where midges wriggled. These warrens were planned as arks for the city; the names of the blocks were painted on their sterns, the estate's blank end walls; they commemorated civic-minded benefactors, all forgotten.

It wasn't by any means one of the worst times for the estate, so Kate Daiges, his head teacher, told Kim when she gave him the job; most of the children were very young, too young to make trouble. The average age in the whole warren, she reckoned, must be around thirty, and she hadn't a clue what was going to happen when the kids needed secondary schooling.

Kim's classroom overlooked the rear of the estate: huge wheeled steel refuse bins, and garage space, let to commercial interests. The refuse lorries clattered into the alley below two days a week; grinding and rattling as they reversed down the narrow passage, spearing the bins on to prongs and hoisting them till they tipped and spewed their contents into a gnashing maw. When a family had moved on, leaving a heap of furniture, a busted sofa, a beer carton of discarded clothes and toys, the rubbish men would lash an abandoned stuffed teddy to the snout of the cart, beside more soiled toys and a sex doll or two. Then some of his class would sigh, longing to have the soiled animal for themselves.

Lessons had to stop while the process was completed, but Kim considered it good for his class to watch, to see the services that kept the city working. Besides, the view into the wings and the underside of things interested him more than the events in the limelight; if he hadn't taken up teaching, he might have become a health and safety inspector, pushing through to the scullery at the back where the young illegals at the sink were being exploited, uncovering the dummy fronts of shady enterprises, enforcing decent standards on corrupt employers and entrepreneurial pressgangers.

His bus-and-tube journey to school took him up to an hour and a half from the northern suburban home of his childhood, where he left magenta cherry trees garish as food colouring and front lawns edged with careful, low maintenance shrub planting, and travelled into the level, broad brownfield sites of the inner city. Cantelowes extended behind the mainline station to the canal; this had once carried a lot of traffic, bringing coal and other essentials to the city from distant mines; it was now used mostly by pleasure craft, its dingy waters death to all but the most tungsten-gilled dingy dabs; scraps of boys angled for a catch, rain or shine. Its waterside had been fitfully regenerated by private enterprise over the last five years: near the school there was a new pub on the wharf called The Fancy, a favourite watering hole for backpackers; ramshackle camper vans were parked on the cobbled alley leading to its canal frontage and trading was good-humoured, if slow, between owners who had come to their journey's end and others, the customers, ready to embark on world travel. Kim had listened at first as they swapped boasts of mushroom trances on rose-coloured beaches and sulphur baths on the slopes of volcanoes, aired ancient visa problems and crowed indignation at dry or homophobic cities, at societies with laws about hair length. These were people who thought the solution to every problem was moving on. They chased the exotic from one port to another; but Kim wanted whatever the opposite of exotic was – could something be inotic? For Kim the issue was how to belong somewhere and then stay put.

The tube escalators at the nearest stop to the school came up inside the station, opposite two hexagonal, bubblegum-pink kiosks which had recently gained their franchises to operate; pointy pavilions from a video game featuring mailed terminators, they winked contemporaneity among the scumbled greys of commuters, luring them to counters laden with multicoloured pic 'n' mix sweets, to windows where a cancan of amputated forelegs kicked to display chequered, pictured, fishnet, spangled and diamanté backseamed tights, alongside lopped torsoes displaying daisy-stitched, dimity and lace knickers and bras and slips to match.

Kim walked across the concourse of the station each morning to the exit at the side, nearest Cantelowes Primary; he'd buy *Voice of the Street*

45

from the vendor he knew, but refuse the begging of the new arrivals in the city who'd flopped down on the ground for the night, sleeping on their bags as all benches had been removed in order to discourage dossing. Some of them weren't much older than the children he taught. Outside the station, across the main artery, there were agencies for them: 'Alone in the City?', 'Contact', 'Youthline'. Occasionally Kim saw railway police working in pairs questioning the youngsters; but their numbers remained steady. Runaways. They were multiplying: quarrels at home, boredom in the country brought them to the bright lights, big city and dispersed them.

Kim still lived with his parents; he meant to move out, but housing closer in was expensive on his salary, and the area was much safer than the inner city for his computer equipment, which was his most valuable, indeed almost his only prized possession, HSWU's matrix and engine.

Araminta McQuy, born St Clair and brought up as a girl in one imperial possession after another (her father was a railway engineer), adopted Kim from Tirzah, at the height of the Tirzahner Orphan Rescue campaign. Minta and Gerald McQuy were in their late forties, aged parents by the standards of the Sixties. It was the local priest who'd put them on to the agency that organised his adoption, 'through their hidden networks', his mother had said. 'They run escape corridors from places that go up in flames.'

He'd heard the story many times since the year he celebrated his thirteenth birthday (in retrospect, he realised that he was probably older than that, maybe even three years older), when she first sat him down to answer his questions, her eyes unblinking to prevent tears spilling from them. She told him how, with his father, she had travelled to Tirzah immediately after the war came to an end, and waited and waited until he'd been found and brought to them.

The whole idea began one summer afternoon, during the four-year-long siege of Tirzah, when Gerald McQuy was feeding the birds with the stale crusts Minta had cut off his breakfast toast. 'Your father knows how important it is for birds to learn the whereabouts of their food source long before winter comes,' Minta told Kim. 'I was watching the six o'clock news, not paying much attention, though. Then it started showing pictures of the siege and of a column walking down the road. There were hundreds of refugees with handcarts and barrows and pushchairs and pathetic bundles of things. It was the first of the civil wars far away that we could see happening in front of our eyes inside our own houses. There'd been newsreels about Suez and Cyprus at the flicks on Saturday mornings, and the Troubles were beginning, but all those wars were too early for the telly. And at first news cameras didn't seem to follow the army and the carnage, not in the same way as the Coronation. Then they started sending reporters to the fighting. I was on our government's side. I really believed we had to do something – it was our duty to go in and try and stop the Tirzahners tearing themselves apart. White man's burden and all that. I was brought up to believe in our *responsibilities*. So watching those people trudging out of the burning city, something happened to me. I felt this cold hand grip me and something happened in the pit of my stomach. It was as if I'd come down with one of those sudden fevers of my childhood, it was that strong. I called out to your father – he was still by the back door pottering about. I tried to say something sensible, but I couldn't find the words, because I was trying not to start crying.

'I was hoping that the war would all calm down, now that the city had been taken by our side, that there'd be no more bloodshed and everybody could start rebuilding their lives.

'You see, we had a soft spot for that country, because we'd been on a very happy holiday by the seaside there – before the conflict. Or rather, before the bandits came down out of the mountains, where they'd been feuding for . . . centuries.'

His mother's voice had faded then, and Kim sitting up solemn and quiet, with his knees together, felt the tension of unspoken confessions, and didn't want to know any more; he wanted to go to his room and paint the cyclopean orc and his vulture steed that he'd bought with his birthday money. His father was sitting beside Minta on the sofa, not in his usual armchair. It was clear they had decided to tell him something together, something he was afraid he wouldn't want to know.

She controlled herself, and went on, 'When your father came in from the garden, I just said, "I so wish we could do something, be of some use. It does make one feel so utterly futile." And you, you', – she leant out and patted Gerald's knee – 'you understood.'

'My dear,' he said.

'There was a man on the news saying that tyrants who launch wars always hark back to imaginary histories of wrong and injustice in order to justify their violence. But when it comes down to it, it's not history, it's men of violence, here, now, getting away with murder. Why should they get away with murder?, I wanted to shout. Then we saw photographs of all these children who'd lost their fathers, brothers – and their mothers. They were being rounded up in refugee camps – and I'd always wanted to have a . . .'

Minta clutched Gerald's hand and then put her arms around Kim; he burrowed deep into the blue lambswool of her cardigan for it felt as if a crevasse had gaped and dropped him out of the present time into another, where the ordinary laws were broken at random, and inconsistently. He was frightened, but also exhilarated: so much was explained by this faltering, stilted confession of his mother and father, so much he had intimated before but not understood.

Stephanie, his best friend at school when he was seven, who showed him French knitting at break and did cat's cradles with him in the corner of the playground, said that his mother looked old and yellow and they didn't sort of match whereas she and her mum did; they were peas in a pod, especially when she was allowed to use her lipstick and eye shadow. But he countered with a confidence for her ears only: his parents really weren't his parents. Secretly, he knew he was a deposed prince of a distant, sunbaked country very far away, but he'd been robbed of his gold and elephant tusk throne and he was now wandering in disguise – though his subjects still recognised him with covert signs in the street when he passed. He'd return in triumph one day. He'd be recognised. He'd be known.

Stephanie liked this story; she lay down on a school bench and closed her eyes tight and whispered the words, 'elephant tusk throne', slowly again and again, and then asked Kim to describe his lost kingdom to her. Animals kept coming into the picture, from various alphabet books he'd been given, though he wasn't sure that the creatures in his mind's eye belonged to the historical past where he'd once lived. 'I want to go there, I want to go there,' cried Stephanie, squeezing her eyes tight shut, like Kim, so that they could watch the colours change in bands and stars in front of their lids.

Minta used to take him to lessons to prepare for his first Communion, but his father never went with them to Mass. She told him, as one of the fragments of information that she relinquished, 'We promised to bring you up in the faith because otherwise they wouldn't have found you for us – it was a bit underhand of us, I suppose, as we didn't really believe, either of us. But there you are, now, and I couldn't imagine what my life would mean without you.'

'You must believe, you must,' cried Kim as a child, 'Otherwise you'll go to hell for ever.'

Minta McQuy laughed. 'I don't think so, pet. If God exists and he's a god of love – which is what they say – he wouldn't let the devil build a terrible place like hell in the first place.' Then she went quiet and took him in her arms and stroked his hair, 'You see, it would give the devil too much power, when he has already so much to do here and is so busy and so successful at what he does here.'

In dribs and drabs, they told him what they knew. It wasn't much; in those days, adopted children weren't encouraged in their attachments to their birth mother. Minta wept when she tried to tell Kim what his mother must have gone through, how she would only have given him up because it was the only way he could have survived. So when Kim read the story of Ishmael at his catechism class, he recognised his alter ego. The nun showed him a picture and in the mock-tearful, hushed tones she used to express her wonder at God's ways, she described how, when Ishmael lay dying, dying in a wilderness where there was no water or food, his mother set him down and turned away and sat herself down a little way off, so that she should be spared the sight of his death. But God took pity on them and an angel came down in a golden glory, with a red drape casually tossed over his smooth and shining body, treading through the air as if solid steps were carved in it, and touched his mother on the shoulder and pointed – west. West.

He too had come west, from Tirzah.

There, said the angel, gesturing towards the setting sun, there there will be food and water, and a place to lay their heads, and shelter, and friendship. 'And family,' said Minta.

Kim grew up 'well-rounded', his school reports said; he had never been trouble, almost to Minta's regret, for she attributed his teenage containment to damage he had suffered before they adopted him, experiences that lay beyond her reach, beyond his conscious memory. The doctor to whom they'd taken him on their return assessed undernourishment since birth; it had stunted his growth, he said, and slowed his mental development. Otherwise, there was nothing wrong, just his time had been moving more slowly than other children's. 'Think of him as a preemie,' said the doctor, 'Their chances of survival are improving year by year – we really can look forward to an absolute fall in the rate of infant mortality – but it's still tricky. They need more attention, and they do grow at a somewhat different pace.'

He developed early, it seemed. A duvet of dark hair appeared on his upper lip and cheeks when he was twelve; others put it down to his general complexion, but Minta knew it meant he was catching up with his age, that, physically, he wasn't any longer retarded by his infancy. Nor was he mentally: he was a diligent schoolboy, with sudden erratic bursts of indignation – the first signs of his later activity in student protests. But she often wished he'd have fun like other women's sons, that she and Gerald would return to find traces of a clandestine party, or even a girl whispering in Kim's room. She would even have welcomed a window flung open to get rid of the smell, as other parents lamented, noisily. But Gerald couldn't see there was any problem in having a son who, unlike so many of their friends' and neighbours', hadn't dropped out, didn't play loud music, hadn't pierced his person in any place, and did not take drugs.

When his parents told him about his origins, that afternoon of his thirteenth year, it still fitted with the earlier dream he'd entertained of his secret, faraway kingdom. But the story also became real for him because it took place in a country nearby on the map, during a war that had frightened everyone in Albion on account of its savagery and its death toll, so near to home.

When Minta and Gerald McQuy flew into Tirzah, they put up at the single newly functioning hotel on the burned out main street; they had the name of a nun in a team of Catholic relief workers and had brought with them £500 in small notes. This cache contravened all the currency restrictions imposed by the government of the day so they stowed it as deeply as they could, in two money belts which they kept on in bed. The sum also represented a large tranche of their combined savings, from Gerald's job as a middle-ranking civil servant (he was employed in the planning department of Lanthorn borough council where he struggled against the new broom approach to urban renewal), and Minta's wages as a part-time clerk in Outpatients at the pioneering local health centre that Gerald's department had supervised, and for which it had been commended.

The Hotel Metropole in Tirzah was connected to the water supply for a few hours daily, and intermittently to the smashed electrical grid. Its former elegance still glimmered through the wreckage: the sweep of the double staircase up to the mezzanine bar opposite the entrance was no longer reflected in floor-to-ceiling speckled mirrors, of course, and the potted palms that had lent the foyer the air of a turn of the century spa had been charred in the bombing, their porcelain jardinières cracked. But the general ambience breathed elegance, and the reception desk, holed here and there, remained a magnificent slab of rose marble studded with pearly fossils, while, upstairs (and with the lift out of service, this was indeed up the stairs) the bedrooms and bathrooms still spread out their ample proportions with the restrained swagger of pre-war luxury. Since the insurgency had abated and international agencies had brokered a relief programme, the glass had been replaced in the windows, and such furniture as could be salvaged rearranged. Temporary emergency measures brought food to the city in astronaut packages, including sachets of ice-cream powder.

There were insects everywhere. 'For they shall inherit the earth,' muttered Gerald, moodily swatting at the flies in a dirty sunbeam. At home, he always removed spiders to the garden by trapping them in a glass and then slipping a piece of card under the rim. Here, there were spiders in every corner, under every protrusion, busily spinning, their old webs torn by the weight of the prey they'd already ensnared and cocooned and laid up for the winter.

'They know how to provide for the duration,' said Minta. '*Their* larders are stuffed!'

They arrived in the hotel, and waited for news. The process was very tortuous, since it was not yet clear if the government allowed foreign adoptions; they took place, but nobody knew – or would divulge – the process by which the petitioning parents were screened, the orphan picked out, the documents produced. Capriciously, suddenly, a child would appear in the arms of Sister Thomas, the nun in charge of the charity's programme, and the family would whisk her away to the airport, before somebody might decide differently and revoke the move.

Sister Thomas, bright-eyed, plump and masterful, cheerily ordered them to pray and be patient. She would contact them as soon as there was something to report.

The days dragged by. Gerald went sightseeing, but Minta had no appetite for adventure. He came back and reported: on the black market in fuel, foodstuffs and books, on the continued felling of every bush and tree in the old, once shaded avenues and gardens of the city, on the ingenuity of the local mechanics, tinkering with torn metal to patch broken vehicles and get burned kitchens in working order again, on a service of thanksgiving he wandered into, where everyone was weeping for the dead. He did not tell her that, as a foreigner with clear means, he was continually accosted, beseechingly, by well-spoken women with modest manners.

One evening, as Minta was lying on the bed thinking she now understood what it might be like to be in prison, there was a knock on the door. She opened it, to a hotel maid. She began to say, carefully and slowly, that there was no need to tidy up or turn down the bed, and that she wasn't going to go out. But the woman stepped in and took a photograph from the pocket of her apron.

There was a paper with it.

It said, in English, in carefully composed capitals:

'I AM LITTLE BOY HELTHY STRONG PLEESE FIND FOR ME RICH FAMILY FOR FUTURE'

Minta looked at the paper between her fingers and held on to it tightly as if it might disappear. Then she looked at the photograph – a black and white passport photo booth snapshot, torn so that only the hands of the person holding up the child to the camera were showing. The child was a blur, but maybe it was her sight that was failing from the pressure building up inside her skull.

She stepped backwards into her hotel room. The woman followed her, or perhaps the woman's closeness made her take the step back in the first place.

'Yours?' she asked, pointing to the hands in the photo.

The woman shook her head, and patted Minta's arm. Her hand was hard and dry. 'You like? You want?' she said.

Minta cried out, 'How?'

The woman reached for Minta's wrist and Minta flinched, thinking she was going to take the photograph from her, but no, she turned over Minta's hand to look at her watch and she tapped the dial at the bottom to indicate six o'clock. Then she looked round the hotel room until she found what she was looking for: Minta's handbag. She pointed to it, and said,

'Dollar?'

Minta hung her head and tried to shake it, but couldn't make the gesture for fear that the paper and the photo in her hand would now evaporate. 'Sterling.' The maid did not seem to reject this and Minta, never imagining she could speak so plainly, asked her, quietly, 'How much?'

Then, very still, she studied the photograph. The child in the image wasn't looking at the camera, but at something happening over the viewer's shoulder, something that was creasing his round eyes into a small frown of attention. The mouth was full, relaxed, but not smiling: this wasn't a baby, as she had dreamed of, not a tiny infant who would arrive, unmarked by experiences she could never know. Her heart shrank: this was a child, not a babe-in-arms, and he was sitting up to face the camera. Then the blood swelled again, rushing to her temples and making her giddy: he could be hers. The boy's head was slightly on one side, bright and alert as a wren, thought Minta, finally trustful enough to hop out of the bushes on to one of their feeders.

The woman took back the message and the picture, replaced them in the pocket of her apron.

'Three hundred fifty pound,' she said, slowly. 'Give me three hundred and fifty pound. When I come back with boy, here.'

Later, as Kim grew up and his face changed, Minta could never remember what he had looked like when he was small, except for this characteristic bright crispness of movement, the readiness of his response as he put his head back or sideways to listen. But she always remembered the rush of hope she felt when she first pored over the photograph in the palm of her hand: the mystery of the small, blurred, round face that she'd been promised would return, enfleshed, to be a child of her very own.

She sat on in the hotel room alone, waiting for six o'clock.

Gerald came back. At first he shouted at her about street riffraff and medical guarantees and under-the-counter transactions and official paperwork.

But when there was a knock at the door and the woman stood there with the child holding her hand, Gerald didn't bluster any more. Minta fell back, with Gerald beside her, as if an apparition had materialised before their eyes and streams of celestial light were flowing down around it, while the woman laid the child on the bed, unwrapped him and showed him to them, whole and hale as he was, smooth and glossy as a horse chestnut newly slipped from its firm casing. Minta dared not look too closely; so near to the fulfilment of her deepest hope, she could not face finding some obstacle, some fatal impairment that would snatch the treasure from her grasp. Besides, she felt at that moment so emboldened by love that she would have taken a child who was blind, deaf and dumb. They both knew that some of the orphans were marked by their mothers so that they would be able to recognise them again, if they were ever reunited: a nick to an earlobe, a small tattoo on the shoulder. But this child was smooth and radiant, so this mother wasn't the sort who'd inflict a hurt on one of her children, even in desperate straits. Minta felt a flow of love towards her. She would continue the work his first mother had begun, with all her heart.

Minta thought she was going to cry; an overwhelming grief seemed to rise up inside her in the middle of her ecstasy: the child seemed so small and so vulnerable and so beautiful. It didn't matter he was older than the infant she had longed for. When she went over to him and crouched down to look into his face, she felt the heat of life glow from his body, and saw in his shining eyes a flicker of curiosity with no fear in it.

'Thank you,' was all she could say, as a flustered Gerald pushed the envelope with the money into the woman's hands; he managed the exchange as awkwardly as a monk instructing a schoolboy in the use of a condom. In return she handed him a blue plastic bag.

'For later,' she said, at his unspoken question.

Minta did not kiss the child; she could only look at him. She could feel the warmth of his presence, she could smell his living breath, like sap.

'You put both arms round my neck, as if to say to . . . to the woman who'd brought you to us in that funny old room in the Hotel Metropole where I'd waited so long for you, "It's all right, I'm happy, so you can go now".' She paused and looked at her quiet son, at the way he had grown. 'There were a few things for you in the bag, including a change of clothes, with KIM scratched on a button.'

Between the station and Cantelowes Primary School lay a wide tract of wasteland through which ran the great sheaf of railway lines from the north of the country. Since the gasometers had fallen into disuse, the huge area around them was being cleared in preparation for a new development. But as the school year wore on, work slowed. The planning stage failed to meet the first deadline, then the second, then the third. Architects came and went. Sponsors flirted, but did not commit themselves. Now buddleia and rosebay willow herb seeded in the ruined brick foundations of the factory sheds, canteens and shops that had once clustered in the space on both sides of the tracks. Environment activists fenced off a part and declared it a natural wilderness: Kim took his class there in the early summer, with pads and colouring crayons. Afterwards they made drawings of tadpoles in the puddles and of the heron that, their guide had told them, unerringly descended on the puddles and ate the froglets.

A Gothic rave took place under the derelict arches close in to the station every Wednesday night; sometimes Kim saw the clubbers in their whiteface and mascara drifting along the road towards the tube as he arrived. When the council's new car pound opened behind barbed wire on the wasteland, it brought yet another population to the area.

At first Kim didn't know where to direct the women in narrow-cut deep pile coats and expensive shoes who would ask him, hesitantly, for the way to the pound. The first winter it was in operation, he fell in with a woman, and accompanied her there. She was flapping at the unfamiliarity of the location, scared because she'd taken the tube on account of the size of the fine, after she'd found her car towed from its parking place in the smart centre of Enoch where she'd been shopping. She was carrying glacé carrier bags, bulking awkwardly in the cold wind against her legs.

It was after school, and already dark; they followed signs in ruined capitals to the pound, past the iron shutters on the rave venue; a huge skull and crossbones was daubed in white overhead.

'You're being *so* kind,' she kept saying.

The way to the pound was so grim he was himself astonished. The woman chattered on: she'd been having lunch with a friend, hadn't noticed the time, her husband would kill her, it was just what they needed, to throw away a hundred pounds on a fine. She was nervous of him, he could see that; it amused him. She was talking herself out of

55

being scared. He was aware that his slim, slightly dancing gait could appear menacing, almost elvish; he knew that he was hard to place and that this unsettled people on first acquaintance. Dark. Educated-sounding. Not a yob, then. A young professional? Who could tell what his business might be? He was careful not to run up behind a woman in the street, to catch a bus, because Minta had explained when he was young how frightened she was. But this woman who had lost her car could see him, hear him, he was on her side, and she was still afraid.

When they reached the steamed-up Portakabin, with its fug of tea and tobacco, he let her deal with the heavies inside who took her credit card and threw her the keys of her car in insolent triumph. But he watched them, and they knew he was watching them. Cropped, bull-necked, beer guts, skin and liver and eyes of rotted cod, the stuff of vigilantes. Ex-cons, most like. Or ex-cops, done for malfeasance. Corruption. Or worse. Outlaws as role models – what shit. Whoever thought crime was glamorous? He thought of bringing the class here, too. A lesson in civic tensions. Second car owners, lapped in luxury, meet the new, profit-making arm of the law.

He exaggerated the courtesy with which he ushered the woman out and down the clumsy steps. She picked her way across the tip, hobbling in her high-heeled boots through the ruts and puddles towards the pound; there were arc lights, which cast such thick shadows it was hard to see. She was crying when she finally found her car. But she did not offer him a lift.

'I'm really sorry,' she whimpered. 'You've been so kind, so helpful. You look a very nice young man, even though you're . . .' She faltered. He understood she meant his not being, well, native. 'But I can't let a stranger into my car. I just can't.'

'Go on, try it', he said. He flashed a small, slow smile at her; her fear stood between them. She was thinking of him trying to kiss her, he could see that; he was aware of the zips on her boots on the inside of her calves; of the folds of her thick soft coat.

'No,' she replied, with a hint of a whimper. 'No.'

7

The Rushcutters' Assault

[G: Skipwith 673.1841: Misc. Mss. G. Fr. 20, papyrus, c. 325–350 CE, translation in the hand of Hereward Meeks, keeper of Near Eastern Antiquities, 1858–76.]

... the crickets were chafing loudly among the dust and stones when Leto became strong enough to leave the cliffside cave and set out down the rocks on the other side from the necropolis towards the freshwater lagoon that lay behind a sand bar near the shore. With the children, Lycia and her cubs, she began walking south; their accompanying shadows moved beside them over the terrain in long thin ribbons, scribbling their presence.

The she-wolf was uneasy; her nose pointed and detected movement, the salt sweat of working bodies. 'We should have started after dark,' she muttered.

Leto was headstrong; she insisted she must find water, people, somewhere else to go. She could not stay in the she-wolf's den forever, with no clothes for herself or the babies and no water that was sweet, not fouled.

She was stumbling in haste on the uneven, precipitous path; in her still depleted state, with the babies tied to her front and back, she was clumsy.

'Here,' said Lycia, 'give me one of them.' She butted Leto's son with her narrow muzzle. 'I'll carry him.' Her own cubs were trotting behind her, as light on their feet as if they were tumbleweed on the breeze.

At first, Leto resisted, and kept on, stumbling, towards the shore; she still had her silk slippers on, for, thin and frayed as they were, they gave her soft feet a little protection against the sharpness of the stony ground. But they also made her slither when the slabs were broad and smooth.

The sea's surface was shining in her eyes, a stretched skin, gilded and tooled that threw back from its surface the horizontal shafts of the late sun like a struck gong.

The wolf stopped, now and then, and sniffed, while her giglamp eyes opened, lambent, as she scanned the view. 'There are men about. More than usual. We have to turn back.'

'No!' Leto wailed. She so longed for fresh water, she could have faced a crowd, naked.

'Give Phoebus to me,' said Lycia. 'We'll move more nimbly.' Gently, her muzzle closed on the dirty rags that swaddled the infant boy. Her own cubs frisked, making three times the distance as they scampered ahead, tacked back, tumbled in a flurry of limbs together, picked themselves up and gambolled on.

They saw the lagoon below them, a wide smile of silver with the smith's small hammer blows setting it to glitter. Fringed with burr reeds and the spiky blades of irises, the sight of it lightened Leto's step and she almost began to run, turning her head now and then to make sure the wolf, with the baby in its jaws, was not taking a different path.

'Wait till dusk,' whispered the wolf. 'Don't go so fast. They'll have gone by then.'

But Leto ran, with her daughter on her back, as soon as they reached the marshy ground around the lagoon; she pushed through the reeds, feeling the suction of the wet earth tug at her slippers.

She undid the scrap of material that bound Phoebe to her back, and, taking her tightly in her arms, walked into the water as she was, closing her eyes as the cool thick silk of the flow clasped her and soothed the hot soreness of her feet and legs and between her legs. She must not lose her footing, not with the baby on her hip, who was looking up at her slightly cross-eyed, with furrowed brow, as if perplexed by her mother's immersion.

The lagoon was mud-bottomed, and swallowed one of her shoes; she felt the silt move smoothly between her toes. With her free arm she splashed her face; the little girl looked even more puzzled, poised to howl in protest. Leto turned back, to find a point of access, a kind of beach, where she could set the baby down while she bathed.

Lycia was calling to her, softly, through the darkness from a screen of reeds.

'Leto, we're here. This way. Wait. You're too exposed there.'

But she ignored the animal, and sank deep into the dark water, into its coolness, drinking it into every pore and cranny of her sore dry body, inside and outside, through her mouth and eyes and floated.

When she surfaced, she heard calls from the shore, and shook the water out of her ears.

'What in hell's name are you doing?' the words bounced on the surface of the lagoon towards her, clear as the opening phrase of a tune. '*Get out of there, now!*'

She saw men emerging from the reeds, with cut sheaves on their shoulders. Her baby was there; she struggled to reach the shore. But she was feeble from the privations of the last few days, and the water stuck round her legs and the mud shackled her ankles as words pelted her too:

'Get out of there—'

'You and your brat—'

'Go back where you belong—'

'You and your kind—'

'You don't belong—'

'Here—'

'None of your kind—'

'Breeding your brats—'

'This is *our* home—'

'*Our* water—'

'*Our* land—'

Their curses reached her in rags and tatters, flying lashes, a sting of pain on one side of her head. She put her hand up and felt a warm pulpiness above her ear, in her hair, where the stone had hit her. She looked across the dancing water to the shore; shapes were moving in the reeds; she caught shouts, gathering huddles, figures bending. She saw the streak of the wolf's form move higher, beyond the reeds. She fancied she heard the animal howl, but no, the papoose still hung from her narrow mouth. The animal was leaving her, with her son, running for cover in the caves riddling the cliff; she could not do otherwise, or could she?

Her dress was stuck to her; she kept her arms crossed over her body as she clambered out through the silt towards them.

More stones drove into the water near her; another caught her on the

59

head again, she floundered, the refreshing element in which she was swimming suddenly heavy as sheet metal, preventing her from moving, from climbing out of its grip. She grasped at the rushes to find her balance and push her way to the shore.

Her daughter. A group of shadows on the inlet crisscrossed where she had laid the baby down.

Her dress was stuck to her; she kept her arms crossed over her body as she clambered out through the silt towards them.

She reached the bank. They had the baby; one of them was cradling her, making goo-goo noises.

'Oooh, ooh, what a pretty little creature! Who'd ever think your mother was a whore?' He threw the child in the air, made as if to let her crash, caught her and danced her up again. 'Dance a baby diddy, what shall daddy do widdy?'

He tossed the infant across to another figure, passing her like a ball.

Leto was among them now, whirling to catch her daughter as they chucked her from one to another. Phoebe was roaring, a red and purple scrap, her tiny limbs spread-eagled like a flying bat as they played. One of the men grabbed Leto as she struggled to catch her child; he clutched at her breasts under her wet clothes, twisted her round by them and pushed his face into her mouth. She jerked back and pushed, using her nails, her teeth, until at last, with a supreme effort she leapt to catch her daughter and holding her close, fell to the ground, crouched over her.

A kick made her fall sideways but she kept curled tight around the peach-soft flesh of the baby, who was slimy with tears and other oozings of her terror.

'This is our water,' shouted one man in her ear.

Another kicked her, 'Next time, we'll kill you and your runt.'

A blow caught her full in the small of the back; they were beating her with something whippy and wet and flat – the rushes they had been gathering in the lagoon. Their panting rose as they lashed her; she curled up more tightly over her baby.

'Teaching our women your dirty ways—'

'Filth—'

'Whore—'

'We know what you're like—'

'We know what you like—'

'We'll show you what you like—'

60

They had cutlasses; they had been harvesting reeds. One man tussled now to pin her legs, another at her shoulders to turn her over. Another breathed hard in her face; hands paddled between her thighs. Their knives shone.

Through her swollen lids she saw them, jagged flashes and flickers, like scraps of leaves tormented by a storm wind that tossed shadows against a moon.

She prayed, to all the powers and thrones and dominions she had ever known or half known or guessed or dreamed. She did not see her life pass before her, but through the broken roaring and grunts and curses and maulings and beatings she saw her divine lover again. She saw his eyes above hers, the pupils widening into a corridor to the velvet where the far stars swim as he bent to kiss her. She saw his wife, tall, pale, with a straight furrow between her eyebrows that continued the parting in her hair, her expression tight as the grip of ice on water. And she felt for them all a piercing longing, for their love, for their mercy.

Then she heard Lycia the she-wolf howling from the ridge.

Leto picked up the high keening noise through all the tumult as the men scrabbled over her, and then she felt them freeze. Her attackers were rising, in disarray; screaming at one another. They rushed, themselves now animal in their panic, a quarry raised and scattered by beaters in the chase. Some ran in terror, dropping everything, others, thriftier, hesitated, casting about to salvage the harvest of reeds they had been cutting.

The she-wolf was loping down through the dunes towards them; they could track the sound of her battle cry as she came.

A flying missile of fur and spit, the animal hurled herself on to the shore of the inlet, scattering the remaining men; one of them turned and stood and slashed at the animal with his cutlass, but she was snarling, crouched back on her haunches, and he dared not close with the bared canines that glinted in the darkness, and he, too, turned to flee with the others.

But there were no others; not any longer. How had they disappeared so swiftly? so silently? First he had picked up their cries of panic, their footsteps stumbling through the reeds and on the dry ground, but now he could see nothing, hear nothing, except the shrill song of the crickets beyond the wolf's snarling.

... men who outrage the gods in heaven are condemned to shed their human shape ... transfixed by the slavering dripping from the wolf's jaws, a rushcutter stood, unable to flee. Semen smears on his stomach, bloodstains on his mouth, his arms, his legs ... he could not run as he felt a bolt of something damp and wet snake over him and cover him and begin to shrink and condense him. His flesh as it diminished turned clammy. But he was not alone in his punishment. Beside him, others who had also played their part in the attack were rooted to the spot. Their fingers lengthened and their knuckles swelled, skin grew between the digits of their toes and knobs and gnarls swelled over their bones. One tried to cry out against his fate, but his voice came out in a feeble gulp. Another tried to run, and found he was jumping on unaccustomed, thin, green legs. They fled, some diving headlong into the water with a wild croaking, others sinking into the mud, their bulging eyes big with alarm, the pulse in their crops racing to the terror in their changed hearts.

Thus are the wicked punished for their transgressions against the beloved of the gods ...

[G. Fr. 22]

... the she-wolf approached Leto where she lay. The animal placed a paw on her shoulder and turned her over.

Phoebe nuzzled her mother; there was blood in her milk.

Lycia cleaned her wounds, gently. Her tongue was lithe and thorough. She murmured, 'I've stowed the baby boy with my cubs deep in the rocks up there – they'll not be found.'

But she could not bring Leto back from the darkness where she was plummeting.

There, as it furled her in its cloudy arms, Leto was moaning.

The wolf said, 'The boy's safe, I've kept him safe.' And then prophesied, 'She, too, the girl, she'll survive. And Leto, Leto, come back. So will you.'

That region is called Lycania today in honour of the animal who came to the aid of Leto in the hour of her death.

... and all wolves shall be sacred to her ...

Praise be to God for His signs & wonders.

... holy Leto, patron of mothers in distress, grant us the favour of your protection now and forever Amen!

8

'People Like You': The Rise of Gramercy Poule

From the cover of her first single, Gramercy Poule's face shimmered, painted with silver-white clouds floating in gold and azure haloes: her forehead, cheeks and chin became a summer sky, in which her eyes, wide-open and startled, stared out, with a swallow in flight applied around each eye, the bird's beak and split tails substituting for false lashes. The stylist had showed her a postcard of a painting by Magritte and she remembered the blue head, swimming with fleecy clouds, from a school trip to the gallery where it hung. The resulting image seized on public fascination with undersized waifs and their empty, spaced-out heads full of dreams, and intensified the effect of Gramercy's scratchy ethereal screaming as it hovered and broke and jumped like a needle in a dusty groove. The whimsy of the portrait didn't convey the impatient irony of the ballad 'People Like You', or the desolate spirit in the songs that she wrote for the album that followed hard upon the heels of the first successful singles.

'And Then Some' was a love lament for a boy she'd been at school with who left her for a friend at a party whom he began French kissing in front of her eyes; the song mimicked the sucking, squelching noises he'd made. It also staged an edgy assault on the dawn of the me-generation, the coming time of the symbiotic explosion of the yuppies on the one hand, and the underclass on the other. Gramercy was neither. Her background was old Bohemia and the Sixties; her mum, Roberta ('Bobby') Grace, a former Southern belle who'd done the masked balls at Carnival time in Shiloh's southern parts before leaving her native land to live with Gramercy's father just in time for all the brouhaha over miniskirts and Mini-Minors. He opened a restaurant, just off the Avenue where it was all happening then, and called it Medlar's, after the crooked and dense-leaved tree that grew in its tiny courtyard. It was one of the first informal, eclectic restaurants to throw off the post-war national gloom of boiled ham in onion sauce, and offer a polyglot diet of avocados and clams and garlic and mozzarella. Medlar's attracted a young, spendy, loud crowd who, men and women alike, wore gladrags and cobalt kohl on their inner eyelids and patchouli oil; they featured in new, excitable magazines and newspaper gossip columns. But like many a sommelier and cook before him, 'Hatters' Poule took to drink, and, on the upward slope of the early boom – too early to make a bundle – he sold up to a chain of new pasta cafés, who moved in and lightened and streamlined the tatty, glamorous crush of his original creation. Bobby Grace continued to do shoots of her legs for adverts of the innovatory hose in many lacy patterns and fruity colours for some while after she couldn't present her face for fashion anymore, but by then she too was chronically cash poor.

'And Then Some' sold 20,000 copies in the first two weeks after its release, and Gramercy appeared on the telly, for the first time. Her dress of parachute silk cut like camiknickers was slashed and fastened precariously at the shoulder with a chipped pink enamelled nappy pin her mother had kept as a talisman from Gramercy's infancy, and had given her daughter for luck. She parried the banter of the presenter with a scowl and a sniff, but told him the story of the pin, so that everyone laughed; nobody could remember terry towels. She explained how she was called after the Park where she'd been conceived one summer, and then she launched into karaoke to her own recording while the shadows of the fans' hands, reaching out towards her like Israelites gathering manna from heaven in the desert, played over the stage and the raking halogen spots multiplied her touchingly fragile figure into leaping wraiths like burning tissue paper.

Her album 'Islands in the Moon' quickly followed the release of 'Freedom Days'.

> The airmiles and the gold credit card
> The car alarm and the burglar lights
> In your 'Desirable Country Residence'
> > But you don't know you have all you need here and now
> > In your mind, in your dreams

Freedom Days/Billy Blake

You say you want to have it all
But you don't know you have all you need, here and now

Freedom Days/Billy Blake

You never know what is enough
Unless you know what is more than enough
   I want to live freedom days

Gramercy Poule could keen like a banshee and howl like a stuck pig, said some of the reviewers, or she could whisper, so close to the mike, that you could feel her hot breath corroding your ear. She was the queen of the sad people, said one writer, while another raved that her voice was like spider's silk, so fine but so strong that, on a single sudden rise in pitch to a fluting, winged dominant (something Gramercy had found in the sweet soul ballad singers, like Marvin Gaye), it could lift a man right out of his boots as high as you wanted to go. And there, at the very top of her range, you'd feel this unbelievably intense sorrow pierce right through your head and turn into joy. The title song 'Islands in the Moon', plus a baker's dozen of other numbers, including 'Telling It Slant', 'Don't Buy It', 'Bivalve', 'Wearing My Whiteface', 'Webs of Shelob', 'What Does Your Navel String Say', 'Wodewoses on Fire', 'Going Down Down', made the charts and a fortune, and Bobby Grace, who wasn't short of money through any improvident tastes of her own, took charge and built up, in those spiralling years of money markets and city bonds, a significant portfolio of investments for her only child.

Gramercy hated the sight of her credit ratings: she went on blasting against greed and grabbiness, against youth success and youth money, targeted by new magazines called *Ego* and new colognes called In Your Face.

Property was also recommended: years of moving and decorating followed. Bobby Grace had strong ideas about paint colours and curtain materials, and mother and daughter fought. Monica, who settled in as Gramercy's manager after bitter fallout with her first, interceded between them, and Gramercy bought another small house for her mother, not so near that she could call round on foot for a bottle of wine, but not so far that she couldn't come quickly in an emergency. There were no emergencies, but a whirligig of photo shoots, interviews, meetings with agents, fashion designers, visagistes, record company officials over on the redeye, dates in local clubs and venues up and down the country, shopping sprees, tours, clubs, parties. Gramercy told the stylists and the press all about the zabaglione in Medlar's, for a long time her favourite and only food, about her pet rat who had been eaten by the cat in the next door flat in the mansion block and how she had been there and seen it happen, the tail flicking between the cat's jaws, about the poets who inspired her lyrics. The reporters wrote down that she would declare that poets were the legislators of mankind, and described her experiences with drugs almost as they happened. She answered questions about what her songs were about as well as she could: she had books, she told her audience, and she wanted to have lots more of them. Her spirit guides were Blake, of course, and Mary Shelley and Tolkien – and, yes, Emily Dickinson. She'd like to wear white all the time, as Emily had. But she drew back from full confession when she saw that her audience was jibbing. Her reputation as rock's latest kook became tinged with a certain jocular scepticism about her throwback hippie tastes among the almost exclusively male comradeship of the music press: she was really weird, it was generally agreed, weird and pretentious. Some said she took herself much too seriously for a teen rock star. Others drooled: 'Check out that incredible gurgle-cum-squeal at the end of "Bivalve" – you'll wonder what you're doing that you've never heard a woman make that noise!'

Sometimes when Gramercy's head was thick and her eyes were spinning and the veins in her arms and legs felt as if the blood had turned fizzy, she'd look in the mirror and make faces the photographers had never seen. She'd screw up her nose and eyes and grind her teeth and pull her mouth to her ears like a child playing monsters and utter deep groans as if an alien baby were straining inside her wanting to be born. That way she could feel, for a moment, that she still had some secrets. But sometimes, her expressions made her cry: she had no idea she could look so ugly and evil and it frightened her, in her cups, that she was apparently an unknown quantity, even to herself.

Phil told her not to worry. 'We all contain multitudes,' he said. 'I *are* others,' he added. 'That's the contemporary version – plural, not singular.' He was studying philosophy and politics, and sometimes, when the whirl of her life set her down for a week, Gramercy wished she could leave her life and join his.

It had been Monica's idea that Gramercy needed a place to hide away, she said, humming. Bobby Grace supported her warmly, since the market in country houses was quiet, but would soon follow the urban explosion, in her opinion. Monica stressed the importance of a good rail connection; Bobby Grace wanted other kinds of connection. When the house of the late Sir Mervyn Feverel-Orbe, Bt., was advertised, under his name, in the Sunday papers, Bobby Grace immediately organised an appointment with the estate agent.

'You met him once, darling. He was in the restaurant with . . . ' she mentioned a couple of names Gramercy had vaguely heard. 'Mervy was really droll, I can tell you. Very very tall and very very thin, with a pink or blue Sobranie dangling from his long long fingers and a swooping, drawling mad cutglass voice. But he was brilliant, too, musical and artistic and – well, you know, he collaborated with all the greats, the Ballets Russes in the old days, Constant Lambert and the Sitwells. He's old world, a last trace of true dandiness, of Oscar Wilde and that whole universe that's gone out with the Dodo and martini cocktails and White Russians drinking tea from silver cups in the Café de Paris.'

'You gave me his fairy tales,' Gramercy said, sulkily, as she always felt when her mother grew excited. 'Ballet stories.' She sounded contemptuous – why did she sound contemptuous?

'But I thought you loved them . . . ' Bobby Grace caught herself when she saw Gramercy's look of rebelliousness. 'Anyhow that's neither here nor there. So: "Prestigious manor house, mentioned in the Domesday Book, the seat of Sir Mervyn Feverel-Orbe, Bt., whose family have lived on the estate since the sixteenth century." Fabulous! Just think of that! "Set in spectacular scenery on the edge of Fellmoor. 6 reception, 6 bedroom, 1 bathroom . . ." (typical!) "Orangery" – *Orangery!* – "Magnificent views of the Nine Maidens, secluded 4 acres, orchard, mature borders and beds" Hah! i.e. overgrown and weed-choked ". . . walled kitchen garden." No mention of heating. "2 barn, garden sheds."'

'I'll rattle about in there.'

'No you won't – estate agents always exaggerate. Six reception probably includes a cubbyhole under the stairs and a bootroom with one of those panels of enamel bells saying "Valet de chambre" or whatever in Gothic script.'

Bobby Grace was even more delighted with the house itself, when she returned from a reccy with Monica, even though the Domesday mention turned out to be a mere 'bothy', of which a doorway and lintel remained in one of the several dilapidated outhouses in the garden where the cucumber vines had burst through their glass frames and borage, grown to spice the summer wine, ran rampant, buzzing with bees.

For five years after she bought it, as the renovation made slow progress under Bobby Grace's tight financial control, Gramercy felt like a visitor in her own house; nobody understood how to cook on the electric cooker or the oil-fired Rayburn, stoves with their own time signatures, so differently paced from the quick gas burners of the city. But Phil liked it there, and, after he finished his course and began writing a film script, he stayed down in Feverel Court. Gradually the rooms grew untidy and comfortable, with his books and his jumpers and CDs and videos strewn about in a companionable tangle. He and Gramercy made a deal: she would pay for everything (or rather Monica would see to the bills being paid) and Phil would line up help from the village and round about to reconstruct the garden and maintain the house and keep the larder stocked with beer and rum and coke and wine and ready-to-cook meals and the freezer with ice cream (Gramercy's staple); he'd collect her from the station, and take her back when she had to return to the city; he'd score her dope locally and feed the ginger cat whom they acquired when he sauntered into the orangery one afternoon and mewed to break your heart. Phil called him Poly, because he had a damaged eye from a scrap. 'He must have lost his territory,' Phil surmised, 'To some young Turk who nearly gouged out his eye and turned him into a ghoul, a Cyclops! Poor old tom cat, past his prime.'

Once Feverel Court was up and running, Bobby Grace found life in the country dull. In the city, she bought outfits she had never been able to afford before, not even at the height of her modelling career, and, as she told her daughter, had a string of beaux, as she still called them in her Southern way.

'Don't you worry, though,' she told Gramercy. 'I'm not going to let any one of them move into my life and take it over. Not after what I went through with your father.'

So Bobby Grace withdrew, with pride.

'Darling, you don't need me any more. I feel I've really achieved something! Isn't that what mothering is about? I'm really proud of you. Just stick to your guns 'n' roses and keep flying.'

She and Gramercy still spoke on the phone every day that they could, though sometimes, when Gramercy was on tour, they missed each other. Then they would talk longer the next day. At the time, her mother liked Phil.

So Phil and Gramercy played house together, and were happy. They were comrades, Phil said. They smoked together and drank together; they made each other up with different faces late at night; they nuzzled into each other's smells in the late mornings when they woke; they quarrelled with sudden storms of tears from Gramercy and furious scowls and sulks from Phil – over money, mostly; they spread out maps of places near and far and planned adventure voyages they never made; they talked about friends who had come to stay and played sardines and murder in the dark with them, and laughed uproariously as they slagged them off when they had gone; they raged at the papers and the music press and the film industry and swore to overturn the whole set-up; they cut out words from tabloid headlines and magazine articles for Gramercy to pin up in her music room and prompt her lyrics; they thrashed out the plotline of Phil's movie and took parts in turn but kept finding they were just parodying golden oldies they'd watched in the afternoon. They dissected Bobby Grace and left her in shreds, then called her up and pressed her to come over; they wondered about Hatters, who was living in a tropical watering hole, but who turned up now and then and embarrassed them in the pub by shouting about his fabulous connections and amazing entrepreneurship. Monica tried to hang around close enough to prevent him asking Gramercy for money – Gramercy was under sentence of death from her mother if she gave her father anything at all. They also discussed what could be done about Phil's parents, Charles and Vivienne, who sometimes came to visit, bewildered and mannerly, from the ruined rain-swept wastes of a northern town. Then they drank some more and smoked some more and kissed and cuddled; they were babes in the wood and they were going to make all the difference through her music, through his writing. They were going to change the world, Phil said, and Gramercy believed him.

9

Kim to Hortense; Hortense to Kim

Subject: Leto Bundle
Date: Tues, 19 May 199– 00:36:09 +0100
From: kim.mcquy<hswu@lattice.onlyconnect.com>
To: Dr Hortense Fernly<h.fernly@natmus.ac.alb>

Dear Dr Fernly

   You were kind enough to give me your card after your talk today. I'm
a schoolteacher (at Cantelowes primary) so we do school outings to your
Museum when we can. That's how I first saw the Leto tomb, and got
interested in the bundle inside.

   If you have more info about the writings from the tomb, PLEASE point
me in the right direction to read them, so that I can put out what's
relevant on my website – http://www.hswu.org. If you had time to visit
it, I'd be glad to hear what you think.

   Thank you for your talk.

     kim mcquy

P.S. The frogs were a revelation. Hadn't noticed them before, carved on
the inside like that. Do you know this poem? I found it last night on the
web @www.dsh.concretepoetry.com

   Frog
   Pond
   Plop

I was reminded of it by your story:-)

71

Subject: Re: Leto Bundle
Date: Thurs, 21 May 199– 09:14:16 +0100
From: Hortense Fernly<h.fernly@natmus.ac.alb>
To: kim.mcquy<hswu@lattice.onlyconnect.com>

Dear Mr McQuy, If you would like to make an appointment with the
National Museum Archives, I'd be happy to arrange for material
connected with G: Skipwith 673/4.1841 to be put out for you. Their
number is 580–9000 ext542. If this interests you, let me know when you
are able to come. I am here at the National Museum most days.
   Yours,
   Dr Hortense Fernly
PS If the frogs interest you, you might take a look at Meeks' translation
of Misc. Mss. Gr. Fragments 16–23.

Subject: Re: Leto Bundle
Date: Thurs, 21 May 199– 22:19:07 +0100
From: kim.mcquy<hwsu@lattice.onlyconnect.com>
To: Hortense Fernly<h.fernly@natmus.ac.alb>

Dear Dr Fernly thank you very much for the offer but it's hard for me to
come weekdays now term's started unless it's after school hours one
afternoon/evening. Is the archive open on a Saturday? Is there a chance
of your being there?
   Yours sincerely, kim
p.s. is there anything you can send/bookmark for me in the meantime?

Subject: Archives
Date: Tues, 26 May 199– 09:04:17 +0100
From: Hortense Fernly<h.fernly@natmus.ac.alb>
To: kim.mcquy<hswu@lattice.onlyconnect.com>

The Archives are suffering from cutbacks like the rest of us, so opening
hours are severely curtailed – late night Thursdays, but I don't stay on,
and I'm rarely here on Saturdays. However, I can arrange for the material
to be out for you to look at in the reading room. We can take it from
there. Yours, HF

PART TWO

In the Convent
(A Petition and Two Chronicles)

I

'Item, One Frog'

Kim McQuy opened the brown, crinkly folder the librarian had brought him from the shelves in the back of the Archives Reading Room. On the inside of the cover, Hereward Meeks, keeper of Near Eastern Antiquities, had inscribed his name in a precise, legible hand above a list; the first, loose, handwritten sheet was headed: 'Inventory (Unfinished)'

There, Kim read:

Item, One mummified frog, bound in linen, basketweave pattern.

Item, Woman's leather sandal; silk and silver gamp; traces of gilding on the leather straps.

Item, Tortoise shell, pierced with holes around the edge. Comparison with examples found in better condition elsewhere suggests that this was strung with stones to make a baby's rattle.

Item, Upper left canine of a wolf (amulet missing accompanying charm, probably used to fend off danger from roaming wild beasts) cf. surviving rings inscribed against scorpion bites, insect stings, etc.

Item, Three infant's (milk) teeth in a drawstring leather pouch, much damaged.

Item, One earring, with gold beads as bunch of grapes. Lazuli work, c. 1250.

When he reached the seventh item, Kim felt his pulse bang, in his eardrums, in his throat, in his heart:

Item, One mother-of-pearl button, inscribed 'KIM' – ? standing for '*Kalē Ierē Mnemosynē*', as in the opening invocation of a prayer to the goddess Memory ('Lovely, Holy Memory!')

He looked around the quiet room; there was no commotion to match his excitement. The atmosphere still sounded as deep and still as when he arrived, as if he and the few other readers were enclosed in a submarine; their several absorption with the words on which they were travelling was carrying them down below the earth to the silent aquifers below where lost things, forgotten things fell, settled, and waited to be raised to the surface again.

'Lovely, Holy Memory,' he read again, with his pulse quietening now to a tingle. No, he said to himself. No, we must begin again. Start a new story. Shake the pieces of the past into another pattern.

He went back to Meeks's precise script:

Item, One cuttlefish bone, once possibly inscribed, but entirely effaced.

Item, Silver lamella or sheet, good condition, engraved with charms, originally rolled up in a silver phylactery (this much damaged):

'Turn away, thunderbolts and lightning flash. Flee, death by fire.

'The goddess Artemis raises her voice to her father on high and its sweetness recalled the music of swallows twittering in the eaves of home. He smiles and nods. "Bind up all the demons," he orders, and the mountain peaks sway to his command . . .

'And the place of meeting was in flames,

And the earth cracked beneath them.' (Homeric Hymn to Artemis) (here the text breaks off).

A rare survival, ?450 AD. Amulets telling such historiolae or short mythic tales, were usually inscribed on wax, parchment, wood, and so have perished.

Item, Scrap of orange peel.

Item, Residue of haschisch resin.

The list ended:

See separate catalogue of Mss., for various fragments and documents on papyrus, linen, vellum; maps, drawings, sketches, etc., comprising:

G. Mss. 1–72.1841

Lat. Mss. 73–89.1841

Eng. Skipwith Add. Mss. 90–122.1841 (GS's diaries and ship's log)

Eng. Skipwith Misc. Mss. Fragments 1–227.1841 (GS's notes and sketches from the Lycanian excavations)

See also related material: Anon., *Adventures of a Ship-Boy. Of the Most Barbarous Abuses of the Press-Gang & the Cat; of his subsequent Adventures among Slavers and of his Providential Deliverance & Happy Return. Written by a Well-Wisher. With an Appendix and an Appeal to Her Majesty for his Pardon and for the Improvement of Conditions in Her Navy* ... Printed for private circulation of Her Majesty's subjects (Portsmouth, 1859) Shelf mark: SK892.1889.

Kim leafed through the folder; Meeks had pinned pages together with dressmakers' pins, now rusted and seeping haloes of reddish-brown dust on to the paper. He began with a slender sheaf somewhere in the middle of the folder, on which Meeks had written:

Evidence of one Karim, formerly an equerry in the entourage
of Cunmar, taken by the commission of enquiry at Cadenas in
1200, held seventeen years after the martyrdom of Leto, also
known as Laetitia *Deodata*; the necessary preliminary to the
Petitio in causam sanctitatis Laetitiae, the submission to the
Congregation of Rites to plead for her eventual canonisation.

[Many lacunae.]

2

The Deposition of Karim the Equerry

(*From the* Petitio in causam sanctitatis Laetitiae)

[Lat. Fr. 16]

'... the lady Leto was exchanged against another child, a small boy with a turned foot – no use to our armies or to the Lord Cunmar. Moreover, birth defects – and this was counted as one – were considered unlucky; but Ser Matteo, Leto's father, was a boastful man, and he declared that surgeons in his country would soon fix the boy's gait, and that he only wanted to show his own people what an Ophiri native looked like; in this respect, the child would serve despite his deformity. He would introduce him to his people; maybe to the Pope himself. The Holy Father took a deep interest in our heathen brethren, he said, as he had a great respect for the learning and civilisation of our ancestors.'

We rebuked Karim for this blasphemy.

'Lady Leto's father loaded his vessel with a great cofferful of treasures from our country; it was a matter of wonder to us that the Lord Cunmar trusted him. Around the child he left in our keeping, laughing that she was the pledge of his good faith, there played a kind of crackly fire, we sensed; she looked so different from anyone else in Cadenas. That strangeness was part of the reason for the effect, but not the whole of it. We used to say then that she had been breathed out when a god, sated with pleasure, had yawned.

(We rebuked Karim for this blasphemy also.)

'That was the Ophiri way of thinking, he persisted. I'm not saying that I think it's the truth. But it's a pretty enough thought.

'When she first came to the Keep, we dressed the child after our own fashion, and would have done so even if she had not grown out of the stiff corsetry in which she was bundled when she was first left with us. Together we attended Lord Cunmar; sometimes in the baths. Slippery with the soap, her light fists following mine on his back, we pummelled him. She could sit on him, then, she was still small; how he sighed and rolled his eyes with the bliss of perturbation she gave him. You see, she did not know her power, but we were all beginning to feel it.

'Now and then a message arrived in the trade documents, from Parthenopolis and other ports of our Inland Sea, addressed to Leto; eventually, someone would be found to read it to her.'

We reminded Karim we had collected such evidence of this nature as we could.

'Leto was placed in the Convent of the Swaddling Bands, when she was seven and her father had failed to return and keep his promise to Lord Cunmar. Even though the nuns are great chatterers and they told the child of other times and other places, of threads that linked Cadenas to metropolitan centres far and wide, Leto told me, after her return to the Keep, that she felt she was suffocating. She experienced her childhood as if she were living in a bottle, like a spirit in a flask cast to the bottom of the sea. All she could see through the glass walls of her captivity was the huge, formless mass of water, now turbid and churning and moonless, now light-speckled with looping rays, and visited by fish with gloomy smiles on their whiskered lips, sometimes revealing a double row of tiny transparent fangs.'

These morbid imaginings, if true, were sent to test her faith; we made Karim desist from repeating such assaults on her unless absolutely central to the question we put.

Next we asked, 'Why did she leave the convent?'

Karim said, 'She returned to court after she had her women's flowers, because the Procurator remembered that he had promised Ser Matteo he would look after her and there were reports of new business from that quarter. Although it seemed Leto was now an orphan, without family or fortune, Cunmar was too crafty not to make a show of keeping his side of the bargain. He was considering an appropriate match for her. But, then suddenly – as children like to hear one say in the story – everything changed. He was seized by a passion for her: you know the rest.'

'Be that as it may.'

So did we order him to continue.

'Lord Cunmar was seized with a passion for her; there was to be a wedding. But . . . '

We pressed him. 'I was given orders to take Lady Leto – she was about to give birth – and kill her outside the walls of the citadel and leave her as if bandits or wolves had attacked her. So we – Doris, her maidservant and I – threw her down on the nightsoil cart leaving that night. We wanted to save her by this means, by trusting her to divine providence.'

We forbade him to blaspheme. We commanded him to admit his part in the death of the sainted and suffering child. We threatened the screw and the rack if he continued to deny his part in her martyrdom.

He shook his head. 'I am proud that my heart led me not my head and I disobeyed the orders of my lady Porphyria.'

'What happened to her after that?'

He continued to lie. 'I've heard rumours, but I know nothing.'

The old man was returned to the dungeons again, the better to refresh his memories and repent his sins, in preparation for being put to the question the following day.

In Kim's head, connections formed, faded, returned. He shuffled back through the folder, and began to read the contents from the beginning.

He could hyperlink the story in Karim's testimony, he was thinking, under the catchword, 'Saint' on the HSWU homepage.

3

Homepage: http://www.hswu.org

Leto Lives!
The Angel of the Present is Here!
To Open the Bundle Click on:

[hyperlinks] 👆
Treasure
Frogs
Prayer
Saint
Wanderer

Join our database: send an e-mail to <hswu@lattice.onlyconnect.com>

4

Kim to Hortense

Subject: Re: Archives: Help!
Date: Thurs, 28 May 199– 02:11:38 +0100
From: kim.mcquy<hswu@lattice.onlyconnect.com>
To: Hortense Fernly<h.fernly@natmus.ac.alb>

- -

Dear Dr Fernly   looked at the boxes of papers after school today
would welcome a steer :- thought you said there was writing *on* the
mummy wrappings – that the bundle was made of them   after the
body was taken away/disappeared/resurrected? thats what I'm after and
thought I was going to find – the charms and texts you talked about –
    best   kim
ps visited room xix – lots of hswu people about   we discussed the
return of the Leto   approval expressed all round for your plans for
the big new display – though I want to see a new building   she needs
space, lots of it   there'll be *huge* crowds – it's growing   the
planetary diaspora needs a figurehead someone like them to focus all
their feelings of belonging and unbelonging there was some surprise felt
I must pass on that you still haven't opened a comments book   which
we've all been asking for since this started – I'd like a see a whole glass
tower/cube/pyramid in a park somewhere – a crystal palace –
    people want to write down their feelings   their wishes   their hopes
– they – we – feel let down
    not by you personally – you're not rubbish like some people – I trust
you

by the way when is Leto coming back   she says she's already hanging
around all amongst us   but people need a focus for their feelings
where they can find a reflection of their experience   a shrine would do
the job nicely cheers kim

5

The Plane Tree and the Lotus

In the body of the letter, past the customary overtures, Gramercy Poule read:

'What is our national identity? What are our national identities? How do we define today, in a world beset by strife, international and civil, an idea of home and belonging? How do we enable this country to maintain the civic pact of openness, tolerance and citizenship for which we have been renowned since the Mother of Parliaments was founded as the expression, instrument and servant of modern democracy? Has our national pride withered? Is even the notion unmentionable in today's climate? Multiculturalism is enmeshed in difficulties and contradictions – indeed the very word is seriously contested. The purpose of this committee is to examine the thinking behind the current critical turn that the question of national identity has taken, and to look at the language in which it is expressed and the laws in which it is enshrined.'

The letter came from the junior minister in the newly created government department of Cultural Identities. It surprised Gramercy, and flattered her even while she dismissed it, scorning it to herself: 'He's just an old sleazebag, most likely, who thinks he might get his end away.'

'Your participation,' the letter continued, 'would bring an essential ingredient to our deliberations. The idea of national identity has undergone profound changes, and popular culture, of which you are a leading light, has been a vital ingredient in these historic shifts. We are anxious to represent a full range of age groups, interests, ethnicities and communities and we would greatly value your input.'

The invitation was clearly the outcome of that party of media and entertainment folk she'd been invited to at Number Ten, when in an access of pride – and even patriotism – she'd expressed her desire to 'do something' in some way. Besides, she was getting on – Keats was a decade dead at her age, and . . . well, Blake at least grew into middle age and stayed wild. Gramercy could still stamp and whirl for her audience, as she whispered and squealed her songs. But there were times when she, Gramercy, flew outside her body and roosted somewhere up in the flies above the stage, among the lamps hung to strafe her fans, and from that perch watched with curiosity her small, panting, gyrating figure as it beseeched the audience to join her down the paths of woe and love and anger: were these the lineaments of gratified desire? Hardly. She could split herself in two and suffer only a slight thinning of her octane, but the experience of performance was different from the utter self-forgetfulness that used to carry her away. She hardly dared admit it, but she was getting bored with her old self. The problem wasn't so much how to astonish others: that was still a doddle, in the concert hall. The hard part was astonishing herself.

The day of the workshop, she dressed the part of an entertainment star: she wasn't going to pretend, to betray her own constituency, her own tribe of incoherent resistance: an off-the-shoulder lilac cotton T-shirt which showed off the sleek gleam of her skin, plum-coloured lipstick, a suit of figured black satin with breeches under a stiffly lined hacking jacket, boots of glove-thin emerald suede, with arabesques cut directly into the leather, giving an effect of wings flaring out at the ankle, with no stitching or lining; a medieval look in which her legs, in cherry tights, looked firm and sturdy and somehow hoofed, like a calf's. She powdered plum eye shadow around her eyes and across the bridge of her nose in the clubbing Sioux style: why not warpaint for this skirmish on new territory?

Monica had approved when she left her that morning: that was a good omen, as she was not easy to please, especially when maintenance would present a problem, as it would in the case of this footwear, light as underwear, made for polished interiors, not Enoch's broken and puddly pavements.

Jeff Noakes, the minister, had been a fan forever, he'd told her at the party, though she could hear, through his phrases, the operator's stratagem of drawing someone out. Testing, testing. It was a strange feeling, being the same age as a government minister. 'Freedom Days', the ballad she'd put out nearly twenty years ago, had made a big impression on him, he ran on, eagerly. 'I had the tape with me when I was backpacking through virgin rainforest, in my student days. Listening to you far from home kept the connection live somehow. If you aren't home, a song can be a pretty good substitute. It was our national anthem – against the corruption of that long, long dreadful time when the last government . . . But *we*'re back now, and it's never going to be like that again.' He laughed, and hummed a phrase or two, 'Freedom Days/Billy Blake/You say to want to have it all . . .'

Gramercy's voice was naturally reedy, but she knew how to use this weakness; she always knew how to use her weaknesses, she had learned the art early of throwing an opponent's strength against him – or her; she bent her voice around the words and around the notes in an eerie warble, punctuated by clusters of trills against her palate and the occasional frenzied squeak – the higher the better to take her audience up with her, through the welter of the backing arrangement.

The gathering at the Prime Minister's was noisy, and she didn't catch everything the junior minister was saying, but it made her feel that she might have done something, something more important than she thought. When she told Phil (he hadn't wanted to come, all political powers stinking equally and irredeemably in his eyes), he looked sceptical: 'You,' he said. 'You're always complaining you haven't any time to yourself as it is. You think you're going to take on some make-work committee which just fritters away public money on itself – when there are *important* things to spend it on. The deforestation of the Amazon, the hole over the South Pole. I can't wait till I see this: Gramercy Poule, the new voice of national conscience, the new catalyst of change. You're so naïve, Gramercy, if you think you can do anything from the inside. Steer clear. You'll only get the smell of them on your clothes.'

His taunts firmed her resolve, and so, when the letter arrived, she didn't throw it aside and forget to answer it, as she did begging letters from charities asking her to be a patron or festivals inviting her to open their events.

A smiling older woman, with a slight lisp and an accent from somewhere, introduced herself as the committee's secretary, waving at the coffee and tea urns. The chamber was very hot: double-glazing against the traffic didn't altogether keep out its roar, but it would be hard to hear anything if the windows were opened. The sandwiches on caterers' oval, crypto-silver and doilied platters were drying fast. The new committee was gradually assembling: some of the other names were familiar, but the only person Gramercy knew was Robert Chowdury, the choreographer who had a company that fused strict Bharati discipline with modern expressiveness in the tradition of Martha Graham. They kissed each other: Gramercy had missed Rob's last show, performed in the ruined shell of the old COCA, the Centre of Contemporary Arts, known to its aficionados (of whom Gramercy was one) as the Concrete Cavern; it was being demolished as too harsh and brutalist for the new feel-good times that were coming round.and was to be replaced by a huge, translucent fibreglass bubble.

'It was sad,' said Rob quietly. 'A beautiful space, austere, uncompromising – we danced in it for its last hours. I like to think we sent the building on its way more serenely, like the body that passes over more easily when professional mourners have performed their laments.'

'I'm *so* sorry I missed it.'

'Darling, don't you worry – you've got your own stuff going on, I know. But it was a good piece.' His veined eyelids dropped as he remembered it. Confidingly he lent closer to Gramercy. 'We were trying to catch today's violence and destruction, not to repeat it, you know, but to repulse it, to make it over. Terminators, terminations: these are Western words. A friend said to me the other day, after watching one of the endless massacres on the telly: "A society that doesn't know any longer how to observe every death with proper rituals, that does not know that death is not the end, but only part of the journey, has lost its way, has had the very heart of its humanity torn out." I counted yesterday, during the news. There were five shots of corpses, or parts of corpses.'

'They're censoring the pictures now, they're so terrible even tabloid editors draw the line,' said Gramercy. 'I heard that the ones the newspapers won't print can be visited on the Internet. Do you think if we saw them we'd have to stop killing? If we saw the worst?'

'Do you?' It was disconcerting how Rob kept his eyes closed so much of the time. What was in his head?

'I used to sing that rough, tough material, as if it was being pulled out of my guts. But I'm not as keen to do that stuff any more, don't quite know why. Before it was like homeopathy: you forestalled ugly people by being ugly, getting in ahead with your ugliness – you know, snarling and screaming like a Rottweiler not because you wanted to be a Rottweiler but because you wanted to pre-empt other people getting Rottweiler-ish with you.'

Rob's eyes opened wide, suddenly. 'That's good, darling, that's really good.' He paused. 'What d'you think we're doing here?' He swept the room with his newly staring glance. Apart from Rob, who was one of the first fashionable hybrid exotics in the capital – Gramercy'd met him with her parents (he went back to happenings and love-ins and multi-media events with swirling coloured oil projections) – the committee was a shaken bingo dispenser of different numbers: Gramercy recognised a popular poet with braids bristling like a lizard's crest down his back, who was celebrated for his whispered incantations; a human rights lawyer who was also a rabbi who regularly offered a soothing, and at the same time agonised comment on current affairs on the morning radio; an abrasive television presenter who grinned from ear to ear when he dished it out on his nightly show and another, twice-weekly, early evening slot; a peeress with freckles on her nose and cheeks and ample arms who pioneered reform of women's health issues, especially among groups inhibited by religious custom. Plus some names that echoed but that Gramercy couldn't place.

She saw Jeff Noakes, and he made gesture for them to come over, to the side of the room, where a barrel-chested man was sunk into a wheelchair, talking with bright eyes and many quick gestures of his long brown hands.

'We're still under terrible pressure,' the chairbound professor of politics, Sanjit May, was saying. His voice was honeyed, the ironies moving at a depth below the formal phrasing. 'Since I joined the department two years ago, we've been audited and inspected and overhauled and remodelled: not much time to teach students to think, we're so busy doing "presentations". I used to feel like the White King looking on bemused while the Red Queen laid about her. Now it seems we shall all turn out to be nothing but a pack of cards.'

The minister shook his head sympathetically, and murmured, 'But we're getting it all sorted – you'll see. Have faith.'

He then introduced them.

'Have you come far?' Jeff Noakes was asking Gramercy.

'Sort of, from Fellmoor.'

'You *live* there?' Sanjit May looked up at her sharply.

'Yes, on the edge of Fellmoor. A village called Feverel. Some of the time,' she answered, too warmly, making up for his alarming crookedness with a show of bluff cheerfulness. 'I do have somewhere here, but I'm not there much.'

Jeff Noakes left them together.

'I loathe the country,' Sanjit was saying. 'I find it so dull. What do you do there? You don't *look* rustic.'

'She isn't,' said Rob, with a gurgling laugh.

'But I am,' Gramercy put in, laughing. 'I have dogs and rabbits and hedgehogs – a whole hospital of all kinds of animals. Plus frogs and foxes and all the usual wild animals.'

'Are you a Green?' the professor demanded, suspiciously. 'Would you give your life for a tree?'

Gramercy was beginning to give a considered answer, outlining Phil's views and her experiences in the country, but her interlocutor fixed her with a look of asperity:

'You're not one of those priggish vegans? Do you rub marigold oil on your forehead and evening primrose on your body? Favour infusions of St John's Wort before bed?'

'No, no, none of that!' Gramercy warded off his bile with a giggle. 'My partner is – that way inclined. I like microwaves and curry. Even beef,' she ventured.

'My God, you probably ride to hounds. Well, we're here to discuss National Identity. Tally-ho and tantivy: the battle cries of the shires. You, however, have mixed loyalties, I imagine. Between the darling sick hedgehogs and the squiresses in scarlet up on sixteen-handers, with colossal withers.'

He didn't wait for her to reply; Gramercy felt more like Alice every minute.

'I'm glad to hear you're a carnivore, however. There's a bit more to life than worrying about your body and what it takes in and puts out. And believe me, I know.' He crooked a finger towards his convex ribcage. 'The inner man – generic use, mark, I'm not leaving you out – that's all that matters. You young people are obsessed with fitness.' If he weren't so dedicated to the scathing mode, thought Gramercy, she would have caught a sigh.

'Let's start,' Jeff Noakes waved them to the table, piled with stapled papers. 'Some of which have been circulated to you by post,' said the secretary. 'But some have been tabled at this important workshop.' She pointed to a scattering of books and reports. 'For background – to take away with you, or, if you prefer, we'll send them.'

The politics professor's wheelchair got snagged in the carpet. He pushed at the wheels to pull it free, but the corner wouldn't disengage. Gramercy was confused: she was the nearest to him, as Rob had already taken his seat and had his eyes shut again. She felt Sanjit May was so commanding he wouldn't ever want anyone to help him, and she held back, stuck through a sense of the man's dislike of fussing, of his angry independence.

'C'm'on, Greenwich Village, whatever your name is,' he was looking up at her from his hooked neck, jerking it to indicate the back of the chair. 'Get hold of the controls and pull me out of this.'

She did so, arriving at the same time as the secretary rushed up, all concerned in the way that Gramercy had felt would irritate. So she tipped the chair off the ruck in the carpet. He was surprisingly hefty – the slackness of his poor dead body, she realised – and for a moment she thought, He'll fall backwards with all that weight, and I'll not have the strength to withstand it, and he'll be lying on the carpet like a goldfish after the cat's knocked off the bowl.

Once Gramercy and Sanjit were in place, side by side, at the table, Jeff Noakes introduced the chair, who turned out to be the amply formed health issue peeress, and then took his leave, making a telephone finger and thumb sign at Gramercy as he left, mouthing 'We'll speak'. She almost blushed.

'Welcome to you all,' began Baroness Ghopil. 'We have some very important work to do, and we're pleased that so many of you have agreed to take part and have been able to attend today. Just feel free to talk, to disagree, to interrupt; minutes will be taken, but everything said here is confidential. So speak your minds. You're all here because you've already contributed, and we need your expertise in this difficult area: who are we now? What does it mean to belong here?' She smiled, dimpling, and breathed: 'Whither Albion? One might well ask.'

The discussion began swiftly; Gramercy was surprised by the alacrity with which her fellow panellists caught Baroness Ghopil's eye and how, in her smiling, companionable, big-bosomed way, she marshalled the speakers one after another. She was skilled at chairing: a longtime trustee of many philanthropic organisations, including the generous Bethesda Foundation, which was sponsoring the publication of the workshop's results.

The discussion soon crystallised around certain questions: was the idea of the melting pot outmoded? Was the tossed salad still viable?

A columnist whom Gramercy sometimes read declared his faith: 'The constitution, the flag, the idea of citizenship: these are the bonds that tie the nation together! This is the ideal secular model – everyone is proud to be a citizen, even if they only arrived last week. You have to be one of many to be part of the one: hyphenated identities are the goal, not grafts of one species on to another to make a new variety. We don't want genetically modified people, do we? We want the organic originals, healthily rooted in new soil, which brings out the best qualities in them. The past culture a nutrient of the present, not a poison.'

There were murmurs; Sanjit beside her whispered, 'Oh, such happy hyphenated citizens of Shiloh, kept on reservations, fat and drunk on casino profiteering!'

The journalist flushed slightly as the mood of the gathering became restless: 'I know that the state of the blacks, the history of slavery, the inner cities are a blot on all this . . .'

August Farrell, the poet with the Leonardo-like braids, broke in: 'Let's be very cautious about using this model: it simply is not possible to say that slavery is a blot, that we can just set aside, or use a spot stain removal to lift it out of Shiloh's history. Exclusion happens there through economic forces, through *de facto* segregation in the cities and the countryside – ghettoes, rich and poor. Housing and settlement planning is key to community – a word I loathe, by the way, but in the absence of another, have to use.'

The Baroness took him up: 'Would it be an interesting exercise if we brainstormed around these words – multi-cultural, multi-ethnic, citizen, community – for a while and saw what we could come up with?'

'Let's start by shedding "minorities",' proposed one voice. 'That marginalises all of us for a start.'

There was almost unanimous head-nodding.

'And toss out "ethnic" just as we threw out "racial".'

'My preference is "multi-communality",' said another.

'"Communali*ties*", surely?'

'I've heard,' intervened Sanjit, 'that "visible presences" is gaining ground in some quarters.'

Gramercy found herself speaking, for the first time, addressing herself to Sanjit. 'But that's putting the viewpoint the wrong way around, isn't it? Don't we want to see for ourselves, rather than be seen by others?'

Sanjit followed, 'As someone who is highly visible for additional reasons, I'm not inclined to like the term. I have to agree with my friend here, Miss Poussin. We want to be seen, but not observed. We want to be paid attention to. That's not the same as being watched.'

'If only we could simply use, "Friends, countrymen—",' said Rob languidly. 'And "countrywomen".' He exchanged a look with Gramercy.

'How about a neologism altogether?' offered the journalist. 'Like *polites* – for members of a polity together?'

'Ugh.'

'Or a historical echo, like "commonweal"?'

'Danger that way lies,' murmured someone. 'We must stay above divisive politics – and Republicanism, well.'

Baroness Ghopil unfurled the shawl of her salwar kameez and folded it tidily on to the back of her chair as she called the meeting to order.

'We're not here to plot a revolution, but to find a *modus vivendi* – and language is not a side issue, but central. However, let's move on. We have a paper tabled – I never like to do that, but everybody is so very busy it was not possible to circulate it in time. Its author is with us, I believe, waiting outside, is that right?' The secretary nodded. 'He will talk to his paper for a few minutes, and then you can discuss the issues it raises. Many of you will know what it concerns already – there has been some tabloid and television interest in this matter, which raises fundamental questions about how we should respond to . . . the "visible presences" or whatever it is you wish to call us former . . . foreigners, outsiders, colonial subjects, or diasporic denizens of our muddled-up world.' She smiled at the table, but singled out Sanjit and Rob, it seemed to Gramercy, then nodded to the secretary to fetch Kim McQuy.

'My name is Kim McQuy. I'm a schoolteacher,' Kim began as soon as he approached the table and looked quickly around the company. 'I was able to come to talk to you this afternoon because, providentially, it's half-term.'

Gramercy's heart lurched: here stood before her, in living flesh and blood, that weirdo activist, the Leto agitator, her very own plagiarist, who'd never deigned to answer the messages she'd left him after accessing his website. Monica had said she was considering a legal letter warning him off, telling him he'd not get another chance. Had she sent it?

'I teach ten-year-olds at an inner city primary school in Cantelowes which has children who speak fifteen different languages.'

Off screen, he looked more glittery in eye and lip, and very slightly built, with ears that seemed kind of pricked, and she could see that his hands were shaking. He caught her eye, and an eyebrow twitched together with the corner of his mouth; she found herself dropping her gaze, his own expression was so serious, so blazing. He was sitting against the light that hot afternoon, so there was a kind of heated luminousness around his dark head, which matched the ardour of his speech. As he went on, addressing the committee, his voice became odder, the pitch a little higher, with a quick, urgent catch of the breath. He was standing – although he had been shown a seat at the table.

'I have a vision – I describe it in the paper you have there. My vision concerns the history of this country, how Albion has always been crossed and crossed again by people coming from here, there and everywhere, sometimes looking for food, shelter, work, but sometimes for experience, adventure, novelty. The diasporas of the last centuries include wave upon wave of refugees, political exiles, persecuted races: the roll call, as you all know, is magnificent.'

In many ways his style was simply that of a born teacher used to facing a class and keeping going to hold their attention; but there were the inflections of the preacher, and his eyes bulged slightly with the effort of his address.

'Some of us are mongrels, yes. Some of us aren't. Some of those don't wish to entertain the mongrelisation of the nation: the process Rushdie has likened to chutnification, the blending of spices and herbs and the fruits of the earth. But it makes no odds whether some individuals are squeaky clean as clean can be – ethnically, because it's our history that is mongrel, our culture is mongrel, as Defoe realised already a long time ago – even before you were here . . .' he pointed at the rabbi 'or you . . .' he waved towards Baroness Ghopil, 'or you . . . or you or you—' He took in Rob, Sanjit, the poet, and ended tapping his breast. 'Or me.'

Sanjit nodded, then boomed out, '"A true born Englishman's a

93

contradiction, / In speech an irony, in fact a fiction." But Defoe doesn't like us much, does he, Mr McQuy?'

Kim swallowed, stiffened. 'Defoe's patriotism made him rail at all the failings he saw in the arrogance of people around him. Ingratitude, chiefly, was the vice of the age. But Defoe was brilliant and complicated, and most people aren't – I'm not. I have simple needs, and that makes me understand others better than many.

'I like mongrels. I like mongrelisation. Newcomers, the stranger who walks into town, the creatures who inhabit other worlds – these are all fascinating to us, they drive history and stories and films and ... curiosity. They put a lift in our step, they stir up energy, they inspire new defences of old ways, and new ways to kick free of the traces of the past we don't want. But today people are scared – of what? Some people are driven here, but this isn't the situation in every case: some choose freely to come because they are attracted to what this mongrel country means, historically and culturally.'

He was holding the panel's attention, Gramercy sensed, in spite of Sanjit's show of amusement, and besides, even the professor's barbed condescension was probably a gesture of self-defence against Kim McQuy's passion. For the group's listening was filled with wishfulness: Kim McQuy was kindling a hope that something, that someone, might change the way things were. 'The alternative history of this country's spirit. Facing forwards, with the future in our faces, not looking backwards, at some exhausted notion of heritage. No forced folk identities, no ethnic songs and costumes and rites to whip up into enmities.

'This is what my vision is about. A new national myth rooted in an old reality that has been forgotten ... Where is the giant Albion now? Where for that matter is that armed virago brandishing her trident? Where is the pinkness of the map? the Union flag? These symbols and figures have decayed one by one.

'Aeneas plunged into burning Troy to rescue – what? First, his father. Some of us don't have fathers. But aside from that, he also took the cult statue of the city. A figure of the goddess he served. But this was more than a sculpture, the way we think of art now. This was a living, potent, magical vehicle of identity, and losing it stole all the remaining energy from the sacked city. Aeneas came out carrying both of them and went on to found Rome, arguably the last great mongrel hub of a chutnificated culture, a mixed spice civilisation, living then in the most fertile phase of natural generation in the great life process of absorption and composting which is necessary for all new growth.

'What we need is something similar. Ever since the identity of this new energy was revealed to me in a dream, she's been adopted by hundreds, by thousands of people who would never have found a sense of belonging through any of our superannuated national symbols.

'She's everyone who's ever been driven from home, who's been stolen away or beaten out ... she's Persephone and dozens and dozens of young women who've been raped – not least Europa, you know that story. That victim gave her name to where we live now. She's Hagar and Mary and ... well, she's Leto.'

He took out a handkerchief – it had been ironed, Gramercy noticed as he shook out the folds, and wiped his forehead and his eyes carefully, before he folded it up again and put it in his pocket.

'Thank you, Kim,' said the Baroness, gently. 'Do take a seat. Your observations are appreciated. Any questions, now?'

There was a silence.

Then the rabbi asked, 'Mr McQuy, were you brought up in a faith yourself?'

Kim was sitting up stiffly now, his bird-like quickness of movements tense in response. 'I'm adopted. I went to Catechism class and my mother – my adoptive mother, that is – took me to Mass when I was little. She was grateful to the nuns who'd helped set up the adoption in the first place, and she'd given her word to them that she'd bring me up in the faith. But my mum and dad were old-fashioned, socialist radicals: bird-feeders and sandals – *with* socks – you get the picture? As for my *biological* mother, in that part of the world, she could have been anything: Orthodox, Moslem, Jewish, Zoroastrian, Reformed, you name it. I'm circumcised, so that makes some identities more likely than others. But who knows which?' He laughed.

'I was one of the Tirzahner orphans – that moment, if you remember (when there've been so many like it since). I've no personal allegiance to any particular creed or church. I'm a jumble. Which is another word for mongrel, but a whole lot less nasty.'

He stopped himself and looked serious again. 'You see there's definitely a humanist and rationalist slant in me and my visions: it's simple, what I desire. I want the world to become a better place.' He looked down across the table at Gramercy. 'And I know I'm not the only one.'

She felt herself flushing, as if caught out in an act of intimacy with him, but she faced him and nodded. He drew in his breath, visibly pleased that he'd made an impact on her.

'I know that there are thousands like me, who want to find a language of co-existence, of fellowship, of peace and justice. Did you know that in nature resemblances lie far far deeper than mere appearances?' He paused. 'The botanists just discovered that the closest cousin to the lotus flower, that sacred symbol of the east, that gorgeous and exotic oriental blossom is—' he paused. Gramercy wondered if anyone would, under his teacherly presence, put up a hand to give the answer.

'You don't know? Well, it isn't the water lily, as you'd expect. It's the plane tree, common Enochite street furniture. Bearing no visible feature in common, it's through and through lotus-like. Yes!'

The rabbi expostulated, 'But how can you claim that your kind of thinking is "rational"? It's a contradiction in terms.' He then went on, less vehemently. 'What is difficult for us to understand, in what you have been saying – and I can't believe I'm alone in this – is what status does the idea of "a vision" have for you? How can a statue – a tomb – this example of one of simply thousands of classical antiquities – come to life and speak to you in a vision? By what power? If not God's?'

'By the power of imagination,' said Kim, quietly. 'It's not a statue, by the way. It's an unknown, dead woman, who's nobody, and who isn't even there. And it's not going to happen by the power of God, but through yours, and yours, and yours. And theirs.' He looked out of the window as if at a crowd of impassioned demonstrators. 'Religious conflicts have riven the world, drenched populations in blood – here, in this country, as well as in the larger communality we inhabit. But human beings need religious sentiment. The crucial question is, not to make any particular religion, faith or creed the basis of the identity of the nation. That's why we need a new secular faith, a church so broad that everyone can belong!'

'Impossible.' Rob shook his head.

'You say here,' the television presenter tapped Kim's paper, 'that "Today we live in new realms of reality: the physics of telecommunications have enveloped us in images made act, just as word was made flesh in the past. Once Hamlet lived in the mind more intensely than a historical personage; now when a character in a soap opera dies, thousands send flowers to the funeral." I have to say, that given my postbag, there's some truth in this, but should it be encouraged?'

'Not encouraged. Recognised. It's a faculty of mind: the poets' power. To make realities.'

A climate of disagreement thickened in the room but did not take articulate shape.

'Surely it's a nine-day wonder . . .' Sanjit began, after the pause, 'the excitement around this "Lady" of yours?'

Kim looked startled, but gave a slight shake of his head.

'It reminds me of Princess Diana,' said Rob. 'That huge outpouring of passion – dried up almost as quickly as it had happened. Just guilt – guilt at collective prurience.'

August Farrell added, pensively, looking at Kim, 'Isn't there a danger that you're pandering to the credulity of people who have no other means to express themselves? It makes me very uneasy. I think we've seen these methods of national cohesion through symbolism before: they're dictators' natural territory. Mumbo-jumbo about solar myths and astral heroes . . .' He shuddered, and his dreadlocks shook with him.

'Our symbols are different: they're not heroic, they're humble, they're not exclusive and warlike, they're inclusive and peaceable.' Kim was nettled, his voice mounting higher, his skin brightening. Gramercy, watching him, felt a different interest spark; she smoothed her bare shoulder absent-mindedly: mentioning his prick, was that a first for a committee room of this kind? One or two gays in the room, too. Can't have passed them by. Yet he wasn't aware, it seemed, of the arousal quotient of exposing himself verbally like that. She wondered, looking at his oddly combed hair, was he a virgin? That ironed hanky – did he still live with his mother?

'We're not irredentists, we're not even nationalists in any of the old uses of the word. We don't want the Leto repatriated – there's nowhere for her to go back to. That's precisely the point. She belongs to us and there's nowhere for so many of us now. We're not into ethnic nostalgia.

'That's why she embodies us, stands for us, can be our figurehead. We're the people who have no homeland – apart from the one we find ourselves in, by chance, by luck, by fate. We're the ones whose footsteps tread out new paths that lead to the door we can call home. All we ask is for this lost woman to be given proper respect. We want a new

97

Cenotaph, to be filled with her spirit and the spirit of people like her. We are the New Ishmaelites. And she is Our Lady.'

After he'd left the room, the assembled panellists breathed out, almost unanimously.

Baroness Ghopil hushed the hubbub, then asked for considered responses; they came, musingly.

'He's a crackpot, a nutcase, completely barking,' said the TV presenter, taking off his glasses and wiping them as if to assure the company and himself that he was clear-sighted.

'No, no,' said the rabbi. 'Ambitious. Opportunistic. A young man hungry for power – by whatever means.'

'I'm sorry to lower the tone, but what's in it for him? We have to remember,' and the columnist gave a dry little laugh, that almost came out as a snort, 'that refugees are becoming big business – and not just for triads and Mafia. We should step very, very carefully, I reckon.'

Gramercy breathed in sharply, but before she could speak, the chair intervened: 'I would like us to be less personal. To consider the possibility of renewing national symbols in the way the crowds whom this "Lady" is drawing suggests. There's Marianne, remember, at the other end of the rail tracks. What Kim McQuy was saying amounts to not much more than the message on the Statue of Liberty's pedestal, after all, in a different era, disinfected of all those problems you so trenchantly recalled earlier . . .' She smiled.

August Farrell let this go, and instead faced the columnist across the table. 'You know as well as I do, that the whole point of letting people in lawfully is to prevent Mafia and triad operations. This chap's hardly clandestine.' The columnist boggled at him, spread his hands, and indicated they should listen to the ongoing discussion.

'But it's hard to separate the message from the man, Shareen!' Rob protested. 'He's got something slightly mesmerising, kind of mongoose-like, don't you think? In another time, he'd have been a Puritan preacher. What he's saying is a whole heap of rubbish. You're not going to get the shires rallying round some Near Eastern mummy, are you? Come on!' He paused. 'But it's odd that when you hear him, you get caught up in it. It's a bit like that nineteenth-century dream that Albion was the lost tribe of Israel, God's chosen remnant. Barmy, but a lot of sensible people believed it and worked hard to make it stick.'

Sanjit said softly, 'One can never argue with visionaries. The only thing to do is to walk away from them. They're irrefutable. It's that dread passionate intensity, you know.'

August Farrell added, 'We simply haven't reached the point when we can forget I'm black, that you're black, that he's . . . if we're not to use labels of colour, we have to have descriptions of origins to stand in for them, we depend on religious affiliations, if not beliefs, to place people. A Tirzahner means not-white, not from here, and it can't be otherwise – the Tirzahners' problem is getting themselves valued for what they are. This McQuy's flying in the face of the whole trend. He wants us to stop drawing up the census with scrupulous distinctions between someone coming from here and someone from there. He can't turn any of us invisible, like a stage magician.'

'Like St Paul, he wants neither Jew nor Greek, nor slave nor free—' said Rob, quietly. 'It's rather sweet. But in Albion, now!' He shook his head. 'Mad.'

Farrell went on, 'He's eager, he's brave. He's got a kind of shiny guilelessness about him. He'll never survive a moment in that piranha fishpond that's politics. Yes, he's a holy fool, a naïf – he may stir up more than he can handle. We'll see. I shudder to think of his hate mail.' He shook his head. 'I must say I fear for him.'

The columnist commented, 'Rubbish, if you don't mind my saying so, old boy. It's us who should be alarmed: self-styled saints end up torching the ungodly. Just consider the mullahs. That tolerance for each and everyone – it wears thin very quickly.'

Gramercy broke in, indignant, intervening in this discussion for the first time, 'That can't be right. He's an idealist, and anyway, it's not really up to him, is it?' she said. 'He's not going it alone. You're exaggerating his part in it – and his power. He's picking up on something that's happening out there – and it won't stop just because we decree he's bonkers. I'm not sure that he's bonkers anyway. He's just lost, doesn't know who he is, feels out of place, with no land of his birth to leave and sing about, no home behind him and no forwarding address either.'

6

Hortense to Kim; Kim to Hortense

Subject: G: Skipwith 673.1841
Date: Tues, 02 June 199– 14:35:47 +0100
From: Hortense Fernly<h.fernly@natmus.ac.alb>
To: kim.mcquy<hswu@lattice.onlyconnect.com>
Attachment: Skipwith 673.1841: checklist

- -

Thanks for yours. I've been away, hence delay. With regard to the Mss.,
didn't the librarian show you the checklist of the boxes' contents? I'm
attaching it fyi. Under the heading 'Fragments', there's a resume of texts
that were transcribed from the mummy bands. These are in the main, as
I indicated, magical charms and spells though I haven't been through the
material closely, and there may be more stuff. There are many papyri
and later, vellum and parchment documents deposited with the marbles
by Skipwith – a vast miscellaneous collection nobody has looked at very
much. There was to be an edition, but Meeks began and for some reason
never finished, lost heart, ran out of steam, whatever. A pity, as it's a
pretty large cache of papers, and, as I say, of an unusual character. But
the task demands multiple palaeographic and linguistic skills, and in the
days of outreach and bottom line profits museum curators no longer
have the time, let alone all the other skills and time required.

Good luck – if you decide to have another go.

Yours,

Hortense Fernly

PS The Director of the museum wants us to put out some kind of
booklet about the Leto Bundle – in time for the re-installation of the

tomb and its contents. For our series of Pocket Guides. He wants it by the end of the summer. That is when the cartonnage will be displayed again in a much better setting – and with the right set of mummy wrappings, and more objects from the tomb and associated materials. You – and HSWU – should be pleased, I trust.

Subject: Re: Leto Bundle
Date: Tues, 02 June 199– 18:32:47 +0100
From: Hortense Fernly<h.fernly@natmus.ac.alb>
To: kim.mcquy<hswu@lattice.onlyconnect.com>

I've had a look at your website now. Much of its contents far beyond my expertise. But it's enjoyable. [She looked at this sentence and deleted it.] You might consider revising some of the references to the Leto Bundle when you've had a chance of look at some more material. Your interpretation is of course your own, but you might add some more up-to-date historical (and more accurate!) background details in the light of the material you're looking at in the Archives?

   Let me know how you get on. Yours, Hortense

Subject: Re: Bundle
Date: Tues, 02 June 199– 22:48:21 +0100
From: kim.mcquy<hswu@lattice.onlyconnect.com>
To: Hortense Fernly<h.fernly@natmus.ac.alb>

Hello Hortense if I may   – yes I did find the checklist   thanks anyway –   Id like to save it to disc so do send list again but in the body of the message – attachments are dangerous as they say – natmus is probably pure as pure but I don't want to risk a virus – and new ones keep evolving – schoolkids not much older than the ones I teach have a fun time introducing them best kim

Subject: Re: Bundle
Date: Wed, 03 June 199– 09:36:47 +0100
From: Hortense Fernly<h.fernly@natmus.ac.alb>
To: kim.mcquy<hswu@lattice.onlyconnect.com>
Attachment: Misc. Mss. G. Fr. 32–35.rtf

Kim, I'm attaching some of the early Hellenistic stuff as well, because I feel sure it'll be of interest to you – given your concerns. (Our virus control is very tight, so don't worry about downloading.) What follows comes from Meeks' holograph translation of the wrappings. Till now it's been a mystery that no matching manuscript had been found in the Skipwith collection, but it's now possible that when Meeks abandoned the task, he reassembled the linen strips around the mummy and left no record of his procedure.

[I'm getting far too technical for him, she thought to herself. And began to delete, then thought better of it. Let him break his head on this stuff instead of all that glib nonsense he's putting out.]

Let me know how you get on – as I say we're excited here at natmus by the rediscovery of these fragments and we'll be featuring them in the new display. We have you to thank for it, as you sent me back to the files.

You'll see the episode described here in rather different, flattering terms, as a kind of witch's duel. As such it's related to several myths about Zeus and his amours. It's of great interest, as the earliest extant fragments from the story of Leto, written down around the same time as the cartonnage was made.

For the time being, this is ABSOLUTELY NOT FOR CIRCULATION - or scanning into your network! I've still got a very long way to go with the material. But I do want you to get a feel for the complexity of the story, for the sheer amount of stuff associated with the sarcophagus. This bit is connected to other bits, but they're much later, at least in the form we have, so the relationships hook up across any ordinary time passing. Don't even allude to anything here, at least not until you've run it past me. All right?

Yours sincerely, Hortense

PS Appropriately, the writing on the wrappings is in sepia - cuttlefish ink (as I'm sure you know).

7

A Witch's Duel in the Hellenistic World

[Misc. Mss. G. Frs. 32–35]

... he caught Leto in a passage one night, on her way from the bath in the women's quarters; he was not allowed in that part of the building, whatever his authority overall. He bunched some of her dress into his hands over her stomach, and bent his head down to find her mouth; she smelled his beard that she had known tight curled as lamb's fleece when he took her riding on the pommel of his saddle to see the long cat stretching her shadow on the honey sand; she swallowed his hot winey breath down her throat. But she broke away from him and ran down the passage, trying not to make any noise at all. She wasn't heavy, but her high silver and silk slippers slapped against the rush matting on the floor; the other young women in their quarters might not all be sleeping, but, in the Keep, there were noises at night it was best to pretend not to hear.

She felt she would like to be heard, to be seen, in order to be sure that what she felt was happening to her was indeed taking place and not a phantom in her sleep. She would like to be watched over, too, by an older woman – by Doris – who had warned her and excited her beforehand by her talk, who had anticipated so often in her stories this flight of her body away from him, towards him, her trembling, her anticipation.

He had stopped her in the passage, whispering to her to come with him, to let him wrap her in his coat so her nightclothes wouldn't shine under the stars so brightly.

'You could make me so happy, little one,' he said.

She cried out against him, but he clutched her tightly and slurred in her ear, 'My dove, let me see your sweet body, let me feel your silken limbs. For my wife can't return the fire that burns inside me so brightly – beside you I feel like a new colt, like a young goat on the mountains . . .'

[Fr. 33]

. . . she struggled to fly from him again, but found that she was curving her body towards the slow softness of the voice; he made a sound in his throat as she came up against him, and his neck stretched high, as he lifted his long head and crowed; his arms had become wings, their wing beats struck her between her shoulder blades until she gasped for air and her breath broke out of her in moans. He twined his lithe long neck around her waist and rose up under her armpit and bit and nuzzled her breast. Then she too sprouted wings, her arms grew into strong pinions, but flecked blue-grey, unlike the silvered moonlight of his big body that flapped and struck her; she unfurled her full span and ascended, throwing her head forward and stretching until, arrow-like, she lifted from the bent bow of his clasp and soared upwards on the current. But he rose with her, and brought her face to his dark, hair-curled belly, and held her there and begged her 'Milk me'.

Her head jerked away from him then, she would not; she gagged and tore herself away from the suffocating closeness of his heat, his smell, his wanting.

As she pulled away, her new wings stretched and lifted her; she soared, but he was coming after her. Together, they were skimming the earth: swan, goose: swan mobbing goose; goose chasing swan. She was laughing now, the whinny of fear as she rose high in the thinner air above; her strength was waning in her wingtips. He was gaining on her. Then she dropped, suddenly, in a flurry of feathers, as if shot from the sky; shrunk into a small ball of quail-tender dappledness, cooing as she squatted down in the dust, fluttering and dragging a wing to plead her weakness. 'I know these tricks,' he answered, mocking her, with a flash of pleasure in his round shining eye as he caught her in his claws and pierced her here and there, breast, lips, vulva, buttocks, with his curved falcon beak and his sharp talons.

*

. . . Leto cried out for help, for a god, any god, of her lost people, of her new family, to come to her aid. And it happened that one heard her prayer, the goddess of the outcasts, she answered her, and Leto began turning shiny and scaly and slipping from her divine lover's grasp, as they went tumbling over the bluffs at the land's end and dropped on to the stiff breezes that sweep the edge of sea and earth; they floated there, descending from wind current to wind current, swirling through, his falcon giving chase – now to the leaping salmon she had become as she sprang from him again, blood streaming from her flanks as she flashed into the coastal waters where he could still see her, with his hawk's eye, flecked against the pebbles, a twisting, squirming banner of gleaming skin and pink flesh exposed where he had mauled her, trailing wisps of blood in her wake.

He hurled himself into the water after her. The light looped and spooled as he unfurled himself far and wide to hold her in his mesh, to wrap her in the bane of his stickiness. She was flailing now, her fins and her tail slapping against the toils in which he was winding her, gasping as they met in the embrace of his several limbs. The sea was pouring liquid light over them and the salt quickened the sensations in every orifice that had been prised open, every rubbed patch and pore where they were combining, where their bodies joined.

He hauled her; she hung, a dead weight, dripping, mute, and just as he felt that he had at last vanquished her as was his due, she sucked the last of her reserves from her body, summoning all her reserves, sugar from her liver, juice from her kidneys and the air brightening her heart's blood, and flung their full mass of energy at him. She drew him into the spiralling tendrils of the several limbs she too could now throw out, each one blistered and stamped with a round mouth, fastened on his body. He was nothing but a man, and a man well past his first youth at that, and she now knew how to entangle him in her flesh, flesh that was all mouth, fringed about with lips and tongue to lick and swallow, to suck and consume. She closed the waving tentacles of her new form around his spent energies and with a last throe of her powers, clouded the water that lapped them in the musky jet of her black ink.

... the children will be born from an egg the blue of a wild hyacinth. Fish roe, cuttlefish spawn, quail's eggs: it would resemble all of these, though it is *sui generis*, a species unknown. On their downy bodies, beneath the first chick feathers, in the starred interlacing of their epidermis, there will be tiny calligraphy, the spoor of their inky matrix, from their mother, the cuttlefish, who squirted sepia at her lover during the rape when they were conceived.

And the time will come when this will be a sign, to those who come after that they belong to a sacred line.

May these words as I repeat them unbind the demons, O goddess, from the body of my daughter ...

[Kim: This formulaic invocation is found on numerous amulets of the Hellenistic world. Its presence here reveals that the myth of Leto's hierogamy, or rape by the god, was told to avert blows of fate, and especially to safeguard young women from similar torments.]

[There follows a lacuna in the text.]

8

Kim to Hortense; Hortense to Kim

Subject: Re: Leto
Date: Wed, 03 June 199– 18:46:07 +0100
From: kim.mcquy<hswu@lattice.onlyconnect.com>
To: Dr Hortense Fernly<h.fernly@natmus.ac.alb>

Dear Hortense Fernly,

After what you've sent me I must talk to you but just in case you're
thinking that kim mcquy's a nutcase and he wants something I want to
assure you I am not I'm not after money or sponsorship I'm not going to
stalk you or fill up your voice mail or ask you to read my latest message
of genius I know that my saying this won't make you believe me but you
talked to me that day in person at the museum and you didn't treat me
as if I'd crawled out from under a stone and you don't know how
rarely that happens. That's a political statement – NOT whingeing.

This is all by way of saying I'm a primary schoolteacher not the scholar
you are and I've read what you sent and I'm excited but would you take
me through it please? The piece you sent me reads like today's news but
in fancier language than your average correspondent in the war zone
can manage story styles change anyway could we meet for a cup of
coffee after school one day? won't take a lot of your time I promise
thanks so much - hopefully kim.
ps the handlist you attached didn't arrive by the way please try again I
want to hyperlink the tomb contents to my homepage

Subject: Leto
Date: Thurs, 04 June 199– 14:38:13 +0100
From: Hortense Fernly<h.fernly@natmus.ac.alb>
To: kim.mcquy<hswu@lattice.onlyconnect.com>

- -

I'll meet you on Thursday, a week today (late night opening). I'll come
and find you in the Archives around 6. Yours, Hetty Fernly

9

A Desert Outpost

(*From the* Chronicle of Barnabas)

[Mss. Lat. 73–77]

'The author of this fragment', Hereward Meeks's notes read, 'was writing around 1200, around thirty years after the events he relates. He was a monk at the Shrine of the Fount in the Pearl Quarter of Cadenas-la-Jolie, a fortified citadel in the desert on the eastern shore of "Our Sea". This fortress changed hands frequently between the different faiths and peoples who came to power in that contested territory, as divers manuscripts in the Skipwith deposit reveal . . .' Kim's eyes travelled to the final sentence: 'Through Barnabas, a chronicler loyal to the Enochites, we catch a glimpse of the trials suffered by the martyrs and heroes of our true religion, who struggled to defend the holy places.'

[Ms. Lat. 73]

When the child Laetitia first arrived, on the boat from the other side of Our Sea, she lived in the Keep; Doris lay at the door of her room, on a mat. She was called Leto then, for her name in God, Laetitia, was given to her in the Convent, later. Abbess Cecily did not consider Leto, the name of a pagan idol (and one of the savage generation of Titans at that), a suitable name for a little child *Deodata*, given by God. In defiance of her dying mother's vow, Laetitia was handed over to the Procurator, the infidel Cunmar, by Ser Matteo, her father, as surety for his trade; he was allowed to load his ship with Cadenate glassware, mirrors and lenses, and other precious manufactures, for he made a promise: 'I will return with a treasure you have never before seen, one that will make you the strongest fortress in the whole of this territory.' And he confided its character in secret to Cunmar, who laughed; for all his warlikeness, that lord loved new devices, tricks and traps as a young boy loves his first catapult. Ser Matteo also brought Cunmar a pair of peregrine falcons from an oak forest in their country, trained to hunt, with tooled leather harnesses, hoods and jesses of the finest quality; Cunmar patted the little girl, and handed her over to his consort and to her attendants. The Lord Cunmar then went hunting with Ser Matteo – in our desert coloured like the sherbets at his table, to test the foreign birds against the kind reared and trained in Cadenas. Not to be outdone, for the Ophiri pride themselves on their largesse, Cunmar picked out a boy to send with Ser Matteo to his country to learn its ways.

Then came the time for the child's father to leave: at the harbour, this lad was there, already fitted out in long, coloured hose and short-waisted tunic in the shameless style of Ser Matteo's paymasters; these had been copied from Ser Matteo's wardrobe by an Ophiri tailor who sucked in his breath as he worked at the strange geometry of the stranger's garments. The boy had a twisted foot, which was cruelly revealed by this flaunting apparel.

When he was about to re-embark, Ser Matteo threw Laetitia up in the air above his head and she crowed with the thrill of it. Prophetically, he cried aloud, 'Cunmar, see how this one's fearless! Good as any lad of yours – even better! You'll see, she'll be teaching you what's what – you saddle-sore battle-hardened Ophiri don't know what's coming to you from my little baggage!' Laetitia caught the words; they seemed to be streaming out to both sides of her hurtling body like wings as if a voice beyond this world had spoken them; her father himself was a shadow tipping away from her, only his hands that caught her as she came down returned her to earth.

So Laetitia at the age of four was left in a special position in Cadenas; she lived in the Pearl Quarter, in the Keep itself, in the same suite of apartments as the Procurator and his wife and their household. But Laetitia's father did not return the following season as he had promised, according to the terms of his agreement with Cunmar. A ship from Parthenopolis arrived, bringing a few paintings and some books, as well as great packages of chandler's tackle – candles, ropes, sails, capstans, winches, and other large metal manufactures – felloes for carts and waggons, nails, axles, knives, and chains. It did not bring the hitherto, unknown treasure he had promised the Procurator in payment; but it did bring a letter for Laetitia:

[Ms. Lat. 74]

> Sottoportego San Teodoro, Feast of The Invention of the Holy
> Cross, May 3, Year of Our Lord 117 –
> Beloved daughter, It has been a bitter January here and riots
> have followed bread shortages, with some loss of life. I am
> endeavouring to raise support in the City to provision a new
> ship, to sail this spring and bring some manufactures which are
> lacking in the outpost in exchange for some Cadenate armour
> and mail, for they are much prized here for their lightness and
> strength.
> I trust in God that you are well provided for –
> Your loving father

[Ms. Lat. 75]

Rumours about Ser Matteo travelled with other cargoes: lost fortunes, shipwreck, diversions into trade to the south-west, beyond the pillars of Hercules; sometimes, stories of promotion, a Cardinal's favour, the bestowal of gems, princely apartments in a great city, a library, a title; others also spoke of a cardinal's disfavour, of treachery and beheading. It was a jumble, it was a broken line or two from fragments of annals that courtiers and nuns related to her, for the outpost teemed with rumour.

The outpost of Cadenas-la-Jolie was founded in the year of Our Lord 998 by the sainted Cyriacus, he who was granted a vision of the Swaddling Bands of the Holy Infant, and who led us to the fragments of those sweet relics where they lay concealed. By divine providence, these have survived the Ophiri sovereignty over the holy places, and they are still enshrined in the convent of that name, where Laetitia of blessed memory was rescued, through the workings of divine providence, from the grasp of the infidels.

For these infidels came to triumph over my people the Enochites who had come from the far west across land and sea to defend the holy places for our faith: in 1170 AD, the Ophiri, led by Cunmar, drew us by guile to fight them on the plain below Cadenas at the battle of Al-Ziza (which we call Lacarina for it signifies the same in our languages); the citadel passed into their hands; many times since then have we battled to regain it, but the Lazuli, our presumed allies in the outpost, are men of little faith. Their soldiers do not deserve the name of warriors before the Lord, since the men wear silks from the renegades of Ophir while their women spoon rosewater jams into their painted mouths without thought of due fasting and encircle their lascivious eyes with ashes for they have no proper dread of death. Their sinful ways brought about the decline of Cadenas, once the fairest bastion in God's earthly kingdom.

Laetitia was drawn into their snares, but, through the mercy of Our Lord, she found grace and repented, and as we shall relate here, she expiated her early vanities and heedlessness and wantoness and shed her blood to cleanse us.

May this chronicle that I, Barnabas, once gatekeeper of the Shrine of the Fount, have set down, bear witness to the blessed life of this pure child, who herself testified to the faith through her travails and through them has surely gained the martyr's crown in paradise.'

[Ms. Lat. 76]

... [the Citadel] stands on an almond-shaped bluff of crumbly desert rock a hundred and forty feet above the spirited sea, where star sapphires bounce in the play of the sun. It was once our triumphant holy fortress, immoveable, implacable, unassailable from without, seated on sheer spurs of golden-pink rock with the swirling pastel desert stretching away to the east, and guarded on its seaboard to the west by a natural harbour; our wise founders extended the arms of this providential haven, narrowing its mouth with fortified breakwaters. On all sides, to sea and land, geography has been assisted by dressed stone walls garlanded at the top with toothed martagons and shored at the foot by a steep slithery glacis that once upon a time took three hundred wretched captives whom we had brought to serve us from Tirzah, landlocked and impious city of the mountain passes that lie midway between the realm of Enoch and the holy places. Tirzah was the original native city of Ser Matteo, the holy child Laetitia's father: like the blessed virgin martyrs Barbara and Agnes and so many others, her persecutions began at home, at the hands of a cruel and godless infidel.

Laetitia's blessed mother died vowing her infant to the care of the one true god (hence her name, Deodata), but the child Laetitia was abandoned in the godless Keep in the fifth year of her short life by her father. The Keep stands in the steep, dark centre of Cadenas, near our holy Shrine of the Fount, in the heart of the Pearl Quarter, where the power of Cadenas was concentrated, and where Cunmar, the Ophiri general and thereafter Procurator appointed by their metropolis far away, kept his state.

The area was named, not after the jewels worn by the wicked harlots, sycophants and catamites of the court, though many who at that time saw the abominations with which Cunmar the Procurator's wife, Porphyria, bedecked herself, the encrusted brocade jackets she wore and the pearl-stitched cuffs of her silk trousers and gem-strewn uppers of her mules, might have thought so without incurring contradiction. It was called after the Pearl Well that was sunk three hundred and fifty feet down into the stealthy aquifer in the rock below the level of the ravine floor, the wet walls of which gleamed with a soft luminescence that had given that part of the outpost its name. Donkeys trod the spiral stairs that an engineer from Parthenopolis had ingeniously devised so that their descent and the subsequent ascent, loaded with the heavy, filled, leather water bottles, formed one continuous unbroken journey, the twists of the shallow gradients passing one another in a double helix without intersecting.

The survival of the outpost depended on its supply of water, not only for all the needs that water meets, but also for our main traffic – in the blue and crimson glass that was poured and blown in the Turquoise Quarter. So the well, and the ancient shrine at its head, was holy to all who lived in Cadenas. But in the course of the bitter conflicts that have torn apart the citadel and its environs, worship at the shrine at the wellhead fell under the control of the Ophiri, and their priests have taken over from us the custodianship of the sacred pierced stone that stands there, and prohibited access to others since the fatal battle of Lacarina. It was forbidden to enter the Pearl Quarter without specific business or appointment; no one unsupervised could stay overnight. Only we in the monastery of the Holy Fount were granted special dispensation to remain within its bounds, though access to the sanctuary of the Fount was, as I have written, controlled by the Ophiri. This was a matter of grievous hurt to us.

At the Shrine of the Fount, under the dome sparkling with gold and ultramarine mosaic, water bubbles from the core of the omphalos, wetting the rock till it gleams like the hide of a dolphin when it leaps from a wave, and winking in the penumbra as if it were flowing with splinters of stars fallen from the roof above. It is the very rock that Moses split with his wand in the desert, brought here from Sinai; the Ophiri also claim Moses as a prophet on account of their Book and allow us access to venerate the true God at the shrine but three times a year.

Without this blessed source of water, which does not fail, even when the desert around and the sea seemed to go molten as the sand in the glass foundry after its firing, the citadel of Cadenas would never have remained hospitable to our settlement. Preserving access to the well, from above, and keeping its waters unpolluted from below, were the crucial responsibilities of the Procurator. He was also responsible for patrolling the borders of our bastion, and for checking the wording on passes and permits so that no strangers could infiltrate unbeknownst to the authorities. Cunmar's duty was to enforce the segregation on which the subjection – and hence the tranquillity and the wealth – of Cadenas was founded. He was to assure that trivial disputes and struggles over footling points of etiquette profitably tangled up energies which might spill out elsewhere to more serious ends. Sumptuary laws strengthened every link in the chain of command. The brothel where a courtesan must learn to make twenty-six movements when she takes a single step is one where she will always be enslaved, for she will inevitably fall short – her neck will bend at the wrong angle on this occasion, her right wrist will flex to the wrong rhythm on another. Cunmar was no stickler on his own account, but he watched for infringements in his subordinates. The long, ravelled threads of surveillance spun by the Keep into the Cadenate communication system formed an essential weapon in his statecraft; they sustained his jurisdiction like a net that is specially knotted to allow certain fish to slip through but catches designated prey in its mesh.

Laetitia grew up accustomed to the clashing music of rival claimants on significant days in the calendar: the wailing of an Ophiri hierophant would rise from their temple, while from below, in the street, another sect, returning from their place of worship, beat drums to call their followers to prayer. If any of our pilgrims heard this baying after heathen gods, they would pray aloud to drown the clamour; this was not always to the taste of the Lazuli priests, who would keep up their chanting ever more loudly to silence us. And so the air of Cadenas rang with the strife between believer and unbeliever, each sequestered for safety and harmony in their designated Quarter. But these settled inhabitants of Cadenas in their demarcated quarters were admixed with a raggle-taggle of sailors, dockers, harbourmasters, longshoremen, hostellers and victuallers in the Poppy Quarter by the harbour; they were required to supply the strangers, those many transients who landed and occupied the arcaded caravanserai that stood on three sides of the port area. There too lived the descendants of the Tirzahner captives; once few in number, they were growing; nobody trusted them, for they adhered to a sect of the Ophiri faith, which sowed division among us all in Cadenas. Ser Matteo, born in Tirzah, scorned his countrymen; he had adopted others, for as a merchant, it suited his ambitions to sail under different colours.

Lord Cunmar strengthened the system of security we had instituted in the outpost when he first took power in Cadenas. Permissions, passes, badges of rank, symbols of identity, controlled us all; our different peoples and faiths in that stony place – Enochite, Ishmaelite, the Children of Isaac, Ophiri, Lazuli, Tirzahner, and all the rest of the godless ones – were forbidden to mix or mingle or merge: the very use of such adulterated verbs excited censure.

Groups of petitioners would gather at the gates of the Pearl Quarter, some of them pilgrims hoping to worship at our Shrine of the Fount, others pleading for an audience with Lord Cunmar. When someone appeared to be leaving, they rose in a wave of hope, but then fell back with a great collective sigh of disappointment when the traveller's purple seals revealed that he was not a pilgrim, but a pharmacist from the Hospital, and therefore could not make way for one of the crowd who wanted to touch the holy rock at the Shrine of the Fount.

The importance of maintaining the Pearl Well's sweetness gave pharmacists licence to circulate in Cadenas; many of them practised as masseurs and masseuses, profiting from their comparative freedom to bring comfort and excitement to more housebound Cadenates of both sexes. Apart from the pharmacists, nightsoil carriers were also provided with passes that allowed them to move through the streets – but only in the two hours before dawn – as they went about their business of collecting the slops and stews and worse to transport out of the citadel on to the orchards and vegetable plots reclaimed from the desert beyond our walls. These two groups could infiltrate anywhere, look into every dark corner and privy, and so they acted as informal eyes and ears for whomever could pay them: I have been glad of their intelligence as to the events in the Pearl Quarter, and would not be able to recount what I do here without their tale-bearing. Doris liked to denounce their bags of sinful instruments, smelly oils and essences; 'that Lazuli woman Porphyria' – she would lower her voice here – 'has corrupted the citadel and all who lived in it.'

There were also other kinds of men and women who moved with unprecedented lightness of foot from Quarter to Quarter under Cunmar the Procurator's rule: moneychangers and arms-dealers had no trouble – they either came with the foreign visitors and prospectors in the first place, or they simply wormed their way into foreign deputations upon disembarcation and slipped through the city on their clandestine business, unchallenged.

During the sainted Laetitia's childhood, when Cunmar had reigned in Cadenas for over a decade, the boundaries between the districts were no longer as clear as they had been. Older people complained that the rule of law had once been less slack, and order had prevailed. Once it had been impossible to smuggle anything through the alleys between the stacked dwellings in order, say, to pass from the Rose Quarter to the Turquoise Quarter: the paths were barricaded with packed cullett and rubble, mortar and rusted metal. If a shard pierced you under a nail, corruption seized your joints and stained your flesh, like tainted meat in the butchers' market in the dog days. But as Cunmar grew complacent, passes became easier to come by if you had the right contacts – and who did not know a guard or a guard's daughter? The efforts of beggar children who habitually disregarded danger, combined with the clever scavenging of rats for scraps on the other side down by the harbour, opened corridors through the walls and barriers and allowed the forbidden circulation of people of different faith and loyalties, increasing the dangers in the crowded fortress.

Among the many who yearned for the old days, Doris, the child Laetitia's nurse from infancy, was forthright in her denunciations of the collapse in standards. 'From one day to the next,' she would complain, 'everything changes for the worse. They make the old mauve permits blue, cancel the yellow ones altogether ... It's a crying shame.'

In spite of the watchtowers that overlooked the harbour, and the beacons that lit the wharfs and warehouses all night, new arrivals spilled into Cadenas, drawn by its reputation for security and wealth. Their presence caused grave disturbances, but Cunmar seemed to pay scant attention. 'Strangers who come off ships without documents,' cried Doris, 'who then hide like mice in the walls, scuttle under our feet like rats in the drains. The guards try to pin them down – but if you penetrate their hideouts you can disappear, trapped in their shebeens for ever. Years later, someone will be redoing a floor, or turning a plot of land, and they will find the bones of one of their victims.' She lowered her voice, pulled Laetitia towards her. 'Someone I know bought a geranium in the market, and it flourished so well that she decided to repot it, and you know what she found?'

Laetitia knew, but she still asked, for the pleasure of hearing Doris say the terrible words again.

'A human head – with bits of cheek and one ear and hair still stuck to the skull. That's what they do to you in the Poppy Quarter.'

For the first two years after Laetitia was left behind, she was the painted idol, the poppet of that pagan court, its pet, its mascot; bundled in woven silver wire veiling, with a brocade sash showing two lionesses passant and raised slippers of beaten silver on her henna'd feet with toenails burnished, she would be seated on the steps of the dais during audiences given by Cunmar the Procurator to merchants, financiers, emissaries from various cities and powers from over the sea; she waited, without impatience, on these occasions, for her father to appear; or at least, for someone to appear who would bring news. Every time she was dressed up by Doris for public display, the hope that she would see him again, that again he would swing her up into his arms, revisited her and made her heart pound hurtingly against her ribs. Sorrow and solitude were her schoolmates in those days; she bowed in obedience to her fate.

Gradually, the confusion about identity documents grew and with it, a happy shiftlessness developed, so that the child Laetitia and her nurse, on their weekly visit to the Convent of the Swaddling Bands, where Laetitia was learning her letters under the direction of Mother Cecily, found they were frequently waved through the gate with a cheerful gesture. Doris did not approve; she liked it when the special status of her charge was acknowledged after careful scrutiny of their identity badges and permits.

. . . two years passed, and Laetitia was no longer called to the hall where the Lord Cunmar received his visitors; or to meals to be sat on his lap and fed from his square, reins-calloused, brown fingers. One day, when she and Doris were returning from the Trendle to the Keep as they habitually did after one of her lessons with the Abbess, the guard on duty that afternoon gave their permit a look of contempt, and took it with him into the guardhouse where the records of every permit and every card were kept, casually meanwhile waving them to take a seat on the bench where some other petitioners were already sitting. From the condition of the ground at their feet, littered with peanut shells, sunflower seeds, and orange peel, this gathering had been keeping a longish vigil.

Doris pulled a piece of material ostentatiously across her nose and gripping Laetitia by the shoulder attempted to give orders to the disappearing back of the guard:

'Don't pretend you don't know who we are,' she rebuked him. 'We have been passing through this gate weekly for several months; this child's identity is . . . well-known to the whole of Cadenas.' She tapped Laetitia's badge.

The guard vanished into the gate office, and another of a higher rank came out to replace him. 'It might be,' said the guard, 'that you have passed through this barrier between the Quarters before. But no longer.' He pinched Laetitia's cheek so slowly and hard that while Laetitia refused to cry out, realising the moment did not call for a response of any kind, Doris started forward to hit his fingers away. 'But that badge you're wearing, my pussycat,' he continued, 'means you should be over there, with them—' he jerked thumb and head towards the shambles of the Poppy Quarter. 'And you, young lady, you belong in the Turquoise slums. These passes you've produced have expired.'

They returned to the Convent of the Swaddling Bands. Doris wept and raged, and made continual efforts to recapture the Procurator's attention through missives furiously despatched with the pharmacists and the nightsoil carriers whom she despised.

Meanwhile, she found herself lodgings near the convent, and Laetitia was left to live on the charity of Abbess Cicely. There the blessed child's education in the true faith her mother had desired for her began at last.

10

Kim to Hortense, twice

Subject: Re: Meeting up
Date: Fri, 05 June 199– 02:12:42 +0100
From: kim.mcquy<hswu@lattice.onlyconnect.com>
To: Hortense Fernly<h.fernly@natmus.ac.alb>

Hello Hetty   it turns out I can clear the whole day next thursday   the
class outing to the mcdonald's rainforest in the docks is happening then
and I've done my stint there in past years and so can be excused – any
chance you coming earlier than 6?
  thanks kim

Subject: Re: Skipwith 673
Date: Tues, 09 June 199– 09:38:12 +0100
From: Hortense Fernly<h.fernly@natmus.ac.alb>
To: kim.<hswu@lattice.onlyconnect.com>

I'll come and find you in the reading room at around 4.00 pm. You can
of course arrive earlier (the Archives are open from 9.30). I would be
pleased to be of help, as in my profession, we too work with memory,
and I'm all too aware of the gaps in the records – history is a very old
man, and, as the saying goes, old men forget. Yours, Hetty

Subject: Re: Leto bundle
Date: Tues, 09 June 199– 18:11:42 +0100
From: kim.mcquy<hswu@lattice.onlyconnect.com>
To: Hortense Fernly<h.fernly@natmus.ac.alb>

- -

Great. I'll be there lots to talk about looking forward :-) kim

Subject: Re: Skipwith 673
Date: Wed, 10 June 199– 10:38:12 +0100
From: Hortense Fernly<h.fernly@natmus.ac.alb>
To: kim.mcquy<hswu@lattice.onlyconnect.com>

- -

**Kim, Just a PS, really : I can see you're really fired up so do bear in mind
Meeks was one of those eminent muscular Christian Victorians who
wanted every document of the past to confirm the truth of the Bible,
and when they didn't, he tossed them aside. If it doesn't fit, chuck
it. . .It's a lesson to us.**

  **I found a note Meeks left in the box saying the text was 'so corrupt it
was better hidden than published'! He used old-fashioned standards of
editorial purity to suppress a picture that challenged his rosy vision of
the past.**

  We think we're better, but are we really?

  Yours, Hetty

Subject: Leto Lives!
Date: Wed, 10 June 199– 16:47:01 +0100
From: kim.mcquy<hswu@lattice.onlyconnect.com>
To: Hortense Fernly<h.fernly@natmus.ac.alb>

- -

**Hetty I know we're meeting tomorrow but I wanted to say there's more
there than I'd ever dreamed of even more than she tells me but it all
figures she *is* she truly is the goddess of diaspora embodiment of
the dispersed and the drowned and every generation who's come in
contact has seen it in her they've recognised it – but not been able to
grasp it fully till now and hswu –**

  History's full of hidden files of memories that have been drowned and

drowned it seemed for ever – so what happened to the unstoried, untold, unremembered? we've found such an extraordinary work we can do together on the bundle – you and me I mean it – I know you feel awkward when I explain my flashes my messages my revelations because in our time this language has lost its claim to any kind of truthfulness But you see that I really knew how she'd suffered – and in ways that are still so alive to us now – and those stories bore out my wildest visions – the rape the kids the orphanage the wanderings – we must go back to start again

I strike people as a charlatan or a madman – but you know I'm not and I can tell you can tell – you're a wonderful generous beautiful woman and I revel in your trust – from the beginning you didn't dismiss me and I'll never forget that – through thick & thin come hell & high water you name it I'll do it anything & everything for you if you need me – please remember that call on me *trust* me I've been having tremendous thoughts – truly –

Kim

ps can't wait for term to end – six weeks to go and two whole months free – I'm inspired and Leto is too – we're communicating *nightly* never miss a day –

II

An Anniversary

(from Annals of the Convent)

[Mss. Lat. 78–83]

The *Chronicle of Barnabas* document broke off, and Meeks's translations passed on to another manuscript, 'written', he noted, 'by a nun of the Convent of the Holy Swaddling Bands at the Hospital in Cadenas. ?c. 1200 that is only seven years after the putative date of Leto's martyrdom, possibly as part of a *Vita* of Leto the Well-Beloved, for submission to the *Petitio in causam sanctitatis Laetitiae*, the proceedings of her canonisation.'

[Ms. Lat. 80]

. . . we survived, we of the faithful Remnant of Enoch, and we survived in grace and dignity, then; the Hospitallers remaining in the building that abuts us still gave us what support they could afford, though when a certain Doris, who had been Laetitia's haughty nursemaid in the Keep, was able to bribe and wheedle her way through the barriers to visit her former charge, she insisted I pen letters to the Vice-Procurator about the continued exile she and Laetitia suffered from the Keep. I took down her dictation, though I was very doubtful of success.

'Your Excellency!' she cried. 'Think of the reputation of Cadenas! We are nothing but poor little women, without strength or influence, but you in your wisdom and justice are known to the whole world.

'There is a taint in the blood of your dominion which risks

envenoming the whole ... You cannot condone corruption and injustice. Please find it in your noble heart to reward the community of the Convent of the Holy Swaddling Bands, and rescue us from the straits in which we are foundering.'

There was no answer, and indeed, we were never sure that the long laboured over letters themselves were ever delivered, as the correct stamps required to pass the gates had become difficult to identify for they changed from day to day according to the vicissitudes of power.

Laetitia joined a group of nine girls of different ages; each of these stray lambs had arrived at various times in the last decade when the Procurator Cunmar ruled in Cadenas. Our girls wore plain straight pale blue pinafores over a paler blue, checked undershift which they washed twice a week; the same gingham cloth covered their heads.

I once caught a glimpse of Agatha, who was Laetitia's neighbour in the room where they slept during the cooler months, twisting the cloth over itself to form a higher turban and bending to try and see the effect in the reflection in Laetitia's eyes. We were strict with them; they had to tie the cloths tightly at the nape of their necks at the back, covering all of their hair and the tops of their ears, flat to the skull; to Laetitia, it made them look sombre as the harbour cormorants, sleek and wet from fishing. But she also told me that she enjoyed the visits of our, 'Red' bishop (by contrast to the Lazuli prelates, who are always dressed in black), for when he came to say Mass for us, our abbess Cicely crowned herself and us in his honour with tall purple velvet turret-like wimples, while our beloved orphans were issued starched white veils, in which the folds from the linen press showed like the chequered shadow of the Keep's precious leaded window panes.

When the nights became cold, as happens in our desert climate, they were issued woollen hose; in the winter we issued them with cuffs which protected the long-sleeved versions of their usual dress, tucked in when they were doing the cleaning and dishwashing and laundry and helping in the garden.

[Ms. Lat. Fr. 82]

Child scavengers who picked over the refuse on the wharves at the Sea Gate called regularly at the back door of our Convent; in return for the occasional bowl of meal, or for a sprig of grapes from our vines or a couple of tomatoes or a bunch of radishes, produce of the vegetable garden our community kept on every available surface of our huddled buildings' roofs and balconies, these harbour rats provided us and our young wards with shells; these were scoured and filed until our girls could cut out pearl buttons from them, make tiny polished sequins and round studs. Some were inscribed with blessings, invocations of protection and prayers such as AMDG (*Ad maiorem dei gloriam*) or OPNVM (*Ora pro nobis Virgo Maria*) in order to spread the good news of our faith. Our girls then stitched ribbons and trimmings with these ornaments, or used them to spangle collars and ribbons and belts, purses and slippers. We lived by delivering their handiwork to a dealer who had procured a pass which allowed him to trade throughout the citadel.

He was an Ophiri, a pharmacist who could move from household to household, with many fingers in many pies; a young man of high colour in his cheeks and a blurred edge to his large wet irises, given to laughing for no reason, except, it was my opinion, that his trade involved him in delightful (to him) and unexpected intimacies. As indeed it did when, together in the small vestibule by the door, we would examine the sparkling slippers and other fancy goods we three sisters and our little wards in the Convent had completed that month; but I learned to control my feelings in such encounters. I know from the ancient naturalists that blushing is unique to the human creature. Its clear signal of shame arouses male lust: we warned our charges.

The young man was never dissatisfied with our work – we gave him no cause, and he gaily provided us in exchange with the unadorned cloth and cut garments and accessories to ornament, as well as the thread we needed to sew on the buttons and beads; he occasionally introduced novelties among the patterns: garments for dowry chests which needed some further, mother-of-pearl detailing. He also handed us a purse with a little Ophiri money with which we could buy what we could not make ourselves, or grow in that season . . .

[Ms. Lat. Fr. 83]

On the anniversaries of our foundlings' arrival in our care, Abbess Cecily would tell the child her own personal history, as far as it was known, while the other girls rasped the shells with sandpaper, or stitched; then there would be honey cakes with curd cheese for a treat, and each of our charges would give the child something to celebrate her new year: a feather, a song, a picture she had drawn, a packet of seeds gathered from one of the plants for her to grow herself, a paper twist of honey-coated nuts, or, most prized of all, a dried poppyhead threaded to wear like a locket.

The little girls called all three of us nuns Mother; but it was tacitly agreed that 'Mother Cecily' was mother superior in more ways than one, and we were poor copies, like a text that has many scribal errors and lacunae; or, like the cotton, as it were, that has been placed in contact with a holy relic to be given to pilgrims, not the living relic itself. Her large eyes with the roan flecks in them fastened with a passionate exalted and holy affection on the children; her voice, when she recited to them the rules of the order, was steady, soothing; it too had bright gold lights in it. She appeared, with her long-legged step and her unusual height more like a migratory bird than a woman: her presence among us gave us a glimpse of grace and power no less memorable than the visit of the flocking storks that made a land bridge in our city and the territory around every Easter. Sometimes, she clasped the children to her; this was not motherly behaviour, however, not in the sense of fleshly connection and even possession intended by the general. Laetitia herself understood the abbess's love: she told me that in these embraces she felt her body bending, becoming that instrument of God's will that only Mother Cecily knew how to handle to achieve the purpose for which God had first formed it. It was she who had renamed the child, giving her the name meaning joy, to celebrate her belonging to our community and our faith . . .

12

Kim to Hortense; Hortense to Kim

Subject: Skipwith 673
Date: Wed, 10 June 199– 19:37:23 +0100
From: Hortense Fernly<h.fernly@natmus.ac.alb>
To: kim.mcquy<hswu@lattice.onlyconnect.com>

Kim, You're definitely confusing things by taking Leto and Laetitia to be somehow connected. The Cadenas chronicles were just thrown into the tomb by chance – they've got nothing to do with it. Don't become one of those conspiracy theorists who see arcane patterns where only random chaos rules. [She deleted this and wrote instead:]

Of course you realise that none of what we looked at has anything to do with the Leto of the frogs episode. You'll be saying next that gods and goddesses are back among us. Neo-paganism! The original Leto was a Titan in classical Greek mythology a religion that doesn't even have any followers any more. Which makes it an admirably rare creature, in fact.

The web's good on mythology – as I'm sure you know! Put in Leto on MissMarple or Etherprobe or any one of the search engines and her CV comes up: the mother of Apollo and Artemis, patron of mothers and childbirth, the goddess who struck down Niobe and her children after Niobe rashly boasted of their beauty. Aka Latona. Related to Leda in some complicated way. But as for the twelfth century material, I suppose you could just about make out a case that the classical story influenced it. . .

[Hortense Fernly stopped. Really I am going along with him far too much. Why?

Because I'm bored?]

126

I'll be coming into the Archives tomorrow afternoon, but it'll have to be brief.

Yours, Hetty

Subject: Leto Bundle
Date: Wed, 10 June 199– 20:16:37 +0100
From: kim.mcquy<hswu@lattice.onlyconnect.com>
To: Hortense Fernly<h.fernly@natmus.ac.alb>

Hello Hetty   it has everything to do with Leto she's the same person then now forever   that's the whole point   she's unreal   so she's hyperreal so she's always live always alive   see you tomorrow and we'll TALK   cheers kim

Subject: Skipwith 673
Date: Wed, 10 June 199– 21:37:49 +0100
From: Hortense Fernly<h.fernly@natmus.ac.alb>
To: kim.mcquy<hswu@lattice.onlyconnect.com>

Kim, I know Buddhism is fashionable especially among health food shoppers. [She struck this. Instead she wrote:] Are you saying she came back under another form? I mean, are you talking metempsychosis?

[She didn't send this e-mail. She would tell him this, and more, later.]

PART THREE

The Keep, Cadenas-la-Jolie
(The 'Cunmar Romance')

I

A Hostage in the Outpost

'These leaves are the most precious manuscripts from the Skipwith deposit, so we can't allow you to handle them yourself,' said the librarian. 'But Dr Fernly wanted you to have a glimpse of their splendour.' She sounded puzzled.

Kim was in an insomniac's state of dazed wakefulness, words and images disordered in his mind and clamouring for attention. He'd been to the courtyard café, but the latte he'd ordered was probably a mistake, however much it masqueraded as a bedtime toddy.

The librarian placed the grey acid-free box she was carrying on a different desk from Kim's, one nearer her own presiding position in the room. She handed him some white cotton gloves, and herself put on a pair before opening the box. Between leaves of tissue, which she lifted gently to the side, Kim saw a vellum sheet, puckered and fleshy, covered in a pale grey-brown script in serried files, so regular and harmonious, that, looking down on it, Kim could hear sounding in his inner ear the rhythmic chant that pulses under high naves from dark choirstalls. Here and there, like the punctuating high note of the cantor, an ornamental gilded capital letter, picked out in the colour of damsons, swelled out of the page.

The librarian picked up the catalogue note in the box and read out: '"Eleven folio pages, written around 1350, on parchment, in the miniature uncials most familiar from the scriptoria of the Lazuli court, and in a highly concentrated cuttlefish ink enriched with purple ornaments and gold leaf. This fragment constitutes one of the greatest treasures in the bundle of miscellaneous manuscripts deposited by Sir Giles Skipwith."'

'These are Meeks's notes,' she added, and gave him the sheet. Kim read, 'Since Fol.1 r bears the words "Of the Deeds of Cunmar, Vice-Procur . . ." I have called this manuscript the "Cunmar Romance".'

The librarian's voice dropped as she read on from the catalogue note, ' "The writer reveals his official allegiance to the Lazuli, but cannot but fail to conceal his fascination and admiration for the Ophiri administrator of Cadenas, known (to his enemies) as 'Cunmar the Terrible', a soldier of fortune from the north shore, who rose to broker power in the contested borderlands of the Ophiri–Lazuli empires." And so on and so forth. Strife. Mayhem. History.'

'Yes,' said Kim, smiling down at the parchments.

'Let me relate now the pride of Cunmar the Terrible, and the cause of his fall,' began the document that now lay before Kim, the vellum originals having been repacked in their tissue nest and swiftly removed to safekeeping.

This translation was freshly typed: Hortense Fernly's initials, dated recently, appeared in the reference number under the heading. She had drafted this copy, he realised; he would be able to ask her about it, when she came to find him.

[Skipwith Add. Mss.: G. Fr. 62]

. . . Little does it become an old man to feel the heat and passion of a youth. But God is infinitely mysterious in His wisdom. The child Leto of the Remnant, called by the Enochites Laetitia *Deodata*, was the humble tool of divine providence in the tyrant's fate, as I shall tell. Through the sins of Cunmar, He brought about his ruin and our salvation.

Ser Matteo, father of Leto, a trader of Tirzahner origin, longtime in the employ of Enochite merchant adventurers on our seas, promised to bring Cunmar a great wonder, a weapon of defence that had not been seen since the time of Archimedes, inventor of many wonders, but not of this one.

Cunmar was intrigued; he put aside his customary caution, for he valued rare and curious treasures. He urged Ser Matteo to continue, and the merchant began to speak of a certain kind of spider: 'She's tiny, no bigger than a midge over a standing pool in the close evenings that late summer brings in my country. You would never notice her, if it weren't for her handiwork, to use a figure of speech, her webs. Brush one aside and the threads stick to your fingers; when you try to pick them off, they won't break, but hold like tempered steel. This silk has healing properties: place a poultice made of it on a wound, and that wound will close. Continue to apply it, and the scar will fade and vanish. Nothing we know, none of our books or our wise men's learning, can give an account of the power of this orbweaver's web. It was perhaps one of God's amusements – to make such a paltry creature as a spider a wonderworker of such strength and cunning. Think of it, Lord Cunmar! If you can possess this skill, there'll be no more plaiting of straw that rots in winter and grows dry and friable in summer! No more siege gear raised by ropes that soon fray! Think of the weight of a fly that a spider traps in full flight! Think of the weight of that projectile, stopped dead by the thinnest threads of the web!'

Cunmar pondered this, and nodded.

'If you dangle one of these spiders in the air,' Ser Matteo went on, 'it will run a line down to the nearest surface and then, if you lift the creature up again, it will continue to spin. You can wind the thread on a spool for as long as the spider lives – these spinners will yield a hundred times their weight in silken fibre – and these insects are plentiful in our woods and in our houses in the autumn. You need only breed them for use.

'Their thread is far easier to harvest than silk – and think of the riches silk has brought. Those worms are the spider's industrious kin; this silk is another, great natural wonder with as many uses as gold, and as imperishable!'

The merchant understood that he could flatter the Procurator's vanity: 'Consider the great kings and warriors who were not afraid to search for nature's secrets: Ulysses who was determined to hear the sirens singing, though no man had ever survived the experience, and Hercules who travelled to the farthest west to pick the golden apples that grow there. Think of the great Khan whom Ser Marco Polo served as I serve you. Not to speak of the great Alexander . . .' Now this was the truest stroke the trader could have struck with Cunmar the Terrible, for the Procurator of Cadenas in his folly fancied himself a new Alexander, in spite of the littleness of his dominion and the baseness of his birth.

'Alexander! His curiosity about natural wonders inspired him to harness an eagle and fly up into the skies and drive fishes to take him to the bottom of the sea: follow his lead, Cunmar, and pluck the mystery of the spider in her lair!

'With the right skills you can apply her thread to many uses – and you Ophiri do not persecute your alchemists as servants of the devil, as we do. You can work with the silk, learn its secrets, *copy* it.'

'Ah,' sighed Cunmar. 'Your great Satan is the ape of God and he proceeds by copying – falsely.'

'Indeed so,' said Ser Matteo. 'Which is why I shall bring you a nest of such spiders as you have never seen and you will milk them of their silk as we pull at the udders of milchcows and then . . .'

'We shall make nets that cannot be broken; we shall rig our ships with invisible lines; we shall harpoon our enemies and reel them in; we shall raise siege engines on gossamer—' Cunmar was laughing, then he asked, 'But you, do you not consider yourself a traitor to your creed and to your people?'

Ser Matteo shook his head. 'The sea-roads are my native soil (if I may mix up nature's elements). My people are traders, and we are in the habit of crossing borders. As for my creed . . . I trust in the mercy of God to all sinners.'

He was smiling as he said this, and Cunmar embraced him, and instructed that his ship be loaded with our blue glassware, our metalwork – chased silver vessels and knives in damascened sheaths.

In his rashness, Cunmar the Terrible at that time also accepted the child Leto as a pledge of their pact.

[Skipwith Add. Mss.: G. Fr. 63]

. . . as a young apprentice, working in a foundry in his native Deuteropolis, on the northern littoral of Our Sea, a spark had pierced Cunmar's left eye; there was excruciating pain, and for ten days he wore a bandage and did not know if he had partly lost his sight. When it was lifted, he could see as well as before, but the iris had burned, and was now half the eerie aquatic green of some desert peoples, half a basalt blackness, and it no longer retracted. With this large, open pupil ringed by its pale halo, he resembled one of the desert creatures who prefer to hunt by night, shunning even the illumination of the moon.

Cunmar first fought with the Ophiri raiders who increasingly harassed our Lazuli merchants' ships, and he rose as Ophiri influence spread. Settlements like Cadenas came under their new mastery: this was when our co-religionists at the holy fount were stripped of their authority over that sanctuary. In the Turquoise Quarter, a few remained: the Enochite Remnant who, as God willed it, were to become our enemies in the bitter struggles to control the outpost. Cunmar continued to serve the distant metropole, and when the farflung garrisons of our empire were reduced, soldiers of no breeding or connection, like Cunmar, were advanced.

Nearly half a century of battle since had left other marks: an upturned chevron on his shin, milky against his skin, where he had caught his leg on a nail in the forge where he was apprenticed; a star-shaped hollow in his thigh where he had been struck by a flail wielded by a footsoldier, whose bravery at that vantage had inspired Cunmar to spare him, even while the spikes of the caltrop ate into his flesh. He was missing a kneecap from his left leg, the result of a fall during his third campaign. Though able to ride again, another unseating gave him trouble lifting his right arm higher than level with his shoulder. His clothes had been adapted; his breastplate had been remade in leather so that it weighed less (at the cost of giving him less protection), and the tunics he wore over it were looser over his back and across around the chest, which softened his military carriage and enhanced other qualities of his appearance: the musing irony in the corners of his mouth belied the soldier's committed partisanship. But riding still kept his bearing tall and his diaphragm muscles tight over the growing heaviness of his belly and torso. His body was a chronicle; many women, and many boys (he knew the ways of the cities of the plain) had put their fingers to his wounds and told them off, one by one, learning the chapters.

[Skipwith Add. Mss.: G. Fr. 64]

The nest of spiders, the promised treasure that Ser Matteo had guaranteed against his daughter, did not arrive; nor were there signs of diminished raids on shipping on our sea roads. Cadenas began murmuring against Cunmar; secret reports were despatched to the Ophiri capital, citing instances of his lawlessness, his misjudgements and his profligacy. His alliance with the foreign merchant was only one false step of many the Procurator had begun to take in these last years of his power.

Cunmar had held sway over the outpost for sixteen years, since the Year of Our Lord 1165 when the Ophiri invested Cadenas. He despatched punctually, every quarter day, the metropole's dues and revenues, recounting in equable tones the events of the past three months, and adding blandishments with the fluency for which he was well known. After the first five years of his governance, no further visitations arrived to inspect the citadel: severe troubles on the sprawling Ophiris eastern border as well as continued strife with our Lazuli empire absorbed much of the central government's attention. So Cunmar began to run the citadel as he pleased. After a long career in arms, he began to exercise power through traffic in goods – in so doing, he flouted many of our customs, trespassing against ancient and prescribed differences and degrees between peoples and worship and culture and morals, and inviting foreigners to tread on grounds forbidden them before. Cunmar overlooked pollution where others know it to lie. It is when a man thinks he is greater than the law, above the requirements of faith, alone and pre-eminent among humankind that woe becomes his lot. Presumption is a sin, against God and man: the Procurator of Cadenas also committed crimes against history, against revered tradition.

The Procurator married, in order to pursue his diplomatic ends, Porphyria, a woman of our faith, who was five years older than him, and the widow of the commander Xanthos, from one of our noble families, whom he had taken prisoner in battle. The ransom for her husband's freedom was promised, again and again, but it was never paid – the Lazuli coffers were drained – and so the captive remained several years in Cunmar's custody: they played chess together and discussed the meaning of honour and the code of war. It was through the influence of this prisoner that Cunmar extended certain privileges to our people in Cadenas; we were glad of this, but in doing so he disrupted the harmonious distinctions, which kept order in the outpost.

Then, it came about that a new pact was struck in the metropole, when our beleaguered Lazuli empire asked the Ophiri for help against the Enochite and Tirzahner armies gathering against them in the west. A general amnesty of all prisoners was declared: so the nobleman Xanthos, who had lived in Cunmar's household for four years, was set free, without ransom, to return to his wife and children. Before they had parted, Xanthos begged Cunmar to care for his wife Porphyria, for his son Chrysaor, and for his other children should anything happen to him.

So when Xanthos was killed soon after, in the bitter fighting against the Tirzahner rabble, Cunmar married the widow, and brought that highborn Lazuli lady to Cadenas.

At first, no one murmured aloud against the breach in the rules that she, a Lazuli, shared a bed with Cunmar. But in this marriage as in other matters, the Procurator scandalised the people, and a great hue and cry was raised against him in Cadenas. It reached the ears of the metropole; the repercussions of his errancy brought about the return of the citadel to Lazuli rule, and the restoration of the sacred Fount to our control.

[Skipwith Add. Mss.: G. Fr. 65]

. . . rumours began that a ship flying the flag of Ser Matteo's company had been sighted. If, as it seemed, Ser Matteo's trade was seaworthy once again, then Cunmar was forsworn, since he had promised to keep Leto by his side as a daughter. He recalled the peevish letters that reached him from the Convent and knew, to his relief, that she was alive. Her loss of rank could be quickly remedied with a change of clothes and a move back to the court. He had also promised to care for her. He suffered a twinge over this, not for reasons of conscience, but for that sense of occasion, which had scarcely ever failed his diplomacy.

So he summoned her from the Convent of the Holy Swaddling Bands.

When Cunmar the Terrible saw the young woman Leto had become, in her gingham pinafore, with her scarf tight over her head, and her wooden box of tokens in her arms, she stirred that quickfire pity that in him lay close to disdain: how could a girl of her age be allowed to be so ugly? He went up to her and looked in her face. She bit her lip, it did not redden; she looked bloodless. She had been a solemn little girl who had sometimes cooed like a dove when he dandled her; or squealed when she twisted from him and he, in play, gnashed his teeth and crushed her to his chest.

This young woman struck no notes of recognition in him.

He told Doris to take off the scarf.

'I should think so. At last!' said Doris, with enthusiasm. To her great satisfaction, she too had been summoned back in attendance from exile in the Turquoise Quarter. 'It's been far too long that she's been cooped up with the nuns and those poor orphans. She's made of quite different stuff. If you give my young lady the use of some clothes and unguents, lotions and perfumes, if you allow her to go to the women's baths – you'll see, I'll make sure she won't disgrace a palace.'

Cunmar paused, then nodded.

Doris could not help letting out a trill, so delighted was she with this fulfilment of her ambitions.

Cunmar said, 'Let's not exaggerate. This is not a palace; but a military outpost. Still, I expect an improvement.'

For Leto, there was to be no more polishing and engraving and punching of buttons or sewing of fancy goods, no more stealthy bulletins whispered up the convent walls, no more rationed access to her mementoes; she wore her earrings every day, and silver sandals were being beaten out to fit her again. Sometimes Cunmar ordered her to join him; he would scoop her up on to the pommel of his saddle and take her for a canter in the desert; he smelled of smoke and spices from the black bags of the pharmacists he favoured and his silvered, tight-curled beard and hair were combed out with potions; he would ride out with her into the sherbet hills and showed her the ruined hulks of desert outposts that, unlike Cadenas, had been abandoned. In this way, her life of iniquity began and with it, the destruction of Cunmar.

2

Kim to Hortense, twice

Subject: Leto Bundle
Date: Fri, 12 June 199– 21:16:37 +0100
From: kim.mcquy<hswu@lattice.onlyconnect.com>
To: Hortense Fernly<h.fernly@natmus.ac.alb>

- -

Hetty! You only stayed ten minutes why? When we're finding out so
much about the bundle – when leto's life is unfolding now for us at last
– but thanks for your help anyway

   your presence radiates makes windows open doors yield – I mean
it   kim

Subject: Leto Bundle
Date: Fri, 12 June 199– 22:07:12 +0100
From: kim.mcquy<hswu@lattice.onlyconnect.com>
To: Hortense Fernly<h.fernly@natmus.ac.alb>

- -

Hetty   ive been thinking because you seemed kind of sad about things
yesterday   and so rushed   but it's important we talk   it's not that leto
comes back in another shape   as. . .a wolf or a goose or a salmon or a
cuttlefish or whatever. . .the way Buddhists believe   this is
different *she* is different   she's always in time present cutting across
ours that's always going by   so she's of all time   of our time   or put it
another way she's a story and stories have a life   and a time all of their
own   when you read   think how real the characters

139

are miranda or frankenstein's monster hamlet his mother too his father even and he's a ghost! I could go on peter pan alice now even harry potter lara croft barney the dinosaur think of the things in your head the pictures you make when you're dreaming or thinking or just imagining things an afterimage in my head doesn't need to be outside my body to be real dreamers experience unreality intensely witchhunters really thought the devil copulated with women and the women agreed because in the night they had indeed known something and it didn't have to be there in a physical sense these are human realities we can we all have experiences every day that dismantle the ordinary ways we know whether something or someone is real or true or *there* and these conditions are intensifying. . .this is the new air we breathe and I'm enjoying it my lungs are full of it I like figments they keep me company all the time when I'm alone I see you in my thoughts when you're not there you're real to me I like thinking about you I like talking to you like this you light me up even when you're not there but you are in some real deep way and I we have to make do with that cheers kim

[And Hetty finds herself thinking, against her better judgement, Does he mean me? Or is this the way he talks to everybody?]

3

'Of the Great Subterfuge of Cunmar the Terrible'

[Skipwith Add. Mss.: G. Fr. 68]

'Now comes the time for me to relate Cunmar's most famous deed, for which he earned that sometime sobriquet, The Terrible. It thrilled all who heard it told, including Leto, for girls on the verge of womanhood can be kindled by tales of cruelty and skill and valour.' Kim skimmed on: here was the shape-shifting god of the classical past he'd heard Hortense describe, changed again, rising up alongside Leto from her tomb and commanding him to listen. In the silence of the reading room, he found himself wanting to shout: the man compelled him to read, against his will. He wanted to destroy him; he wanted to shake Leto into awareness, prevent the plot unfolding. That was what he had to do: put her story out, as widely as he could. So that it wouldn't happen again. He believed it, he was sure he could make his plan work. He was there to make a difference to the old story, the one that happens every time.

... The maxim of the fox, 'Know your enemy', Cunmar learned, gradually, in his years of soldiering for the Ophiri empire; he began to turn observations he had made of his enemies' ways against them to forward his own ends.

He delighted in travestying the holy tenets of the faith, though he reserved the worst of his scorn for our Enochite brethren: 'They believe,' he would say of men of our faith, 'that the spirit is like a shadow, bloodless, insubstantial; their ghosts have no bodies, they glide through closed doors, they walk on fleshless feet, they touch you with bloodless hands. There is no colour in their other worlds: their heaven is a blaze of light, their hell all murk and darkness. Both are filled with bodies that look like bodies but do not bleed or breathe or eat or drink. You need only look at the pictures and statues they put up in their churches to understand this. By contrast, after we quit this world, the earth is perfected in our paradise – and the men and women in it: warm and vigorous and full-throated. Every rose is essence of rose in every aspect of roseness, fragrant and blooming and dewy with the freshness of the morning and, in its singularity of hue, the full expression of that hue's depth and extent.' In this Cunmar at least spoke true: their abominable beliefs grant eternity to their lusts.

'They love and worship the flesh and the blood of dead men – and sometimes women's as well. They buy and sell parts of their saints' bodies as relics, because these are still flesh, still coloured, not in any thing ghostly.

'They fear that the shadows we cast in the sunshine are messengers from this other world, where all colours, and bodies and flesh and blood dissolve and become wraiths. For them, shadows exercise influence over the bodies they possess, over the persons to whom they stick.'

And he boasted, 'This was their folly, that I used against them. I entered the minds of my enemy, and prised their defences open. I chose to haunt them – to raise living ghosts before them.'

The great siege of 1165 was in its fourth weary month: the Enochites had sealed the harbour of Cadenas and were thus preventing supplies reaching the outpost from the sea, while the land approaches were cut off from the south by their cavalry encampment. In the Rose Quarter, the tanners were marking up the price of hooves for soup from the horses and beasts of burden fallen in the fighting – the flesh was reserved for the army. The Pearl Well was under assault from slaves hacking into the rock to reach the spring; their actions fouled it. Desperation was growing inside the city, and against us, especially, the few remaining Lazuli in the outpost, since we were wrongly suspected by many Ophiri of secret loyalty and even collusion with the besiegers. Cunmar said (and alas, he did not lie): 'Although they worship the same god, their conflicts are deeper and more bitter than our differences with them: the closer sects are to one another, the more terrible their hatred – that is the way it is, as we know from ourselves, let's admit it.'

But some elements were not persuaded. There followed riot and lynchings in the Turquoise Quarter: a young Lazuli nobleman was dragged out of his house and accused of spying for the Enochite army outside the walls; two of our brothers were caught in the doorway of their church: they were suspected of betraying some method of access to the Pearl Well. They too were beaten to death by the crowd.

Cunmar studied the situation: the garrison was weak from lack of food, the besiegers still had the season's coolness on their side for another six weeks at least. None of the promised reinforcements had arrived from the metropole and its extensive allies, either by sea or land.

He decided, he told Leto, that since the way of the lion was failing, the besieged must adopt the way of the fox:

'I gave the orders: the battered bodies of the two monks [Basileos and Gregorios of blessed memory] and of the young nobleman, to be delivered to the Rose Quarter: there, the tanners to behead them and flay their bodies carefully, preparing them as those leatherworkers prepare a hide; the head was to be rendered whole and restored to their likeness in life as accurately as possible.

'Meanwhile I sent a messenger out to the camp of the besiegers under a flag of truce. I offered the commander an exchange: we would hand over these recent victims for honourable burial, and post the threat of capital reprisals against any more killings of this kind in return for a lifting of the sea blockade.

'But Lord Laurent, who was in command, then entertained no fellow feelings for any Lazuli, as I well knew: they had not joined forces with his men in this phase of the long war.

'He told the messenger, "God knows your cruel savagery already and will mete out to you divine justice. He will deal for all eternity with those who die at your hands, according to their deeds. Fighting for His true faith, I can offer you nothing on this earth except my undying and implacable enmity."

'With these haughty words, the Enochite lord retired into his tent and dismissed our ambassador.

'So when the messenger returned, I had the three heads impaled on stakes; the two monks' were posted on the Sea Gate of Cadenas, the noble youth's over the arch at the eastern entrance, facing the camp of the Enochites. For two days and a night the victims were displayed in their dishonour. But on the second night,' and here Cunmar lowered his voice to lean into Leto's ear, 'I directed that simulacra be made to resemble the dead men's heads. They were compacted of straw and clay and wax, and were secretly substituted. The decaying trophies were then joined again to their carcasses. The process of flensing and curing rendered the victims' skins waxen and translucent, and I specified that they be carefully stitched together, that every rent of the assaults upon them be closed and sealed, every wound sutured, so that like the pig's bladders you children use in play and the jester bounces on his target's heads, they could be inflated.'

When he described this to Leto, she huddled closer to him, in fear of the spectres he had made. Thus does a seducer soothe the terrors he himself has conjured.

'Towards the end of the second night,' he went on, 'while the counterfeit heads were still in place on the walls, I had the grisly trophies raised on lances, the head fastened at the point, the feet fastened to the haft. I then mounted my light-footed mare, and ordered a company of horsemen to follow. We were to raid the Enochite camp for much needed supplies, I told them.'

Did Cunmar place Leto on his knees and pretend to ride with her? Kim saw them in his mind's eye: Cunmar paddling in the young girl's body, and he shivered.

'I took two of the lances with the hoisted corpses and stowed them in the scabbards hanging from my saddle; Karim my equerry, riding close behind, held the third. We left Cadenas by the postern gate in darkness and rode up to the slope above the enemy so that the sun would rise behind us. I had observed that from the ridge our shadows would fall towards the camp so we held our position there as the sun broke over the rim of the desert behind us and the enemy began to stir.

'The Enochite ranks in the camp below first saw the dead men hovering aloft, then felt – and saw – their shadows fall across their lines.

'The outline of the effigies was ghostly; they did not block the swelling sunlight like the stuff of living beings, but allowed it to pass through, glowing – the Enochites began scurrying and looking up and trying to ascertain if they could believe the evidence of their eyes.

'This was the ghastly plight of the men whom they in their barbarousness had denied burial rites,' Cunmar continued solemnly. 'But to them, they appeared to be living ghosts, since the real bodies (as they thought) were still rotting on the battlements in grisly display.'

That day of destiny saw the Enochites run from the advancing squad; they scattered in panic to find armour, weapons, horses. Cunmar had surprised proud Lord Laurent, and his troops tumbled over one another in disarray, until, as happens always in the desert morning, the breeze lifted sharply at daybreak. With his two trophies raised up high, Cunmar, flanked by Karim with the third carcass, and the company packed behind him, began streaming down the slope towards the enemy.

'The flayed victims' bodies filled, as I knew they must,' he turned Leto to face him and look into his eyes as he continued, 'and the dawn gleamed on their waxy hides, they seemed to swell bigger as they floated. Like phantom riders from the pit of hell, like souls of the dead conjured by devils, they rode with us in the raid on the Enochite camp.'

On that occasion, Cunmar seized enough provender and victuals to refresh the garrison. But above all, his exploit unstrung the besiegers. It grew in the telling, too. I have given the unembellished version, as I learned it from within Cadenas in those days; but the Enochites did not know how the ghosts came to walk and ride into their midst that morning, and their speculations fed their fears. So they failed to press their continuing advantage that spring. Cadenas remained in the power of the Ophiri, but only for another thirteen years.

[Skipwith Add. Mss.: G. Fr. 69]

'Hereward Meeks notes here,' Hortense had written, 'a definite change of tone in the manuscript': 'The passages which follow offer an excellent example of the classical rhetorical device, preterition, or writing of what you pretend to be beneath consideration. We should give Saint Jerome the benefit of the doubt (perhaps) when he lingers on the bevy of girls and other delights and fantasies that tormented his solitude in the desert, but the writer here, self-identified as a monk and hagiographer, must be amusing himself in full awareness of his double game; unless, and this is not to be set aside lightly, this section was interpolated by another, mischievous author.'

... 'What is a man?' asked Leto of her nurse. She was keeping company with the male for the first time since she had left the Pearl Quarter at the age of five.

'Men'll come in two forms, by and large,' the nurse would say, with a cluck and a chuckle. 'At least where you're concerned. Of course there are many other kinds, but you're unlikely to meet with them, unless you're unlucky. There's the quick sort and the slow. The quick sort treat women like field cooks making an omelette and should be avoided: they want you hot in the pan, instantly, and they break you up, throw you in, and finish.

'This quick sort are dry and twiggy like old firewood. But the slow are firm and slippery like fresh trout.

'You can tell quick types from slow types: I'll give you some rules of thumb which will come in handy when Cunmar lines up some candidates, as he's bound to do soon, you being the age you are, you're too dangerous to have around with only me to watch out for you. And when your father comes back (any day now), he's not going to want to find you a whore or an old maid, which are about the range of choice we have, my dear little lady.'

She was painting blue on the inside edges of Leto's lids.

'First: quick types avoid looking a woman in the eye. They're scared of a devil who, they've been told, lives curled up in the veins of a woman and can slither out and milk a man silently, invisibly, emptying him out until he becomes that woman's slave. She'll then eat all his money, his lands, his children, oh yes, she's altogether insatiable, is this devil, who comes with webbed claws and forked tail and bat's wings and a pretty face with a little dewy mouth hiding her sharp teeth. All disguise, all illusion, all mischief. This devil has many names, and I've heard men from north, south, east, west bring her up – it doesn't matter if they're Enochites or Tirzahners, or Ophiri, or Lazuli, whatever.

'She's very dangerous to you, not to them. For these men go quickly on to the attack, claiming the attack came first from you; they appeal to this devil to cover their worst savagery. I know, my husband is a quick one: but I strike back at him, I tell him that if he comes at me again like that the snake inside me will bite. This keeps him off, for a time.

'I'm forgetting to tell you how to spot them before it's too late – if you're given any choice in the matter, as I hope you will be.

'Another sign to watch out for: the male friend. If he mentions, in the course of his opening remarks, that friend so-and-so is like this, and then says this-and-that about him, that's a giveaway he'll be a quick one: he won't be able to contain himself before rushing away to tell so-and-so what he did and how he did it. Puff puff, the Great I Am.

'Another telltale sign: a short beard. In my view. I've heard some women say that a scratchy man close to one's skin is as necessary as putting salt in soup; but I'm not convinced.

'The slow ones have long, soft beards, which smell of gardenias, and they like to kiss, all over, and their silky hair curls silkily around their soft lips . . .

'Let me tell you about the slow ones . . .'

So that bawd would lie down alongside Leto, matching her limbs to hers, and tickle her gently with her fingertips trailing over her body, in readiness.

[Skipwith Add. Mss.: G. Fr. 70]

. . . does blood call to blood? When Ser Matteo returned, seven long years after he made his promises, he opened his arms to enfold Leto and cried out in his language, 'My daughter! My daughter!' She shrank from him, and when that bold maidservant pushed her upright and forwards towards him, Leto ran to Cunmar and twisted herself under his elbow, where he cradled her, as she peeped out to look at the man who was calling himself her father. Cunmar was less of a stranger to her than her own flesh and blood.

Ser Matteo was crying out, 'Why, you have become a young woman, and so lovely we'll be able to marry you well. Ah, what a jewel you are, who have lived and learned the ways of a princely court!'

He did not yet know that Leto had resided for the last few years in the orphanage at the Convent of the Swaddling Bands, learning the livelihood of maids and seamstresses and laundresses.

The boy with the twisted foot had returned, too; he was now a tall, bearded young man, and he still limped, but his boots were made so delicately that, unless you knew to look, you could not tell that the sole of one was two inches thicker than the other. He exchanged words with Cunmar; permission was given for him to have brought into the chamber a little organ, which he sat before and played, most solemnly, while two members of Ser Matteo's crew plied the bellows at the instrument's back to keep the music flowing as angels do on cloudbanks in paradise, as sometimes painted on ornamented parchments such as this.

Cunmar patted Leto's hair, where she huddled against him, and we wondered that she felt so intimate with him after an absence that had lasted half her life, and that he, who was fastidious about contact with underlings, should allow her presumption. But he was fingering the texture of her hair under the pearl fillet with which it was threaded, and looking across at her father, whispering to her – and in due course, she trotted across to Ser Matteo and curtsied, but he caught her up in his arms and squeezed her against his chest and spun her till she cried out in protest, but he only laughed and set her down and pinched her cheeks till the blood showed in them.

Cunmar then began to make a formal speech, perhaps to dampen Ser Matteo's paternal effusions, and the merchant, his attention engaged, did not stop Leto from leaving him to return to stand by Doris, though she was all eyes for Cunmar, it was plain. Like a cade lamb, that does not know its progenitors, will become attached to the hand that feeds it, so Leto took refuge with Cunmar the Procurator who had shown her sudden kindness, who had plucked her, it seemed, from the severities of the convent and brought her to the comforts of the Citadel; and likewise, just as a ewe that has lost its own lamb can be persuaded to accept an orphan if this lamb comes draped in the pelt of its dead offspring, so Cunmar recognised Leto, in her Cadenate finery, as something of his own.

He felt the girl cling to him: she had not learned to act her age. Where the nuns had failed, the court would provide. In the presence of her father, he would provide her with a husband, give a handsome, but not inappropriately ostentatious, feast for her wedding. It would perhaps help stabilise the present ambiguities in the truce to make a display of Ophiri generosity, goodwill and enlightenment. He would call in a singer; a couple of acrobats to tumble and cheer up the Keep; even some comedians; the court was dull, and its future – and his own – always uncertain.

His thoughts turned then to the son of his wife Porphyria, Chrysaor, whom he had raised as his own, and who, at twenty-two, was still a bachelor, and pursuing his learning, Lazuli fashion; Cunmar resolved then that he would do very well for the groom.

But the passion that the evil one had inspired in him did not permit him to relinquish her; in the shameless way of that Ophiri faith, he resolved to keep her for himself. And her father, equally fallen in the sight of God, did not refuse this pact; rather he exulted in it.

There were only two sheets left; Kim glanced up at the Archives room clock. If Hortense Fernly came, as she'd said she might if she could fit it in, he would have finished this bundle of papers, and be able to play the good pupil in her eyes.

[Skipwith Add. Mss.: G. Fr. 71]

. . . [Chrysaor] sprang forward and fell on his knees before Cunmar, his ruler and his father, where he stood under the bridal canopy holding Leto's right hand in his. His eyes bulged out of their sockets and I thought blood might spurt from them as it does from a species of frog when it feels itself confronting danger, for Chrysaor's interruption was bold, and placed his life at risk. Indeed Cunmar's right hand flew to the dagger he wore in his belt, and Leto, losing the mainstay of her bridegroom's hand in hers . . .

Kim stopped, read the sentence again, looked at the beginning of the paragraph, and understood, that yes, Cunmar was the groom, and this was Leto's wedding. He glanced up at the clock. Two p.m. only. He kept seeing Hetty come through the door; but the hoped for figure would turn out to be someone else.

He bent his head again to the page.

. . . stumbled back into the arms of Doris who caught her and propped her; she seemed an effigy, a statue arrayed in stiff finery for a feastday with the expression of anguish twisting her brows, the Madonna in a swoon at the moment of Christ's expiry. For Cunmar struck Chrysaor with the flat of the blade across his face; the prince reeled back, holding the wound, he did not cry out or falter but threw himself forward and clasped the knees of the man who had taken his father's place ever since his own father died.

Chrysaor spoke for many of us when he began:

'This wedding is a shameful thing in the sight of God and man, and I beg you, my father, whom I love and respect, according to my mother's wish, not to do this thing and bring dishonour on us all.'

Ser Matteo sprang forward as if to strike him.

Cunmar did not bend to prise the youth's hold from his knees, but raised his arms and lifted his head as if the contact befouled him, like a

149

swimmer who finds the translucent envenomed limbs of a jellyfish have wrapped themselves in a trail of fire around him and knows that he must not use his hands to unwind them and spread the fiery poison. But nobody ran forward to stop Chrysaor's pleas, for we were glad that the princely youth had thrown himself between Cunmar and his shameful act.

He rose to his feet again, and, facing the Procurator, went on, 'The girl Leto isn't worthy of your love – she's a schismatic, who came to us as merchandise – not much better than a slave, who speaks no language as a mother tongue, who belongs nowhere.'

Ser Matteo surged forward again, his blood heating; Karim and one other seized him by his arms and held him back, struggling as Chrysaor raced on, ignoring him. 'Imagine, you are taking to your side a used bargaining counter, a soiled chit of exchange that has been passed from one hand to another. We should keep our affairs in their place and you, you above all, who can draw up battle plans, trick the enemy with your subterfuges, set in train complex trade agreements that have enriched us here and have contributed to the wealth of Ophir, you above all know that everything has its place and her place is not by your side in Cadenas, as the spouse of the ruler in this citadel.

'This woman Leto has no history. Who is she? The man who calls himself her father is a merchant, a heretic and a usurer, a man of no rank, who appeared, a sail on the horizon, abandoned her here among strangers so lightly she was clearly of little account to him – to her own family, and he from a country where women wield too much power in the household, administer their own estates and even defend their fortresses at the head of their rabble soldiers.

'No, he would not have left her here as a warranty of his word, and then gone ahead and broken it, not returning in the interval he promised, if she was of any consequence. Besides, the wonder he promised you is fool's gold, and you know it. Nothing will come of that nest of spiders you have stabled at the Keep. Nothing. She does not belong at your side, at my side, not anywhere.'

Ser Matteo twisted about, crying out imprecations against Chrysaor, but Cunmar looked at him keenly and stroked the air to calm him as he began to reply to his stepson's challenge. His furious look swept the assembly. 'None of this matters,' he declared. 'I myself am the living proof that in Ophir destiny shapes us, after we have seized it in our hands and bent it to our will. The future moves according to the will of God, but when I find a young horse whose spirit is wild, I don't say, it's the will of God that this horse remain unbroken. Who made the bridle, the spur, the saddle, the reins? Who rides that wild colt, that wild mare? The Lord God made the wonders of nature for us to explore and understand: the spider is a model for us, not a monster whom we should shun. We should learn from the ways nature changes and adapts and survive. This also is the will of God – to alter the course of things: the future is a wild creature, and it's our human gift that we can tame it and shape it to our ends. I will take this girl to be my bride and we will enrich Cadenas together, you shall see.'

'No!' cried Chrysaor, clasping Cunmar's knees once again: 'Some things are immutable. Think of her way of being, of what she is, of what she has become in that place: these are women who grow the hair on their shameful parts and do not, out of respect for modesty, shave them clean, who live together without curb from brother or husband, who do not observe any of our dietary laws, but will eat anything that is put before them – swelling pig's bladders with the offal to meet the cravings of their clammy, mere-wife appetites, whitening their hair and their skins with lemon juice in the sun to ensnare men to their rank beds.

'You have a wife, my exalted mother Porphyria, bequeathed into your care by my noble father after his death in pledge of the love and friendship he felt for you and which you reciprocated. My mother is your lady, in the eyes of God and in the eyes of man. And in her son's eyes, who now clings to you and implores you not to do this terrible thing, which will shame us all. My mother has shared in your renown, and now you move, like a man whose eyes have been put out and whose ears have been stopped, to repudiate her as if she meant nothing to you and your past was an alien place where you had never travelled.'

Ser Matteo writhed himself free of Karim's grasp and drew; Chrysaor sprang at him, and the trader fell to the ground, his blood seeping into the embroidered floor coverings. Leto curled more tightly into the body of her maid, her sobbing shook her body in spasms, like a small craft knocked by a tempest towards cruel reefs when the tiller has snapped and the mast is broken. Many of us felt pity for her, as I did.

Cunmar lifted his head to order Ser Matteo to be carried away and tended; then he took Chrysaor in his arms so that he could look into his face where the weal of his dagger blade across it blazed, a brand of his courage.

'Old lion, young lion,' he began. 'When I was your age, I too thought my heart would break if I lost the love of a girl. But it isn't so. The heart heals and the fire in the belly leaps up again for others, for many others. I've stolen a girl I promised you: unkind father, who should make way instead for the energies and ambition of the son who wants everything his father has and more. You shall have another young woman, one whom you prize more than it seems you prize Leto, one born in this place, who shares your high condition and knows your customs and speaks your language and worships in your churches too – since these matters seem to count for you. A young woman, even younger, who has not been bartered and made captive to the stratagems of power – I can think of one or two, right now! Though your words move me and I feel remorse for my earlier rage' – at this he laid two fingers on the weal – 'I shan't relinquish Leto, I do not need to – I feel only pride in my union with her, for she has restored me to the vigour and the splendour of a self I thought had withered on the vine of my old age.'

Chrysaor pushed away his father's arms where they held him and once again threw himself to the ground, this time with his lips against Cunmar's feet in their perfumed sandals, which were threaded with silver, and he moaned in his disbelief, which we all shared, and renewed his pleas.

'I'm not speaking for myself! How could you think I would be so base and underhand to couch a sorrow of my own in the guise of public wrong? I was obedient to you in the matter of my marriage, when you summoned me here to introduce me to the bride you'd chosen for me. As I made the journey from the capital, I didn't yet know what the circumstances were, and you hadn't then decided to take her yourself. I'm your son who loves and honours you in all things and is bound by your commands. It isn't the character of the bride that I find wanting – she's delightful, of course, I freely admit. It's her lack of . . . status, rank, family, ties, belonging, the unfortunate fate that has made her what she is: a cast-off from her native land, someone who doesn't belong here or anywhere and cannot, who has survived only through the mercy of your arrangements for the proliferating unbelievers, infidels, outcasts and strangers who live in proximity to us in Cadenas. She is impure, by birth, by upbringing, by chance and by choice: her conduct with you shows it.'

His tears splashed his father's feet as he held him by the ankles and railed: 'My mother's virtuous, loyal, and loves you chastely – don't dishonour her. Don't marry this young woman. Keep her in your bed till you tire of her. As you've done before. But don't share my mother's state with this stranger to our ways.'

Cunmar lifted Chrysaor to his feet once again, but this time he wasn't weeping, but angry, for his eyes were screwed up as if he was facing blind into the sun.

'I'll go to your mother now,' he said. 'I'll speak to her, to make her understand that I mean no disrespect to her . . . but I have other needs.'

So he left the hall and us who were gathered there, with a single glance to Leto where she whimpered and words of command to the assembly: 'Take her to her rooms – this marriage will take place another day.'

4

Hortense to Kim

Subject: Skipwith 673
Date: Tues, 16 June 199– 12:14:32 +0100
From: Hortense Fernly<h.fernly@natmus.ac.alb>
To: kim.mcquy<hswu@lattice.onlyconnect.com>

- -

Kim, What are you asking me – and all those other people out there – to
believe? I confess I'm at a loss. We're looking at a heap of miscellaneous
manuscripts, jumbled together in a tomb by a fluke of history – or, if
you like, the hunger of imperialist antique hunters – and you're asking
me to accept that this is some continuous story about a single individual
– who doesn't die either? In haste, Hetty

5

In the Necropolis

[Skipwith Add. Mss.: G. Fr. 72]

... A daughter, a son, twins, twin babies: she could not quite say 'my' daughter, 'my' son – on account of them she had been exposed, driven out, left to die in this rocky place, under a tree that gave a patch of shade. Their coming had found her out, and Cunmar the Procurator, who had held sway in Cadenas and promised so much to her, had not stepped in to protect them. The hours of Ophiri power in the outpost were numbered: for months after the foiled wedding the bride was kept in her room at the Keep, and denied access to her lord. Only Karim brought her news, news that was broken in pieces like a dropped water jar: one day, the Procurator was under Chrysaor's control; then he was treating for his life. Another day, he was gone, back to Ophir to raise an army against the new authorities in Cadenas. On yet another occasion, she was told that Cunmar was dead. Never did he send word to her himself. Yet, when she heard a commotion from outside the walls of the Keep where she was held, she still hoped that he was there, that Cunmar the Terrible would carry her off in a surprise raid, such as he had conducted in the days of his glory.

But instead, when her condition could not be disguised, she was visited in her cell by a judge and two clerks, from the Lazuli court of justice, and sentenced: 'No child of yours will survive to see the sunrise one more time. You are to be taken outside the city and there you shall die.'

The spirit of the child bride, once cowed by the violence at her nuptials, was now fired up by her impending motherhood; like a mother cat who crawls away to litter, she spat and hissed at the assassin they sent to fetch her – and she found herself fighting her friend, Karim, Cunmar's bodyservant, screaming at him, 'Turncoat', and struggling until he too began cursing and crying out in a muddle of pain and pleading.

It is elementary statecraft that new rulers use the servants of the powers they have supplanted because those servants go in fear of their lives, and are willing to perform any deed, however cruel, to survive.

How clumsy Karim had been, treacherously carrying out his murderous errand, shrieking at her, foam flecking his lips as he pushed his face near hers, gibbering: 'You're to be killed, and your bastard with you.' He was clownish, grappling with her with one hand and trying to stab her with the other, she thrashing and kicking: two drunkards flailing at each other and staggering. Had he thought she would come quietly? Did they all think she would not struggle under attack?

When she was living in the palace, she used to go down to the stables to help him groom Cunmar's mare. When she observed the patience of the pack ponies and other, well-trained horses as they waited for their feed at the trough, she wanted to hit them. But hitting only made them meeker. Would they never rebel, toss the hay from the mangers in contempt, refuse to be pacified? In that cool arcaded precinct below the Keep, they munched the hay the stable lads baled for them, their tender velvet lips curling over the dry stalks, blowing through their quivering nostrils and inflating their bellies as they fed as if playing themselves like bagpipes. Leto would smell the sweetness in their feed, and her teeth would clench with impatience. That miserable supply was enough to keep them captive, standing and chomping on the same diet all winter long.

That is why I am not the same, Leto told herself, that is why a girl is not a mare. I will not be patient. I will not learn patience.

Karim did not know how to handle the girl as hard and round as a melon, who was about to give birth. He could not get a hold of her without feeling shame at his orders to seize her, and she took advantage of his awkwardness and was able to sink her teeth into his sword arm until the bone under the muscle stopped her bite. She clamped her jaws tight as she could and held on through his howling till the gouts of blood in her mouth sickened her. At fourteen, she still had sharp teeth; Leto still had a child's fancies, and her favourite foods were fruit and sweets, which, though they do their own damage, do not blunt the ivory edges of incisors as meat does.

A guard had pulled her down the steps and into the street, heaved her up on to a cart where Karim was waiting for her – then a cloth, soaking wet and cold and minty, flopped on to her face; it was a nightsoil cart, with lidded buckets, but they still stank. Even through the gauze soaked in peppermint held over her mouth and nose, she caught whiffs of corrupt meats and hot fresh waste. Crazed Karim, her childhood, longtime friend, weeping at the order for her death, he had clutched her in a kind of embrace before he flung a scratchy blanket over her and began driving them out of the citadel.

Lying in the rocky place where he had left her, the young woman laughed; the sound was dry and clacked against her dry tongue. The death messenger, he who had been her ally, her childhood friend, he had accepted the errand. Cowards! All of them. Not to do it themselves. And to think she would not put up a fight.

When she looked outside the byre, she realised she was lying in a necropolis, among the tombs. He had taken pity on her, he told her: 'I'm leaving you here, but I'm not going to kill you,' he had said, putting his ear close to hers in fear that anyone might hear. But there were only wild animals to hear in the place where he left her and where her babies were born. Karim the intended killer had not been able, at the last, to fulfil his orders.

'I can't do this,' he had screamed at her. 'But if I leave you here, you can never come back. You must keep away.'

So Leto was spared death for herself and for her offspring, but cursed to wander on the face of the earth, one of the fugitives whom the fates cherish even while they are wanton with them, harrying them hither and yon as a cat bats a shrew for sport. She could imagine the equerry delivering his report: 'Yes, my lady, you can rest assured that you will hear no more of Leto – or of any bastard brood born to her – she's been disposed of – in the burial ground of . . .' Maybe he had cut the heart from a calf to show her to prove it, a bloody lump – 'This is all that remains of her, my lady.' And the eyes of her enemy would glitter with satisfaction in her wrath and her vengeance.

There was a gash on her shoulder where the dagger had cut her on its passage towards her throat; it was when the dagger slipped and cut her shoulder that she had bitten him.

Now, that time since she'd been wounded stretched from where she lay under the sky to the farthest star.

[G. Fr. 73]

. . . flies droned near; she brushed them off the babies, but let them settle and buzz in her sweat and lesions, too tired to struggle against their persistence. She wished she could sink far below wakefulness, deep into the felted dark, where even a candle flame would sputter and fail in the saturated depths of that oblivion. And yet, deeper even than her yearning for no pain, for numbness, for death even, the nestlings at her flank lit a taper inside her: her mind was forming pictures of the future, of schemes she must attempt, of means she must use. These plans were physic; they administered a fluttering, winged medicine to her ordeals as her needs and her children's began to assert their claims on her: she wanted water. She dreamed of a clean basin and a brimming ewer and linen napkins and talc and rosewater and lotion and dry, scented towels. The memory of a sweet taste rose in her throat, a buttered pancake flavour, runny with syrup, flavoured and sprinkled with almonds and pistachios as her nurse served in the mornings when she came in to wake her when she was a girl, installed by her lover in his palace. Its bathrooms – they made the kingdom where her lover ruled one of the most luxurious places in the world, so travellers from elsewhere and far afield marvelled.

She thought of her lover and she longed for him, she cleaved to him, in spite of everything, for he had trembled when he held her and made her own child's body feel as tall as a thunderhead in its power over him.

A choking pain rose in her throat; and she fell back against the ground, anger and fear scorching her cheeks and neck as she clasped the girl child in her arms, lying alongside her son.

Consciousness came and went; she was drifting in and out of this place where she found herself, where no lights in the distance guided her to human habitation. The late night air was soft-fingered, though, unlike the desert below the crag of the palace; so she was farther away than she had thought, somewhere near the coast and the warm onshore winds of the dunes and freshwater ponds trapped behind them. Water. Her tongue swelled against her palate and rasped and she was dreaming, ablaze with wanting to drink, to drink deep, to plunge into cool dark water and merge into its flow. She rolled on to her side; put out a hand to the baby boy she had laid down on the ground. He lay very still. She could have used one of his father's slippers for a cradle, or hung it from her back and carried him in it. The boy had arrived after the girl; he was more purple-skinned and his matted curls kelp-dark; from his position he was staring up at her and his sister, unblinkingly as if she were as far away as the sky.

She probed her shoulder, where his tears and her blood had mingled. She was foul with her own emissions as well; her dress was stiff with stains, from the birth, from the struggle, from the flight. Again, pools of fresh water formed and smiled at her, calling to her with a sound of flutes and pipes and bells – to slip down and dance in their depths, to be washed clean.

She looked about her to get her bearings. She needed food, and clothes, too. For herself and for the infants. And people; people who might help the three of them.

They were in a stone building that had once served as a byre, perhaps, but had lost its roof and was no longer in use; the thin straw under them was grey and brittle. A twisted tree was growing from one corner, its crooked branches silhouetted like script in black ink against the sky, where the stars were fading now and a bird, far above the ground where she was huddled, was singing to the first light of dawn visible from its vantage point. It was trilling to another, who answered, displaying more frills and rills. She could not see them, though they sounded strong enough to pick her up in their beaks and soar upwards with her and the twins together.

She tried to puzzle out where she might be: it was March, so the dawn did not break very early. Though it felt to her as if she had been carted for a lifetime last night, the whole journey could not have taken longer than two hours; if she was right, and the mild warmth of the morning air indicated the presence of the sea, they must have taken the coast road – north? She only had her thin, silk slippers on her feet – the pair of indoor shoes embroidered in silver thread that she was wearing when the groom appeared in her bedroom with his orders and his knife. Her thirst scraped in her throat, worse than her hunger, she was lumpen with the sore weight of it; next time she fed the babies, they would empty her, drain her to a flaccid camel's hump.

He had left her a water gourd, a blanket, a piece of bread, now crawling with ants. She wound the infants into the blanket, side by side, and felt her own eyes fill at the news of her own death. 'Shame she was taken so young,' some might murmur in her lover's palace, while his wife's lids would lower to hide her pleasure.

With her soft indoor feet and smooth hands Leto gave every indication of her status, she knew. There would be passers-by soon, coming to tend the graves of their loved ones perhaps, or on other business; she must try and appeal to them. It might anger them, that she brought them nothing but three mouths to feed. She felt at her neck – the gold chain and the phylactery her lover had given her, to protect her with a charm. She undid it with shaky hands and knotted it into a corner of the cloth Phoebe was wrapped in. Then she pulled her earrings free from her lobes, and tied them into her son's meagre covering. She would conceal them until she had to trade – for milk, for apricots. She craved a ripe apricot. Or an orange.

Someone might see her once again as a bargaining counter, they might hold her for a possible ransom. She should try and convey this, before anyone did her and the babies harm.

But they could not stay where she'd been abandoned to give birth; the three of them needed to move from the cemetery. The sun would bake them; that single crooked tree gave no shade. She began to prepare herself to leave, before the sun rose higher. She dribbled some water from the gourd into her mouth and eyes, and tied one baby to her back and one to her breast; they were quiet, still stunned by their entry into the world; she was grateful for this, though it alarmed her, too, as if they might already be failing.

As she picked her way across the limestone, she remembered the scrap silver left by the city's metalworkers: after they had punched out slugs to make charms for a bracelet, a curious, haphazard template was left behind which they melted down and used again. Could this be happening to all the dead who lay here in the higgledy-piggledy scattering of tombs? Would their flesh be melted down to be recast in another, perfected form?

Some more tombs, banked one above the other in ledges on one side of the area, were marked with sigils in the Greek style. They were hollowed out from the rocky outcrop that lay ahead of her and formed a natural amphitheatre, as if the dead lying in their sarcophagi on the shelves were an audience awaiting the grand spectacle of doom to begin on the stage towards which Leto was making her slow progress, her thin leather soles giving her no protection on the jagged stones and slithering on the larger, smoother slabs. Some of the rock tombs were sealed by blank stone; yet more were empty, awaiting occupancy or looted, dark gaps in the spongy rock. They would give shelter – and shade, Leto noted. In a cleft that ran slantwise across the rockface to its foot, she saw tufts of greener, bushier plants, marking a kind of trail; she made her way towards it, slowed by the difficulty of the ground.

She heard something shuffle and clatter, and stopped. A tortoise appeared, clambering, pigeon-toed over the uneven stones, manoeuvring to find the fulcrum of each obstacle beneath it, and toppling down into the crevice between, on to its back. It retracted its limbs, then began to wave them, scrabbling for purchase on the air above, its gnarled dark head twisting in panic. Leto found that she could still laugh at its plight, so much more helpless than her own; she bent to the yellow and black cryptic shell, and righted it. The tortoise pulled in its limbs, but she could see its eye, like light at the bottom of a well glinting on the surface of the black water. Did tortoises get thirsty? Was it heading for water?

She picked it up; it would make a first plaything for her babies. Then she continued to trudge towards the shade of the caves in the cliff-face . . .

6

Kim to Hortense

Subject: Re: Leto, You, Yesterday, Today, Tomorrow
Date: Thurs, 18 June 199– 02.04:42 +0100
From: kim.mcquy<hswu@lattice.onlyconnect.com>
To: Hortense Fernly<h.fernly@natmus.ac.alb>

- -

Dear Hetty – you've seen how Leto lives on *after* she's stoned to
death   you've read the strips that show her scrabbling to survive after
that nasty little episode   think of it this way   think of her and the
babies as stars   whose light is reaching us only now across time   you
accept when you hear a thunderclap that the moment when the bolt of
lightning fell happened a few moments before   in class I get the
children to count between the flash and the rumble and reckon it's
about a mile away a second   if they're scared imagining the distance
takes their mind off it when you look at the distant stars Andromeda is
the most faraway that you can see with the naked eye   but you can't in
Enoch too yellow at night   so I look at the sky on the web
www.hubble.org when you're looking into space you're looking into
time   what you see happened a long while ago   its called lookback
time   that's like Leto and her two babies   they happened a long time
ago but their presence in the light is coming nearer all the time   the
actual speed is one foot a billionth of a second not too difficult to
remember   it was there and now it's reached us through the bundle in
the tomb

when light moves her presence through the ether or the interstellar
medium as they now call whatever it is out there between the stars she

picks up dust and smears and scars   and that's what we call history

shes getting nearer all the time but we don't know when we'll see her in the here and now   when in time present the light and space become one   and so we start again – hswu!

But Hetty it's not just the story in the bundle – it's how it links her and me and you all together – your spirit's beautiful you know you understand you cast a special brightness all around you – I feel *irradiated* as I say when I'm near you – you're all charged up with these beautiful ancient things you've handled and worked with all this time – their light is saturating you and so you're magic in the true sense – when I was looking at that eerie silver sheet of charms I felt your mind was travelling into mine and fusing with it and lighting up the cobwebby shadows in there and it made a shudder run down my spine–

when the sarcophagus comes back we're going to have a huge celebration – you'll be amazed by the crowds that will gather – Shareen Ghopil says that on balance her panel will support the idea of the new shrine a proper setting a new temple for our times – housing the bundle the question now is – where?

Hetty – Hortense – Dr Fernly – you were the first to listen really to listen and you're going to be the one everyone wants to talk to – it'll be you who'll be bringing the beautiful face of Our Lady back and you'll be asked to go on the telly talking about everything that happened before she reached us – you'll be the interpreter the voice everyone will want to hear –

after looking at the bundle together – your curiosity – your interest – sustain me

even the poor toxic deadbeats behind the station can't dim the rush I get from all this

its late must go to bed my heads full of the vertiginous stars yours always *I mean it* kim

7

An Earring Recovered

[Skipwith Add. Mss.: G. Frs. 1–3]

Hereward Meeks: 'On linen strips, much damaged, with several lacunae. The hand on this group of manuscript fragments used to make the shroud of the mummy shows regional characteristics, c. 250 AD.'

[G. Fr. 1]

. . . the tortoise shell, a bone, a reed, a pebble would do for toys, for the twins to rattle and whistle . . .

. . . she applied spider's silk to Phoebe's welts after the beating. The wounds were fading but not disappearing. The livid bruising paled in the delicate web of her flesh, but lumps of keloid tissue had hardened under the lesions, and as the child grew, they stretched under the skin of her back and legs into taut wedges of inert, paralysed flesh. When the little girl first began taking her tottering steps, Leto thought that Phoebe was imitating the wolf cubs' gait, as she ambled crookedly, often dropping to crawl again, but as their first year of hiding passed, she could see her daughter was developing a lopsided, angular walk; she would skip forward three steps at a time, come to a stop, and then start up again, while, to counterbalance this asymmetry, she leant her head over to one side. Beside his sister, her son toddled purposefully ahead, his head balanced securely straight between his shoulders. The difference in their growth filled Leto with anger; she massaged Phoebe's scars, trying to ease the knots and stimulate her limbs' ordinary growth; she crushed and packed tight poultices of capsicum leaves, dotted with their fiery seeds, to

164

try and draw out the pliancy that her childhood body deserved. Phoebe submitted; she did not roar with pain at the treatments Leto tried and tried again, for the battering she had received as an infant had numbed her sensors of pain, brutalised her nerve endings and cut her off from the quick flood of pain – and pleasure – that would sweep over her brother all of a sudden, provoking furious bellows of red rage in his tiny clenched body, or catching him up into crowing gales of laughter.

But what Phoebe could not feel bodily wreaked havoc on her at night: like a wolf cub, Phoebe twitched in her dreams . . . she fended off attackers with her fists bunched as she slept . . .

[Gr. Fr. 2]

. . . for three years Leto and the twins lived with the she-wolf Lycia; she saw a new litter of cubs grow and leave the cave but still she shared their dwelling and their food for she could not yet find a way to return to the society of her own kind . . .

. . . but also, scavenging after dusk, they found many useful things in the surrounding territory. Leto's prized possession was a knife. It had a short blade twined to a handle that was a little large for her hand, but it served. She came across it when Phoebe was chasing a last persistent cricket of the day; she was following her and saw the knife, fallen through the crack between two boulders; its owner must have been gathering wild fennel or thyme. Phoebe could slip her hand in between them and draw it out . . .

[Gr. Fr. 3]

. . . when she thought back to the assault, the loss of her gold necklace and her earrings galled her most bitterly. One day, as night was falling, she left the twins and went down to the lagoon again, and her heart was tight in her chest and drumming, like a call to battle from a long way off. She heard the frogs croaking and as she came nearer, plop-plop into the water. She waded in, like before, but this time she was strong and clear. She began fishing in the mud. They were cool to touch when she slid them out of their hiding places. They palpitated in her hand, with their hearts fit to burst. The creatures' bulgy eyes popped even wider as she pinched each one of them by the neck between finger and thumb and slit the panting belly open. One after another she tossed them on to the bank, where she'd once lain, and she was certain that fortune would work on her side and deliver up to her the frog with treasure hoarded in its guts.

And so it came about: she killed dozens of frogs, no, scores of them, hundreds, one after another. She slit them with her knife from gullet to rectum. Some were puny, too small to be guilty, perhaps, but she did not spare any. Then, she found she had caught a gnarled monster, and she knew. She cut him open, and there lay the unmistakeable glint of gold. It was one of her earrings: the fine bunch of tiny bead grapes in soft gold gleamed against the shining slither of the bullfrog's pink and green innards.

For a while she kept plunging her arm into the mud, and bringing out more of the silly trembling brutes, flipping them over, cutting them open. She wanted to find the other earring, she wanted to retrieve the necklace, too. When she left the mountains, it would show who she'd once been. It would be something that she could use to persuade others to help us, something, too, that she could sell.

Now she had one memento from the lost world of gifts, of made things, of precious objects of virtue. But she never found the fine gold chain twinkling in the frog's gut, or the other earring, and she quit the murders and turned back up the mountain.

. . . carrion birds tossed themselves into the wind from their roosts in the cliff-faces overlooking the sea and with deep swirling wingbeats located the source of the powerful and appetising reek rising from the wetlands, and in a great din of cawing, swooped to feast on the rotting remains of Leto's revenge.

8

Kim to Hortense, again and again

Subject: Re: Re: Leto, You, Yesterday, Today, Tomorrow
Date: Thurs, 18 June 199– 22:46:11 +0100
From: kim.mcquy<hswu@lattice.onlyconnect.com>
To: Hortense Fernly<h.fernly@natmus.ac.alb>

- -

Hetty please come and find me this weekend in the reading room I
know you're not meant to be working then but I need to talk to you im
finding out so much its not special to me you know everybody when
they hear a story sees things in their mindseye I just pay more attention
to them they're the future echoes of the real coming through time
  your kim

Subject: Re: Re: Leto, You, Yesterday, Today, Tomorrow
Date: Sat, 20 June 199– 20:32:15 +0100
From: kim.mcquy<hswu@lattice.onlyconnect.com>
To: Hortense Fernly<h.fernly@natmus.ac.alb>

- -

Hetty I waited and every time someone came past I thought its going to
be her with that ship-boy book you've taken out (and I now can't get
hold of) where are you? I dont even know where you live and ***
directory enquiries say 'we don't give out numbers without an address.'
  I need to talk to you Hetty
  your kim

167

Subject: Worries
Date: Mon, 22 June 199– 07:12:21 +0100
From: kim.mcquy<hswu@lattice.onlyconnect.com>
To: Hortense Fernly<h.fernly@natmus.ac.alb>

- -

Dear bright shining Hetty through my nights I'm rushing for school but didnt you get my last emails? haven't had a reply – I am paying attention to what you say truly   I'm not completely carried away by my own concerns. I do want to learn from you yes! you're an integral part of my whole project – I will write with you and your work in mind and I can't move ahead without you – you're the one with the key to the meaning of what I just see 'through a glass darkly' – one of my mum's favourite expressions which she still says sometimes when she's more lucid than at others –

as I understand it you were trying to explain to me that there are two possible reasons for Meeks abandoning the edition – apart from overwork exhaustion or sudden lapse of interest:

a. Meeks decided there was no historical value whatsoever in the bundle's chronicles: when he began testing the information they contain against other sources he found they were full of implausible events and straightforward mistakes – but you said he'd obviously mistaken the kind of texts he was dealing with: not the annals of some real life history but another kind of story another way of telling

b.   Skipwith's notes etc – Meeks got nervous at what he was finding about the goings on on board the Shearwater

you see how I do pay attention to what *you* say –

hswu isn't invested in historical truth – but we need the historical record to show how things panned out how the story we know is only part of the story – like the Truth & Reconciliation commission said – there's healing truth and there's other kinds – yes! this leto bundle matters – Hetty, please reply to this email – I 'm being interviewed by jacko kirby – you've probably never heard of him or his prog but he's a dj who's big with kids as young as mine as well as older ones – I'm going to tell him everything I know so much more now – thanks to you

yours always yes! please write soon –

Kim

Subject: Where are you?
Date: Tues, 23 June 199– 23:16:37 +0100
From: kim.mcquy<hswu@lattice.onlyconnect.com>
To: Hortense Fernly<h.fernly@natmus.ac.alb>
- -
Hetty! where are you? answer me!

I'm going again on saturday to read more – I need to see how much
matches what she's told me, what I've already seen –
send me a word – kim

Subject: Where are you?
Date: Wed, 24 June 199- 19:12:23 +0100
From: kim.mcquy<hswu@lattice.onlyconnect.com>
To: Hortense Fernly<h.fernly@natmus.ac.alb>
- -
Dr Fernly, there's a lot to discuss as I'm posting new info about the Leto
bundle on my website Skipwith's stuff excellent and lots of it so it's in
the public interest for you to reply to my messages.
  Please
  Yours, Kim

Subject: Where are you?
Date: Thurs, 25 June 199– 19:05:43 +0100
From: kim.mcquy<hswu@lattice.onlyconnect.com>
To: Hortense Fernly<h.fernly@natmus.ac.alb>
- -
Dear Hetty I telephoned your office in the school break today – its
difficult for me to find gaps in the schedule as the new government
tests for six-years olds have been taking up a lot of space – (I need to
talk to you)
  as ever, kim

Subject: Skipwith 673

Date: Fri, 26 June 199– 09.46:16 +0100

From: Anna Vignole<annav@natmus.ac.alb>

To: kim.mcquy<hswu@lattice.onlyconnect.com>

Attachment: Anon., *Adventures of a Ship-Boy. Of the Most Barbarous Abuses of the Press-Gang & the Cat; of his Subsequent Adventures among Slavers and of his Providential Deliverance & Happy Return. Written by a Well-Wisher. With an Appendix and an Appeal to Her Majesty for his Pardon and for the Improvement of Conditions in Her Navy* . . . Printed for private circulation of Her Majesty's subjects (Portsmouth, 1859) Shelf mark: SK892.1889.

Dr Fernly is away and in her absence, she asked me to let you know that the material you requested has been relocated – you can now use the attached reference to call it up. She did want me also to draw your attention to its date of publication, for reasons she said you'd understand.

Yours sincerely, Anna Vignole

PART FOUR

On Board HMS Shearwater

I

Stowaways

When the ship first anchored in the bay the woman watched from among the tombs: many a boat had passed by, a sail on the horizon, like a broken promise. But this one stayed, and its crew appeared to be loading it with cargo of rocks hewn out of the necropolis and carried down to the sea.

She told the children: 'We must find a way to reach it.' Her blood was pounding as she wondered and watched.

The crew ferried themselves from the moored ship in a small tender; Leto could also see another, bigger rowing boat, hanging from a cradle on deck; one day, they winched this longboat down into the water and four of them rowed to the shore. There seemed to be two men left on deck, one a speck, maybe a mere slip of a boy. She left to reconnoitre, taking once again the path from the cave of the wolf and her cubs towards the sea across that rocky place, and as soon as she reached the flatter ground she heard the hubbub and saw for the first time the long man with the pale flat hair and flushed cheeks. He was sitting on the ground rubbing a stiff cloth over the marks on one of the fallen stones, and now and then he stopped and stood up and looked about him, and held out his arms as if the mountain was a wind and he was spreading himself before it to fill and lift. A team of men were working among the monuments, under the direction of an armed guard of some kind, who was mounted on the only pony; the men were loading stones into baskets and heaving them to the waiting line of mules who stepped with heads bowed and legs apart down the steep flank of the necropolis to the shore; there, the men untrussed the burdens from the animals and gave them a

173

nosebag of feed and some water before whipping them to make the climb up the cliffside again for another load.

Slabs and fragments of the tombs were left standing on the beach, like an ancient city exposed by the withdrawal of the sea, waiting to be loaded aboard.

Leto stole closer. *A new life*, she thought. *A new world in a new place far, far from here, where nothing will be known about me or about the babies. Where they won't be recognised and ashamed: somewhere we can become anything we want, where we can put on a new life like a suit of clothes, if only we could find some.*

Mister Jed Strugwell, the ship's cook, rummaging among the kegs in the hold for the smoked pepper sausages he'd chosen from such regional foodstuffs as he'd been able to stomach in the market of their last port of call, found the tarpaulin differently arranged, and cursed, assuming that Teal had been pilfering food. The look-out boy's thin, sad, weakling physique and longsighted peer offended Mr Strugwell's standards of manliness in sailors and sailing.

'A little lesson in discipline, that's what's needed,' he barked to himself, with some satisfaction at the crime he'd uncovered; he'd long desired a pretext to lay his hands on the boy. 'Nobody else on board to see to him, is there?' Strugwell had cooked for many a crew, and was in a high temper on this voyage. The merchant navy's proper business was manufactures, trade, goods that could be sold and exchanged. Not piles of old stones and boxes of dust which jeopardised the proper handling of the vessel in anything stronger than force four.

He stomped over to the goat where she was tethered under the gunwhales and felt her udders.

'This damned animal – eats like a horse and never fills.' He undid the halter and began leading her out – 'Some fresh air will put an edge on your appetite, but it'd better make you yield more.'

Leto heard the cook approach their hiding place. She pulled the children closer to her, and covered their mouths and curled up so that her face was burrowed deep into the smells of tar and salt cod and pemmican that were stacked and suspended around and above, presenting only her back concealed under empty sacking she'd drawn over herself and the twins. The timbers under the cook's tread creaked as he went – to fetch the lantern, it turned out, for when he pulled the tarpaulin heavily aside, the weave in her protective covering scattered pinprick lights on parts of their bodies. Phoebe reached for one of them and danced it slowly on the palm of her hand, then bent her head forward, poking out her tongue to lick it. The child wanted to swallow it, as if it were a star, and her mother quelled her, brusquely, tucking her in closer to her body.

Leto pressed her hands tighter on her children's mouths, while the drumming under her own ribs sounded so loud to her ears she feared the angry cook must hear it, even over his own imprecations, the rhythmic soughing of the water against the boat's sides, the reciprocal sighing of the ship's timbers as the sails lifted her, and the slop of water in the bilges below them.

Before the cook descended into the stores, she'd been drowsing to the rock of the boat; it was a fine evening for sailing, and HMS *Shearwater*, lying low in the water on account of her cargo, was pulling steadily through a calm sea.

The cook turned over the cargo, looking for missing items, talking aloud – more impatient that he couldn't determine what had been tampered with than pleased he could find no damage. Then he was gone, with his string of sausages in his fist; the small stars that had drilled into their hiding place went out.

Leto took her hands off the children's faces, patted their limbs as if to mould their slight flesh back together, whispered to them, 'It's all right now'.

Phoebe whimpered, and reached for her mother; reluctantly, Leto let her; the three-year-old really should be happy with the goat's milk by now, but the girl still needed the soothing and reassurance of her mother's breast, which she kneaded with a small hand, almost indignantly, as if it didn't meet her needs with enough eagerness. Phoebus woke at his sister's writhings and opened his opaque, shining eyes and asked with the solemnity of small children, 'When will we be there?'

'Soon,' she said.

'Tell me what it will be like there,' he insisted.

'I will, soon. I'll tell you all about it.'

'Lycia told her cubs never to wander far – she said every city was dangerous to wolves.'

'We're human beings, my sweet, and we'll be able to lose ourselves

175

there. A city of the size of Enoch with so many people will be big enough for us to hide in.'

'But I want to come out of the dark down here. I want to be He.' He grabbed at his sister, who shook him off; though she was smaller than her twin, she had a whiplash tension that made her strong, and she attached herself even more angrily to her mother's body.

'I've found you, I've caught you, now it's my turn to run,' Phoebus persisted, cheerfully grabbing her again.

'Sshhh,' whispered Leto, urgently. 'Soon, soon, you'll be able to play again.'

She was very afraid, and pulled the two children tightly towards her, wishing her body could open and fold them into her deepest recesses and close herself, locked fast as a bivalve, so that nobody could open her and prise them out to hurt them.

'Tell me more, PLEASE.'

'I only know what I've heard.'

Phoebus prodded his mother, and she tried to assemble the fragments she remembered.

But life – or was it death? – was playing tricks on Leto. Every time she moved or was conveyed from one place to another, as when she was abandoned in the tombs or now, when she came down to the shore and embarked under cover of the night on to the sailing boat bound westward, the distance she put between herself and what lay behind her became also a space of time, its measurements in feet and yards, in ells and furlongs transmuted into units of duration which transported her beyond the world that had been the Citadel and her home, where Abbess Cecily prayed, with her long freckled hands joined composedly, and Doris prattled excitably, where Cunmar's hands tightened round her ribs.

It seems, she worried to herself, that living with Lycia has deformed my human soul. But she said nothing of this to her children.

Her lost loves still danced in her mind's cave, but receded from her as they turned and gestured, the sound of the wind and water outside tearing the sounds out of their mouths so that, as she strained to hear, she couldn't catch the words and she found herself running after them, but her legs rooted to the ground. Yet if she could not remember, who was she?

In the tombs with Lycia and her cubs she would watch the fire that she had learned to lay and set light: the wolves shunned all fires of hunters and travellers in the area but they learned to watch hers. The wood she and the young wolves carried up the cliff was dry and light and soon blazed; it was mostly live oak, and it burned brightly, spurting white tongues of light from the cracking bark. Sometimes, her mind also caught alight in this way; she would stare into the heart of the flame, and when one tongue curled through to the heartwood and burned incandescent, the burst of light was so dazzling she could not look: the flash from metal in the sunshine, something that shot through her with anguish of longing and loss. Sometimes in the winter, when the sky grew laden and there was cloud cover, you could look at the sun; a pale halo of lambent light under the drifts of mist. When you looked away, though, you might stumble because even shrouded, the disc scored deep into your eyes, burning out their core.

Mother Cecily and her nurse Doris and others in the convent had gone over the past again and again. Cunmar too had entwined her in tales of his past triumphs.

Memories were their constant companion and surety; the past gave them compass points on the map of their lives.

And Kim, piecing together her story as he read Skipwith's bundle of papers in the Archives, heard Leto say softly to herself:

But my memories are like splinters under my skin, they weaken me like spears stuck in a pig's neck. For they attach me to the past and I've been flung out of time and don't know what past belongs to me.

Leto's voice was coming through faintly. Kim put his head down on his folded arms and closed his eyes, smiling to himself as he listened closely.

The present has a way of turning translucent for me, of opening up to me. Do animals remember? They know how to tell friend from foe, bane from berries – the yew from the redcurrant. They recoil from fire, unlike my babies, who'd have put their hands to the dance of the flames. But do animals keep particular memories, in the way human's experience memory?

It isn't memories I need any more. The longing to return, to reel back the rope that's being payed out will weaken me. I can't be weak. Nostalgia for all that I've lost will shackle me. I – We – need the future. We need a future.

Her voice was growing fainter, overlaid by another, more insistent.

The librarian came over and tapped Kim awake, shaking her head at him. 'We don't allow sleeping in the Reading Room, I'm afraid.'

In the hull, Leto was making decisions. She would soon have to come out of hiding. The twins couldn't tolerate the darkness and the muteness and the immobility much longer, and besides, she wouldn't be able to hide the smells any more or someone would notice the wrong kind of droppings in the goat's hay.

Phoebe's head was lolling; she was quietened, drowsy. But Phoebus's brow was furrowed: he wanted Leto to leave her thoughts and talk to him. His eyes stared at her hugely, the look of a child who is recovering from fever. Soon, they must climb out of the hull and into the light again.

They slept, but woke to the wind, which rose in the depths of the night. The laden sloop began to groan and shiver under its lash, and the sleek mass of the sea heaved under the hull. Leto watched the children: they were curled together in a kindle, tiny hands raised near their faces as if in a gesture of entreaty.

The following morning, Sir Giles Skipwith, Bt., was sitting on the deck, under a shelter he'd rigged from one of the sails, with the portable desk he'd devised set out on his knees; he'd had a strap attached to it so that he could hang it round his neck. 'Like a pedlar!' he'd explained to the carpenter on his estate. His hands were free to work and there was a socket for his inkwell, and a lip on the near edge so that his writing and drawing implements wouldn't slip off. It was a gently misty day from the haze of early summer; the coast was visible on his right, the long promontories watchful like hunting dogs with their heads between their paws at the command, 'Lie' from their master. Captain Winwalloe at the wheel was quiet, apparently dozing, since the course was set and the breeze steady and strong enough to carry the boat with its cargo of marble; no other vessels appeared. The boy, Teal, was sitting in the prow, scanning for pirates. It was on account of the pirates that they were steering close to the shore for as long as they could, though not every harbour was secure.

One of Skipwith's sketchbooks of the site was spread out in front of him, and he was annotating the drawings there, collating them with his notes; he was partly content with the results, but needed to work fast to add details from memory. When they reached home, he'd commission an engraver to redraw the monuments. His efforts at the picturesque weren't 'lamentable', his mother's favourite term of disapproval. For an amateur cartographer, they were accomplished, almost 'delightful, dear old boy'. But every day, the gap grew wider between his pencilled outlines and the sculptures as he had beheld them in their setting among the rocks, before they were disassembled for safekeeping back home. His manuscript notebook was altogether most handsome: he had not wasted those daydreaming hours practising scrolls and flourishes on his ascenders and descenders during the tedium of morning school. He had a specimen box, compartmented with cotton wool pockets for fragments and small artefacts which he was entering into his register of the excavation.

The day was clear, the early morning breeze still fresh from the dropped temperature of the late summer nights, the sea was still soft and velvety and the ship moved to its cradling hold; they were made on days like this, thought Skipwith, to fit together as bodily as a bean lying neatly in the wadded mould of a pod. The sun's glare had not yet hardened to bounce off the surface of the water and flash, but stars winked deep down in its amethyst depths. His spirits expanded with the beauty of it till he felt his head might burst. Never had he imagined he would stumble across so much, that he would be able to rescue so many riches of the classical past, bring them back to safekeeping and to intelligibility. Twenty-four of the thirty-six cities mentioned by the sources for that area identified from their broken ruins. He felt he knew how God had felt at the creation when he brought order out of chaos, being out of nothingness. He, Skipwith, had found a trampled wilderness, strewn with stones, creeping with snakes, scorpions under the stones, crawling with tortoises and prowled by mountain lions and hyenas and wolves, a barbarous and desert place abandoned by the old gods and avoided by the new, and had gathered them so that they would speak again and tell their stories without risk from weather and war. Yes, it was god-like to halt time, to lift its fell hand from a world that was nearly lost.

When Strugwell and the boy came back that morning from the market with a hank of sausages wrapped in a scrap of old parchment – what a stroke of fortune that had been! It was greasy from its employment at the butcher's stall, torn by the nail on which he'd hung the pieces for use as wrapping, but clearly Greek, exquisite sepia uncials, some sort of chronicle. Then the furious ride back to the market, the cob steaming and heaving as he spurred him so that he'd catch the vendor before he disappeared; the wild search for the butcher, who had shut up shop before the furious heat of the day struck, but someone had directed him to his house and he'd roused him from his afternoon nap, and given him some money to remember where he'd purchased the scrap. Then the wait, because the sun was in the zenith, but as soon as they could set off again, he'd changed mounts and ridden to the mountain town where the butcher had told them the refuse trader lived. He'd enquired in the hamman, where everyone always knew everything, and it had turned out to be easy to track him down. A dealer in detritus and waste, with a cave for a storehouse. It was secured by a wooden palisaded gate and inside it, in the dark, Skipwith saw hundreds, perhaps thousands of documents stashed higgledy-piggledy, all mixed up together in a pile that rose under the steady powder of limestone dust from the cave's roof – how long had it been there? How far back did the pile begin?

'House clearances,' said the dealer. 'My father-in-law and his father before him.'

Skipwith bought the lot, by weight.

'What am I going to sell now?' The trader shrugged. 'You've emptied my stores.'

Skipwith was busy ordering more donkeys to cart the stuff back to the boat.

As the paper was boxed up, he saw bills, letters, receipts, wills, house deeds – but among this notaries' jetsam, there must be more of that chronicle, and perhaps more like it.

Still stowed behind the stones in their lagging of oiled canvas, Leto noticed how her children's noises were taking shape. No longer mere squawks and gurgles and cries, she realised, but ribbons of words that they spilled to each other, like kittens batting at something dangled in front of their eyes. They were impatient to rove, too; she would follow them as they explored, her heart knocking, as they tried out their new steps. The twins tumbled around on the cargo of rocks, the binding ropes giving them handholds when the boat pitched. Leto crept after them, in their dim playground, keeping her ears pricked for footsteps from the deck above, so she could snatch them into a hiding place at the sound of someone approaching

Apart from the cook, fetching up supplies, the long-limbed, flushed young man she had observed directing the haul of stones would climb down the companionway into the hold. He would rest a hand on the trussed haul from the tombs where she had lived, and stand there in the semi-darkness for a time, quite motionless, as if he wanted to drill through the oilcloths of the stowed packages and penetrate to their interior.

On deck, Sir Giles Skipwith arranged the papoose of a frog corpse at an oblique angle on his pad so that it appeared to be poised to leap off the edge of his desk. He was attaching a label to the frog's right foreleg, identifying the tomb by number.

Teal, the cabin boy, appeared at Sir Giles's elbow; he liked to watch the archaeologist working, and Skipwith enjoyed being watched, and, as he thought, admired.

'Of no extrinsic value, Teal,' he explained. 'But every item must be recorded, down to the smallest shard. That is how the great chronicles of civilisation are made: from fragments. This creature was probably used in magic: "Double double toil and trouble/Tongue of frog and eye of newt . . ." in the cauldron, "Boil and bubble" – you know the kind of thing!'

The boy was rapt, but did not look as if he understood.

Skipwith ensconced the weightless, papery cadaver on its cushion of cotton wool.

'AMULET?' he wrote in fine black script.

'Here,' he said, 'take a hold of this.' He handed him a crayon. 'We'll make a start on your letters, Teal, and you shall be able one day to do as I do.'

The boy was bunching his fist round the crayon as if it were a hammer, but was looking at Skipwith instead of paying attention to the task. His eyes were screwed up, and he was biting his lip. Skipwith tapped him on the forehead, and adjusted his fingers around the implement. 'Now, we need something to practise on. We can't use paper – never know where we'd find some again. We'll make as if we're on the beach – there's a fine place to write. Fetch me some salt – there's plenty of that about and we can always make heaps more!' He laughed, and pulled at his clothes; they were stiff with brine. They'd spread the salt on something – the deck or the top of a crate and it would make a fine screen on which he'd trace letters for the boy to copy.

But Teal wasn't paying attention.

'Come now, my boy, you lost your wits?'

Teal looked scared. He stammered, 'Can't go down there, sir—' His voice petered out.

'Yes you can; if you're frightened of Strugwell, I'll square him. Tell him I ordered it.'

'No, sir, I can't,' the boy was shivering.

'Don't be a little fool—'

'I'm not going.'

This was preposterous. Skipwith tossed his fair hair off his forehead with impatience. 'I'm ordering you to.'

'But I don't want to be the one who finds them, 'cos then,' he sniffed, 'it'll be me that's ordered to kill them and I don' want to go near such things nor whack 'em on the head. They're devils, not natural. If they get a nip at you you're a goner . . .' He danced on his feet and threw his head back, mimicking being throttled and foaming at the mouth.

'What the devil are you gabbing about?'

'Rats. Rats as big as . . .' he stopped, searched. 'Dogs! I heard them down there, snuffling and crying like babies.'

Skipwith examined the boy's face. It was red and blistered and smeared with dirt; the fair, almost white eyelashes dusted with salt, but beneath this crust, he could see Teal was truly frightened.

He unlatched the strap of his desk, lifted it off his lap, tidied away his writing tools and drawing materials, folded it all up into a compact box and took it into the cabin.

'Show me.' The treasures he'd found were thickly wrapped in waterproofed sheeting he'd had dubbed and oiled; then crated up in strongboxes. The smaller items of his magnificent haul – the fragments of carved reliefs and sculptures, the splinters of inscriptions, the pottery shards – were packed in crates the same carpenter from home had made to his specifications and would be proof against any rodents' gnawing. But he did not want to risk finding the manuscript hoard shredded into rats' nests.

He swung his long frame down the companionway into the low, stuffy darkness below deck in the fo'c'sle; the boy hung back, outlined in the square light of the hatch, whence, in a shaky whisper, he gave Skipwith directions.

'On, on, farther, behind your marbles, sir, right in the very depths of the fo'c'sle.'

On the first night, Skipwith had sensed a presence when he was standing on the deck under the violet Lycanian sky giddy with stars, unable to turn in, so acute was his excitement that his marbles – the tomb sculptures and the temple bas-reliefs – were on board and bound at last for Albion. The marbles were stowed forward and the heaviest of the pillar tombs aft for ballast; while in the hold amidships, the mummified bodies and their beautiful painted masks – the pinnacle of his discoveries! – were wrapped in oilcloth and slung from cradles above the sculptures and the stones. He was trying to quell the mad din in his heart that broke out when he saw again the extent of his hoard, when his ears had picked up something – was it giggling?

His consciousness did not fully register the sound, but it came back at Teal's pinched, scared face and a current of fear prickled up his back to the base of his hair.

This was nonsense; the boy's superstitious ignorance was clearly catching. All such folly is, Skipwith noted grimly.

Kim looked up from the diaries he was reading in the Archives, and closed his eyes for a moment as he took in the scene.

Giles's father, Sir George Skipwith, Bt., an elegant and urbane widower at the time, married Fidelia Ormonde, the tall and clever daughter of a portrait painter, during a tour of diplomatic duty in Parthenopolis where the painter was chronicling the Bonapartist regime in exile. Giles was her only child, and the product of his father's old age, a most beloved boy who precociously enjoyed the company of adults, both in the kitchen quarters and in the drawing room, until Sir George decided, 'He must become an English gentleman, my dear'. So off went Giles to the university, to All Saints' in the fens of Albion, with a tutor who was a balladeer and poet; he learned to pronounce Latin as if the language were a kind of Anglo-Saxon rather than the ancestor of his mother tongue. From the window seat of his rooms he'd look across the court in the darkness, and scan the powdering of stars on the secret face of the fenland skies; they called him away, singing their melancholy harmonies as they combed light out of the blackness and scattered it below, so sharp sometimes that on moonless nights, he cast a shadow on the cobbles as he returned to his rooms. He felt connected to vast distances, not with the investigative tools that Isaac Newton had set up in the same court two centuries before, but by something more deeply interfused, as the poet he admired had written. He was out of sorts when he was staying put; on the move, his finds led him on from one to another. He never could gather all the pieces, just as he could only decipher the stars intermittently, in broken phrases.

When Sir George died and Giles inherited the baronetcy, he was invited to the newly resplendent terraces of Regent's Park and other domiciles of his father's circle, was initiated into the Hellfire Club and had his portrait painted for the Society of Dilettanti, wearing a turban with his stock loose at his long supple throat and smoking a long clay pipe. He travelled, making maps, tracing on to living terrain places that figured in the histories and the mythologies he had read and was still reading; he visited monsters and found them to be geographical wonders – the spurting blue gas fumaroles of fire-breathing Chimaera, the groans of toppled giants deep in the craters of volcanoes, the current seething through the straits where Charybdis swallowed ships twenty fathoms down. He noted the way seaweed rooted and bunched on the hulls of boats drawn up on the shore for their winter careening, and saw in their strong lithe spathes and dangling fronds the long necks and bedraggled plumage of the fabled barnacle goose.

Skipwith published, on his return from his first exploration of the near east, a pamphlet on the geography of the Alexander Romance; it was warmly reviewed in the *Gentleman's Magazine*. 'Sir Giles Skipwith has most ingeniously distinguished two of the principal breeding grounds of eagles in the regions conquered by Alexander: it was in one of these that the story sprung up, he proposes, that the emperor harnessed the giant birds to transport him aloft, by attaching them to a scaffold above which a goat was tethered, for ever out of reach. Thus the birds, straining to devour the tantalising meal, flew upwards, drawing up the emperor in a basket below them. Sir Giles is of the practical persuasion called Euhemerist, holding that for all the prodigies and marvels in the ancient world, there must exist some historical or physical explanation. Alexander's maiden flight reveals the practical mind that informs our culture, and has led to its great scientific revelations, in contrast to the barbaric imagination of the more ancient epics, which treat of flying gods and goddesses as a matter of no remark, and offer no contrivance by which they could have accomplished their swift turns about the globe, presenting only magical appurtenances, such as winged helmets and sandals.'

But Skipwith could not settle to an English life. Planter families returning full of complaints from the post-abolition sugar islands proposed their daughters endowed with their still considerable fortunes; Giles duly flirted, but a lassitude soon overcame him, and he found he did not have the energy to argue his many differences from their point of view.

He went travelling again; he was gifted at languages and his digestion was doughty. He enjoyed nothing better than marking his maps and turning a spouting mermaid from a Dutchman or Portuguese seaman's portolan into a rocky outcrop or an ocean vortex. He hunted for correspondences with epic and romance, that had turned a dry and dusty and featureless wilderness of rocks or a relentless expanse of water into a landscape of horrors and wonders; yet his own careful research and collation did not undo their marvellousness, not in his eyes. That the past was real and had taken place was infinitely more miraculous to him than the fantastical shapes in which it was so often clothed: he'd give all the cloud-capp'd palaces for a single cast shoe from a medieval farrier, all the gorgeous pageants for a deep dry midden in which the oyster and mussel shells, the pomegranate husks and the artichoke stalks of the vanished villagers were interred for him to retrieve.

When he first reached Lycania and came across the drowned sanctuary of the necropolis and its temples, the dry chamber tombs high in the cliff-face, the steles carved with reliefs and inscriptions, he viewed the rubble with mounting delirium of excitement at what was there, and fury at what had already been lost, plundered, destroyed. He determined to rescue what remained.

Using all the charm of his father's memory, he approached contacts in St James's to raise money for the return expedition.

'It's for the nation,' he said. 'We're the guardians of classical civilisation now. The only ones left.'

'"Some talk of Alexander", and all that sort of thing, what-o?' hummed one acquaintance.

'Indeed. Absolutely. Though the site predates Alexander, he came through there, and of course, they never could stop talking about him afterwards, commemorating him – we can't know what we'll find until we can look carefully at the fragments we can recover.'

His friend was glad to assign him a banker's draft of forty guineas. And so it went on: he persuaded the navy to provide a vessel and he accumulated the wherewithal to leave, with enough silver (and some gold) to buy provisions for the sea voyage, for the pack mules and their drivers, for the *douceurs* to soften any local difficulties.

Two years later, after this spell of feverish negotiations in a metropolis he found increasingly brash and shallow and foolish, he joined the *Shearwater* and set sail again, for Lycania.

The hot afternoon when Sir Giles Skipwith came down below and, at Teal's insistence, clambered through the hold towards their hiding place, Leto was ready for him. The twins were communicating loudly to each other and she couldn't quell them any longer: Phoebus would trill till he made bubbles of saliva, and Phoebe would laugh and then imitate him, exaggerating till out came a sudden fart and so delighted the two of them that Leto had to clap a hand over their mouths to keep them quiet.

She struggled out of the tarpaulin, and, clutching both children to her knees, stood up to face him.

'Stowaways!' muttered Captain Winwalloe. 'Never in my life have I been inflicted with stowaways.' He looked aghast at the woman with the two children. Their bodies slumped against hers, unhealthily, he thought; they appeared to have been charred, they were so ragged and dirty. Yet the woman didn't seem cowed by her circumstances, but was casting about around the cabin, her eyes flickering over his table, as if searching for something. Instinctively, Winwalloe covered the ship's log and planted himself firmly in his chair facing her.

A smell hung about her, rank and feral, or, worse, diseased – something like the reek of that foul toadstool he liked to uproot and smash as a child when he found it in the hedgerows of his childhood home: stinkhorn.

Skipwith stood to the side, leaning against the wooden wall of the cabin with his arms folded across his chest, silently observing. When he had found her, under the tarpaulin, she was crouched in the hull with her babies like a Madonna of Humility on the ground. He asked her who she was in several languages; but she had shaken her head mutinously. He'd brought her above, stumbling and blinking at the light.

'What the confounded devil can you have been thinking of?' Winwalloe glared at her. 'What possessed you to smuggle yourselves aboard my vessel?'

The stowaway looked him full in the face, and the captain baulked at her expression. It was like looking into the eyes of a statue, one of those classical jobs that Skipwith was so enamoured of; that had no irises or pupils and didn't blink either, so that they seemed to be all soul and no body. She was standing there, a thin, drained, foul pillar of rags, and he would like to blast her with his words and his glance till she turned into a pillar of salt, with caked hair, and he could order her to be tipped over the side and melt into the empty expanse of the sea, leaving not a trace. But something about her made him quail. He told himself it was because she was a woman with children, that she was small and weak and needy and he was a captain of a ship of the line, a man in power, with men at his command, and a national history of chivalry to live up to.

The stowaway was fishing inside the girl's wrappings, where she'd tied the pouch during their sojourn below. She found what she was looking for – a gold bead earring.

She held it out to the captain. She said her name, and asked for food with gestures to her mouth and the children's. Winwalloe recoiled from her approach, as if she was threatening him. So she put it down on the table between them. She gasped as she did so, her voice cracked from hunger and thirst. Her breath was foul.

Skipwith moved from his position in the wings and picked up the earring. Winwalloe looked over his shoulder.

'Exquisite work, very pure, so soft some of the beads are a little dented,' said Skipwith. 'It's broken and the hoop is missing.'

'Good, so she's got an eye for rich pickings,' said the captain. His scowl deepened.

'She wants to buy food, Geoffrey, don't you see?' rejoined Sir Giles. 'If we were Ancient Greeks we'd offer hospitality freely – provide nourishment for unexpected guests. However beggarly and brutish.' He swung the gold grapes of the earring in front of his eye. 'Don't you think you could tell Strugwell we have some company?'

The captain spluttered. Various solutions spun through his head, each one making him more nauseated than the next. If he had the woman thrown overboard, and her brats with her, the order might not be easy to justify; he could have it done *sub rosa*, and fail to enter it in the log, but then that fanciful dilettante Skipwith might not go along with it and he'd have to come clean and there might be unpleasantness. But how could they keep a woman on board? A woman with two wailing sprogs to boot? They could hardly spare a boat and send her off on her own with a pair of oars and a barrel of their precious water.

They could maroon her, put her off on one of the islands, making sure there were springs and sources of food – berries, fruits.

But he was a captain in Her Majesty's navy, not a pirate from the Barbary Coast. Still, the solution hung in his mind.

In spite of the crust of filth, she was young and rounded; her breasts showed high and small under her thin torn clothing; her thighs, too – hell and damnation – he could see her legs and her small feet and neat toes, in spite of their crust of grime.

Skipwith was saying, 'I think she may be someone, don't you know, Geoffrey. Why shouldn't the jewel be hers?'

'Of course she's someone, you think I can't see her standing plain as day in front of my eyes? All too much flesh and blood. Though I'd like to think I was hallucinating, I can tell you. Why, for heaven's sake, why, why this ship?'

He switched direction to address his expostulations to the woman's face. It looked stubborn to him, untender and cold, in spite of the children, one of whom stood clutching his mother's legs, the other on her thin jutting hip.

'No, Geoffrey, I mean someone – who counts. A fugitive from . . . I don't know. It's romantic, don't you think? A tale of high misdeeds probably lies behind this. I vote we treat her with proper consideration.'

'Where in heaven's name are we going to stow her – and her brats – now that we've found her?'

The captain was furiously at a loss. If he left her exposed, tied up on deck or below, the crew'd be at her for far less – or far more depending which way you looked at it – than the value of those gold beads. Where could they put her? She couldn't sleep amidships with the men. Perhaps she should be tied to the mast below, and a guard mounted at the hatch to prevent anyone gaining access to her. But the men'd conspire and have their way. He shivered – he couldn't allow that.

He was cursing the fate that had delivered him, in the course of an absurd mission on behalf of saving classical civilisation, into this hideous quandary.

They were on course, with no landfall in sight that wasn't infested with bandits and pirates or worse, and they needed to keep out to sea, out of sight of the raiders who lurked in the concealed harbours of the shore and the islands peppering the chart; he wanted to keep making headway to more friendly waters. The original plan was to sail up the coast and then round the peninsula, avoiding a gulf crossing with this weight of cargo, then put in for water and provisions in the sheltered harbour off the straits. If they changed it, it would still be three, four days at least before they could locate civilisation and put in to a secure mooring. Three days was a long time to keep that kind of woman on board without incident. Besides, he didn't need to ship supplies or water and he didn't want to change course.

They'd have to maroon her – that would be best. Row her ashore and leave her and the children wherever they landed. But the problem remained: coming in to shore would expose them. Which of these islands wasn't sheltering raiders?

Now he had it: that scribbling dreamer Skipwith could give up his cabin – he was so interested in her and her baubles, he could make way for her.

'Don't lose courage, old boy,' Sir Giles responded, to the captain's challenge to his chivalry. 'I've an idea. We'll use one of the crates – it'll serve as her quarters. One of the document crates; we'll deposit the papers in my cabin for the time being. Punch some airholes in the sides, and padlock it. Lock her in there at night, keep the key on my person, and they'll be no trouble. She can stay there, with her dirty cherubini, safe and sound,' said Sir Giles, smiling. 'Until daybreak, when there's less opportunity for mischief. I'll keep an eye on her in the daytime, till the men get used to having a young mother around them. They'll adjust, you'll see. I'll vouch for it. She'll not introduce licence to the *Shearwater*, as God is my witness. Let's leave aside Sodom. The men might even grow fond of the little family in flight – you never know the secret tenderness of the human heart, and it's not often that you get to see children playing on one of His Majesty's – sorry Her Majesty's – ships.'

'I'm putting her off in the next anchorage we can be sure of, Sir Giles.'

'We'll see.'

The crew watched the little group emerge from the captain's cabin: the stowaway holding on tight to her children, Skipwith, Captain Winwalloe, and Strugwell, who had been summoned and ordered to give the stowaways a bucket of slops to wash in, a clout, biscuits, water. Teal's eyes crossed Phoebus' who suddenly flashed a smile, to which Teal grimaced back, his sharp face impish: at thirteen, he was closer to the three-year-old than to any of the men on the boat; one child recognised another, and Teal's heart gave a jump. The rest of the crew stared ravenously at the same children and at their mother but did not smile. They rather frowned and hooked their heads as if the species was unknown and repugnant to them, and she looked away, frightened. Lone men, without connections, without possessions, encased in their hardened carapace, like stag beetles waiting for some plunder to fall into their clutches.

The boat was under way in a good breeze, and clouds were high, now and then plunging the brilliant sparkle of the waves and the shimmering blue of air and sky and sea into a chill shadow as Leto was hustled past the staring crew to the stern, where she was shown a canvas bucket on a rope; she lowered it to the sea and began hauling, but the filled pail was heavy for her cramped light body and she failed; they were watching her from a distance, silently. Then Teal was running up, and took the rope and swung it, brimming full, on to the deck so that she could rinse off the accumulated grime of the last week in the hold from the children's faces and feet and arms and hands. She spoke to them under her breath; the salt was terrible and stung the abrasions and bruises they'd sustained down below.

Kim saw the sailors in his mind's eye watching her as she sluiced herself down. He could feel her thinking, *I couldn't look up and catch their eye.* They were seeing the body of a woman: had they ever been looked at or touched with love or interest since their mothers had borne them?

Another mind picture came up: of sailors playing with the twins, on the deck in the sunshine. Could this happen? She wouldn't try appealing to them now. She must concentrate on the leaders for the time being. For her to look back at the men, she knew, would make them see their lack, and the weakness that lack dug deep into them. She was the thing they didn't have here on this boat and probably never would have. She didn't want to spark the men's fury by inflicting a request for reciprocity on them. The children might enrage them even more: the pleasure in trampling the weak, the glory of destruction, the rush to the head that causing pain brings.

Leto resolved: *Keep your claims very weak, very small, very meek: like that mongrel bitch in Cadenas who was being kicked by a donkey after she came too near the donkey's feed or something, and you were standing there, and it looked as if the hooves would rip her to pieces, but she rolled over on to her back right under the trampling and the donkey, seeing her adopt this posture of submission, left off thrashing out with its legs and contented himself with butting her out of the way until she limped off dragging her head and tail and belly as near the ground as she could, whimpering.*

She could save herself and the twins like that; she knew she mustn't be proud.

Or they'll want to break me, she warned herself.

If the twins didn't exist . . . but she stifled the thought even as it rose. Then, again, it presented itself, insistently: she would have so much more freedom to manoeuvre. There would be things she could do. If they didn't need her constant vigilance.

'It's a miracle that you haven't fallen ill, my little mites,' she whispered, clasping them, 'that, Phoebe, you gurgle when I tickle you as if the things that happened were long ago and have faded.' She kissed them both, with the sailors still looking on, and the sun and the moon did not seem more beautiful to her than her twins.

After she had finished her attempted wash, Teal handed her some clothes: Skipwith had provided them with shirts and kerchiefs and even a pair of breeches. She wound Phoebe and Phoebus into cloths and turbans against the exposure on deck, where they were now tied by the leg with ropes that delineated a circle of activity and allowed them to crawl under a hammock for shade. On the other side of the boat, two sailors began prising loose one of the sides of a wooden crate with a claw hammer: this was to be her cell, she understood.

She was sitting against the side of the longboat, at the end of the rope, out of the afternoon sun, with Phoebe and Phoebus comfortably sleeping after she'd fed them two ship's biscuits softened in goat's milk with a mash of salt cod that Strugwell, his eyes scrunched tight with indignation, had heated through in the galley. The tall ribbon of Skipwith's shadow fell across her.

'It's fortunate that you're so small, though even so, this box will be somewhat confined.' Skipwith indicated the crate, now fitted with a door and padlock. 'Still you and your children will be safe from . . . prying eyes inside it. In due course we'll be able to introduce you to a little more comfort, I trust.'

The stowaway looked less feral now that she was dressed in one of his spare shirts and had tied, with a piece of ship's hemp supplied by Teal, a pair of breeches around her waist. Her hair was caught back in a length of twine, too. In her boy's outfit, she didn't look much older than Teal; if it weren't for her twins, you'd take her for a child herself.

She turned over and clasped his feet. He was wearing a kind of soft leather boot.

'For God's sake, girl,' said Skipwith. 'Don't grovel. Stand up.'

He was furious as he hoisted her by the elbow, to feel her limpness, her lightness.

'Nobody's going to hurt you – or your babies – not on this vessel, not while I'm on it. This isn't some pirate band of ruffians, but the Royal Navy, do you know what that means, and we're not engaged in warfare, but archaeology. Treasures of the spirit, not the body—'

He was wasting his words – how could she understand?

'I wanted to ask you,' he said, opening his hand where the gold earring lay in his palm. 'Where did you get this?' He paused. 'Say the name of the country, the city, the place. I might understand: say Ophir, or Tirzah, or . . .'

'No,' she replied, 'Cadenas-la-Jolie. The earrings and my necklace were torn from my neck when I was attacked, before the wolf rescued us. Later we went back and I fished the pond for the frogs and slit their throats till I found that piece you have in your hand.'

Skipwith nodded; he understood the name Cadenas and the shake of her head at least, though her words fell scattered in his mind. But he knew the workmanship; he had a fragment, three beads, which may well be its fellows retrieved from the marshland near the tombs. They were lying in one of his specimen boxes, labelled, 'Lazuli work, circa ?1125'. Beautiful lost wax casting, the work of skilled goldsmiths – but whose?

'Cadenas-la-Jolie,' she amplified. 'They sought my life for I incurred the emnity of the Procurator's wife, Porphyria, and of her son, who then came to power in the outpost and overthrew the ruler, Cunmar, whom I was to marry.' Skipwith was listening intently; he was trying to make out words. 'Chrysaor imprisoned Lord Cunmar,' the stowaway told Skipwith. 'After the celebrations of what was to have been my wedding. I never saw Cunmar again, so I fear that he is dead.'

'What are you?' asked Sir Giles. 'Are you a Lazuli? A Child of Israel? An Ishmaelite? An Ophiri? You're fleeing some persecution or other, I imagine.'

The boy child was becoming restless, and started climbing up his mother's body; she put him on her hip. The stowaway stroked his face, unsure how to respond to the tall fair man with the drooping hair who was so curious about her.

All of a sudden, the child mock-growled, 'I'm a wolf.' And buried his laughter in his mother's neck. Skipwith nodded, absently, ignoring him.

'He is, you know,' said the girl child, now tugging for attention. 'And so am I.'

The stowaway pressed their hands in hers to silence them, but Skipwith, having no familiarity with children, simply continued to fix his attention on their mother.

Quickly, Leto made the sign of the cross.

'Haha!' exclaimed Skipwith. He thought over the possibilities: was she a converso? Ophiri in origin, or something other, but inducted into the faith? By choice? Or duress? But she could be lying about her allegiance, trying to please him. She had a whiff of Romany about her, but she'd boarded them where he'd never come across gipsies, and besides, they kept together. A snatch of the old song that one of his nurses used to sing ran through his head: 'What care I for my goose-feather bed? What care I for my money-O? I'm off with the raggle-taggle gipsies, O . . .' *You* ran away to join the gipsies; they didn't run away to join you. And they never expelled their own, but preferred to mete out punishments privately, within the tribe.

Patched up as a kind of Rosalind or Viola in breeches with her hair tied back, this young woman had the making of a nice looking page. Maybe his Mamma would like her? The children could be costumed in jewelled and feathered variations on the turbans she'd wound around their heads, in silks and satin. His mother Fidelia would cut a charming figure with such picturesque attendants. The three of them could indeed be Moors – though they were rather on the fair side. Youngsters did grow darker and hairier as they got older, and there were many fair-skinned even blue-eyed women on the Barbary Coast, not all of them captives. One never can tell. I know that deciphering the signs can't be done hastily but has to be approached slowly, patiently. And even making the sign of the Cross, she could belong to so many sects. Those territories teemed with variations and the most fustian heresies still had their pockets of adherents. Monophysites, Nestorians, Arians, Monothelites, such refinements of distinctions. Did the son of God have a human memory? How could he know everything and remember only this and that as we do? Was he endowed with free will? And if so, how could he choose when he could see into the future? But a human heart – does he have a human heart? Yes, YES, – and it came to him why his musings were taking this direction: the formulae the stowaway was now uttering took the shape of a doxology, which he could understand, not from the way she was pronouncing them, but as the sounds formed on paper in his mind's eye.

It struck him that this scarecrow woman with her savage offspring was speaking a kind of Greek.

He spread a paper in front of him and leant on the longboat's hull behind him to write on it. She looked at the words he'd written: 'Who are you?' she read.

She took the pen from his hand, and wrote her name.

'Outis.' No one.

Skipwith laughed. 'I know that trick. We can't have that.' He pressed the paper towards her again.

'Leto,' she said aloud.

'A big name for a little woman. A Titaness!' Skipwith smiled. So she was called after the cult goddess of the region, appropriately. This custom had never caught on in Albion, to name children after Jesus Christ or Aphrodite or Hercules. He pondered a while, then decided, 'It's charming, it's an improvement on "Nobody", but it still won't do, not if we're going to take you with us to Albion. We need to have you fit in. How about . . . Lettice, instead?'

*

Captain Winwalloe watched the stowaway from the bridge: preternatural girl-woman with twin children, puny and pallid from the dark where they'd been hidden, but gabbling to each other like much older children. She'd gold on her. Still smelly, even after a wash on the deck, standing in her borrowed clothes, slopped down in seawater from a bucket on a rope wielded by Teal, who whooped as the woman shivered and shuddered. You could see everything through that white lawn gentleman's hosiery that pretentious Sir Giles Skipwith had given her to wear. No damn point in her pretending to be modest and keeping herself covered. Sharp sticking out bits and dark patches. Too scrawny and too small for his taste; he liked a good croup to grasp as he thrust. She'd shiver into little bits, like porcelain. Even at this distance she made Winwalloe feel stout and bellybound, ungainly and, the long and the short of it, out of sorts.

Strugwell frequently listened in to Skipwith's exchanges with the captain when they sat dining, spooning the provisions he offered them into their mouths. He understood clearly that that damned clever lord, who was forever jesting, teasing people except where it concerned his marbles in the hold, pooh-poohed the portents and prodigies of the sea that he'd spent a lifetime avoiding, and at times, he'd found a consolation in the gentleman's confident scepticism:

'"Here be dragons"? I think not,' Skipwith would say. 'A trick of the earth; gas escaping from the rock, followed by spontaneous combustion, takes the appearance of flickering flames such as might be spewed by a fire-breathing dragon of olden times. That monstrous she-devil the Chimaera is nothing but a chimera,' he laughed. 'Nature, Geoffrey, nature. Quite magical enough on her own without needing myths or religion to explain it.' A pagan by imaginative inclination, Giles had a developed sense of the contingencies of religious faith; his archaeological explorations had removed traces of trust in the behaviour of believers.

Captain Winwalloe disliked his clever passenger's scoffing, and he was sometimes moved to rebuke him aloud for presumptuousness against divine providence; like most naval men, he was highly respectful of fate's powerful caprices. Strugwell on the other hand learned from Sir Giles's rationalising and took some comfort from them – his explanations and dismissals could set some order to the jumble in the cook's soused mind, and blunt some of the many goads that roused his temper and his terrors. The churchyard on the shore where he'd grown up was full of the dead whom the sea had claimed: men who had slipped from the deck out fishing, men who had been lured on to the rocks, men who'd rowed out to help a boat in difficulties in a gale and been engulfed themselves, smugglers and wreckers, too, who worked under the rose in the blackness of moonless nights and mistook the currents along the cliffs. In his granite village on the promontory everyone knew that some of the men who the sea took went of their own will to go with them – the immortal and fatal spirits who live under the sea and rose up to press their cold and fishy flesh against a sailor's body and interlace their flowing limbs with his less supple, human frame of bone and muscle.

Years of surprising survival at sea and the loss of many sailors who were his comrades-in-arms in a variety of assaults, accidents, punishments and plagues, had made him superstitious. When they talked among themselves, the crew loved swapping tales of bloodshed, hauntings, curses and woes; however familiar they were, however many times they'd been repeated, they still could thrill a sailor with delicious trembling fear of the unknown forces invisibly gathering in the ocean and the sky, watching for their moment like sea hawks hanging on the uplift of air from the lip of a cliff.

Strugwell had made a pact with his hammock partner, the second mate, that if an accident should befall him, his friend would take the surgeon's needle from the medicine chest and sew up his nose and mouth tightly before winding him into his shroud so that no fishes could swim into him and gnaw his insides before they'd decomposed in the natural way of things. Round his neck, he wore a badger's penis on a cord: Georgie, the shepherd from home, who'd given it to him when he was a boy, had said it had a bone in it, and that badgers had the only penises in the world to have one, and that it would stiffen his manhood through fair wind and ill.

Whereas his captain was in high dudgeon about the stowaways, he, Strugwell, was more alarmed than annoyed about it: the woman, that mother didn't seem altogether right in the head, twins were a peculiar lot anyway and these twins were honest-to-god strange: they weren't like any offspring he'd ever seen, the way they jabbered to each other all the time and that girl, who could walk and talk and jump about and climb all over everything and eat like a horse, still at her mother's nipple. There was something funny about the way they looked, too – something in their eyes. Something deep down, like looking at a waxwork; in port two years ago, he'd visited the show of Mrs Salmon's where you could look at the most notorious murderers wearing their own clothes as they were at the time of their topping. They'd glass eyes in their pink, sweaty faces and you could look right into the orb and see all the bits, the filaments of the iris and the dark hole of the pupil and the light passing through the jelly. They looked back at you, too, and it was really hard to believe they couldn't see you. Those three strangers looked in the same blind way, especially the young ones who stared at everything so frankly; their mother reminded him of the statue of that Sarah Malcolm, the indoor servant who'd murdered her mistress and two of her fellow servants – for what? For gain?

The children's mother was all skin-and-bones, which Old Ma Malcolm wasn't. She was more like one of those Jenny Hannivers on display in Mrs Salmon's as well. Brought up with some catch in a fisherman's net, with wrinkly black hands and a face like a pear that's dried up in the store. They said this Jenny was a mermaid, and Strugwell thought he'd have no trouble sailing past this wizened hobgoblin even if she did know songs that no man could hear without tearing off his clothes and leaping into the sea to reach them. Every day in this sea, they saw porpoises. They'd conduct the boat out at the prow in fair weather, glittering arcs slicing out of the water and swooping down again; they'd disappear as suddenly as they appeared and seemed to come for no other reason than the sport of it. Flying fish too, in squadrons. One or two misjudged the leap, and landed, panting, wild-eyed on deck.

Maybe that's what she was, really? Would the captain chuck her and her brood back into the sea? They'd swim away, Strugwell was sure of it; her legs would turn scaly and finned, and the twins would ride the waves calling out in their godless tongue on either side of her.

Sir Giles was very animated that night, at supper with the captain at his table under the awning by the tiller. The night was fine, the breeze strong enough to swish the heavy boat through the sea's dark toils, which opened silvered lips as the boat entered them. Skipwith's voice was always loud, and while many men whom Winwalloe had known sat quietly wrapped in the swinging chords of the sea at night, Sir Giles called out to him:

'We'll be putting in to Parthenopolis in a fortnight, you reckon . . . ?'

'If there's a following wind, but the bay of Feltimye can be treacherous and the winds are fickle this time of year – it's late, much later than I hoped, as you know, Sir Giles.' Winwalloe was bitter: if Sir Giles hadn't held out to carry more and more rocks down to the shore and load the *Shearwater* to the gunwhales, they'd have set sail in more clement weather with a lighter burden and made better headway. As it was the *Shearwater* was groaning like a winded nag.

The captain was decisive: 'We'll land them in the next harbour where we can put in safely.'

'But she's a woman, Winwalloe – and young. You know what that'll mean, in these parts.'

'It's not our responsibility. My charge is to bring the marbles – and yourself – back to Albion. No more cargo. No livestock. Except the edible variety. Of any kind.'

'Consider her a prisoner – imagine we've captured her in battle. She might be valuable. A bargaining chip. Besides, does Her Majesty's navy hand over prisoners without ceremony? Marooning – surely this is fit only for stories for boys, the "bloods" I read when I was very young?'

'She's a stowaway, sir, and we're not at war, not with our neighbours here. If she weren't . . . what? A woman, and a woman with two children, damn it, I'd throw her back in the sea where she came from.'

'Do you think she came from the sea then?' asked Sir Giles, amused. 'A siren? I've the reputation for collecting wonders. Maybe she's a curiosity, a figure from an old map. Shall we ask her to sing?'

Winwalloe flushed. 'This is a ship in Her Majesty's navy, sir, and I'll not let your fiddle-dee-dee attitude deflect me from my duty. Which is to bring you and those rocks we've loaded safely to port. That's my duty, as I say, and we'll have no women. And no singing. I'll not vouch for the stability of the ship if you start more of that kind of nonsense.'

Later, Strugwell approached the captain.

'How long is it we're to provide for . . . ?' he jerked an angry head sideways towards the companionway that led down to the lower deck where the stowaway was now locked in the crate with the twins.

The captain stuck out his beard and said, 'Ask Skipwith to secure the costs, or part with his rations.'

'Captain? Do we have enough water? Three more mouths – and gullets.'

'Those are your orders. It'll be two, three days, at most. Then we'll be rid of her and her brood.'

'Captain?'

'I'm putting them ashore as soon as it can be achieved safely – for us. That means Feltimye.' He struck the map.

'I'd be pleased to conduct them ashore, when the time comes.'

The captain's attention was caught, since Strugwell's character did not lean to chivalry.

'I couldn't help hear what His Nibbs was saying.'

'Sir Giles, to you.'

'Sir Giles said she was *valuable*. You know what I mean. If you let me take the longboat alone with them, I . . . we . . . could bring back some provisions of a better class and quality than what's on board.'

'What?'

Strugwell had sailed that shore before. He'd even spent time in a jail there, once, after an eventful night, before the consul got him out.

'She'd be no worse off than she was and better off than she might be – we could be boarded by lesser fry among the brethren any day and there's no telling what'd happen to her then. Massacre of the Innocents. You know, captain, what I mean. They've got palates for tender flesh, and cooks not like me, who'd not blench at . . . As for a young woman like that, they'd be in her plackets, excuse me, soon as look at her. Not that she has any plackets.'

'Strugwell.'

'Yes, captain?'

'Enough! Back to the galley you go. Not a word more.'

'But you'll consider my request, captain.'

'You're dismissed.'

Strugwell glanced at him as he saluted, shamblingly, and left the cabin. He heard the friendly knell of hypocrisy, not outrage, in the captain's order.

2

A Cheval Glass

There was someone else there when Sir Giles Skipwith conducted the stowaway into his cabin, on the second day after she and her children were discovered.

She took in this third figure out of the corner of her eye. He was standing back, in a corner by a washbasin on a stand, a grim, gaunt silhouette compared to Skipwith himself, whose elegant limbs and languid flesh seemed to flow around his quarters like a bale of silk velvet displayed by a merchant. Her eyes swivelled towards their silent witness and then back to Sir Giles, who offered no explanation.

She was very tense; ordered to follow her captor – and benefactor – to his quarters and to leave the children up above, she'd quailed and protested and pleaded, but Skipwith had mocked her:

'You're not plants, you know, grafted together at the trunk. They're in safe hands – Teal is going to keep an eye on them, aren't you, my boy?'

Teal was indeed with the twins. They even appeared to be talking together.

'You see, the universal language of the race – the young know it. It's called play-acting or make-believe,' said Sir Giles, genially, and pointed his peculiar prize in her breeches and bare feet down the companionway to his quarters below.

This room offered for a brief respite greater comfort than she could have imagined on board a boat, but Skipwith's intentions towards her were hard to grasp. The bed stood in a wooden boxframe, with heavy green curtains, a table with writing materials, notebooks, a lamp and several books set into racks, more books in a crate, a portrait on the wall of a lady in a huge hat with black plumes streaming sideways while behind her, a mountain was gusting smoke like a cauldron on the boil on laundry day in the Convent.

A mountain on fire – it must be . . . Skipwith followed her look.

'Parthenopolis. And my esteemed mother, Fidelia, neé Ormonde, Lady Skipwith. A mettlesome temperament,' he made a pass in the air as if with a fencing foil, 'and a clever woman, interested in education . . . of the deprived, of the barbarous.'

She was watching him. His insouciance was frightening to her, as if the encounter he was planning was to be nothing but a cold and calculated frolic – with the silent third as audience, as assistant . . . or, even, participant?

Fear of this long, pale man did not turn her insides molten, as Cunmar's embrace had when he first seized her. But the thought of what Giles Skipwith could do shrivelled her will. She had the children to defend, and she desperately wanted him not to hurt them, nor use them to have power over her. Long past hoping for any reciprocal understanding with her fellow man, she was wholly bent on circumventing this new danger.

'You're trembling,' he said. 'Sit down.' He pushed her on to the chair by the desk and leant over her. She saw the other figure in the corner withdraw, suddenly.

Clutching at his full white sleeve, she began, beseechingly, 'What do you want?'

'Oh stop that whining!' he answered, shaking her off. 'Really. I've no designs on you – you're about as appealing as a plague rat, quite honestly. Not my style to force anyone, either. I brought you down here because I want you to trust me. I'd like us to . . . converse – I'm curious about you.' He pushed a book open towards her. It was a notebook, with a sketch of one of the tombs where she had sheltered, inscribed with invocations to the gods to ward off demons.

'Does this make any sense?'

The figure in the corner remained very silent. Was this a test? Would she place herself in greater jeopardy if she showed she could puzzle out the glyphs he'd traced?

Leto gestured to the corner, where the other figure was hidden behind her.

'No, I want you to concentrate. If you can play the wit with me and

201

write down your name is "No one" in Greek, you must be able to decipher something of this.'

She pushed the notebook away; her eyes seeking out the figure crouched near the wall.

'What are you frightened of? That?' Sir Giles got up, moved towards the mute figure. 'That's my *psyché*,' he said. 'As the French call it. Latest thing, acquired in the elegant salerooms of the Palais Marly. Expensive. Best crystal, silvered. Come, you'll certainly never have seen one before. It's an innovation.'

He pulled the stowaway up and led her across the room. As she drew nearer, the dark dwarfish figure that had been skulking in the shadows twitched and cringed at her approach.

'Ha!' exclaimed Skipwith, 'you're starting at your own shadow! And mine. Look.' He paused, his lips curled up over his teeth. 'So, Lettice, there you are. You've never seen yourself in a glass before?'

He took her up to the cheval glass on its pivoting mahogany stand and moved so that he materialised in its narrow glass; she saw his likeness appear behind her and above her as he took her hand – she tensed still tighter – and held it out towards the doubles in the glass, and the figure from the corner reciprocated and her fingers touched his, except they were behind the smooth plane that was cool and hard.

She shook her head. In the Keep, she had used a small silver hand mirror, chased with cupids and dolphins, with a naked Venus for a handle, and she remembered how she could see her face in Cunmar's bright armour, when the breeze lifted his surcoat. But the glassware they blew in the Turquoise Quarter took the form of beads, vessels, flasks, phials and alembics, not this shining sheet of water turned solid.

Sir Giles Skipwith believed she was shaking her head because she did not know. He pulled her nearer to its surface, and traced the contours of her face in the mirror.

'You,' he said. 'That's you. Take in your image, look at yourself, it'll be interesting to know what you find there, what you see. Tell me.'

'That's not me,' she said, again shaking her head. 'That's not anyone I know.'

Skipwith placed his hands on her shoulders from behind her. His long face appeared in front of her.

'Do you feel me holding you?'

A nod.

Under his hands, she was quivering. Like one of the songbirds that, when flying south, roosted in the orange and lemon trees in the courtyard in Parthenopolis at his grandparents'. Every year, from one generation to the other, the migrants always found the small, enclosed garden of the Ormonde studio, in the heart of the higgledy-piggledy city, unerringly, even though the cool dark tall house shut its ochre face against the street and nobody could know, unless invited in, that such a paradise even existed within its walls. One summer before his grandparents died, the gardener's boy and he had played together at trapping the birds, in nets they strung through the branches, not to kill and eat them as delicacies, but to keep them in cages, to sing in the house. He had marvelled then as one fluttered in his hand that the tiny head with its rolling eye could contain the map of such vastness and the coordinates of a journey for which he now would need a hatch full of charts.

He said, making sure his voice did not show his sense of her poignancy: 'And you see that – in the mirror – I'm holding this person you don't know?'

Another nod.

'Don't you see then, that it's you?'

She stayed mute, her face unresponsive, a dull shock in her eyes, as she turned her back to the glass.

There was a silence between them.

Looking at the stowaway in her boy's rig as she took in her reflection in such perplexity and dismay, he could feel her body as she stood stock still in tension next to him. Although its sour ill health repelled him, as might an animal dragging a festering limb, he was also gripped. Sea voyages – and he had made many – were not exactly monotonous, since the dangers were lively (and not from the elements alone), but they were wearisome to a spirit as restless as his. He was happier on land, making new encounters, acquiring smatterings of new languages and crates of new treasures. When he was on board, especially on the return home, he often felt dull; he craved stimulation that games of piquet with Winwalloe could not satisfy, nor working on his notes and inventory under Teal's baffled gaze. Moving by sea often gave him the impression that the world moved past the boat, and that those on board were fastened to the same spot while it sailed by. There were some islanders, he'd read, who made maps on which the land moved, not the traveller. They charted their crossings by showing the numerous islands of their archipelago moving past the boats they sailed. They draw accurately, thought Giles, this suspended animation of a sea passage: we are stuck in our time, after all, a mere tick in the clockwork of time; whereas the land has been there almost for eternity, growing, heaving, splitting, spilling, declining, in a constant slow frenzy of change. At times, excavating the past opened up a vision for Giles of such revolving, spinning universes, speeding through time and space and hurtling into the void so fast that he felt like writing his name on everything to hand, putting his stamp on anything he came into contact with so that he should leave a mark for the thousands coming after who might never ever know that he – and his kind, his world, his culture – had even existed. Nothing but defaced rocks, worn inscriptions remained – from all that tumult and excitement and splendour that had been the past.

The idea of a stowaway already was a source of pleasant interest; but the mystery of this fugitive with her twins delighted him more.

She was spellbound, it seemed, by the image in the glass.

Giles thought of the story of the wild brother whom Valentine catches just so, by showing Orson his reflection. There were twins in that old story, which his grandfather Ormonde used to tell: one twin was brought up in town as a prince, but the other stolen away by a she-bear in the forest when his mother was asleep. Skipwith could not recall exactly what had happened, except that Valentine did not know that the wild man who was terrorising wayfarers was his long-lost brother. He wanted to capture him alive – so he didn't hunt to kill, but trapped him instead in a net and then took up a mirror and showed him his savage visage – and Orson the bear-boy was rooted to the spot at the horrific picture he presented. Just like this wild creature, he thought, whom we've found on board . . . 'And thus the wild boy was taken to the city and his brother's palace and learned the ways of civilisation', he wrote in his journal, concluding, 'this is a promise that the print of nurture can take, as my mother believes so strongly.'

Leto saw in the glass that the girl whose father had staked her in a trade deal, whom Doris had chivvied and Abbess Cecily had moulded and Cunmar had held so tight, was now dead. Another had replaced her: a burned, weather-beaten scarecrow, a beggar with a thin, set mouth and hair in stiff clumps and a panicky look in eyes and forehead.

'I've something for you, Lettice,' said Sir Giles. He wanted to reward her for what she had done, for the strangeness of the scene he had just witnessed. 'I keep some of these treasures in my cabin, but you shall have one.'

He held out an orange.

Seeing the dilation of her eyes, he laughed: 'You can have it – and others like it. Not now – later. You'll see – we'll be friends.'

3

Some Oranges

As oranges go, this one was withered. But Leto had not seen one since her days in the citadel: there, orange trees grew below the walls, in orchards mixed with vines and almonds, the lemon trees' trunks standing ankle-deep in puddly loam linked by runnels cut with a sharp spade into the red-gold earth. Before dawn, when the citadel's gates were first opened for the nightsoil carts to leave (as she knew), the farmhands and fruit pickers would gather and wave their passes, shouting at the gatekeepers to let them through; then, their documents checked, they'd rattle out with their donkeys and carts and tools and move through the groves lifting the sluices here and there in the irrigation channels to water the roots in the cool freshness of the new day and plump the fruit; they'd gather the ripest to bring to market later that morning, where Doris would bargain for one or two of the best to bring to Leto for her breakfast in bed. In the days when Leto was living in the Keep.

In the convent, the fruit sometimes appeared, too, on feast days, after supper.

Cadenate oranges were smaller than the one Skipwith gave Leto as a reward for sitting still during that first lesson when he showed her, alongside the inscriptions from the tombs, their approximate equivalents in his native alphabet. The fruit fitted neatly to Skipwith's hand, round and hard like a soup stone heated in the fire, whereas Leto remembered them small enough for her to cover with her child's palm when she took one from the kitchen without asking. Skipwith's gift had shed its leaves, some dirt had caught in its navel and the skin was pitted with pores; after a few weeks' store in Skipwith's baggage, the fruit had aged like a human face over decades.

The sun is very, very old, she thought as she held the fruit, but everything moves within its own timescale, so that although the sun is older than the brightest planets, its glowing orange sphere looks each morning as if it has burst into new life, swollen with shining sap that it shakes off in flakes and beams to light up and fill thousands of its reflections – oranges and melons and apples and figs – as it climbs. Its bright flow does not dim or dry up: it goes down in a ripe, juicy welter and bursts out again undiminished the next morning. By contrast even her children changed daily, and as for herself . . .

However shrivelled, Skipwith's orange was scented: there was precious juice trapped inside and its sharp sweetness pierced through the drying rind and wrinkles. She hid the fruit against her ribs and stole under the sail that Teal had rigged outside the crate to give them shade.

The twins were lying on their stomachs, each of them tied by the ankle with a rope to a capstan. They were practising seeing stars by banging their heads together.

'Stop that!' Leto pulled them apart and showed them the fruit.

When Leto bit into it, using her front teeth like a rodent – for she had no knife and her nails were torn and blunt – the perfume of the peel pricked the air, and the children blinked at the sudden fragrance. They had never seen an orange before, for the tombs were too exposed and the ground too dry in the mountains to support the trees. Leto began pulling off the rind in sections with her fingers, but in its thinning, dry condition, it stuck to the endodermis more tightly than in the case of a riper fruit; below, there was a bandage of yellow pith but the juice ran and the fruit's lively, sweet pungency rose from its flow over her fingers as she parted piece from piece and gave them to the children to suck. They both looked wary at the taste; the bitterness of the skin lingered. She persevered, picking at the tough rind. Inside, the orange's segments lay, a little shrunken, in transparent chemises of pale membrane; she pulled away the pith and prised out the first piece of the fruit's luminous iris, where the filaments were packed tight, clinging together, and runny; the juice spurted into her palm as she parted one from another. With one hand she fed the segments to the twins, with the other she crammed a larger piece and then another chunk into her mouth. Now that she had broken into the orange, she no longer split off the pieces carefully, following the fruit's inner structure, but tore into it so that her children, their initial suspicion melted away, could take the pieces in their fists and push them blissfully into their own mouths.

When the orange had all gone and they were licking their fingers and their lips for the last stickiness, Leto became aware that Teal was watching them, like a dog who's been well trained to sit and not to beg as its owners dine, but who seems to howl his hunger from every mute limb of his body and silent gesture. When he saw that she had noticed him, he turned away and bent again to the sail which he had been patching, pushing through the thick canvas a thick needle and even thicker thread.

'She's our greatest find,' Skipwith was joyous as he joined Winwalloe, who was leaning over the navigation charts and drawing the rhomb of their progress against a ruler. 'She demonstrates that self-consciousness doesn't exist in the mind unless it's taught. She didn't recognise herself in the glass – imagine! She's a marvel, a fabulous piece of living evidence for the thinking of our ancestors. A primitive, who knows some things and is completely innocent of others. She seems to read and write – I can't find out how much. Astounding, no? You know, bear-children, wolf-children can be captured with a mirror because the sight of their own features gives them such a shock they lose all their defensive instincts and turn docile. I reckon that's what happened – all unwittingly I brought her face to face with a self she'd never seen, and she reeled from it! Imagine not even knowing what you look like!

'Geoffrey, old boy, it's the key to the attitudes of the past. Nobody before – oh, when was it? – the fifteenth century, Venetian glass – knew what their faces looked like. Except in glimpses in metal or ponds. She's just experienced Narcissus' primal discovery – except that, ha, I don't think she fell in love with what she saw.'

The captain gave Skipwith a weary look. But Skipwith continued to rejoice: 'She's a perfect subject of study: she's canny, that No one. And she comes from somewhere – we don't yet know where – where no images of the self have adulterated her relation to the world of phenomena. She's been living like an animal with her children like pups – on the run from something, in the ruins of the necropolis. I've managed to establish that much by questioning her. She's not much older than fifteen, I reckon. I want to observe her very carefully. She holds all kinds of clues. A rare chance. Wonderful priceless raw material – a treasure above rubies!'

Captain Winwalloe saw Strugwell hovering at the cabin entrance – and waved him away, impatiently.

Skipwith continued, exultant, his dish of brown hash hardly touched, but his glass emptying rapidly. 'We may've traced and identified more lost ancient cities than any of our competitors, and brought back treasures doomed to fall into utter ruin, but I feel almost more delighted with this living fossil of ancient intelligence than I am with all our discoveries in stone!'

'You mean that she's a savage,' said the captain.

'Come now, old chap.'

'And you put a high value on such things, where others don't.'

'Geoffrey, do put aside this old seadog curmudgeonliness. You're an enlightened man, you don't have to entertain common prejudices. You see a young woman, some sort of foul siren with smelly feet, as a risk to our voyage and our whole enterprise – but I – I see a key to a puzzle, the greatest puzzle – the human mind.'

Winwalloe muttered, 'You're a fantastic dreamer, Giles.'

'That is exactly what I'm not, Geoffrey! I'm an explorer, a scientist – I look for the natural, physical laws that govern all the stuff and nonsense carried in our heavy baggage of beliefs. I want to explain, not accept all unknowingly. Saint Thomas is my patron saint: Thomas the Doubter. He had to stick his fingers in Christ's wound before he agreed to the truth of the resurrection. I'm convinced there's a perfectly reasonable explanation for almost every occurrence, however preternatural or supernatural it might appear. But on account of our ignorance and idleness, we don't know how to explain it – not yet. For example, I'm beginning to realise that most people are entirely mistaken about mermaids.'

'They're walruses,' said Winwalloe.

'No, no, my dear fellow! Anyway that simple-minded school believes they're manatees – even worse. Sea cows! Aquatic mammoths. Even uglier and fatter.'

The captain pulled open the drawer of the table and put out two packs of cards.

'How about a game, what?' He wanted to stop Skipwith talking.

Skipwith accepted a pack without answering and began shuffling. 'A shilling a point? What d'ye say?'

The captain sighed. His debts to Giles over the piquet they'd been playing were mounting.

'I'll offer you a deal, Geoffrey. Give up your authority over our stowaway and invest it in me. I'll cancel your debts for it. If I recall rightly, they're standing at 34 guineas, 5s. and 6d., I'm afraid.'

'I'm not a slaver.'

'I'm not proposing to buy her. Consider her salvage. Wouldn't you be able to assign me your interests in salvage in return for – your losses?'

The captain didn't reply.

'Come on, what d'ye say to it?' Skipwith pushed the pack over the table. While Winwalloe cut for the major hand, lost, and began paying out the cards, first five together, then three, then one, with a stack of eight left in the middle, Giles continued, 'I need her. For my work. I'm not going to say anything more now than this: I just realised that sirens aren't admiring themselves, they're mirroring the world and other people in the world. They lure you and enthral you by showing you your own face in their mirror – this must be what Homer meant when he said they'd knowledge of the future and were fatal to men. Narcissus wasn't in love with his own image – he thought it was someone else – that's why he became besotted.'

The captain poured himself some port and pushed the decanter over to Skipwith.

'You've the major hand, Giles,' he reminded him.

'Are we agreed, then? – Before you look at your hand!'

Winwalloe nodded. 'But you will have to explain matters, when we reach port.'

Skipwith was looking at his cards; he reordered them, pulled three and changed them for three in the pile on the table.

Winwalloe threw five and scooped up the remaining five cards on the table to replace them.

Skipwith's ardour was brightly blazing and was not to be damped. He would start his enquiry now, on the *Shearwater*; he'd find out the depths of the stowaway's ignorance and misapprehensions, the pattern of her understanding of the world. Then, once they reached home, he'd begin her proper education there and, while educating her, make notes on the ways she thought and her feelings and responses and see if a human creature who had no grasp of herself as a face and a body and a being in space could learn to be a lady according to the customs and expectations of modern society. And beyond that – his mother Fidelia would impart the accomplishments required of a young woman; she would spring at the opportunity of moulding the raw material of a wild girl and her cubs, too – they'd live in the fresh air, grow strong and well and ruddy.

He was possessed of his vision: his propitious fate had delivered this wild creature to him with a purpose.

His hand was very strong: he opened the bidding with a quint.

Winwalloe nodded. 'That's good.'

'I also have a tierce. And a septième.'

'That's good, too.' The captain was leaning into the lamp on the table to see his cards better, as if by examining them they might change.

'And fourteen tens.' (How astute he'd been not to use all five of his possible discards, but to hold on to the three tens, throwing the jack of hearts and the queen of diamonds, hoping for the fourth ten and keeping his length in spades.)

Winwalloe groaned.

'Come now, as they say, the night is young.'

Skipwith laid down the card for the first trick with an exultant declaration of his opening score.

'So I lead, my dear captain, with sixty-eight in my hand . . . Sixty-nine . . .' He began paying out his long suit in spades. 'Ninety,' he said, 'with an unbroken run, as you know, old boy, we move ahead by leaps and bounds.'

Winwalloe's fingers hovered miserably over his hand, trying to pick the right discard.

'Ninety-one . . . Ninety-two, ninety-three, ninety-four,' continued Skipwith, implacably. 'Ninety-five.'

Now, with his spades out, he had to use his memory. He'd have to lose the king of hearts that he'd unfortunately picked up from the table to the ace in Winwalloe's hand, but he'd play it last. That left him exposed to his opponent's diamonds, including the ace-king, so he mustn't allow Winwalloe to lead, though he might be able to use his singleton ten of diamonds to capture the king, and bring his ace of diamonds down in the last trick.

He saw a way, and led the ten of clubs: 'Ninety-six.'

Winwalloe slowly fished out his king, laid it on the trick, muttered as he took it, 'One'. He looked wretched, as if Skipwith's playing would make the card disappear. Even if his luck changed, this single round had augmented his losses by an amount that seemed irrecuperable.

On the afternoon of the third day after their discovery, when Leto came up the companionway from the cabin, the eyes of the whole crew were on her and Skipwith. Strugwell was watching from his post by the chicken coop, where he took out his fury on this turn of events by cursing the hens for not laying more, kicking at the wire till they fluttered and squawked in panic. Behind his eyes, he could see that woman writhing and squealing in the cabin; kissing and swallowing as that fop stuck himself into her, shouting no doubt. They were spreading a malignancy through the boat; turning it to a floating stew when such things should happen on land, down dark alleys in cities that could be left securely behind. Carrying the infection with them: Strugwell's whole being churned at the thought of such dissipation on board and he picked out a chicken whose neck feathers had been pecked out, leaving the scrawny mottled skin exposed, and twisted the bald place till she stopped squawking.

The children stirred various emotions, by contrast; on the afternoon of the second day, for alliances and enmities moved fast in the closed world of the ship, they had almost become mascots; the second mate had stopped carping at Teal for neglecting his usual post and duties, and first showed the boy, Phoebus, and then Phoebe, when she wanted to be included, how to pull at the goat's udders. They were apt learners, curious as kittens.

'What kind of a name is that?' asked Teal when Phoebus told him.

Phoebus pointed to the sun, with a solemn gesture, then to himself; this was followed by a quick grin. So the crew started teasing the child, calling him, with not a little touch of sarcasm at first, Little Sunshine, and Sonny Boy, until the nicknames grew shorter and shorter and the note of mockery faded. As for Phoebe, she was already called Bebe by her brother, and this stuck.

The captain no longer gave the order that the twins should be shut back up again in the crate, and even smiled at their antics as they scrapped and tumbled together in the shade under the longboat which they had demarcated 'Home'. As the captain looked on, misgivings at this softening of naval discipline shadowed his eyes even while he held back from protests. For soon, the problem would be over.

When Leto came up that second afternoon, she was holding a second orange Skipwith had given her in her hand, and she ran over to her children and squatted down with them and began peeling it; its sharp sweetness pricked the air.

Teal said, 'I want some'. Since Leto had been discovered, his lessons with Skipwith had ceased. The boy only came to mind when Skipwith needed him to keep watch on the twins, and he wanted to engage the attention of Leto, who would only comply with his early tests if Teal stood somehow between the children, the cook and the rest of the crew.

Leto plucked off a segment of the orange, and handed it to him.

On this occasion, the crew were watching; oranges weren't taken on board, or any fruit for that matter. A luxury, useless and expensive, perishing fast, spreading mould to other foodstuffs, taking up room: there were dozens of reasons that Strugwell rejected fruit.

Now the cook caught the whiff of the orange on the air, and sniffed, and he lunged out and snatched the piece from Teal's hand and dashed it on to the deck and then seized first Phoebus and then Phoebe and pulled what remained of the orange from their grasp. Clutching Teal by the hair and ear, he hauled him away, bouncing him like a stuffed doll along the deck and down the companionway to the galley.

'No more fun and games for you,' he roared. 'This ship isn't a bloody nursery.'

Leto shrank into the crate, cradling the twins against the sounds of the beating that rose from the galley and were amplified in the hull, resonating out over the calm of the sunny sea.

So two more days passed, on the open sea under the gently waxing moon after nightfall. In that time, they did not see another vessel.

But on the following day, Skipwith noticed markers in the water, where nets had been sunk below the surface by fishermen for collecting in the evening; the occasional gaff-rigged small craft began to appear in the distance.

'We must be nearing land,' he said. 'Why? I thought we were making straight for more friendly waters.'

Winwalloe's weathered countenance turned pale with determination. 'I'm in command of this ship, Giles, unless you've forgotten. And we cannot proceed another seven hundred miles with this stowaway and her accursed sprogs. She's an evident danger—' His eyes met Skipwith's for an instant, and his reproach was clear. 'We're heading for port, for Feltimye. It's a comparatively civilised place, sees a lot of traffic. We're putting them off there.

'She's caused quite enough trouble – the order of the boat and the men have been disturbed. That lad's mind hasn't been on his duties, either. Occupied with keeping those children out of mischief – have you ever seen such climbers? In and out of the tackle and the rigging and the sail store as if this was a playground. I've penalised Strugwell for that outburst by docking his pay, but that's not adding to the warmth and fellow feeling on board ... And you're not yourself, Giles. Stop to consider. Have you given a thought to your inventory, your notes, your sketches, the apparatus you need to present to the Admiralty to preserve your finds in the way they doubtless deserve? If I wasn't a man of good, common sense, I'd say she'd bewitched you.'

'You can't mean this. You know I won the girl off you fair and square. I want to take her and her whelps back home, train them up to our ways, and see what happens. She's a crucial part of the expedition's discoveries.'

Skipwith's habitually light manner was failing. The captain did not meet his eyes. 'Oh in God's name, don't, Geoffrey, don't do this. It's shameful. It's ungentlemanly. I never thought I'd be reminding you of your relation to your maker, but in this case, you will be doing something, I swear, that's wrong in the sight of God. Of your god. Who happens to be hers, in case you've forgotten? You can't just hand her over to the heathen. I'll denounce your actions in the Admiralty, in the newssheets, in the report on the expedition that I'll see to the press, up and down St James's. I won't allow it.'

Winwalloe was trembling in his attempt to control his indignation. 'You are threatening me, Sir Giles, when I am doing my duty as the captain of this ship to deliver us and the cargo safely home. Go ahead, make your complaints. I don't think your interest in this common female criminal will convince many of your lofty ideals.'

'In that case, I will call in my debt, and you, as a gentleman, are required to honour it.'

The captain jibbed, and made another attempt at asserting his will. 'You have the most extraordinary notions of value. First these battered old featureless bits of rock and stone, retrieved and shipped at such a cost to man and beast, and now, in broad daylight, even when the port is locked way and the night's fancies are banished, you want to persist in your folly about a worthless vagrant and her savage brood. I feel, as the commanding officer on board this ship, and as your friend, Giles, that I can't even entertain the idea.'

'If that is so, I require you to write me a banker's draft now, for the full amount, Geoffrey.'

The captain put up his hands. 'There are many days' sailing still.'

'No, there'll be no more piquet between us. I expect that note, in my hand, today.'

'You're cold as steel, Giles. I wouldn't expect it of an Englishman, of Her Majesty's guest on this ship.'

'I could say the same to you, of an officer of your rank, indeed. And it shall be made known, up and down the city, that you do not honour your debts when they're called in.'

So the bargain was struck, it seemed.

Skipwith, sitting across the table from Leto in his cabin, opened the map and indicated their passage.

'We've another week before we sail through the straits, and up to Parthenopolis, where we'll take on supplies, water, and so forth. Then depending on the winds, a few more days before we reach the Pillars of Hercules. Once safely through them—' He paused. 'We'll face some wild water, but we'll survive. We'll make libations to the old gods for calm conditions,' he said, laughing. 'Then we make for the south coast of Albion and put into shore; we'll travel by coach to Enoch. The marbles will follow. You'll be coming with me. You and the children. You'll be under my protection. My mother will help me educate you in our ways. You'll see, in a short time, you'll become just like one of us.'

4

The Bronze Fly

Sir Giles Skipwith showed his new protégée, Lettice the stowaway, the map of their destination; he pointed to the long cloud shape that the city of Enoch made where it lay along three bends of a wide, thrusting river; he described its towers and temples, its arsenal and barracks, palaces and smaller dwellings. 'It glitters,' he told her, 'from the glass in the buildings – imagine! Glass sheeting used as if it was cheap as straw-baked brick.' It was a city in ferment, as he described it, pullulating and loud, a crossroads, a hub, an entrepôt, a market for a myriad goods and services and currencies and manufactures – and foodstuffs. 'It's the city built by Cain – and did Abel build one? *Could* Abel have built one?' It was a place on this earth teeming with angels of the old order, who may be fallen into the corruption of the world, but were mighty, vigorous, full of energy for new enterprises, more strivings, fresh inventions.

'He painted a bright picture to us,' Leto told the children. 'He said, "I want you to feel at home there". We'll be safe, and you won't be hungry any more, or thirsty. You'll be part of somewhere – you'll belong.'

She couldn't help letting a small sigh escape.

Teal was sitting on a bale of rope, within earshot, playing quietly on a whistle, observing the twins and their mother. He put it down and called out to the little boy.

'Enoch's where I lived when I was your age,' he said. 'Near the river. I know it – as well as I know my own mother.' He stuck the whistle back between his lips, and breathed out the sad tune,

   '"O where's all the men of this house
    That call me Lamkin?

And where's all the women of this house
       That call me Lamkin?"

'But I haven't seen Enoch for a long while now. You'll like it, Lettie, when we get there.'

'Tell us something about Enoch then,' demanded Bebe.

Teal hummed at her,
       ' "They're at the far well washing,
         'Twill be long 'ere they come in." '

'No, Teal, please tell us something real.' The little boy was solemn. Teal's bruised face brightened as he continued teasing the children,
       ' "O shall I kill her, nurse?
         Or shall I let her be?"

'What do you think, Bebe? Shall he kill the wicked woman?'

The little girl laughed and sang out with him:
       ' "O kill her, kill her Lamkin,
         For she ne'er was good to me." '

'I'll tell you what I learned, today,' Leto began, as the twins squirmed, giggling at Teal. 'Listen, come.'

But Teal went on, teasing them:
       ' "O scour the basin, nurse
         And make it fair and clean,
       For to keep this lady's heart's blood,
         For she's come of noble kin." '

'Do people do that in Enoch?' asked Phoebus.

'Oh yes,' said Teal.

'No, no,' said Leto, and hurriedly began whispering a smiling story, about Enoch, that Skipwith had told her, remembering a tale of Parthenopolis from his grandfather:

'The Bronze Fly.

'Once upon a time, Enoch had a severe problem with flies. Flies everywhere, in the soup, in the eyes of ponies, swarming on the food displayed in the markets; when you went to bed you had to wrap yourself in a cloth from top to toe to stop them buzzing you while you slept. The ill were especially vulnerable. The rich would pay someone to fan them all day and all night. But it was impossible: more and more flies spawned and grew – some of them were small and black and darted about, stinging people . . .'

'And animals,' put in Bebe.

'Yes, and animals. Even the most placid milchcow could be maddened by them and go on a rampage.'

'Flies come to Enoch when it's thundery, in late summer,' said Teal. He was still piping, softly, looking out to sea with his back to them. But Leto could sense the boy was listening; every day he moved his vantage point closer to them, and the children provoked more frequently the quick smile of comprehension that unfurrowed his thin face for a flash.

'Other flies were huge and electric blue and bumbling. But all of them were foul pests and in their wake they left tainted meat and rotten fruit, dirty water, disease, death.

'So the people of Enoch were desperate. Then, one day, a man appeared and said he could free the city from the plague – on condition they rewarded him handsomely. He wanted to rule over Enoch in return for ridding the whole city of flies, and they said, yes, but secretly, in their hearts, they plotted not to do anything of the kind.'

Phoebe was cuffing her brother for more room, closer to her mother. Leto rearranged them to sit side by side, and hushed them.

'Go on,' urged Phoebus, pushing at his sister in return. 'You stopped the story.'

Phoebe opened her mouth to bawl.

'Listen and be quiet,' said Leto, moving her hand as if to smother her. 'Don't you want to hear about the fly-catcher?'

She was feeling very weary.

Phoebus was cub-like when he romped, but usually alert to the danger zones in the games that he and his sister played. He was the sunnier child, but something vulnerable also stirred in his depths. A deep seam of solemn concentration ran through his cavorting: his urchin ways arose from a determination to please, because he knew, from all they had been through together, what the consequences of failure might be. He kept a close watch, and Leto recognised something of her own tenacity in him.

Phoebe was much trickier, for she would draw her brother on, and then, at the first opportunity, she would start to wail, and batter him with her fists or bite his arm until she left ring-marks in his flesh, and cry for her mother to punish him. Again and again, Leto would try to make peace between them.

'Try not to be so rough. She's smaller than you.'

Phoebe was much smaller, but her head was big, too big for the tiny, peaky features that appeared in her round face. A furrow between her brows gave her the anxious look, sometimes, of a little man in the moon, frowning with down-turned mouth, isolated and melancholy in the night sky wiped of stars by his bright presence. Sometimes, Phoebe even filled her mother with a kind of revulsion – not all the time, but often enough for Leto to have to make an effort to quell her irritation. The child was clinging and whiny, but Leto knew her whining wasn't only the effect of the assault on her when she was a baby. She called her mother's attention to her puniness and frailty in ways she knew better not to do with others, for whimpering invites kicking, she had learned young. So with strangers, she was mutinous, using Leto as a shield, ducking into the shelter of her mother's lap, her arms, only to peep out now and then, with her thumb stuck angrily in her mouth.

Phoebe was thumping her brother now. 'He hit me first!' she wailed.

'Do try, Phoebus.'

But Phoebe squealed, and so her mother stroked her head as she took up the thread of the story. The child's hair was sticky with salt and matted. Phoebe's neediness only brought back many things Leto did not want to remember or relive.

She made an effort and began, 'The fly-catcher made a very, very big fly, which looked just like a real one. But it was made of metal, like a clasp or a buckle, and he had it trundled by carthorses to the main gates of the city, and winched up to the top. And the other flies, when they saw it, they fled. Every fly in the world, even if it didn't see the bronze monster the wanderer had made, kept away from Enoch because it looked so ferocious, so hungry, as if it would eat anything and everything that came its way.'

'And then?'

'And then suddenly, what?' Phoebus prodded her.

She wasn't certain she knew; Skipwith's version had been very quick. It was strange how difficult it was to describe a safe place. Perils faced, dangers overcome, sickness conquered, troubles quelled, all manner of evils staved off – she had no other way into the secrets of the haven she still hoped might lie ahead, within their reach.

Homesickness for the Citadel stabbed her. Even for Karim, who had turned coward, even for Cunmar, who had bragged and overestimated his power and failed to protect her. She pulled the twins closer, the vital principle pulsing under their warm flesh reassuring her that the future was possible.

She was improvising:

'So the fly-catcher went to the ruler of the city and to the councillors and asked for the reward they had promised. But they said, "Please Sir Fly-Catcher, can't you help us with the leeches which are breeding in our water supply and poisoning all our wells?"

'And he said, "All right, I'll do my best. But then you must give me my reward."

'And he made a beautiful, intricate leech that was twelve foot long and articulated from head to toe so that it slithered and wriggled as if it were alive – and it terrorised all the leeches in the whole province because it was . . . twelve foot long and as thick in the waist as a thirty-year-old oak tree.'

'Ugh,' said Phoebe, squirming with pleasure.

'Yuck,' echoed her brother, a little uncertainly.

'The same thing happened: only this time, the fly-catcher, the leech-killer, was getting impatient and angry.

'So when they said to him, whining, that the population was suffering from tapeworm and that sometimes children opened their mouths and out came a snake, twelve inches long, he thought to himself, should I bother with this ungrateful city any more? But he did. He made a coiled and scaly dragon out of gold. It had only one-eye, like a tapeworm, and a big, loose, baggy mouth ready to snaffle up anything. He set it up on a marble plinth in the main square of the city and it so alarmed all the smaller, skimpier tapeworms that were planning to invade the intestines of the people that they flung themselves into the marshlands far beyond the city walls, where they were all caught by herons very quickly.

'Then he went to the ruler and the councillors and he asked for his reward.

'And they said, "Sir Fly-Catcher, Sir Leech-Killer, Sir Worm-Slayer, we are very well now and we don't need you any more. Thank you for your trouble." '

The children giggled. Teal smiled: he was beginning to catch the drift.

'He protested, and showed them the agreements that had been drawn up, signed and sealed. But the lawyers in the council scoffed, and pointed to the small print. When he still stood his ground, they started threatening him, and then hustled him out of the council chamber under armed guard and marched him to one of the city gates, the one where the fly was suspended.

'They threw him out of Enoch and he fell in the mud outside on his face and bruised his right hip and his right elbow, but he turned himself over and he spoke out in a big voice to the bronze fly above him.

'It began to shiver and shake and its bronze feelers to rattle and its metal wings to whirr and rustle until it roused itself fully and looked about with bulging eyes, took off jerkily from the gate and landed with a bumpety-bump beside its wounded maker.

'He gave it a key, and instructions what to do with the key, and the fly took off again, its shadow darkening the streets where it passed so that the people screamed and ran under its flight path, until it came to the west gate of the city, where the silver leech was hoisted in trophy. The fly manoeuvred the key into the place in the leech's head where its brain would be if leeches had brains, and wound it up. It began jerking and slithering down from the wall into the street, where it slipped through a manhole cover down into the city sewers. Enough citizens of Enoch saw it dropping itself down coil by coil for the word to spread fast that the most gigantic and indestructible and disgusting leech ever known in the history of the world had slipped into the water supply of Enoch, from where it would suck the marrow of human bones, the lymph from human tissue, the blood from the hearts and livers of every man and woman in the city until they were sucked as dry and friable as the last withered leaves rustling on the twigs of winter trees.

'But the leech would pick on only those who were strong and powerful – its mechanism was wound up so that it avoided children's bodies and old men and women's.

'The bronze fly, seeing its orders accomplished with regard to the silver leech, whirred on with zeal and reached the main square, where it landed, scattering all the market stallholders and the shoppers and the ceremonial guardsmen who dropped their musical instruments and ran for their lives. The fly inserted the key into a hole in the side of the giant tapeworm's head, in the small round lidless slit that serves for an ear in lizards and dragons, and the giant tapeworm began to move, to writhe and undulate and spool where it stood so that its oiled metal scales scattered sequins of light all around. Then this loathsome kind of a dragon – this terrible machine – suddenly darted off its plinth and began to rampage through Enoch. It swallowed everyone who came across its path and minced them in its mechanical guts and turned them to scrap metal fit only for cheap cauldrons for boiling soiled linen.

'Meanwhile Sir Fly-Catcher got up from his prone position outside the gates where he'd been tossed, and, hearing the screams of fear and howls of dismay rising all over Enoch, he sauntered off with a smile twitching the corner of his mouth and a merry song on his lips.

'Nobody ever saw him again in Enoch, though there have been other wonders that might be his handiwork in other places – but they can wait for another time. Sometimes you may spot him going by and you'll know him by his song:

> "Tirra-lirra, my sweet pretty,
>
> Your shadow walks with you,
>
> But not as close as I,
>
> Oh, never as close as I,"

sings Sir Fly-Catcher, as he goes jauntily along.'

Teal was breathing into his whistle to Leto's singsong.

'Because the fly and the leech and the great tapeworm didn't attack or eat the children of Enoch, the children paid attention, and, as they were growing up and taking charge themselves, they always remembered the mean way their ruler and councillors had behaved. And they resolved to be different.

'Since then, Enoch still suffers from flies and leeches and tapeworms and other problems and parasites and poisons. But not as badly,' she added, seeing the twins' expression. 'And the main thing is, Sir Fly-Catcher, Sir Leech-Killer, Sir Worm-Slayer taught Enoch a lesson. And I'm told that, in consequence, Enoch prides itself that it is the market and factory of the world, but that its people are always paid a fair wage on time for their labour.

'This happened some long time ago, but the story hasn't been forgotten and its effects are still felt.'

'I don't think I want to go there,' said Phoebus in a tiny voice.

'I do,' said Phoebe. 'I want to see the big fly.'

'But it's gone, it's flown away,' her brother scoffed.

'No,' Leto promised them. 'It must be there still. In a museum. Enoch has many museums – for all its treasures. This boat is bringing them more.'

5

In the Caravanserai

Sir Giles Skipwith, lying in his starboard cabin, sleeping smilingly in his heavy curtained mahogany and brass box bed, did not hear the longboat draw up on the *Shearwater*'s other side, did not wake to the sounds of Strugwell unlocking the crate where Lettice the stowaway was quartered, using the key that Captain Winwalloe had made available to the cook; nor did he stir when the cook pulled Phoebus out, squalling and screaming, and dropped in an undertone the terse threat to his mother:

'Want to see the boy again?' He paused. She was struggling with cramped sleep. 'Follow, then.'

Skipwith did not hear his ward, Lettice the stowaway, object of benign experiment and future daughter of Albion, whom he had won honourably at cards, scramble to her feet and snatch up her scared girl child, he missed the thumping of a body clambering down a ladder against the ship as Strugwell got into the longboat, which Teal in the stern was steadying against the *Shearwater*'s side as best he could. Nor did Giles wake to the sound of her scream, or to the threats of Strugwell that he would throttle Phoebus, whom he had by the neck in the crook of his arm, if she didn't leave off that noise, or the clatter of hull against hull as the dinghy pushed off, or the splash of the oars as Strugwell seized hold of them from Teal at the rudder and began straining hard to put distance between himself and the *Shearwater*. He was dreaming of cards, of opening hands magnificent and costly, flush with crowns and sceptres and ringing down coin for him; the stowaway woman was now an ace, now a jack in a tight fitting suit and rakish cap, bringing him a twist of fortune that almost made him chuckle aloud as he slept on in the silence that poured down from the fiery stars that perfect spring night, as the young mother and her children were carried ashore.

Teal was behind her, at the helm, and when she turned to look at him, he did not meet her eyes, but kept his look straight ahead; his small face pinched with tiredness; brought along as Strugwell's sidekick, doing what he was told. She could not read his thoughts. She was on the bench facing the cook, who had tossed Phoebus down in the prow like a bag of provisions.

'Give him to me now?' she asked.

'Do you want to get him drowned? Just sit still.'

Phoebus was whimpering, but she obeyed.

They entered a small harbour, as the sea turned to smoked silver in the first light of morning. Fishing tackle, hung up to dry, stood against the sky like gigantic cobwebs, and large butterfly eyes painted on the bowsprits of the fishing boats loomed through the grey freshness of the dawn. The cook pushed her up and off on to shore; after her sojourn on board, the ground tilted sickeningly underfoot.

Using a coil of rope lying in the bilge water, Strugwell tied a length between her ankles, then looped one end around Teal, the other around his own waist. Still with Phoebus in his grip, chucked under one arm like a roll of bedding, Jed Strugwell headed off, jerking his head to them to follow. People were stirring, in the cool of the morning, and they stared at the sight of the big-boned foreign man in his soiled breeches and tunic, with the limp child slung from his hip, and at the ragged threesome he was chivvying along.

'Don't you make a sound, or I'll . . .' he warned.

But the stowaway would not have made an appeal to the bystanders anyway; she knew better than to count on the kindness of strangers. To Teal, Strugwell need only start raising an arm for the cowed boy to flinch.

They left the small harbour square and turned down a covered market colonnade, where brightly wrapped women were settling down in front of large baskets of goods; the cook strode down the length of it to the end, Leto shuffling as best she could after him in her trammels. Phoebe was clinging to her like a squirrel up a tree; slung against her mother's breast with the silk scarf woven with silver thread that Skipwith had given her, one of the few things she had managed to scrabble together from the crate when Strugwell summoned her. The child was still so flimsy, still all fluff and no substance, still a nestling at three years old. She was bound to her offspring; all three of them victims as if buried alive in the same grave, grappling with one another, and as they struggled they only breathed in more earth to choke them. Their mother felt a rush of fury. Would she never be rid of this burden? Could she have left the girl on board, for Skipwith to take to Albion instead of her for his experiments? Would that have been the better choice? The twins were holding her, to an interminable destiny of maternity.

Phoebe was too scared to cry now, but her eyes were so wide that her whole face seemed to have become a single mask of fear. Her mother was floundering, as the salt in the sodden and chill rope quickly opened lesions in her legs.

Small octagonal tables were set out under the canopy and a few slow-moving men were gathered, drinking some bright green liquid from tall beakers. Strugwell looked about him. Then he shouted across, calling out a name, and one group of drinkers laughed, and nodded, and pointed to a house across the street; a small boy came up and tugged at Teal to bring him to the right door.

With Phoebus still dangling in his grasp, the child's face bright red from his head hanging down and jouncing to the cook's stride, Strugwell rang the bell to the side of the vast carved portal; the mother, hovering by, tried to reassure her son by making a silent face. A true note sounded, from a clay clapper within. Eventually, the scraping of the bolts was followed by the opening of the small door set into the larger one. Strugwell conferred. They entered. The door closed again; some moments passed; he muttered to them,

'Now, don't do or say anything until I tell you to.'

He was quivering with anticipation, as they waited just inside the entrance. Phoebus was deathly quiet now in his fright.

Deeper inside the building, the night had not yet drawn to a close: perhaps daylight never did penetrate the tiny, high inner courtyard, where a small fountain played on the patterned tiles of the floor and a sequence of slender arcades provided shelter that was neither indoors nor out of doors, but a zone in between. Men were reclining on couches there, smoking, talking, drinking. The murmur that rose from the company was muted, thick with slumber. Steaming scents of peppermint infusions and varied incenses suffused the enclave, drifting over other smells of spitting fat and roast meats. Though it was early morning, it was still night inside these walls.

Leto's heart leapt; she might be abandoned here, among the aromas and the slow slow business of this harbour hostelry, this caravanserai. She was thinking, *This would be a better life, better than anything we've had till now, better than the wolf's den, better than the ship's hold or the crate on the* Shearwater. To her then, slavery appeared a sweeter life by far than any she had yet known.

She was reminded of the Keep and of Cunmar's stories about his people, who were more likely to cram children with kisses and sweetmeats and cry when a favourite has scraped his knees in a fall and feed them than beat and starve them. She told herself she and the children could be happy there in the nocturnal comforts, for she was angry with Skipwith, and angry with herself for trusting in his promises, for paying attention to his plans, for imagining herself – and the twins – as Enochites, moving freely through that vast, bustling city.

The bolt of the door shot home as the youth on the gate left to deliver his message. Her heart was pounding as they waited for him to return. Strugwell was running with sweat. His long forearms and shaggy calves exposed, his shirt and breeches patched and grimy, bursting out of his jacket that had gone at the armholes, he looked as comfortable in that pleasure house as a mule in a lace bed. He had never dealt with Ibn Hamiz directly before, but he had handled a consignment of blue-and-white porcelain that had been salvaged from a sunken ship; Ibn Hamiz and his great annual caravan to the metropole was the booty's ultimate destination. Now he was going to meet him: a legend among sailors.

Had Hamiz been a poet? Ballad-singers gave him the authorship of some of their tales. But he had left his inland, desert birthplace, and, rigging up a small craft with a single sail, moved southwards, showing all the daring that later made him a most feared pirate on the northern littoral. He gathered there a gang of followers, for he was attractive to many men – some called them malcontents, but others, as the songs sang, saw them as free spirits – and they ranged through the Inland Sea from the Pillars of Hercules to the harbours of the Ophiri to the east. From their island fastnesses, from a harbour that lay concealed behind toothed, red cliffs, he would dart out in rapid, light ketches that could outpace almost all the laden boats that were lumbering home along those sea roads; the swiftness and cruelty of Ibn Hamiz on his raids became the stuff of tales of terror, some of them no doubt enhanced by himself. Then, he tired of this way of life as well: after fifteen years of lucrative predations, he took his great spoils and set himself up in his palace in Feltimye, and concentrated on the traffic in . . . almonds and angelica. And in other goods and treasures in demand in the luxurious metropole to the east. His sumptuous style of living in his harbour stronghold, where the windows were made of perforated alabaster and the fountains were tiled with cunning geometry, where the baths flowed with almond oil and rosewater, continued his renegade's glamour among all traffickers and sailors of those waterways.

All this made Strugwell sweat with excitement. He had brought Ibn Hamiz something special and he expected a commensurate reward, and he was hitching up his belt and adjusting his balls in readiness for the deal he must strike, when the gatekeeper came back and conducted them along one side of the arcade to a private room.

Excitedly, Strugwell said to his captive, 'No making scenes now. And no crying.' He glared at Phoebus, and with a rough hand pushed the curls off the boy's face. 'Must look pretty now.' With a thick finger to his lips, he commanded Phoebe to stay quiet.

Then he prodded their mother to precede him as he made his way into the circular room off the central courtyard.

Lanterns hung low over the couches, the stars pierced in their polished metal sides glowing deep crimson. Against damson-coloured cushions, fringed and embroidered in golden gimp, lay the former pirate with whom Strugwell had business. Strugwell was taken aback: he hadn't expected he could have become so very indoors in appearance. For Ibn Hamiz wasn't ruddy, nor was he burly: the renegade who'd inspired terror on the sea by his savagery, and deep and widespread envy of his accumulated, ill-gotten treasure, now had a large, blue-veined nose and swollen hands, with blackened nails, and he was inhaling deeply from a coiled pipe on the low brass table. As he did so, the water-cooled flask belched a slow, sparkling bubble.

The cook jabbed at the marine chart he pulled from the waistband of his breeches.

'I've brought you, sir, something very rare, and that's God's truth', began Strugwell.

The figure on the couch patted the air languidly, as if Strugwell were an over-eager hound, and raised his eyebrows, appraising their ragged band.

The cook pushed Phoebus forward towards the disdainful, lolling figure on the couch. His mother sprang after him, but was jerked by the rope till she lost her balance and fell against the cushions arranged at right angles to the couch. A servant pulled her to her feet; another instantly sprinkled rosewater from a special thyrsus on the places that she had sullied by contact.

The merchant in almonds and angelica sat Phoebus down on the divan beside him, tickled his cheek, and offered him sweetmeats, powdered with fine sugar and dripping with honey and nuts. The boy checked with his mother first; she hesitated. Eating together creates a bond. Eating from his fingers will make an even closer bond between them. One seed, or was it seven seeds? It took so little to be captured by a living death.

But at Phoebus's look, hollow with longing, she nodded. Phoebus had never had a sweetmeat, only raw honey from the comb when they lived among the tombs.

Ibn Hamiz caressed the boy's cheek, with fastidious fingertips, testing the sunburned skin, but keeping him at a distance, and he watched, smiling, as Phoebus took one cake, then another, and then another. When he had finished a fourth, the merchant opened the child's tunic, and looked at his throat and chest, lifting his arms and kneading his thighs. With a wave of his long hand, on which the veins stood out, he pointed to the boy's crotch.

'Go on,' muttered Strugwell to Leto. 'Show his jewels.'

She knelt in front of her son and the merchant, and lifted the boy's tunic.

The merchant nodded. The child was, as was to be expected in merchandise from Enoch, uncircumcised.

'It can be done,' said Strugwell, still very loud. 'Easy.' He made a gesture he knew well from his kitchen, as if shucking a peascod.

'Ahaha, that's very true,' he replied, and Strugwell recoiled from his mockery. Again, the cook was startled, in spite of the rumours he'd heard: he could hear, in the merchant's rumbling consonants, the sound of his native country.

Then the merchant peered more closely, and, taking the edge of the tunic from Leto's hand pulled it up to lay bare the boy's whole torso.

'Where is the navel?' he asked, passing his hand over the thin, smooth stomach. 'This is uncommon.'

Leto tugged the tunic down again.

Strugwell said, 'I've been trying to tell you – they're wonders.' He paused. 'They're treasures: beyond price. He doesn't have one! And nor does she!'

Phoebe, standing on her feet and ignored while Phoebus occupied the others, crept near the table and surreptitiously took a cube of pale rose translucent sweetness, studded with almonds, and soft and snowy with sugar. Phoebus, too, as soon as the two men began bargaining, wriggled off the couch to be nearer the table and its heaped trays of bonbons and pastries. Teal followed suit; they competed for the pile, but as the plates were emptied, the attendants heaped them up again. Soon, even these children, never before acquainted with puff pastry or sherbet or sugar, were satisfied and sat back, licking their fingers.

'How much for the boy?' shouted Strugwell. 'He's the prize. But the whole lot is real value. They're like you like them, and they'll fatten up nicely.'

'Buy me too,' their mother began begging. 'Don't part us. Take me with them.' She lay huddled on the floor, clasping the merchant's arm and kissing his hand passionately till her tears bathed him. He looked down at her fastidiously, and Strugwell made a motion to pull her off. But Ibn Hamiz tapped the cook's arm with the stem of his pipe to restrain him, and then indicated a hexagonal stool set some distance from the table. Jed Strugwell folded his big limbs on to the tiny seat. He was protesting, 'We haven't got all day, I've to get back to my ship. You've got to make a decision now. How much for the three of them? Teal, out of the way. I don't want him buying you as well. You're coming back with me.' But the ship-boy didn't move; he was sniffing entranced at the smoke rising from the flask.

Meanwhile, Ibn Hamiz was indicating that the children's mother should lift her face; keeping his distance, he signalled for her to open her mouth so he could peer at her teeth and gums; he made no nod. Then he beckoned Phoebe over, and tested her flesh, looked her curiously up and down, and when he found she had no navel, too, he glanced over at the raw-boned sailor from Enoch who had brought them to him.

Strugwell leapt up from the stool, pulled out a map.

'See here,' he said. He jabbed at the edge of the sea on the chart.

229

'Mermaids. We found this lot at sea. Mermaids aren't fish-tailed, not the way it's painted in pictures like here. Sir Giles Skipwith says they be birds, really. Sirens aren't fishes, but seabirds. This little lot landed in our ship; they're petrels turned human, dropped from the air. You'll never find any other like them. They're wonders, I tell you. You should hear them patter and tattle, like nestlings squeaking for food. But this lot don't squeak, at least not much. They coo and sing, like they really are birds.

'They're rare, not of this world, more rare and precious than anything. I could take them to Enoch and show them there round the fairs for a fortune, but my captain thinks they're ill-omened—' he stopped short. 'Captain Winwalloe gave me orders to get them off the ship, seeing as they're eating our victuals and causing disturbance.'

Ibn Hamiz tossed his head, and an attendant in the corner approached, to whom he gave orders.

He said to the cook, 'The woman is young, but she's all used up. She'll do in the scullery.' He paused. 'Take the children to be washed. And the woman. Dress her like one.'

Strugwell made gestures at her body, shaping breasts, belly in the air. 'She's fertile. She'll have more like this lot. That's worth a lot of money,' he emphasised. 'They say you require foreigners to be special guards in the capital. The boy's healthy, he's pretty, it's diabolical the way he talks at his age. He'll soon grow strong.'

Ibn Hamiz indicated a second pipe on the table. 'Smoke, Mr Strugwell, to seal our pact.'

Strugwell did so, and coughed.

'Try again, it's pleasant, you'll see.'

The cook obeyed him. He breathed in the blue, scented smoke, barely controlling his glee at the merchant's consent.

Teal exchanged looks with the stowaway and her twins, and, when the time came to say a silent goodbye, he was crying; they had not been so long together on the boat, but they had changed life on board for the ship-boy, and he was now condemned to return, without the solace of their company. But at that moment, from the very depths of the boy's cowed and beaten being, out of that spirit that had been maimed by repeated brutality, he dug up a flicker of flame that was to make a bonfire of his tormentor's glory and greed.

6

A Lump of Haschisch

The caravan would leave for the capital in five weeks; Phoebus would be taken then with three others, for training as palace guards in the metropolis. But in the meantime, the boy's new prison house became a playground; after a day of wariness, he joined the little gang of young boys and was soon skittering and rushing through the rambling rooms and corridors and courtyards of the winding establishment. Now and then someone fetched him a slap with a laughing shout of protest, but he was mostly indulged, with titbits to eat from the cooks and the maids, prodding of his ribs to deploring clicks and many exclamations at his beauty, accompanied by vigorous spitting to the floor to prevent the jealousy of demons harming a favoured child.

The second week, Phoebe came to her mother to report in tears that she'd been banished from her brother's games; lying on her tummy under the low table by the cauldron where Leto was washing dishes, she wailed into the dirt floor. Her mother shook her head.

'Phoebus can't own up to you as his little sister in front of those big boys – it's far too much to ask of any man!'

Now dressed in pink silk trousers under a white damask tunic, Phoebe petulantly kicked off the embroidered slippers she had been given and complained that the women in the household tickled and pinched her and chucked her under the chin. But she, too, would be going with the merchant's goods and baggage; and she was already growing into her future part; she would be sold as a drollery, a funny-looking girl who was no beauty, but would amuse a connoisseur with her antics and her temperament.

The twins' mother still did not know what plans the great merchant had for her. As she carried out the long and heavy sequence of tasks allotted to her in the scullery from first waking to the last moments when she fell, like a lump of lead, on to the ground to sleep, the impending loss of the children was wedged inside her, an ache that continued unappeasable.

The thought of being parted from them shadowed Leto's every move. As she pulled the wood from the pile and built up the fire under the hot water cauldron, as she hauled water from the cistern in the centre of the yard, and filled jars to sluice into the copper basins to do the dishes, she kept seeing the scene unfold in her mind's eye: the two of them hoisted on to the waggons with the baggage, with herself standing there, clutching at the load, running behind them, collapsing.

There were five women on permanent detail, besides herself, in the pungent and steamy back courtyard where the cooking took place in one corner, where there stood a brick oven with low grills laid over wood fires on one side of it, while in another, the cauldron for the laundry squatted mightily on a platform of bricks. The laundry took place once a week, and she was conscripted to draw water and keep the fire going for the washerwomen as well, back and forth, back and forth, with the buckets slung on a yoke. Across the yard, the cooks daily brewed and boiled, grilled and broiled lamb and sausage, rice and beans, peppermint tea and coffee. She wasn't allowed to handle any food herself, but she was apportioned, at the end of the day, generous amounts of leftovers to eat.

These times, in the scullery, were the first she had spent apart from the twins since they were born, for longer than a few hours – she'd foraged without them in the mountains, and there'd been the time spent in Skipwith's cabin, at her 'lessons', but otherwise they'd been stuck fast together. But Phoebus didn't even always come to sleep beside her any more, and she found that she craved him: his was the only love that was left to her besides Phoebe's, and the little girl was so demanding then, she didn't give out strength, but seemed to drain her mother for her own use.

So her mind twisted and turned, however arduous her tasks were, as she cast about for a way to prevent them being taken from her. She had once possessed great gifts of transformation, but she had mislaid the trick of them on her way down the years. As her reflection stretched down over time it had thinned and faded, as she had seen in Skipwith's cheval glass; the light that carried her form no longer gathered enough power to change things; she was lit wanly now. So instead, she entertained ideas from other kinds of stories, not of metamorphosis and escape, but of romance, rescue and recognition: of a young nobleman who, passing by, might peep into the kitchen yard and see through the grease and the grime and loosen her filthy hair from its headrag and see that it could be soft and scented and silky and bright. That Lycia, so so far away now, would fling herself to rescue Leto again, all teeth and tongue and foaming saliva and carry her off in her jaws to safety once more. Was any of the cats that meowed and prowled around the refuse a magic creature who would all of sudden give voice and talk to her and find a way out of the plot she was caught in? Perhaps somebody would turn up with a perverse love of slatterns and skivvies and want to spend a fortune to take her as his slave of the hearth, meeting all his insatiable desires for dirt and degradation. And want her so much she could set conditions. Yes, she would grovel on her hands and knees if he . . . Only if he . . . Might she find, in the refuse from the kitchens, in the piles of uneaten scraps in the dishes and pans she was scrubbing, a magic token, a ring she could rub and then vanish? Would a single feather plucked from one of the fowl being prepared for the table have the power of lifting its owner high above the rooftops? Or would Ibn Hamiz remember her with a sudden movement of mercy? Would he summon her, would he suddenly consider that the mother of wonder children must be a wonder herself? Would Skipwith come after her? She even hoped for that. She had been too wary with that man and his self-love. She hadn't made him understand enough or he could have prevented the captain and the cook's greed. They could be approaching Enoch by now.

She plotted as she did the dishes: she could show herself to her enemies as she had been when Cunmar loved her. She could amaze them with what she knew and what she had seen. But soon after, she would realise she was all used up, though she wasn't yet seventeen years old. She saw the experienced trader's dismissal in that expression of distaste when he examined her; she knew she wasn't playing a part in a fairy story.

'Yet sometimes, I have to admit to you,' Kim heard her whispering from the screen, *'I liked being on my own.'*

The children would be off playing somewhere else: Phoebe was beginning to find her way round the household, and Phoebus, after a week's banishment of his sister, was now prepared to admit her existence to his fine, big new friends. They found her comical and appealing and let her take part in their make-believe. Phoebe was cast as the prisoner, the victim, the hostage, put in a chair, or against a door and told to stay there while the four boys, in two teams, fought for her future. When she got bored with her part, she trotted away to the bathhouse, where one of the maids cuddled her and fed her sugared almonds and marzipan.

Sometimes, as Leto was rubbing wood ash into the big terracotta vessels to draw up the fatty deposits of lamb stew and pigeon pie, and then plunging them into the clear hot water to rinse them, she felt peaceful. With her back to the bustle of the courtyard, wrapped in delicious smells – fruit logs burning and meat spitting into the charcoal, rosemary crushed to spice a dish, nuts roasting in a copper pan on the oven, garlic frying in oil – then the heartache eased and she even felt happy, and she wondered what life would be like without them.

'Maybe I should let them go,' Kim heard Leto from behind the monitor as he worked on the HSWU website through the night. *'Maybe they would flourish, as possessions of the court in the capital. Better than the continual series of catastrophes into which they were tossed, living with me. That's when the idea began to form: maybe I should give up the children. Maybe I was preventing them from thriving.'*

And Kim's thoughts turned to his own first mother, who had handed him over to Minta and Gerald; he tried never to think of her, or seek her out. He thought of the young women who hung around the station at Cantelowes.

His life had begun again when she gave him up; he was glad of it.

Though Leto had not cried before, except to bend the merchant's heart, the caravanserai's comforts were weakening her defences: now that she had food and shelter and – even – safety from violence and attack and death, it seemed, she found that she could mourn the future that she had lost.

People came and went in the courtyard. The guard changed and became less vigilant, so two house masseurs who were rivals for one of the cooks began to steal into the working women's enclave. They were

234

feverish in their courtship, and Leto, overhearing, felt a quick stab of envy at the giggles and kisses she overheard.

The name of the city in the valley, sixty miles north west of the port and the first stop the caravan would make, glittered and thrummed in their talk. Tirzah. If only she could join the caravan, somehow. Then maybe they could all reach the city together; disappear there, as she had hoped about Enoch when she was with Skipwith on board the *Shearwater*.

She hardly dared think of it, since, for fear of more bitter disappointment, she was trying to manage without hope altogether.

In Ibn Hamiz's household, the preparations for departure changed the mood from ambling pleasure to a sharper restlessness. There was a ceaseless flow of farriers, clients, merchants, middlemen, brokers, petitioners, pedlars, factors, vendors, craftsmen, beggars, dragomen, tooth-pullers, leech-dealers, while a myriad hangers-on swarmed through the compound; they haggled and huddled in its labyrinthine passages; in the hubbub, whispered deals and shrieking protestations – of probity, of cheapness – mixed into the thumping of freight, the thud of wadded bales; in coops chickens fluttered against their bonds, and the goats, waiting tethered to a post in the outer yard, bleated with apprehension. A week passed, then another; though the date of departure was drawing imminent, it was still not certain when the great caravan would move off.

Leto kept very quiet, trying to discover how she could join the train, who in the rambling household had the power to help her, who might give in to her entreaties. She paced her work in the scullery to the other women's rhythm, to make sure they couldn't reproach her with idleness, but not to irritate them by excess of zeal. She watched, and she was watched. Guards controlled access to the women's quarters; her post at the dirty dishes was far from the outer doors by which she had first entered, and she slept on the ground beside it. But not everybody's movements were as restricted as hers, and the children were the most mobile and the quickest to adapt and to learn. They told her things they'd picked up in a scrambled way, and Leto pieced them together with other bits and pieces she deciphered, and the rhythm that moved the tumult of Ibn Hamiz's teeming household gradually acquired shape and measure, clarity and pattern.

As Ibn Hamiz lay screened off from daylight at the centre of his operations, his influence coiled through the involutions of his establishment. Like the tendrils of some rampant, fast-growing and blooming vine, the kind that cascade in phosphorescent brightness on distempered walls outside in the sunshine, the former pirate's power curled through his household, hooking on to this servant and that child, tangling them all up in a web of relations, formal and informal, legal and other: he was weakened by his habit, and his savage life had aged him, but he had granted many favours, he had secured many deals against as many boons and as many threats, he had taken from people in such a way that all his profits appeared to be gifts; he had provided for many and he still did so. He was beloved and he was feared.

But Ibn Hamiz was ill.

The rumour began with the servants who attended him in the curtained alcove.

He was sleeping, sleeping, sleeping all the time. Business wasn't being attended to. In the middle of negotiations, he slumped into oblivion. Decisions were being made without his full awareness. His body no longer smelled of perfumes and haschisch, but emanated a dead whiff of camphor covering something else, something rotting.

The repercussions were quick and light but, to the twins' mother at her stack of dirty dishes, they were palpable. The caravan seemed about to burst its bonds, its great agglomeration bulging in readiness, yet still the order was not given to go. As the wait frayed the drovers' and merchants' patience, the stores began to be pilfered, the serving of meals became erratic, the laundrywomen became locked in excitable gossip with one another and the flow of visitors grew into a mêlée, crying for this and that, and demanding answers. But the overseers with their manifests and bills of lading were confused; contradictory instructions kept being given as different members of the household grappled for power.

In the alcove, Ibn Hamiz waved their demands away with a light moan.

Panic gripped the household, as fights broke out between contesting powers: between Ibn Hamiz's sons by different women and between them, the mothers of the chief pretenders, between his favourite bailiff and his overseers, and between their wives. The profuse tentacles of his powerful reach, which had caught up his business and his family into a tightly woven web, were being pulled down, just as a creeper is torn by a gale from its moorings against a wall.

Death: the simplest plot device of all. The one Leto never thought of when she was casting about helplessly for a way to join the caravan.

In the mounting quarrels and confusion, Phoebe suddenly heard a pipe playing beneath a window on to the alley that ran down one side of the building.

The words floated in to her head on the music:

> 'So many hairs as she unbound
> So many tears fell to the ground.'

Teal. It was one of his songs. The little girl tried to pull herself up on the ledge and look out of the window. But she was too small to climb up and so she called out into the air,

'Teal, Teal, is that you? It's me, Bebe!'

But her own piping was weak, so she ran to fetch Phoebus, who hung out of the high window, and saw that it was the ship-boy down below, sitting cross-legged, begging. So he ran to find something to throw, until the song broke off,

> ' "Gin I may choose how I shall die,
> I pray you, draw your sword on.
>
> "But first your mantle lay aside;
> A maiden's blood may spatter wide.
> 'Twere shame your clothes should a'be dyed." '

Teal uptilted his head to look up and cried out with joy: 'You're there! I was so hoping you were there. I knew you couldn't be far away, but I didn't know how to find you.'

He leapt to his feet, and he now put his mouth to the wall so that his words could travel up the surface without shouting.

'Tell her I'm here,' he whispered into the wall.

'Teal, Teal,' they chanted.

'Yes, yes, it's me. Tell her to come here, to talk to me.'

They ran into the courtyard with the news. Leto looked quickly around. She wasn't allowed to leave her corner of the yard, but vigilance was slackening these last days. She was tugged through the building by the twins, until they reached the window.

Their whispers crawled up and down the wall.

237

'Why are you here?'

'I jumped ship. Couldn't stand it.'

'Oh, no, Teal, you'll never be able to go back, you've turned yourself into a wanderer, a deserter, you'll face death if they find you.' The children's mother said all these things, though she was overjoyed to find him again. Then, still sending her words softly down the wall, she added, 'There's coming and going all through the house now. Take advantage of the chaos. Just walk in, as if you've got business. If you're challenged, say you've been summoned by—,' she mentioned one of the names she'd overheard in the inheritance struggle. 'Try it.'

'Why don't you come out?'

'We're more conspicuous than you. And the twins – they're the most valuable things, you know that. Everyone knows they shouldn't be let go, whoever gains control of all this treasure.'

When Teal was reunited with them in the back yard, among furtively squeezed hands so that they should not attract attention by their joy, he told them his story:

'I was sitting on the floor by the table an' it was staring me in the face what that old slaver was doing – he was after softening Strugwell up with that drug so that he'll get a better price from him. Well it worked. After you'd all gone away, Strugwell starts stumbling about when he's making his goodbyes. That leather bag of gold an' silver's riches like he's never seen – so it's more than enough for him, more than he dreamed of, see. Though it's cheap to Ibn Hamiz for you twins! Twins like you count for a lot with them, by all accounts.

'While he's staggering to his feet he falls down an' starts giggling on the cushions like a girl, his red eyes streaming, his legs helpless with the laughter. I'm far too small to stand him up again, so Ibn Hamiz calls to two of them standing around to help him up, an' while they're doing that they're not keeping an eye on me. An' I've this sudden flash – don't know where it come from – I lift the glass on the brazier an' take the burning brown sticky lump that's smoking in there. It burned me – look!' Teal showed them the brown mark of a weal in the palm of his hand; the calluses from hauling on the ship's ropes had afforded some protection. 'But the pain's right worth it an' I'm able to spit gobs on the lump soon as we're out in the street an' heading back down the alley. I

238

was afeared Ibn Hamiz's men'll come after us to rob us, to take back the gold. But he's a big man, a well-known trader, a power in the land, an' we are just small fry, he'll not bother with us.

'Strugwell's blinking an' shambling 'gainst the walls like a bat out in the light for the sun's blazing out there by then midday an' nobody about in the heat but us. He's still swearing at me, fetching me blows an' that, but he's all undone by the stuff he's smoked, an' he keeps missing me. When he can't land his fists, he just roars, laughing like he's performing some invisible Punch & Judy show, acting puppeteer an' audience all rolled into one.

'We get to the harbour an' he staggers over to the fountain there an' makes me fill the pail an' dowse him. He's standing there gasping an' shaking the water out of his eyes. "Drink some," say I, "come on, you need water." "Yes," says he, "give me water to drink I've a godalmighty powerful thirst on me." So I takes the copper scoop on the chain at the fountain an' I fill it up to the brim. I've the lump of haschisch in my hand an' I crumble it into the scoop. I'm trembling as he carries the scoop to his mouth for he's that unsteady I'm afeared his hands'll shake so he'll spill it everywhere an' all my plans with it. But he puts both hands round the bowl to keep it level an' he tips his head back an' pours the whole lot down his throat. He makes such a face, you should've seen it! "Stinking foul water they have here!" he shouts. Then, "Give me more!" I fill the scoop again an' then we start towards the dock where the longboat lies – but we're not gone far when he falls down, straight as a tree – a crash like a mast breaking under a southeasterly turning cyclonic. I couldna believe it, I couldna believe it. But I weren't waiting more than a moment to see that he's without sight or hearing or feeling or anything – out of reach, an' that's when I takes to my heels.

'With the money.'

'*With the money*?'

'*Yess*! I'm half-crying half-shouting with the triumph of it. Then I'm hiding out in the back streets till I see the *Shearwater* gone from the mooring. But I had to find you again so I've been begging around playing my pipe, with my face blacked up, pretending I'm blind too, otherwise some might take me to sell. Thought you might hear an' you'd know then, "That's Teal, that's him".'

Phoebe cried out, 'Teal, I heard you first! It was me, wasn't it? I knew that song you play:

239

"O scour the basin, nurse
    And make it fair and clean,
For to keep this lady's heart's blood,
    For she's come of noble kin . . ."'

And she jigged about as she clapped and gurgled at her success. She was happy, Leto noticed, and she was plumper and glossier than ever before.

'And the rest of them?' Leto could not name Skipwith directly.

'Well I kept scarce, didn't I, couldn't go near the boat, but when Strugwell doesn't come back they must send the boat for him – lower the tender this time. They probably picked him up. With his head sore as a baited bear. I don't know. The captain would've wanted to know where the money'd got to, but if Strugwell told him what happened he'd have him flogged half to death.

'They'll be past the Straits by now and sailing north, coming into shore, bringing all those stones to Enoch. Sir Giles really treasures them stones more than anything.'

And the ragged lad, under his crust of grime, looked thoughtful. 'They're the real thing for him.' He paused. 'Well, that's all done now. No more Her Majesty's navy for Teal. I've deserted and if they catch me I'm done for.'

The day came when those closest parties guarding Ibn Hamiz could not conceal any longer that the merchant was dead; the light unearthly smell of camphor turned to a gaseous stench; flies grew fat and stuck, heavy with satiety, to the walls, the floors, the furnishings of the enclave as the great man decomposed behind the curtains of his sickbed. The news started a rampage through the household, as one rival's supporters began to fight another's for control of his wealth. In the rush, some of his numerous dependants seized what they could carry and packed it on to carts and waggons, claiming as their own trade goods that Ibn Hamiz's careful ledgers would have itemised with provenance, and sums paid and sums due. The sounds of wailing mixed with cries of rage and pleas for calm. Overseers struck at these looters with clubs and whips, but the ransacking continued.

The guards of the doors of the warren, not knowing which of the contending heirs would prevail, now threw in their lot with one party, now with another; some joined in the chaos to filch what they could.

Elder members of the old man's family shouted their loyalty and tried to persuade others to follow them, but the factions fought among themselves, and, in between them, the pilferers and profiteers made off with piecemeal spoils from the great baggage train that would otherwise have set off, magnificent and orderly, under a drilled squad of overseers working together.

Terrified of the muddle, of the marauders and their rapacity, Leto took the bung out of the cauldron where she rinsed the dirty pans, and hid the children inside, with unwashed dishes on top of them, and then took scraps and leavings of old meals from the midden and tossed them in.

She was shaking, when Teal came back to the yard after an interval reconnoitring their possibilities.

'Someone'll kidnap them, to sell them for themselves,' she clutched Teal. 'So I put them in there.' She was wild-eyed. 'I can't defend them or myself if . . .'

So Teal responded, 'We've got to run while we can. Waiting here for something to happen's no good.' He pulled a charred log out of the fire and rubbed his hands over it and then over his face. 'Blacken them too.' He pointed to the cauldron. Then he bent close to her.

'I've got the gold safe,' he whispered. 'Mister Strugwell's gold, Captain Winwalloe's gold. The price the old man paid for them – and for you. It's yours by rights. I kept it close all this time, strapped under my thigh. Too scared to show anyone or buy anything with it. So it's all here. For me. For you.'

In the Reading Room, Kim tidied up the pile of papers and books on his desk. *Adventures of a Ship-Boy* ended with Teal's return to Enoch, eighteen years later, a kind of Crusoe, a battered, time-tried, grown man, but still in the prime of life; he was jailed, and faced a court martial, but the climate of opinion warmed to his story and, if the book did indeed record a true case history, petitions such as this anonymous volume were got up for his reprieve from the gallows.

Were they successful?

The book, published during Teal's imprisonment, didn't reveal the outcome. Kim stood up slowly, picked up the pile of books and documents and returned them to the desk. It was peculiar, the closer

Leto came, the less she seemed to speak to him directly. She was travelling nearer, moving towards him, into his zone of time and space, and yet – it felt as if she was dispersing, her signals breaking up under interference from so much that he'd been hearing, like bands of data from a radio probe bringing him news that he could not yet decipher.

PART FIVE

Tirzah and After

Topography displays no favorites; North's as near as West.
More delicate than the historian's are the mapmaker's colors.

ELIZABETH BISHOP

I

The Road to Tirzah

In a crooked, creaking cart that Teal had commandeered, they had cheese and tomatoes, ham, bottled peppers, wine and oranges, clothing, a rug. On top, Teal had strewn some hay from the stables to hide the goods. His progress was jaunty, even as he hauled on the wooden pole of the vehicle. Phoebus was scampering ahead, doubling back and darting off again, so impatient to get ahead that he was covering twice the distance of his slow mother, who was sometimes carrying Phoebe, sometimes putting her down, urging her to walk.

'You're a big baby, and I can't carry you, not any more.'

Phoebe was wilful; she began to shape a bawl, twisting her mouth to insist on a ride.

'I'm not listening,' said Leto, and couldn't help laughing at the sight of the child's charcoal-smeared grimace of woe.

'Come here, sit in the cart,' said Teal, kindly. 'I'll pull you.'

Delighted, Phoebe stuck her thumb in her mouth and jumped into the barrow.

Leto shook her head. 'Teal, you give in to her too much.'

The dawn had brought with it a lifting gust of air so fresh and light that all her past shames and disgust seemed swept clean, as if her mind were a stale room on which the windows were now flung wide and the old linen stripped, the rugs beaten and the floor strewn with lavender water and mopped to a pale gleam.

When morning lifted the air to a new lightness, they were already far from the sea, with no one in pursuit, or so it seemed; Leto then felt her feet begin to move dancingly along the dusty, broken road. For it appeared that in the disarray of the dying trader's household, all the renegades and fugitives were looking to their own; an unspoken code was preventing further filchings and pickings from their fellows-in-flight. Ahead of them, bands were scattered with their laden barrows and bundled booty; no doubt there were others behind them. But each remained invisible to the other, even when they felt them moving nearby, so that what they were doing might seem not to be done.

The four of them had money, they were free, for the first time for so long; she was moving unconfined, the road ahead was open, the country spread out on either side, some marshland where water buffalo sank voluptuously in the cool and rushy mud, the blade of an egret perched on their backs, feeding, Leto imagined, on blood-rich ticks or other parasites in the beast's hide, using its stately rump as the perfect conveyance for hunting other prey – freshwater fish, big flat mussels, and of course plump frogs.

'I'll get down now,' said Phoebe, after travelling a little way like a ship's figurehead in the cart. She skipped off to join her brother, cuffed him as she caught up with him, and then darted ahead, hooting with laughter.

'She just wanted a bit of a fuss made of her,' said Teal.

'So she does,' sighed Leto. But as she said it, she wanted to bite back the words.

It was hard for her to think about the twins, about what they were like, about their differences of character, and to face her own changeable, different feelings about each of them, because such thoughts plunged her back into the past and its hurts and loss. The best part of her recent adventures, she realised, was that she'd had no time to reflect on anything but the jeopardy they were in and how to extricate themselves. But now, as soon as they began to walk under the open sky towards a future, with food in their bags and money under their belts, she found herself assailed by this puzzling antagonism to the ties that bound her to these children, who struck her, sometimes, as complete strangers. Especially Phoebe.

The times when the man who'd fathered them had seemed to love her and she had loved him and believed him were disappearing off the edges of her memory, leaving a dry and dirty residue: all at once, she remembered from long ago, Abbess Cecily swathed from head to foot in white veils at work on cleaning out the drawers of the hive on the terrace of the convent after the swarm had abandoned it; the husks of the dead cells and their dead occupants had to be scraped from the wooden forms. The pile of dirty, broken wax and disintegrating bodies of the insects grew on the cloth the old nun had spread by her side as she worked. The honey that once flowed in Leto had run dry; she was all husk, turning to a sere and bitter dust, and her twins, the children she had struggled so long to guard and nourish, had been hung around her neck. By the man whose step, falling softly in his beaded indoor shoes on the polished floor outside her room, made her heart jump and sent her flying to a seat to busy herself intently on some task so that he should not know she'd been as alert to his approach as a dormouse to the shadow of a hawk.

Were they like him? Phoebus had his eyes, with the thick and curly eyelashes of a people who need protection from the relentless stare of the zenith above their homeland, and, she remembered grudgingly, he erupted with the same winning, mischievous self-delighting laughter that so often curved his father's lips when he came to find her for a snatched moment, a quick caress, a kiss, before he was gone. Phoebus knew how to charm – his mother, and others.

The sun was climbing; a few torn scarves of cirrus floated high up in the blue. A waggon swayed towards them, loaded with fresh-cut hay; the driver raised his hand in greeting as they clattered past on heavy wooden wheels, and Phoebus ran alongside, cheering on the heavy bullock under the wooden yoke and laughing with the little boy who sat up on the bench. It seemed a vision out of time, of a bucolic ease so deep and solid that it had escaped the hooked talons of history. They were moving away from the *Shearwater*, away from the caravanserai. Leto, who had long ago learned to weep only when it might serve, found spontaneous prickings behind her eyes as the two little boys, the one on the cart and Phoebus with his fright of a blackened face in the road waved at each other frenetically, making a game of it, having fun at their own exaggeration of normal greetings, raucously holding the other to the gesture until they had travelled out of sight.

A few more carts, carrying hay and other feeds, rolled slowly by in both directions, going home after the morning's work, to eat, to sleep as the custom was, though the heat of the day was pleasant and airy, since summer had not yet ripened. The landscape around them shone under the high sun, every leaf and blade shimmering in the soft breeze that now and then lifted a flight of lapwing from one field to another.

Leto turned off the road, following a ridge between the water meadows towards a spreading tree that would give them shade. A few crickets hopped in the sparse grass around, and pale green velvet lockets of future almonds clustered on the tree's broad branches.

Teal went to fetch water from the stream; Leto broke the bread and cheese, and passed the pieces to the children. Phoebus was intent on catching a cricket, crawling on all fours as the insects hopped around him. Phoebe was ignoring him, and trying to climb on to Leto's lap, watching her brother jealously, but with a touch of contempt for such doomed, childish attempts, her mother felt, with a moment of reproof.

Teal was urging the boy to come and sit and eat, and for a moment Phoebus stopped the hunt and munched on a bite or two of the hard cheese and harder bread, but his concentration was soon recaptured by the activities of the crickets, as he jumped to catch them where they sprung.

When he had eaten, Teal took out his whistle and lay down on his back and piped to the sky, and Phoebe and Leto began humming under the music the song he had sung on board now and then:

> ' "Gin I may choose how I shall die,
>   I pray you, draw your sword on.
>
> "But first your mantle lay aside;
>   A maiden's blood may spatter wide.
>   'Twere shame your clothes should a'be dyed."'

As they murmured along to Teal's whistle, Phoebus left off his cricket hunt and came and lay down beside them, and they gradually all drifted off into sleep.

> 'So many hairs as she unbound
>   So many tears fell to the ground.'

When the day began cooling, they hoisted their packages again and set out back down the road to Tirzah once more. Their progress was slower, for the children were tired after the morning's efforts, and on the uphill stretches Leto and Teal couldn't pull them in the barrow for long.

'When will we get there?' asked Phoebus.

Leto said, 'Soon.'

'What will we do when we get there?' asked Phoebe.

Teal said, 'First we'll find lodgings. We'll find friends as well, people to help us. Then we'll eat lots.' He sounded uncertain, then remembered something. 'I'll work. Maybe learn letters too – go to school. You lot too.'

'I don't want to,' said Phoebe. 'I want to stay at home.'

'You'll change your mind.'

'You'll come with me,' said Phoebus. 'I'll look after you.' And he put a paternal arm around his little sister, who shook herself free.

Leto thought, Tirzah, where my father came from, they said. Maybe someone will recognise me – 'Ahah!' they'll cry, 'Ser Matteo's little girl! You're peas in a pod, would have known you anywhere, look at those eyebrows! That chin! That nose!'

Then she faltered. But would the twins look right – would they belong?

At a bend in the road, after a shallow dip and a gentle rise, Tirzah came into view in the valley: the curl of the river caught the light and flashed for an instant. Slender arched bridges crossed into it like the radial spokes of a rose window, leading into the cluster of tiled roofs, some yellow and black, alternating as on a wild tortoise's back, some a high glaze emerald green, the vivid ensemble softened in between with plumes and clouds of trees and climbing plants. They couldn't see into the streets and squares of Tirzah, since the houses were packed together, but smoke rose here and there, in spite of the springtime warmth, giving signs of activity and occupation – bread ovens, thought Leto, or family kitchens. The sun lit up the prospect so clearly that the stacked buildings seemed painted by one of those illuminators who can render the fly on a petal of a scarlet geranium on a distant windowsill. Chimney pots in baked clay, smoking white; whitewashed bell-towers rising near the brilliant gleaming glazed domes in their vivid livery; narrow grey spires and pinnacles of more shrines; the occasional dominant cube of a great edifice, and yet other buildings squat and low-lying: Tirzah was far, far bigger than any place Leto had yet seen.

At this moment it looked to her as if the city had descended, whole and twinkling, from the sky, like one of the models held in his hand on a cushion by a patron saint in the illuminated manuscripts the priests had

249

used in the convent; it beckoned to them, inviting possession, yet kept its own counsel. A great city, humming, singing to itself, calling them to a new future. Yet Skipwith had said that, compared to Enoch where he was conducting them, Tirzah was a mere village.

Teal pummelled his eyes as the joy and terror of a new life there seized him, and Leto kissed the children and pointed, wiping her nose on the back of her hand in her commotion.

The twins were bewildered at their mother's unusual show of feeling, but then, reassured that she really was happy at what she saw lying ahead, Phoebe did a little dance on the spot, overcome with excitement at their prospects, while Phoebus clapped his hands and whooped aloud, crying out the city's name, 'Tirzah!'

The approach took them down a gentle incline; Leto put her hand to the barrow, where Phoebe and her twin were riding together, as the going was easier downhill. The road changed, too; the beaten earth became a hard smooth surface, which ran to the verge and broke off, like a tough uneven crust of mineral deposit on the rim of sulphur springs; this new ground underfoot, unfamiliar to the little band of fugitives, wasn't rutted by cartwheels or stamped with the hooves of oxen or donkeys or other animals. It wasn't paved here, either, but became a solid, dark surface, although intermittently it was shattered by a huge pothole, its broken edges showing strata of grit and sand and stones.

'Looks like battle scars,' said Teal. 'Heavy cannon. Not long ago, either.' He glanced around, uncertainly.

There was no more traffic coming towards them, nor any overtaking them either. The scattered members of the caravanserai must have gained on them, or chosen a different route, or hidden themselves in the countryside.

The emptiness began to grow eerie, for nothing stirred now except the wind in the grass and the occasional crow, taking off slowly from the meadows upwards and then flapping down to settle again elsewhere. As they approached, they began to see the gaps between the houses ahead, missing teeth in the glittering assembly of edifices, with smoke wreathed in the crevasses; the silence became compressed into a dead weight, as if the very air were stuffing its fingers into their ears and plugging them till they could hear only the pumping of the blood in their temples. It was a silence of held breath, of sucked-in responses, of anticipation, of fear. The city, which from a distance had appeared to teem and seethe, was now as still as if it had drunk poison.

Leto hesitated; Teal halted. The children twisted in the cart, clambered out, felt too the warp that held them.

The ground didn't buckle under them, to bring into contact two faces of rock that had lain far apart for centuries, yet time was bending down to them to lift them on to his high shoulders and then, with a heave, standing up to fling them forward into a space where Tirzah, seen only a short time ago winking and basking in the springtime light, lying aglow in the pastoral cradle of green meadows and greener hills, now sank under a long dark shadow as they drew nearer, and shook to the rumble of approaching armoured matériel and the boom of guns.

The next bend in the road took them along a ridge, running parallel to the perimeter of the city, which lay just down the valley, over the river. In fear now, they were looking for shelter, but ahead of them the way was blocked. A small crowd had disembarked from assorted strange vehicles: shiny, metallic, painted a glaring crimson and blue, with windows, and then a tall, larger, house-like, long post chaise with lines of blacked windows, and a four-square, loricated rampart of metal, like a titanic woodlouse with the proboscis of a stinging insect. The passengers squatted in the shade near these unfamiliar, lumbering conveyances, waiting. There were some women, one with a baby on her hip. Some of them were smoking; a few of the men had long thin guns, on which they were leaning.

Leto wondered, Should they turn around fast, try and escape? Back to Feltimye? The crowd did not look agitated, however. It seemed becalmed, the men, women and children numbed and silent, hardly moving, as if she were dreaming them and needed to dream more to bring them to life.

They were all turned towards Tirzah, watching, and when Leto followed their gaze, she saw now the gaily chequered roofs become scorched by fire, the towers crack at the seams and the walls turn black with smoke, while the sky ahead of them, so flawless a few miles back down the road, was dirtied by columns of more smoke rising greasily here and there, while smuts were now being blown towards them on the wind. The whitewashed walls were no longer gleaming, but streaked and smeared with the traces of burning. And, as the little band watched and waited, the preternatural silence was rent, again, and again, by a deep thumping from engines hidden somewhere. Invisible explosions followed; the earth shook so that the view in front of them vibrated as if she were trying to hold it in her hands and they were trembling too hard.

'It's just another raid,' said one old woman, finally breaking the muteness of the group at a standstill. 'We've just got to wait till it's over.' Her voice was patient. 'I was visiting my son,' she added, 'In the barracks back in—' She mentioned a town in the hills.

Leto stood before the smoke-dimmed, smouldering city feeling a chill grip her heart, as if the darkness of solar eclipse had fallen on her world. Then a sudden quick shadow passed against the sun, and again, and again; three times, in the clear sky, the light was for a moment blotted out; and with a huge roar fire dropped out of the sky. Yet the air above their heads was still a flawless blue, the few clouds fresh as cream. Then there came a blast, and another, and another, very close, very loud, but Leto still heard through their concussion the high scream of Phoebe.

Afterwards, Leto said many things about that time, during the first phase of the long siege of Tirzah, when they walked into the shelling of the besieged city of their future, and could not find their way back. She would repeat her sensation that everything had stopped stock still before the lurch and the blast that brought down the fire from the sky. She would remember, 'I felt time was being balled up by a gigantic fist.' Or, she would say, 'I felt bodiless, as if something was lifting me high, high, high out of the world, and then dropping me back down, with a crash.' Phoebus was gripping her round her neck, straddling her hip. But Phoebe had drifted apart from them. Leto was, she would repeat, spellbound; she didn't even throw herself and the boy down on the ground. She was looking over towards Phoebe, crying out to her to come near.

Then the explosion happened again, and again, and in the smoke and the flames she lost sight of her daughter and fell on to the hard, hot road.

When she moved again, which seemed aeons later, in an underwater world where all was slowed and clogged, she found the little girl shivering, lying in the road naked, with her hands fluttering helplessly over her raw flesh. She wasn't screaming any more, she wasn't able to speak, and her eyes were rolled up in her head; nobody could hold her, touch her, cover her. Flying metal had pierced Phoebe's flesh; her face, hands, legs, torso were spattered with welts; her back was flayed. She looked like a rabbit skinned by a hunter to spit on a fire.

But in this butchered body, her eyes were moving, and so was her mouth: she was alive, her face said so. And so was Phoebus, clinging now in terror to his mother's legs. They'd both been hit by the bursts of shrapnel, but their wounds were slight, by contrast to Phoebe's. In the smoke and the dust, Leto began whirling, looking for help, looking for Teal. So many were spattered with the burning metal, stumbling, fallen, and so many were lying motionless, bleeding heaps on the road.

Phoebe was gibbering, shaking as she lay on the road to a kind of hoo-hoo-hoo sound like a lost bird; there was no help to hand, not for a while, not until the paramedics appeared in a freshly marked Peace Front ambulance with the journalists behind them in a dented Mercedes. The team wrapped Phoebe in a shiny foil pupa and laid her on a stretcher in the shade.

Many bodies sprawled around them. They looked like children playing 'Ring-a-ring-o'-roses, we all fall down', Leto thought, incongruously. Then Leto, as she hunted through the victims, came upon Teal's whistle, which lay blackened and twisted in the ashes.

Later, when she knew something more about the siege conditions and the attackers' weapons, she learned that the victims lying around her on that bombed approach to Tirzah were spread with a fiery glue that had been packed in the casings. Phoebe's skin was burned off her body as if by acid coating an etching plate, biting the print of its passage everywhere it met naked skin. Where this bubbling glue came into contact with clothes, they vaporised instantly, so that the metal scraps and slivers of the nerve agent's shell could bury themselves deeper into the victim's flesh.

Leto clutched Phoebus tight; she did not wail, she needed to keep controlled and alert for Phoebe's sake, and for his, too. But at that moment, she would have walked into the fire of her own accord in order to cease to be, in order for the abyss into which Teal had fallen to close over her head too.

In the Basement of the Hospital

For more than two years before the time when she and the children first
walked into the war, the ordinary processes of Tirzahner livelihood had
been disrupted, and with the disruption had begun the urban migration:
cowherds and milkmaids abandoned their pastures in the hills and
descended into the town bringing with them terrified reports of rapine
and pillage. The besiegers included young soldiers – seventeen, eighteen
years old – who jeered at their captives, under encouragement from
their leaders, as they stripped and raped their women in front of their
eyes: this was men's way of talking to one another, trading insults. The
bodies of wives, daughters, sweethearts, mothers, served as communal
notice boards: nail your message here, sign here, or if you can't sign,
make your mark! Then, during the five-year-long destruction of the city,
the fugitives who had run to safety inside its walls assembled shanties in
the shadow of new international department buildings and company
headquarters from the crates and containers in which supplies were
flown in to service the various denominational groups who were working
in Tirzah alongside the clumsy, relentlessly churning turbine of the siege:
peace-keepers, press corps, TV crews, medical observers, every kind of
volunteer, aid workers, travel operators, and, naturally, the black
marketeers with their drums of bitter coffee and wormwood dust for tea,
and their medical supplies with the expiry dates obliterated, defaced and
altered.

The soldiers who were defending were encamped outside, in trenches
and barricades of junk; but for the inhabitants, their attackers remained
faceless, anonymous, an amorphous and ever-present menace that took

the form of fire and flame and bursts of thunder: riders of the apocalypse, with hooves bagged in felt so that they were upon you before you knew it, the bomb working its way with its victims before the sound of its explosion shattered the corpses' eardrums.

Leto survived with the twins: part of the broken city's jetsam, they worked to salvage anything that lay to hand and could be turned to use. The men who gave her work now and then would pick her out of the crowd that gathered at the back doors of businesses of one kind and another in the ruins – she offered herself for cleaning, principally. At the end of the day, when they'd assess the women's work, they'd call her out, referring to her as 'Ella' – simply 'her' or 'that woman'. She did not fight against this new name: 'Leto' was outlandish to the locals, and her life in Tirzah felt so cut off from the former sense she had of herself before, that she no longer owned the woman she had been.

The burning had left Phoebe's skin peculiar as developing paper. When she began to heal, her new, taut, pink sheath of a body took on an ethereal shine, so that she almost seemed transparent, like one of those marine organisms that float in the currents or like leucocytes in the bloodstream. Her flesh, uncovered, gave off an eerie luminosity, otherworldly in its lambency, but also morbid. The involutions of her innards and the light flutter of her heart and lungs shadowed this odd translucency, reminders of vitality, and with it, of incipient mortality; over them the twisting ropes of scars formed a raised lattice. The glue's chill flames had dematerialised her, so that she seemed all made of the eerie twilight of the new moon, mottled and crisscrossed by the branches of battered, keloid tissue that caused her torment.

What Phoebe needed as she began to grow, what her mother began to pilfer from the Hotel Metropole where she cleaned and from the clients she serviced there, were oils, foundation creams, unguents, soft lathering liquid soaps, anything that could ease Phoebe's tight painful skin and make it supple over her developing bones.

Every morning, her mother would empty the phial of creams she had squeezed out (it was very important that she took so little it could not be noticed) and massage Phoebe's arms and throat and back; then, with the foundation cream, she'd smooth over the angriest part of the scars. In this way she tried to soothe the vitreous, stretched flesh that had become her tiny daughter's burden. But there was a salve she knew she wanted; made of a rare spider's web, it was reported to have legendary healing properties that made it change hands on the black market in medicines at the price of far more obvious treasures. The wives of the government leaders and the generals used it to rejuvenate their complexions; doctors rarely got their hands on it, even when they were dealing with the bombings' worst casualties. Distributors were hoarding it, against even worse times; or so it was rumoured. The wonder of it flickered in the back of her memory, reminding her of a whispered promise she could now barely catch. The struggles of the present day were wiping Leto's mind, moulding Ella to their necessities.

The small family took lodgings in the shantytown huddled on the riverbank in Tirzah; and Ella first worked by day in the hospital as a cleaner, which she was lucky to get through one of the staff she'd met when Phoebe was a patient there. By night she did other things, in the rat runs between the shelters. Then she moved to the Metropole, where the clients offered richer pickings for her needs and the twins'. As Ella, one of the cleaning staff, she took the pair with her every morning, leaving them in the laundry store while she worked.

Weeks went by in the broken city, the weeks turned to months and then into years; the remaining inhabitants of Tirzah could not rouse themselves from the torpor that war had inflicted on them, the brand that despair burns on the minds of its victims. But Ella conceived a raging will to pull her son out of this hellpit, he who had miraculously survived almost unscathed and now did not bear a trace of that day on the road to Tirzah. She didn't want him to suffer any longer the unrelenting neediness of their struggle to survive. Observing the foreign clientèle in the Metropole, with their ready money, their expensive toiletries, their books, their fine, warm clothes, she began to form a plan. She also witnessed a succession of worried couples from Enoch who lingered listlessly for weeks in the stricken hotel, then suddenly left, with a child in their arms, emitting a flurry of joyful cries, bundling themselves off behind enemy lines (spreading more cash around) to the occupied airport. Phoebus was the sunnier child, the most winning, irresistible, in fact; he wasn't damaged like his sister; he would be accepted somewhere where he'd have a better future. There, he would thrive.

She would abandon him. Then, later, she and Phoebe would rejoin him, she told herself. Her determination had brought them this far already; she was determined this wouldn't be a final parting.

So Phoebe was told her brother was leaving, for a while, to be safe somewhere else. For his part, he looked at his mother pensively; but did not cling. She felt they had an understanding: this remedy was a temporary measure.

'You won't be caught up in the fighting when – if – it breaks out again,' she whispered into his warm head, stroking the soft skin of his left ear where the fold still gave him an impish look. 'You'll have a better chance, there.' She wasn't abandoning him to strangers; she was lending him to . . . stewards, guardians, people who would teach him, feed him, raise him better than she could. All over the world parents sent their children away to be educated; it was the custom of the wealthier classes, in fact. Nor would the separation from her Phoebus last for ever.

When the time came and Phoebus left, she told herself over and over again that she had done well, for his sake, and for his sister's.

Another year went by after that day and the siege dragged on. Ella herself could find no way to leave; being outsiders already, her kind couldn't count on the generosity of the plundered and scorched countryside, not when scarcity stripped men and women to the teeth, to the bone. She would have liked to find a far, far away place to hide, to bury Phoebe from men's eyes, but who would take an odd, mutilated girl with them on this exodus? Nobody could be trusted, even in better times.

Phoebe would not be parted from her mother, anyway: 'I can do things with you,' she pleaded. It was true; she liked being the only one to command her attention; it consoled her for the physical absence of her brother. She would help tidy away the linen by climbing up on the shelves, and sort the laundry and start soaking it in the basins – they had to save water – when Ella left her there to perform her unnamed, extra duties in the hotel.

There were some men who liked – well – Ella wasn't going to put it into words. 'It can't come to that,' thought Ella. But it might. The little girl was growing up.

Another year passed, their third in Tirzah: Phoebe was nearly six.

'Come here,' she pulled her daughter to her, roughly. 'Let me tell you something. First of all you don't look anything like your age, and that's a protection you need, in this kind of city. Hold on to it as long as you can.

It's the only advantage of . . . the damage that's been done to you. I do this job because there isn't any other way. Your brother's safe, far away. We're going to find a way to make you safe, too. We'll follow him, we'll find him. Everything will be better.'

'Yes,' said Phoebe. 'I'd like that.' She paused, then asked, 'Will he be with Teal?'

'I don't think so.'

When the end came, just before the sixth winter of the siege, a winter that would have finished off the remaining survivors, foreign helicopters flew in over the last blazing barrage from the guns in the encircling hills, over the line of tanks trundling down the main road from the north towards the charred and splintered city, and landed on the roofs of the large nations' embassies; they lifted out a few favoured, counted-on, wealthy locals, all of their own nationals among the personnel, and some members of the foreign press. Cars loaded with the possessions of the besieged started to head for the nearest border, but many ground to a standstill well short of it, as the petrol ran out even for the rich who'd made a killing during the long siege from drugs and medicine and brothels and other necessities, while several other vehicles hit the snub noses of the many mines, spread-eagling their passengers and their treasures on the cratered tarmac. Children, whose eyes were quicker at detecting the weapons' shallow mounds, were sent in by the attacking army to glean the remains.

With the victory of the enemy, and the consequent promised pacification of the country, those who had been trapped in Tirzah for three long years now tried to thread their way back to their villages again; there were some old men in this shuffling column, some boy children under six, but for the most part women made up the ragged numbers, women with infants and toddlers in their arms, on their backs, sometimes wheeling their own broken, frail mothers in pushchairs before them where they clutched bursting bags of their remaining possessions on their laps. When an old woman collapsed on the march, they tried to tie her corpse to their meagre heap of belongings, and another one took her place in the last of the wheeled vehicles, be it a child's pram or a shopping cart. But miles into the hills, with everything burning and smoking around and not a scrap to eat or a well that wasn't choked with putrefying carcasses or poisoned by explosives, these feather-light bodies were left on the side of the road with a quick, frightened prayer. The weeping was dry-eyed; a kind of howl that started in the pit of the stomach and rose to the head and hardly needed the throat; a possession by sorrow; loss made palpable, a chemical miasma seeping through the gut, the brain, the eyes. No one wept the way women weep in ordinary times; they had too little water for splashy, rheumy tears.

When the victorious soldiers reached the hub of the city, the Square of the Swallows, where an obelisk of Egyptian rose granite stood, imported from an historic victory of Tirzah's conquerors a long time ago, and more recently inscribed with a patriotic salvo written by the national romantic encomiast on a brass plaque on its pedestal, they swarmed off their daubed, webbed brown tanks like woodlice freed from under a rock, aimless and panicky, their officers kicking over the stone to set them loose and standing back as they rushed in fours, in threes, in pairs, shouting, embracing, bayoneting this obstacle and clubbing that, kicking and cuffing, to force the event to feel like a triumph to them, to make their mark, to tell on history and sever the old times from the new ones. They were the liberators from oppression, the bringers of light and plenty; they were the coming men. They stamped through the municipal palaces, wrecked the headquarters of this and that organ of state, where the cabinets voided their contents on to grey carpets like the young infantrymen who vomited after combat and performing the rape and mayhem that pleased their officers. They slewed the books in the national library this way and that, grinding the swollen and stuck together pages into the glittering needles of the glass dome that had received a direct hit early on from the big guns that ringed Tirzah. What the snowmelt of last winter, the rains and the mud had begun to destroy, was finally shredded by the cullet fallen from every shattered window. The victors did not loot the books, but swept on, down the main street to the smart hotels (including the Metropole), where they stove in the doors of bedrooms and ransacked the bars, though the cupboards were bare and had been for a while (a handful of intrepid black marketeers were well concealed, waiting to choose their moment). The soldiers made their billets in abandoned dwellings or, if they unearthed some lingering occupants, too ill to flee, they threw them out, and still shouting and kicking, triumphantly took possession of their home. They smashed it if it was humble; they seized it if it was comfortable. The housing in the

259

centre of the city was splintered and blackened and squalid and cramped by comparison to the residential suburbs, but the water had been cut off by the shelling many months before and the long low houses with shaded gardens that had once been luxuriously furnished had been plundered for firewood to keep the besieged alive during the winters.

The batteries on the hills stopped firing, and it felt, in the unaccustomed silence in the city, as if Tirzah were now truly isolated, that there existed nothing beyond its borders except shadows, the flimsy, drained shadows of a past that was being blotted out by the huge, hulking, enfleshed figure of the present time, who had arrived in his cleated boots with a clatter and a loud cheer to block out any lingering memories and thoughts. The artillery ringing the city had guaranteed, it turned out, that the stalker from history's long nightmare remained on the other side of no-man's land; now, after more than five years' fighting, he had come to his new home. When the column of the fugitives passed out of sight, it seemed they had all fallen over the edge of the world into a bog of primal slime, which swallowed them up.

Here and there the conqueror was greeted with a sweaty, ingratiating invitation to a cellar, where something was hoarded, or to a table where some pepper sausage and hard dry bread was laid out like the petrified food of the dead in an old tomb. Some of the troops struck poses for one another, brandishing their guns at the foot of the obelisk in the Square of the Swallows, as if they were taking a memorial photograph. But as the only film in the country had long belonged exclusively to the press corps, who grimly guarded it, it, too, had become a rare and expensive treasure – and now the press corps were all gone, the last one dangling from the helicopter's rope like a circus performer as it scissored straight up into the streaked sky.

There seemed to be nobody left who mattered to witness the moment of victory. Tirzah was a place of husks and rags, and the survivors who stayed behind were mostly too old and fragile to move, though some of them were not so very old according to their birth papers but had been shattered into premature senility by what they had seen and, in some cases, what they had done. The victors took possession of the emptiness and the silence, carrion crows flapping their torn black wings on a carcass after circling above while the animal twitched in its death agony. The foreign airlifts left behind native-born staff, and the fleeing citizens of Tirzah did not gather up with them either the many foreign guest workers and illegals, many of them women such as Ella.

One or two doctors, several nurses, three journalists and a handful of aid workers remained behind in the wreckage with the abandoned. The medics, Ella heard, were holding out in the city's ruined hospital, where the taps dribbled rust and the surgical instruments were grown blunt after overuse trimming the mutilations of the siege's victims. During the last bombardment and the rampage of the victors, the little group took refuge in the basement of the building; the old boiler pipes to the laundry room boomed deep as tubas if you accidentally knocked against them, but the X-ray cubicles were still solid. Two nurses, Anna and Paulina, carried down the patients that had been left behind: two children with terminal cancers, three amputees from the defences of the city, two army recruits, and a senile man, a remnant who had already lost all his family in the siege.

When these last days came, and the foreigners and their favoured friends were scurrying out, catching the last airlifts, and even the TV news networks had been ordered to leave by their national representatives, the manager of the Metropole boarded up the stucco décor and carved marble panels of the elegant hotel lobby as well as he could, barring its doors with bomb debris, and made off to the countryside, carrying as much of the cellar as he could stuff into pillowcases and wheel on a luggage cart.

Ella thought of the young Dr Martin, whom she had seen at work with the wounded. Séverine Martin, from the international agency FemMédecs du Monde, had once stopped Ella in the street and bent down to Phoebe's small height and given her a pencil she had in her pocket, murmuring affectionately. Ella could see she was curious about Phoebe's injuries, that in her eyes she was a case, a specific casualty. But she was at least kind.

'What are you putting on her?' the doctor had asked, very quietly, over the little girl's head. 'These VX-2 injuries . . .' she shook her head. 'We've seen many die of those terrible burns. Your little girl was . . . lucky. Perhaps we can help her. We can do skin grafts, it's remarkable what we can do. When we get out of here.'

'Nothing.' Ella was sulky. They were standing in the street, in the sun, and she was late.

The young doctor shook her head. 'One of the cruellest weapons ever used in war – to our shame, for ever. But you have covered up the scars – with something?'

'Just make-up,' Ella responded. 'It eases the pain.' She didn't tell her she had acquired a small pot of the precious salve, for the doctor would want to know how she had got her hands on it. It was helping, but slowly. (Sometimes Ella wondered if she hadn't been cheated, and that the fabulous spider's webs had been adulterated with other elements. Sometimes she wondered about their properties altogether, but then the whispers she sometimes heard in her head became troublesome and hurt her.)

'Come and see me, please. At the hospital.' The doctor turned to indicate the building, rising clearly visible above the jagged spars of its bombed surroundings. One wing looked perilously carious: all the glass had blown out of the three topmost storeys on one side. 'We're still operational, you know. Just. I would like to help *la petite*. Please.'

Ella hadn't taken Phoebe, then; she knew they would have had to wait for the doctor for a long time as she toiled round the ever-growing casualties of the guns on the ridge and snipers from their hides, and Ella couldn't afford not to turn up at the hotel as expected; regularity, punctuality, no demands, no problems. Those were the manager's rules. Any phones ringing asking why a bathroom hadn't been cleaned, why a tray hadn't been taken, or why the massage number wasn't answering, and she would be out of a job.

As the wholesale evacuation was taking place, in the syncopated confusion of the flight of the refugees, against the roar of the helicopter blades, the bursts of the loudspeakers marshalling the fugitives and the shouts and howling of the scattered survivors, mother and daughter crept through the streets towards the battered hospital.

A few others had had the same idea: Virla, also from the hotel, whom Ella often passed on the back stairs up to the sixth floor where Virla had her beat. When she saw Ella and Phoebe, she began running, shouting incoherently as she overtook them, for Ella was moving slowly, half dragging, half carrying Phoebe; as Virla passed, she grabbed Ella by her hair and pushed her down on to the broken pavement.

'Don't you follow me. No way,' she hit Ella again, 'No room for you, no no no!' But Ella shoved her; made her way past her. Virla took off again, towards the hospital, and Ella began running too, hauling Phoebe by the arm till she shook herself loose in protest.

When they scrabbled at the boarded-up windows of the basement round the back of the damaged building, there was no movement, no sound; light was breaking and Ella was full of fear that they would be spotted by the patrols. But at last a woman's voice rose fiercely through a crack in a sandbagged vent and asked what they wanted; Ella cried out the doctor's name.

There was a pause, and then more urgent whispers, and they were directed to a door concealed behind a stack of smashed equipment, unhinged, wrecked cupboard doors. Resentfully, Virla trudged quietly alongside Ella and Phoebe and followed them into the dark, sandbagged basement. A tense group of survivors was gathered around the young foreign medic, while, in the dimness, Ella could hear the groaning of the hospital's last patients where they lay dying.

'How are you, little one?' said Séverine Martin, stroking Phoebe's cheek. 'I'm pleased to see you—' she stopped herself, Ella knew, from saying, 'alive'. 'And Mémère? How is Mémère?'

Now, in the dark beneath the broken building where she had worked, Ella felt a quiver of self-pity, touched by the doctor's considerateness and courage. She squashed the feeling, harshly, and gave her brusque thanks only. She told herself, *When you last trusted a stranger, look where that got you. Never accept consolation; it's always treacherous. Hope is that bad sprite, who flits in front of your eyes, deceiving you with her brightness, her glinting wings, her star-crowned wand. A whisper, again from that lost past, floated through her mind: Remember the wolf. So, refuse that feeling of common sympathy, for this medic doesn't care about you. Not about you. Just for the mess of suffering humanity, in principle, in general.*

There were no candles; only cracks of light from the high narrow bands of the basement windows, through the gaps between the sandbags. Yet her eyes became used to the gloom and she began to pick out her companions: Virla, now moaning on the floor in a corner, Paulina, a nurse, praying by the mattress on which two children were laid out, curving mounds so slight they seemed already weightless as in death, another woman stacking some debris to make a screen. Soon, Ella realised, to separate them from the corner they had to use for a latrine. Other shapes were slumped against one another, muttering a mixture of prayers, entreaties, curses, and cries, figures missing limbs with soiled bandages were stretched out side by side in one corner; there were several more children, many younger than Phoebe. More women, again. The remnant, thought Ella, we are always the remnant. We are cuttings from the pattern, and we fall from the tailor's shears on to the floor, fit for stuffing cushions or padding shoulders; we are the disappeared, made invisible. Yet those discarded twists of cloth can utter, they fall into patterns and figures dropped at random like numbers cast from a lottery urn, but this will yield shape, arrangement, with ingenuity, with patience. And rags are pulped and flattened and changed into the heaviest, ridged paper. And then, horizons of meaning widen, for there's no limit to what stories they may then bear. Figure: ground. Interchangeable, inconstant, it just depends which your mind fixes on: the bespoke suit spread in deliberate plan and sections on the tailor's table or the kelp-like twists of living cloth fallen from the shears.

She pulled Phoebe into her lap and stroked her, half-singing in a quiet, barely audible drone, so that the vibrations of her voice travelled though her fingers rather than the sound rising to her ears, and as she murmured and swayed, she watched and listened.

Gradually, they began to talk, very quietly, to tell one another where they had come from, what they had lost.

The inventories looped, massed, became a towering pyre; beloved kin, cherished belongings burned up in the war, lost in the siege; families dispersed and become untraceable, moorings here, in Tirzah, cut.

'I have a son in Enoch,' said Ella, suddenly. 'We're going to go there and find him. He'll be doing well. He'll become a doctor, perhaps. Or a lawyer. Or an engineer. Or a teacher. He will take care of us. When this is over.' She began to speak, more rapidly. 'I am glad now that I sent him away from here. I knew it would be terrible here. I wanted him to be safe – somewhere, elsewhere. So we left him—' She hugged Phoebe and rocked a little.

'You must keep your strength,' whispered the doctor. 'Don't talk, try to sleep.' They could not stay long, she knew, not without water or food. Aloud, she said, 'We don't know how long we'll have to stay here. When it'll be safe – or at least not so dangerous as now, outside.'

Soon after, the old man began to howl; the sound rising and falling like a siren wail. It maddened them, and they implored him to stop. But his wild eyes showed he did not understand, and the hole of his mouth seemed to gape so wide it would swallow them all.

'They will hear him, we'll be dragged out, he'll be our death,' wailed one of the fugitives in the basement.

Doctor Martin shook her head where she sat, wearily crouched against the wall. She had no drugs left for the old man in his dementia. The little morphine she had she was keeping for the children; the vial was wrapped and tied to her waist.

When the old man's cries did not stop, the younger nurse, Anna, took up a metal dish, a curved receptacle for instruments, and raised it above her head. When the threat did not put an end to his noise, she brought it down hard on his temple.

The doctor groaned, 'No! We must hold on to what is left of our humanity, please, no!'

But the man fell sideways; the blood from the wound trickled feebly.

Phoebe clutched her mother. 'Is he dead?' she whispered, into her body.

'No, no, of course not, he's just quiet now. Come,' Ella pulled them both up, to creep closer to Séverine. 'You don't mind,' she asked. 'If we're nearer you?'

'Don't be afraid,' the doctor murmured. Then she repeated the words again, needing to convince herself. 'Don't be afraid.' She paused. 'They say the age of miracles was long ago. But I'm not sure.' In her drawn face, she managed a dim twinkle for Phoebe. 'Something will happen.'

She was counting on aid workers returning, hard on the heels of the victorious besiegers; her own organisation, she knew, would return swiftly. As soon as the army and its warlords and the war machine's bosses had done with jubilation, they'd need services up and running, and, to get them, they'd have to agree to terms with the international agencies. There would be a semblance of order restored, soon.

She was almost muttering to herself, to give herself courage, for she too was weak from the long work of the siege. 'So many dying, so many limbs, so many bodies . . .' She began to cry, and Ella did not put out her hand to touch her, for she did not believe in consolation and she did not trust pity.

In snatches through the long hours, she slept too; now and then muffled weeping and whisperings of some of her companions in the close basement interrupted her. Later, one of the children woke with a

265

sudden, piercing cry. Phoebe was sleeping, but at the sound she shuddered and groaned and curled herself into a tighter ball. Séverine Martin woke; she went over to the mattress, where the dying boy was gasping. In the basement, the air was stifling now with the smells of decay, disease, and the restless sleep of bad dreams and foul bodies. The last dose she'd given the child had worn off. Quickly, she unwrapped the vial and, with a much-used syringe, administered half of the remaining supply of morphine. The child's body was a dry twig; it gave a last shiver all over, then lay without movement. The doctor shrank from the bedside, covering her eyes.

Ella was watching.

When she'd pulled herself together after the shot, the doctor roused Paulina, then, reluctantly, Anna: 'We have to take the bodies out of here – help me.'

The three of them staggered under the weight of the old man as if he were already encased in lead.

'I think we have to take the chance, to go out,' said Dr Martin, 'It's nighttime. If we leave him in the corridor, there are grave risks attached, and our resistance to disease is already weakened.'

'It's madness,' said Anna. 'Snipers.'

'It's dark – look. We must take him out. For everyone's sake.'

Ella turned her face to the wall as they dragged the carcass to the barricaded door. But they did not have the strength to go farther and collapsed, by the sandbags, the corpse fallen sideways. The nurses began to laugh, uttering sharp, crazy notes, as they tried to straighten the old man's clothes, arrange his limbs, find something to cover his face.

Phoebe, seeing this, scared, was burrowing in Ella's breast; her mother tried to fend her off, but, occasionally, the damaged girl still needed that comfort.

The doctor was peering out of the window slit just below street level. 'We must try, we must, to get him out of here.'

Together, the nurses and Dr Martin pulled apart the barrage of sandbags against the door to the area outside, the space between the basement and ground level, and dragged the body just outside. A gust of air freshened the atmosphere; Ella turned her face towards it. Watching from the door, Séverine Martin reported, 'There's still a lot of confusion, movement, explosions. You'd never think there was any more glass to be shattered. Everything's burning, too. The night's lit up. And the rats!

Rats are too clever to burn in their holes. And the stray dogs – they'll have become dangerous.' She turned back to the room and addressed the nurses. 'Leave the child. We can't dump him like that, a bone for a pack of pie dogs. We must carry him out of here. Perhaps upstairs – have you the strength? He weighs no more than a ... swallow.'

But it wasn't so. In death, the child's corpse slumped leadenly. Collapsing on to the floor, the nurse wailed, 'I can't go any further, not any more.'

The nurses stood, listless, in front of the obstacle. 'We can't,' one said. 'It'll kill us.'

The young doctor surveyed the basement, grim-faced. Against the walls, on the floor, lay the remnant of all the victims she had tried to help; some fitfully sleeping in the half coma of thirst and famine, others groaning; soon, the second child would die.

She closed the door to the street above and heaved one bag up against it again. Slowly she returned to her spot on the floor near Ella and Phoebe.

'Don't try to carry him out,' Ella whispered. 'We can bury him in a sandbag – he's only small. Then sew it up again. For a time, it will do, no?'

On hands and knees, heads hanging from exhaustion and inanition, the two of them parted the bulging sacking; Dr Martin's scalpel was still sharp enough to saw the fibres; then they scraped at the sand, hollowing it out, as if, Ella remembered from a faraway past, they were transplanting a flower to a new bed, a slip of geranium that had triumphantly taken in a tiny pot and needed space to grow.

The child was sunken-cheeked, with eyes like a baby gibbon's, so round in their deep sockets and staring wide and deep. Ella refused the choking in her throat, and pushed the body into the bag, flexing the tiny blueish legs further discoloured with greyish patches, the motions recalling to her now, even more incongruously, the action of stuffing a fowl. Grimly, furiously, she took the needle from the doctor and pushed it through the coarse fabric, ignoring the punctures of her fingers as she sutured the cadaver into its makeshift shroud.

If they could not come out into the air soon, they would all die, and the rats would come to the feast.

She sucked her finger where it was bleeding: could one eat one's own flesh and be nourished? she wondered. Could one become a closed loop, drinking one's own piss and picking through one's shit for scraps as flies and beetles and even birds do on cowpats and other droppings, digging out seeds and berries that have passed through without being broken down?

'I can't sleep,' said Séverine Martin, weakly. 'Not any more. It's dawn, another day.' She was slumped against the wall, her eyes open wide and lustreless as if old coins were already placed over them to close them. She put out a hand to Ella. 'Talk to me. Let me hear a human voice.'

'You said not to talk.'

'Yes, but it feels we're the last left on earth, and I want to hear a woman's voice. It's the first thing one hears coming into the world and so . . .'

Ella shifted Phoebe's weight, for the little girl's head was lolling heavily against her. The doctor looked sidelong, marvelling.

'I thought so, you're still nursing.'

Ella didn't answer.

Séverine coughed a laugh. 'How long has that been?'

Ella didn't reply. She said instead, 'It'll dry up here. Probably has already. It's comfort, not for food, you know. It eases her when . . .' She was angry the doctor had noticed.

After a pause, she said, 'Phoebe was burned. It was a near-direct hit. She's lucky to be alive. I haven't weaned her – because . . .'

'When was it?' muttered Séverine Martin. 'How old was she?'

'She was three years old.' Ella paused, stroked Phoebe's head lightly. She wanted to say, it was a long time ago, we walked into the war, but we didn't know that then. We were on our way to . . . freedom, so we thought. Tirzah!

'And were there many of you?'

'There was Phoebus, and Teal, and Phoebe, and me. Teal was hit; he was killed.'

She could have added, *It was a lovely day: sunny, with a light breeze and puffs and high cloud. Perfect flying weather, but I didn't know those things then. We stood in the road, I remember. Looking out over Tirzah. It looked so beautiful, that first time we saw it. And then, something changed. Time bent, and we were tipped over into . . . now, today's time, the present day.*

But instead, she continued, 'There were soldiers who came. And press arrived, later. Phoebe was in the papers. Someone took her photograph when she was lying there on the road and sent it all over the world, they said.'

'The little girl on the road? The massacre at Tirinčeva?'

'Yes,' said Ella.

There was a silence, and Séverine Martin looked at the mother with her big child at her breast with a kind of avidity that made Ella hold Phoebe tighter.

'Let me try,' Séverine Martin dragged herself towards her.

'No!' Ella pushed the woman's head away. She fell back, against the wall.

But then the doctor pulled herself closer again, slowly laid her body alongside Ella's and her daughter's. Her voice was thick, her tongue swollen. 'Forgive me. It's a comfort to feel – another human being.'

Ella was too exhausted to fight her, and so let her lie there without pushing her away. She wondered if she could build a connection between what happened then, what was happening now and what might happen; her mind was working. But she made no gesture of reciprocity. Séverine's hair against her shoulder smelled of sweat and disinfectant; her lips were thick and cracked, but the dull eyes were still feverishly open.

'Then we saw the planes coming in, very low,' the doctor's body was growing heavier against her; Ella was talking under her breath. 'We were standing on the road. I was holding my little boy on my hip, and I didn't know where to turn. I just stood there, crying out to Phoebe. There were three planes, one after another. I had him safe, but Phoebe'd got separated from me – she's always been headstrong! The first bomb landed in the road just ahead of us and we fell down in the blast. When I opened my eyes again, there was a terrible stench . . .

'But we survived, it was a miracle we did. But Phoebe – Phoebe – it had flayed her.'

She put her hand out and smoothed her daughter's hair, following the three crowns where the hair grew in whorls softly with her fingers. 'Can't you do something – to help her?'

'Let me,' said Séverine, pushing her head to Ella's breast.

'No,' said Ella.

But then the doctor lifted her head and made her a promise: 'If I make it through this, I'll tell people that she's the child – the child in that photograph of the massacre at Tirinčeva. We'll make her a new skin.'

She struggled to get closer, 'I swear it. We at FemMédecs will help her. A new skin, yes, so nobody would ever know what had happened to her.'

She began to nuzzle, begging, 'It'll save me perhaps. Please.'

'But I'm all dried up, how else could it be?' Ella pushed at the heavy lolling head, shifted away from the hot, rough lips.

'It'll make it flow.'

'Not when I'm parched.'

'For her sake.'

'You're taking what's hers.'

'Let me. Please.'

Ella hadn't the strength to fight her, not with Phoebe stretched out listlessly, not with the others half waking around them. Not too much fuss was best, not too much commotion. She didn't want to alert anyone. She calculated: the doctor might survive, and she might remember and maybe, maybe, they could call in her debt.

It was a miracle that women, starved and broken by disease, could bear babies, that she, with her flap breasts, flat and shrivelled from lack of food and drink, could offer a drop of moisture to this young woman. But as the doctor's dry, hot mouth sucked, Ella felt the faint, familiar tingle of her milk rising from somewhere under her heart.

As Séverine Martin's whole body grew softer, Ella unwound the silk scarf with the silver thread that she had managed to hold on to through everything that had happened to her since Skipwith first gave it to her. She tore at it, and because it was now very worn, the threads gave. She stuffed a piece into the doctor's pocket. 'Take this. After this is over, I'll come and find you. With my portion of the scarf. Then you will know it is me and remember that you've given your word you'll help.'

3

An Encounter in Pontona

The monkey swung off the carnival float and knuckle-leaped towards Gramercy till he had his long arms around her chest and was kissing her so the breath was squeezed out of her; she knew he was the Chancellor of the Exchequer of the late and unlamented government, even though, all fat and white, he wasn't a bit like this stringy taut gibbon hanging round her neck. Then a mighty reek of urine overcame her. She struggled and twisted tighter in the quilt, which bore, on its underside, she saw, when she swam out of the monkey's clutches and the cloud of piss, the stain of some previous occupant's late night booster from the mini-bar. Even in the best hotels.

Where was she? She struggled to remember. The band was two-thirds of the way through a six-week world tour, and she was as lost as a contact lens in a mixed leaf salad.

She had an uncomfortable way of noticing other people's traces: a toenail paring astray in a bathroom once, in a spick-and-span crisp white linen luxury resort no less; an old pair of some previous occupant's knickers on the shower curtain rail where she'd hung them overnight to dry. Rather grey from wear, so Gramercy rolled out some toilet paper to pick them off and tossed them in the bin. But she hadn't ever complained to management about these leavings; these were accompanying ghosts, and she'd written a song about them. In some part of herself, she felt close to their owners, they were, as the lyrics of her song put it, 'Familiars in solitude,/strangers on the move/like me'.

A short while before, an hour or so ago that felt like years, or, judging from her wrecked state, more like an interrupted instant of sweet sleep,

271

she'd put herself away for the night in the huge pile of bedding, the wadded and padded heaps that provided comfort for the single traveller in five star hotels, offering the big body of mattress, pillows, quilt and valance in lieu of company. She'd never smelled anything like it, except when she failed to read correctly the costumed signs that, with increasingly perky ambiguity, designated Men's and Women's loos – breeched figures in top hats didn't read male to her – and pushed open the door of a latrine. You always knew it was the men's, even before you saw the monumental grinning orifices of the urinals; you knew it from the smell. So, here it was again, rearing up into her face in the small hours.

But there was no shameful puddle under her: the reek went with the dream and, as the dream still gripped her, so it lingered.

The wand of the telly lay on the bed. The porn channel was now dead: she'd been watching something in the dark to put herself to sleep; that was going to cost a bit, if she'd left it on for hours. Now that she was awake, the stench was beginning to fade and she could see, nothing was stirring in the room, no monkey, no pisser. Only the low hum of the electrics in the room disturbed its torpor.

But she'd been plugged into the dream like a child who puts a finger in a live socket; she needed something to stop it shivering up and down her, like diabolical endorphins with their spermy tails wagging.

It was probably due to dehydration, a sugar low, after the concert. Pontona, that was it. They'd played some small towns with big stadiums; in this affluent and elegant city, a crossroads at the heart of the continent, the hall had been small with cool steel and smoked glass décor and cunning little halogen lights like hot stars, and no backstage tattiness either. Gramercy was beginning to recognise the EU's Midas touch; certain countries were adept at extracting its juice. The hall was full – many more older men than usual had turned out to hear her. She seemed to attract the white-collar class, nostalgic for the lefty ideals they'd let go, unlike their equivalents in Albion, or so her roadie, TB, said. She'd made an emotional appeal on behalf of Tirzah, a ghost city after the siege, and only a few hundred miles away; she'd sung her ballad, 'Incarnadine', composed during the destruction.

Gramercy unwound herself unsteadily from the heap of bedclothes, lowered herself from the bed, made towards the mini-bar by the crack of light from the curtains and opened it. The glow struck the room, a burst of radiation, huge and blue with yellow edges. Cans and bottles and packets gleaming and luridly presented were stacked inside the light, like ingots in an old bank robber movie; she pulled out a miniature vodka and by the fridge's light fumbled for a glass, mixed it with orange juice, looked in the ice bucket, found it empty.

Ice was what she needed, she realised with sudden fury, her skin was so hot she felt it might peel off her like a werewolf's at the call of the moon. She swallowed some of the drink to take away the lingering whiff of piss from her nose and throat. Not nearly cold enough. Refreshments must be fresh. This was oily and almost warm, so she felt around the bedside table, and turned on the lamp and lurched towards the door. In the corridor, by the lift, a throbbing metal cabinet offered ice, she'd seen it on arrival, she remembered; the porter carrying her bags pointed it out to them, to her manager and her roadie and her lead guitarist. They'd all be sleeping now, more or less quietly. She might call one if the night went on like this. Talk to one of them, till she was bored enough to sleep. But she wouldn't, not her, though she might tell them the next day that she'd thought of doing so and watch the effect of her reproach.

She pressed the button and a lovely tumble of ice, shaped in soft ovals like soaps, clunked into the bucket. She took one and pressed it on her forehead, where she burned.

With the relief came clarity, and then the jolt: she hadn't brought her bedroom key. She was in her strap platforms from the concert the night before; she'd pushed her feet into them before she made for the ice machine. Anvils on the end of her bare legs, and wearing a nightie she'd bought from a mail order underwear catalogue when she'd imagined she could exercise some allure on Phil (it had circular stitched cups that made her breasts look bigger – why was he the only person in the world who didn't crave her? Why wouldn't he come with her on tour and keep her safe? Because he was, well, what was he? – remote, high-minded, holy), she couldn't go downstairs to reception. The carpet in the hotel corridor was ornamented with crowned monograms. The crests pointed both ways: 'In the unlikely event of an emergency, a path will light up in the gangway and guide you to the exits', announced the air hostess in the plane after take off during the safety instructions. Light up, Gramercy begged the crests, light up. This is the event of an emergency. She looked one way and the other from the central axis of the lift shaft:

Rooms 1510–1524 one way, Rooms 1525–1540 the other. Her eyes hurt, something was pushing them out from the back of her skull with hot hard fingers. Beyond the comfortable judder of the ice machine, the silence was terrible. It was like the ash that fell from Mount St Helen's and muffled every living thing under its downy coverlet, it was like a fire blanket that stifles the leap of fire, it was like a sound system failure when the amplifiers just die and nothing, not a bang not a whimper, comes out of your instruments except a sudden high-pitched scream. Maybe she should scream, maybe hell was a hotel, maybe there weren't fiery stakes and pools of ice and devils with grapnels, but just an empty corridor and nobody, only the leavings of the crowds that had passed through, paring their toenails, rubbing the stains unsuccessfully from their knickers, making cascades of piss, wanking in bed in front of the special, locked, charge-by-the-hour channel. Maybe she was dead, thought Gramercy Poule.

Now she couldn't remember the number of her room either.

Still holding on to the ice bucket, which was condensing in delicious cooling drops where she clutched it to her stomach, she stumbled towards the telephone hanging on the wall between the two lifts. What time was it? It couldn't be too late, or too early; it had been around 2.30 when they'd left her to sleep. Must be 5 a.m., must be someone on the desk. She picked up the receiver, dialled 0, heard the ringing. She'd ask for one of the gang – she'd ask for TB's room.

'Yes?' came the hesitant reply. 'Ah, jus' a minute. I give you English menu.' There was a bleep and a tape began, a dulcet-toned out-of-work actor doing his worst: 'For an outside line dial 9. For Room Service dial 1 for Housekeeping dial 2 for Bellboys and Valet Parking dial 3 for Hairdressing and Beauty Salon dial 4 for Crèche and Babysitting Services dial 5. To reach a guest in the hotel dial 6 followed by the room number. Hold for the front desk ... Thank you your call is held in a queue we are sorry to keep you waiting this is a busy time.' The plangent strains of Albinoni's bloody Adagio swam into Gramercy's ear, a full semitone flat from the wear on the tape. She hung up, put her head down into the ice bucket and sloshed her hair in the melt at the bottom; she took two of the soaps and fitted them over her eyes, they were nicely socket-sized.

She dialled 1.

'Hi,' a cheeky voice replied. 'What would you like to eat now?'

'Help me, please help me. I've locked myself out of my room.'

'. . .'

'I'm in the corridor upstairs and I can't remember which room it was.'

'. . .'

'Please, please help me.'

'Reception help you, Madame. I can no bring you nothing without a room number.'

Gramercy wailed her name. To no effect. Only useless people knew her, adored her. Then, after a pause, the only kitchen staff up at that hour asked, 'Which floor you on?'

Gramercy saw the number written opposite the lifts: 'Fifteen.'

'The penthouse floor? I call maid. You stay there.'

From down the corridor, in the stifling inertia of the top floor, Gramercy heard a phone ring.

She discarded the bucket, tottered towards the sound.

The door of the laundry store was ajar. When the telephone rang Ella was in there, half-awake, lying on one of the slatted shelves. She slithered out of the narrow gap without disturbing Phoebe, who was lying on the inside of their makeshift bed, towards the wall, so, when Ella pulled open the door, Gramercy saw them disengaging; she could almost feel the heat of their bodies in such trusting nestling intimacy from where she stood in the corridor. The cupboard was about five feet wide, so curled up together, the woman and the girl just fitted on the shelf. This closet was cramped quarters, with a mop and pail and two or three brushes standing up against the shelves. They had piled up most of the linen from the shelf they occupied on the one above and lay together on the towels they'd kept for bedding, like a bitch and her whelp in a basket. The girl was sleeping with her head flung back and one arm crooked above it: her skin was so thin it looked like old carbon paper. Even though they were sleeping together, it never crossed Gramercy's mind that they might be friends, or lovers: she knew them instantly for mother and child, for their fleshly intimacy conveyed the tenderness of the familial: it came to her all of a sudden how she used to snuff the scent from her mother's things on her dressing table, matching the aroma of this box of powder to the smell of Bobby Grace's cheeks, of this hair

275

spray to the vapour that moved with her towards the door when, her hair newly backcombed, she was going out for the evening. Gramercy would have liked to have climbed on to the shelf with them, to crawl between them and be transfused, to press herself against their doubled soft squirming flesh until her lifeblood beat to theirs.

Ella stood up in her pink uniform and stockinged feet, searching for her shoes with her toes as she looked at Gramercy with an expression in which fearfulness, shame, obligingness and defiance all flickered. She picked up the receiver, deftly looping her hair through a tie with her free hand to lie on the nape of her neck in a coil.

There was an exchange or two between them, and Gramercy saw her draw a passkey from her pocket like a nurse consulting her upside down watch while taking your pulse.

Ella bent over her sleeping daughter's shoulder with an almost absent-minded gesture, whispered something in her hair, placed her pillow against her body, and closed the door of the cupboard.

'You come,' she said, beckoning Gramercy to follow her.

'And . . . ?' Gramercy pointed to the closed door. She wanted to ask if the girl could be left shut up in a linen cupboard on her own.

Ella shook her head, clearly dismissing her enquiry, and set off down the corridor.

She remembers me, she knows my room, Gramercy realised with a rush of relief. I saw her yesterday when I was dressing for the concert she came and turned down the bed and put a chocolate kiss with a sleep well message from the hotel management on my pillow and I thought, yuck, but now, I see they know about solitude, the chocolate kiss is a substitute it releases something in the blood that's like love she has love she can stroke and caress that daughter of hers absent-mindedly she doesn't have to ask or wait for an answer that's the love between mother and child it doesn't negotiate a peace every time.

Inside Room 1518, Ella untwisted the bedclothes and plumped the wrung duvet. Gramercy was fumbling for her bag – for her wallet – she fished out a note – £20 – too much? Perhaps. She looked for a tenner. She didn't have one. She lifted her head to give the woman the £20 note, and Ella took it, nodded, smiled and tugged at the strap of Gramercy's nightdress and flicked her fingers upwards, indicating she should take it off.

Holy smoke, thought Gramercy, her mother's favourite ejaculation suddenly appropriate, you think I want a fuck I can't imagine anything better than a climax now, but what kind of an outfit is this with the maids sleeping in the cupboards and performing special services at any time of the day or night for a measly tip that I was giving her anyway because she's rescued me.

Ella was still plucking at the silk of her nightdress, and steering her gently towards the bed, her face was calm and quiet, not as if she's coming on to me. Gramercy's thoughts were breaking on her consciousness in ragged foam as she pulled the garment over her head and plunged on to the bed. Ella climbed on to it with her; they were both small women and the heap of the hotel mattress was still out of scale even for the two of them together. Ella didn't express any reaction at her nakedness, or even look at her, but pulled Gramercy's concert sandals off her feet and set them down neatly side by side on the floor, bending over with an easy suppleness from her position on the bed. She was squatting, with her legs tucked under her, at right angles to Gramercy's stiff body with the tattooed dagger on her left thigh. Gramercy was scared; this was like the first time with a new lover when you didn't know if he'd turn into a raving flagellator. Phil's face flickered into focus, then faded; Ella's brows were gathered, she was intent on something serious. And she'd just got up, after a night spent on a shelf in a laundry cupboard. For an instant, Gramercy's eyes met Ella's. She could grasp nothing from their shaded irises; then Ella was putting one hand under Gramercy's shoulder and the other under her hip and was turning her on to her stomach.

Her neck hurt in that position, and as if Ella understood this, she lifted her hair off that place – it was still wet from its steeping in the ice bucket – and began to knead the muscles of Gramercy's nape, digging in with strong cool fingers. To get a better purchase, she hitched her uniform higher and climbed on to Gramercy's body, settling herself into the small of her back, one leg on either side, as she worked at the vertebrae of her neck and then with the flat of her palms fanned out to the muscles of her shoulders. Points of fire flared in Gramercy's flesh under Ella's fingers; her flesh was a potbound plant, her muscles roots swollen and knotted and gasping for air and grappling for space, and Ella was teasing them out, the taproots and the threads. Her fingers were combing Gramercy's muscles and replanting them in some fresh moist soft earth, now sifting it to make it more hospitable now slapping it down firmly, and as she

277

worked, she dug herself in more deeply into Gramercy's body, straddling her bottom so that the maid's weight, however slight, pressed Gramercy's cunt into the mattress until she wanted to laugh at the waves that quivered there to rise and meet and melt the pain of Ella's diagnostic probes. As Ella moved down her body, gathering energy and concentration, Gramercy felt her body heat rise and its smells filled her nostrils squashed against the pillows, and there mingled hotel laundry and soap and warm hair and new sweat, and she heard with increasing awe the grunts she made as Ella pummelled her.

Ella concluded by snapping each toe till the joints cracked; after the tenth digit obligingly loosened, she climbed off Gramercy's body, pulled down her pink uniform, once again looped her hair smooth on her neck and said, in English, 'I leave you now, goodbye, Signora. Thank you.'

Gramercy fell at once into a dreamless, odourless sleep, her body limp with the bliss of surrender.

Now I'll get us emulsifying lotion and good soap and shampoo and some needles and thread and tissues   so no more torn-up newspaper today or tomorrow and we'll be given lots to eat lots downstairs too   Lauro in the kitchens will give me and Phoebe lots of food and wrap up some for us to take as well   it's been difficult these last days trying to find Dr Martin   last night I was so hungry I was dreaming we went fishing – for anthills in the sea with lobster pots and fishing boats we set out over brown water   it was nighttime lights were dancing deep down where the ant grubs were fat and protein-rich   that's why we were setting out to hunt them   they had clustered eggs like honeycombs dug deep into the ridged sand below the boats   our shadows moved on the sand deep down below   the ant grubs rose to the bait we fixed inside each pot   don't know how they swam into the pots   Phoebe came too she was happy playing in the boat with ants hatching from the haul in the baskets we pulled up on board   I taught her how to eat the eggs they were like round brown balls and she said, all smiling, They taste of chocolate   Luigi promised to do his best to get us more medicine even cheaper maybe he told me 150,000 lira for one month's supply   he will appreciate the singer's clothes I hope especially the high-heeled shoes for you can see she's worn them he has collectors who will give him real money for tights and other things with sweat on them from big stars I don't know if she is big enough   I have to find Dr Martin again   at the head office of FemMédecs they said I should call back this week she would be back then   I will go by there again today now that I have this money I can skip an afternoon   the landlord still wants money for last week and if I give him some we can have key to the bathroom but if I could find more we could have room alone together and I could look after Phoebe with no people crowding always having to explain no danger to them   not contagious not infectious just the shivers and the shakes from something happened to us a long time ago   not TB not HIV though she has turned blue and sometimes yellow sometimes   maybe this young singer will bring us luck   she feels lucky like fate sings through her every day and gives her pretty shoes and necklaces and flowers and dresses   but her body was twisted up and scalding hot not with fever of the flesh   something else burning her from inside she all alone here maybe that bothers her   I loosen her and cool her maybe then fortune'll give me something in return it's a fair trade I say to fate with a big grin showing my teeth like a wolf defending herself so you can't tell if it's a smile or really a snarl just to show I'm no pushover   you have to look fate in the eye not give in without squaring up to her

The next day, the ice bucket was missing from her room: the only piece of evidence that Gramercy was able to produce to persuade Monica and TB and the others that she wasn't making everything up.

She wasn't going to tell them she couldn't find her nightdress. Or the pair of tights she'd worn at the concert – silver Lurex. Or her sandals. She'd have to buy another pair. She'd tell Monica she broke the heel and threw them away. Pontona was a good place to shop for shoes.

The funny thing was, Gramercy was pleased that her night visitor had taken something of hers; the intimacy of the thefts made her feel the connection between them wasn't severed. But she knew she was being weird, that she should feel outraged. Or at least vulnerable.

'Gramercy,' said TB, as calmly as he could. 'You know we don't think you're lying. You're just all stressed out. You need to relax more.' He was worried. They still had six more countries to play.

'Did you have cheese in anything last night?' scolded Monica. 'What about E-numbers? Surely they don't stuff food with E-numbers here?'

Gramercy shrieked back, 'It was not a dream. I know the difference between waking and dreaming. I had a nightmare and it woke me up. After that, I was wide-awake. That's why I left my room in the first place.'

'It could be the flowers,' Monica went on, 'they're taken out of the wards in hospitals. They're poisonous.

'Or you're allergic to something.'

Monica moved TB out of the way to get closer to Gramercy where she sat, stubborn and inflamed, on the bed.

'The hotel manager is coming to see you,' she said. 'We insisted – we made ourselves understood. Actually a lot of them downstairs speak English.'

The manager, when he appeared, was a fan, one of those men in her audience who'd had to give up revolutionary dreams. He bowed over Gramercy's hand and kissed the air six inches above it very gravely. 'I was catering and management student in Enoch,' he began. 'It is a grand honour for our hotel you are here. Please accept our deepest apologies. It will not happen again. This bad trash . . .'

'What!' cried Gramercy. 'You've got completely the wrong end of the stick. I want it to happen again. I want you to find her. This Rosa—' She stabbed a finger at the cleaner's card from the dressing table: 'Look, it says, "Hello, I am your cleaner. My name is Rosa. Thank you." Oh shit.' She began crying. 'I'd just like to give her – and the girl – tickets for the next concert,' she added, lamely, for that wasn't what was chiefly on her mind. Though she'd do that, of course, if they could be traced.

The manager continued, a look of embarrassment and misery overwhelming his suaveness.

'I have sent away the housekeeper – for allowing these intrusions. It was not Rosa's time yesterday. Rosa was not here last night. I have checked. Please accept . . .' he waved at the room. 'Compliments of the hotel.' There was a knock on the door. More flowers appeared, and a bottle of champagne in another ice bucket.

'I don't want flowers.'

The manager turned to Monica. 'You see,' he began. 'It's a big problem for us, refugees, thousands of them. Everyone wan' to come here – then go on – to other places, make money, have cars, doctors – foreign aid give handouts, then these people use money to do other things . . . give papers to illegals. Refugees. Gipsies. They work for little money – what can we do? We have big shortage of trained staff – it is a problem. When one of the permanent staff – we're not cowboys, we pay salaries, insurance, pension, everything, all the trimmings as you say – wan' to take a holiday, wan' to sleep late, don' wan' to work, we have to go to agency, and they go and find one of these gipsies – at the bus station, in a bar, in one of those places they know they hang out.

Saturdays is baddest for this. It's very dangerous. For you. For us. They rob our clients. She take something?'

Gramercy shook her head.

'She could've hurt you,' he said. 'Dangerous. They are very dangerous.'

Gramercy grew more impatient. She wanted to know, 'Why shouldn't she come back and do the same again? Tonight?'

The manager finished his sentence, waving his hands in the air, 'Agency gives them a little money, but most they take it. They can' complain, the police find them . . . So one night here, one night there. They're not found, if they keep moving.'

Monica put a hand to Gramercy's cheek. 'Come on, love, we'll find someone just as good. It's only a massage.'

Gramercy ignored this. 'I see. By asking after her I've driven her out. So fuck it.'

The manager replied, with a quick spread of his hands, 'If we find her we will tell you, of course.' He looked over towards the window. 'But they're everywhere and it's a big place out there.'

4

An Animal Refuge

When Gramercy looked back, over the ten years she loved Phil, she could not see any crack in the brickwork that could have let in the chill wind that caught him up and spirited him away.

But when the numbness of the first months after his departure began to fade, the fresh pain of her solitude quickened her memories and she was able to look back and assemble the pieces, bit by bit.

'Making a difference begins with small things,' said Phil. He had become a vegetarian and was building a compartmentalised compost heap in the garden to sort vegetable waste from animal remains, in which he included eggshells.

After the first stray cat, the menagerie gained new members very quickly. The next acquisition was the baby hedgehog: Gramercy came back from the north one afternoon and found Phil nursing it with an eye lotion dropper.

'I found it half dead in the road – but it seems to be rallying.'

Gramercy was very touched by the sight of Phil's gentleness and the small round bundle of soft spines in his square strong hand. She bent over and kissed his fingers, nodding vigorously when Phil said that animals were the key to a holistic life.

The hedgehog took up residence in a box in the garage.

After another tour, she came back to three terrier pups, with black patches over one eye, waggling bottoms with short fat little tails. She fell in love with all three, as, peeing with excitement, they rubbed against her legs. They were given a basket in the bedroom, with an Indian silk embroidered cushion to curl up on. Phil bought a trainer's guide to dog rearing, and soon Hook and Jonty (for Long John Silver) and the bitch, Bonny, were leaping after balls and jumping over sticks; Gramercy was proud of Phil's skills in handling them. 'You've got a real gift with animals,' she said.

The numbers grew: Phil rescued squirrels and rabbits and foxes and birds, including a darling owlet, all white down and fluffy feathers; he acquired discarded pets from chance acquaintances or contacts made on the grapevine in the local inns that he visited: a chameleon, leaf-green with a tail like the crozier of a fern, joined the collection, assorted specimens of breeds that were cute small, but soon grew too large. He penned in the ducks – Cayugas with petrol-lustrous deep emerald tail feathers and plump white Jemima Puddleducks; he added a pair of geese. The last frightened Gramercy; they opened their wings wide and poked out their stiff necks and screeched at her when, a comparative stranger in her own garden, she arrived back again from Enoch, where she'd been filming a promo.

'Don't you think you've given yourself enough responsibility?' she asked Phil. 'I mean, you're spending all your time cleaning out trays and pans and buying feed and scraping perches . . . the house is a lavatory.'

'You're losing touch, Gramercy, with what matters. Those consumer-ist values are getting to you, they're contaminating you. Soon you'll be just like everyone else in the plastic economy.'

Gramercy blinked. It was as well she hadn't said that she didn't really enjoy so many creatures around her, especially as an ammoniac miasma hung around the house even in fine weather when the windows were open and penetrated as far as the bedroom. She rolled herself a cigarette of dark tobacco.

'Perhaps we could just take a rain check on any more – for the time being.'

'"Take a rain check!" You're joining the new colonials – the money masters teaching you language. Where've you been? You know these animals need help, they need care, they need *me*. I've never been happier than doing this, I swear to God. But you wouldn't understand.'

He began to taunt her about her desire to make money.

'You're in danger of selling out. Look at all this!' He'd wave sweepingly at the walls, the twenty-four-inch telly in the corner, the hefty tasselled curtain cords on the luxuriantly floral and belling drapes, the French apple wood armoire they'd found together at the annual country antiques fair in their local market hall, which now flowed with rivers of CDs and tapes and old vinyl on to the apricot and indigo kilims that lay on big square baked tiles from Mexico; he'd glare at it all as if spectres were hiding there, spectres from the grim carnival of corporate funds and turbo-charged capitalism and global companies, until his gesture concluded to indicate her, where she stood sullen and muted, fighting the anger that made her want to shout, 'Aren't you living here? Aren't you enjoying living here? Isn't it comfortable?' But she never railed; she was trying to see it from his point of view, the undeserved money that kept coming from songs she'd written half drunk, or worse, years ago. And she never let the slow poison Phil dripped into her form into words, reproaches, or even questions. Not then. But later, she began to piece together how her sense that he was doing her an injustice dropped sharp flinty deposits between them, so that approaching each other in tenderness required passing on naked soles over this boundary, where Phil's anger had hardened into sharp-edged rubble.

Now criticism of Bobby Grace enveloped her, and malice undid their old comic character. He'd accuse her of inheriting her mother's frivolous, empty-headed, pleasure-seeking tendencies, of caving in to her ghastly, chintzy tastes. He sneered at her for her urban pretensions and expectations. He damned her collusion with exploiters and fat lazy multinationals. And laughed at her taste for self-pampering frippery: he scoffed at the rummage bag of body oils, hair gels, sparkling eye shadows, lip glosses, nail varnishes that spilled round the basin in the bathroom and at the battery of cosmetics that crammed the cabinets. Phil forbade her to wear leather; she developed athlete's foot and her nails warped and yellowed from the fungus that invaded after trying the plastic footwear he ordered for her from an animal rights charity catalogue. 'You should wear flip-flops,' he said. 'I can't wear flip-flops,' she wanted to scream at him. 'I make the money I do because I sing like I'm wearing slingback stilettos that I can hardly walk in – that's the whole point.'

She repeated to herself, to others, to Bobby Grace, that he was working through his disappointment over the film scripts that were never made.

Later, Bobby Grace said, 'You buried yourself alive with that boy. Honestly, your generation get a lot of flak, but we were so so much wilder. By your age, I'd had strings of beaux – you could have some fun now, darling. Get out there, you could have anyone you want.'

Monica said, 'He was frustrated, Gramercy. You're *driven*, you get on with your music, you're a success. What happened to that film script? To that brave new world he was building? Hot air.'

'Film scripts', said Gramercy. 'It's not his fault they weren't made. Nobody wants his kind of stuff. It's too good. They want schlock. "Inspirational" rubbish about loners rescued by a wonderful, gifted, special child. Or video nasties. Or gangsta comedy. Not people who are dreaming of a new world. Not *idealists*.'

'Men don't like being new men. They'll play at it for a while but it sticks in their craw.' This was Monica, again.

'Yes, he was convincing and you had some great years. You're allowed to be sad – but you can't let the sadness take over.' (Bobby Grace, cajoling.)

Gramercy heard Phil had moved in with someone they both knew, slightly, in the business. George Rodriquez, who had a house in West Hollywood and specialised in ambient music. He'd made a success of it, too: 'Sounds of Sunshine and Water – The Voices of the Rainbow' stayed in the general CD charts at around number fifteen for months on end.

'They're moving into the animal niche now,' said Gramercy, doubtfully. 'He and Rodriquez are working on therapy for your pet with behavioural problems – that's the new project. Music to soothe your doggy's nerves ... sessions to get in touch with your moxie's inner child—' Bobby Grace was snorting at the end of the line. 'By the way,' Gramercy continued. 'Do you think Phil's really gay? Deep down?' She dropped this in lightly, though the possibility had suddenly seemed a solution to many aspects of their struggles.

'Oh *please*,' said Bobby Grace. 'What's the matter with him? Do we have to listen to this shit?'

She made no comment about Phil's sex life.

Gramercy missed Phil; she began dreading going to bed, for insomnia plagued her, bringing with it a train of ghosts of missed chances, lost times.

'You should go easy on the drugs,' said Bobby Grace. 'I know you can't stop working at night, but you've gone and wrecked your hypothalamus, upset all your Circadian rhythms, turned night into day and day into night. And I'm not turning spiritual. This is mother's common sense. Stick to herbal teas – but check the labels, in case they're wake-up tonics.'

But Gramercy couldn't; besides, if she went to bed drunk or stoned, she could sleep for a few hours before the phantoms sidled in and their gibbering and squeaking began.

There were so many aspects of their lives together that had blurred; in the small hours, splinters of memory returned to pierce her and she gathered them, trying to fit back together the mirror that suddenly he had walked through to leave her. She hadn't paid enough attention to what was happening. Gramercy Poule wasn't yet thirty, but she felt she had arrived at old age, with a lifetime's riches behind her and nothing in front of her except memories, and so many of those were fragments and blur, or had completely vanished into the swirling smoke of their rapt intimacies or the blue fug of the venues she played.

For a while, she smoked and drank more, ate ice cream from the tub, and turned over the press cuttings books Monica kept up to date to see if she could recall what had happened, who she had been, then.

She produced another album, 'Mandragora'. The critics praised the new, smoky timbre of her voice, the flutes and jew's-harp and celeste on the backing, the surprising shifts of key, and discerned a folk influence from the moors in the long, meandering, broken storylines of her songs. 'Spoor' was written for Phil: she chanted a list of the bits of the body that she loved ('. . . nail, wrist, vein, pulse, knuckle; curl, nipple, skin, throat . . .'), whispering it hoarsely into the mike, as if it were a lullaby crooned gently into his ear to make him shiver. Her audiences sang along with her, hypnotically, swaying to the heartbeat of her bass guitar. But when she listened to it now, she realised it sounded cold and oddly menacing, as if she was an anatomist taking him apart.

One day, on the telephone, Gramercy tried her mother, again: 'Do you think it wasn't just me – but something else?'

'Darling, if you're asking me if you were the problem, you know what I think. The answer's no. Of course not.'

'No, I mean, what about Phil, his . . . *sexuality* – did it, did he seem . . . sexy to you?'

'Oh, well, he never came on to me, if that's what you're asking. No worries there. I'd say, aside from that, he seemed pretty normally weird to me.'

286

Gramercy wanted to say to her mother, 'Sex was never a big thing with us . . .' But she felt a fool not to have noticed that their babes-in-the-wood cuddles spelt danger. Phil never complained, never asked for more; she hadn't wanted more – it was a relief to her that he was so different from the howling, lurching and slavering cocksmanship that the music business promoted as the red-bloodedness proper to the male. She'd felt that their love was . . . well, loving; 'Phil's my best friend,' she'd tell the press. 'We tell each other everything, and what's more, we often don't need to say anything because we know each other so well we understand without words. We're psychic – like dogs, you know, waking up as soon as their master turns the corner of the street on his way home. A sixth sense.'

Sex had a live current of hatred running through it: sometimes Gramercy wanted that, the harsh weight of a man humping and nearly smothering her, forcing his cock between her lips as he straddled her. It was always afterwards, that kind of encounter, behind the scenes, in the backwash of a concert, dark and nameless and angry, a fan goaded to stud status by her reeling and keening body's exhibition on stage. But she never expected those kinds of afterwards to have a sequel. Those bouts were purgative, the violent debasement necessary to bring her back to equilibrium after performing her public masquerade of desperation, fury and everlasting love. She hadn't wanted anything like that from Phil.

But Gramercy was beginning to remember, bit by bit.

One summer night, she was coming into the kitchen from the conservatory that gave on to the garden at Feverel and she saw Phil moving near the animal sheds and the birdcages. There was nothing unusual about this, but something about the set of his spine made her notice his manner; he looked intent, not as if he were finishing up the routine evening feed and settling the creatures down for the night. When he didn't re-emerge, she went down the garden to the end to find him, but in the doorway she stopped and turned back without greeting him or even letting him know she was there. He was leaning over the rabbit hutch, muttering to the big meek animals as they lolloped after the vegetable parings he was tossing into their pen, a bit of carrot and some cabbage leaves, a few shreds of outer lettuce, and his words, which Gramercy couldn't hear, caressed them softly; then he reached in and grasped the biggest one, the buck, seizing him by the ears and burying his face in the soft speckled fur on the animal's belly. She hung back;

there was some unbreachable intimacy between the man she lived with and the absurd, oversize, trusting coney that he was fondling. It came to her that Phil had been concealing his unhappiness from her. She saw him all at once as a small boy, who's lonely and without friends, stuck out at some school in the country. But her pang of sympathy with his state turned quickly into savage disappointment. Phil was left at Feverel on his own when she was working, but he had always said that was what he wanted – not to traipse in her wake, form some redundant appendix to her entourage on the road – to work at his own projects in quiet and solitude under the shoulder of the moor. He had not shown her affection, or even a need for affection for so long she could not last think of a time when he nuzzled her or plunged himself blindly into her as he was now doing – rubbing his whole face in the jack rabbit's pelt and pressing it so hard to his throat and chest that she could see the creature struggling against his captor.

Then Phil was opening his shirt and, holding the animal away from him with one hand, he was encouraging, with gurgles and grunts, its strong hind legs barbed with sharp nails, as they thrashed against his chest; he then flung himself down in the corner of the shed with the mutely writhing animal; its lip was lifted to bare teeth, which, Gramercy noticed, were as long and yellow as old piano keys, but Phil held the head away as he rammed the rest of the creature against his crotch, unbuttoning his flies with his free hand.

She turned away, and would have liked to hoot. Doing it with a rabbit!

But she didn't. She withdrew silently, as forlornness excavated a gaping hole where her heart and liver lay: she couldn't really find it funny that Phil was taking refuge with his animals. We've drifted, she thought, drifted miles apart.

She tried to make love to him that night, nicely, slowly, calmly, but he lay mutinously clenched against her. His skin was repellent in its chilliness, putty-like and limp and he brought his legs up to cover his genitals as she tried to coax him to respond to her caresses. She was trying to keep focused, in the dark of their bedroom, on the sharp, clever utopian dreamer she loved, with his long hands, and his slim pelvis and his funny, endearing, crane-like gait, as if his knees were double-jointed and he was wearing invisible stacked heels; she could see his face, moulded in shadow turned away from her approaches, mutely stuffed into the pillow as she had done herself as a child when assailed by a hundred nameless causes of fury and misery and misunderstood-ness.

'Phil, please—', she was pleading with him. Any chance of the blessed relief of sex, the skies lightening after thunder, fled as her voice swelled with disappointment and reproach and bafflement. 'Please let's try . . . to talk, at least.'

'Why?'

'What do you mean, why?' She was limping. 'Because we're not . . . talking.'

'I'm asleep. It's late. I'm tired.'

She tried to turn him to face her, but he was balled up to resist her; she began clambering over his body so that she could look into his eyes. Always look into your lover's eyes, the phrase from the old sex manual she'd read when she was trying to find out about all this, floated back into her mind.

'Phil, we must talk.'

'I'm not the insomniac round here. I need to sleep. I want to sleep. Now.'

A wave of fury rolled over her; she plunged towards him, pushing her mouth on his, to kiss him, to force him to kiss her in response. His lips hardened into the bite of a vice, but, before he clamped tight, she touched his tongue, soft and floppy and damp, like a flannel slimy with soap, as it fled hers.

He pushed her away, his arms that had lain so bonelessly, like the limbs of a victim of a wasting paralysis, lifted her off him, as once he had lifted her so easily when they used to run around in the house, playing their children's games.

He was shouting, 'Leave off, for fuck's sake, Gramercy. Just leave off.'

This was terrible, this was the plain where there is no water, the tundra where not a blade grows, the howling icecap where cryogenic gales drive away polar bears, even, the deserts of the heart, the dried up crevasses of harlots' cunts: she was sobbing, she was pounding him with her hands.

'That's it, beat me, go ahead,' said Phil. 'I'm just a wife, an old-fashioned wife you can beat up. You and your life have turned me into a housewife, circa 1955 – except I don't sing as I go around dusting.'

'That's not true,' Gramercy wept. 'You chose to stay down here, you offered to look after things while I toured and recorded and . . .'

'No, you're doing exactly what suits you. Your life would be no different without me. I make no difference. You hardly notice whether I'm there or not. You know, Gramercy, I once painted bright green spots on my cheeks, with some of the paint left over from the conservatory, and you never noticed them. I did it for fun, to make you laugh, but when you walked in you didn't look at me, so I kept them all day and you never reacted. So I wiped them off with white spirit – and then you just giggled and said, "What's that smell – have you been sniffing stuff?" ' He turned to her, now, more kindly, put out a hand to her face, sleepily. 'You can't help it, girl. That's the way you are. Go to sleep now. Try to sleep now.'

She did, eventually, after she'd had a slug of malt and two cigarettes and half a tub of chocolate chip ice cream, crying downstairs in the kitchen as through the windows she saw the first light touch the edges of the purple-brown bracken on the moor, where ruined walls enclosed land that had been abandoned, after the struggle to farm that forbidding terrain proved too great even for the desperate men and women who hoed it and dragged out thousands of stones.

Perseverance, wept Gramercy. I must show perseverance.

Days later, she alluded to the episode she'd witnessed in the hutches, making a clumsy attempt to chaff Phil about the stink that hung about him when he came back to the house from the sheds.

'That buck rabbit,' he responded, without missing a beat. 'He sprays all the time – anyone and anything. He's ferocious, out of control. He's weird.'

Though some of the animals had died, and others escaped, when Phil left the sanctuary he'd made was overflowing with the original foundlings and acquisitions, plus an aviary full of birds of all kinds, some missing one digit on one claw, some with lesions on their ceres through infestations of parasites or similar problems, others whole but now too tame and fat to set loose.

Gramercy advertised for homes for them; she asked about in the pub for local zoos who might be interested; Monica put up a notice in the local shops and sub post offices, at Feverel and farther afield. They needed someone to come and help Gramercy look after the refuge, now that Phil had gone away.

5

A Scrap of Scarf

In the tree-lined suburb of St Maure, lying alongside a canal much painted by the Impressionists, the headquarters of FemMédecs occupied a zigzag brick-and-stone turn-of-the-century villa *ornée*; it had been left to the society by a handbag and luggage manufacturer as a memorial to his beloved daughter, a pioneering female paediatrician who died of leukaemia before she was thirty. Doctor Séverine Martin, stationed for a period at home in order to recoup her strength after a prolonged stint in another war zone, called in on the offices to pick up her mail; though meant to be resting, she'd attended an international conference on the uses of poisons in contemporary warfare. She found several messages from one Steve Catnach, a journalist whom she'd first come across during the siege of Tirzah twelve years before, and who'd covered the agency's work on and off ever since. He was writing a cover story for the weekend magazine of *The Fanfare*, and he wanted to interview her about recent developments – if she was free, he added tentatively, he could give her dinner.

She deflected the small, tired flicker of lust she detected in this invitation and asked him instead to come to the office at lunchtime; they would go round the corner to a small place she liked in the neighbourhood, where the canal transport workers stopped for their midday meal; they could eat well there, and talk undisturbed.

It was, Ella reflected later, a sudden burst of unusual good humour on the part of destiny that brought her and Phoebe to Dr Martin's office the same day as this journalist from Enoch. Steve Catnach seized on them: they became his story, the one that would make his mark on a paper to which he had just transferred, rather expensively, from a rival organ and consequently needed to justify his salary to the rest of the writing staff who, at the daily morning meetings, had little loving kindness for his contributions.

Ella had slowly worked her way west, leaving the desolation of Tirzah three years after the end of the siege, and attaining, through many vicissitudes, some partial security in Pontona in the heart of the continent; there for nearly eight years, she established herself among the thousands of clandestine workers, many of whom were waiting, like her, to move on. For she never lost sight of her twin goals: first, of finding Dr Martin and holding her to her promise, and second of reaching Enoch, where they would surely track down Phoebus and be united again. By dint of patient enquiries in furtive hotel telephone calls, banking on rich clients paying by credit card and not noticing the odd extra charge, she'd traced FemMédecs' regional rep, and found out that Dr Martin was indeed now back in her native country, between tours of duty to trouble spots. With the money Luigi had paid her for the valuables that she came across in her hotel work (that singer's sweaty nightie, dinged sandals and silver tights, bagged at the knee and stained at the foot, had fetched quite a sum, and Luigi hadn't cheated them out of it), Ella and Phoebe went to the immense vainglorious temple of travertine that was Pontona's central railway station and got seats – one adult, one child – on the night train going north. They gambled on eluding the frontier checks. At the first cry in the speeding night of '*Documenti! Documents!*', Ella pushed Phoebe above the sleeping freight of the train into the luggage rack, and covered the girl with someone's coat (Phoebe's body was so slight, it disappeared); Ella herself squatted down behind the luggage, where it was heaped at the end of the carriage, pulling a sports holdall on top of her. She'd had plenty of practice eluding guards, and could keep her nerve.

Now, in springtime St Maure, after a continuous journey of three days from Pontona, with the money from Gramercy's things running very low, she told the receptionist, 'Please say that I am the woman Dr Martin knows from the siege of Tirzah and I have my daughter with me, the girl with no skin . . .'

The young male receptionist looked glazed and began shaking his head wearily. Ella took out the scrap of scarf, with the silver threads now tin-like in their tarnish, the weft threadbare. 'Show Dr Martin this, please.' He looked at the poor scrap dubiously, but Ella pressed it on him. 'Just this little thing, please.'

To the young man's surprise, Séverine Martin uttered a cry when she saw the scarf, and tears sprang to her eyes so that her glasses misted up and she took them off to wipe them as she exclaimed, 'They're here! Where?'

She flew from her office and found Ella and Phoebe in the reception area, sitting across from Steve Catnach who had just arrived and was waiting to announce himself.

'Docteur Martin,' he said, getting to his feet and putting out a hand to shake hers.

'Excuse me for a moment,' she said, waving to him as she passed him by, to take Ella by the shoulders and look at her through her tears and kiss her. Then she turned to Phoebe.

'You've grown!' she said, though the girl was still puny. Then Séverine Martin sighed, and passed her hands over her eyes under her glasses, saying, 'I never thought I'd find you – that you'd find me. After I was taken out – by air ambulance, you know – I was unconscious, from . . . hunger, and you . . . I didn't know what had happened to you. I tried to find out, but there was such confusion. Nobody knew.'

Ella nodded. Phoebe said, for she often spoke now for her mother, 'Mum knew that. That's why we came to find you. Besides, you're famous, so you stick out.'

'Ah, *ma petite*,' said Séverine Martin, touching Phoebe's cheek. 'It's not common for me to become emotional, not at all. I've a crocodile hide – oh!' she heard what she had said – 'I'm sorry, I mean to do what I do you have to stop feeling things for this one, or that one. You cannot become attached. But this is something I've hoped for. For ten years I've thought so often of you and of that time. Ah, I've dreamed to see you two again.'

Ella said, carefully, 'So you remember? What you said then?'

'How could I forget?' The doctor paused. 'I have the other piece, I've kept it in my case, with my instruments, all this time.'

Phoebe said, 'I didn't remember what you looked like. I thought you were older.' She smiled, and her small round face grew bright. 'I'm well, I'm strong, but I . . .'

'The pain still comes,' said Ella, indicating her daughter's arms, her back, her legs.

The journalist could not contain his curiosity: two of the continent's drifting horde of female beggars, mother and child in their headrags, with busted and grimy sneakers on their feet, with their dirty old bags of belongings, now greeted with rapture by a heroine of the war. 'How do you guys know each other?' he asked, with determined cheer.

'Now you . . .' Dr Martin hesitated.

'Steve, Steve Catnach,' he reminded her.

'Yes, Steve. Steve, you are very lucky to be here to see this. It's an extraordinary moment. This woman . . .'

'Ella,' said Ella.

'Ella.'

'And Phoebe,' added Ella.

'This Ella saved my life.'

And so, over lunch at the local *estaminet*, the plan took shape. Steve Catnach would tell the story of the women's vigil in the basement of the hospital, as he was told it (which was not the whole story, for both women tacitly agreed, without conferring, not to give the full details). He would find the photographer who had taken the picture of Phoebe after the bombing on the road that summer day more than a decade ago, he would track other witnesses of that notorious and tragic blunder, he would start a media campaign to bring the young girl to Enoch, where revolutionary skin regeneration techniques were developed far ahead of other countries' medical expertise, and he would commit *The Fanfare* to organising an appeal and getting the necessary papers to admit Phoebe with her mother into the country.

'It'll give the paper a profile,' he said. 'Put some clear blue water between us and the competition, who can't make up their minds about the refugee question – talking of quotas and pressure on schools and social services, danger to the democratic ecology, and all that – and then mouthing about human rights and our great history of tolerance and openness. We'll show we're the family paper that isn't scared of coming off the fence. That we're not the kind to pussyfoot about, we know what compassion means and instead of just blah-blah, we do something about it.'

294

But it would take a little time. Meanwhile, Ella should hang on, managing the way she had done till now.

Doctor Martin put in, 'But you'll advance her some money, no? So she can find somewhere to live, have a permanent address, for example? Then we shan't lose her again?'

Steve Catnach had no difficulty, of course, in finding the photographer who'd taken the picture, even though the massacre of Tirinčeva had sunk in public memory beneath the waves of other conflicts, other disasters, other images of children dying. But the picture was one of the ciphers of atrocity that set the standard for the later records: the picture agency had sent Phoebe's phantom down the wires, beaming through the air her fragile flayed body, her mute howl. The photograph had gone quivering through airspace to be reassembled on the front page of newspapers here and there, and subsequently, everywhere, including annuals and encyclopaedias of the world's best photographs, with increasingly apocalyptic titles.

A veteran of many hotspots, the photographer told Steve Catnach: 'I got there with the medics, just after it happened. I think you can feel the horror from my photograph, how hot the tarmac was and how raw her body was. I was proud to get that picture. It brought home so much of the true nature of war. It got to people. It changed things. It's what a war photographer dreams of, that scale of opportunity.

'The wire service photograph is in black and white so it doesn't show her flesh like prime cut. I had two cameras, one with colour, but for commercial reasons in those days we always shot in black and white too. But I do remember the moment in bright Technicolor; she was haloed in a blaze and the sky was so blue, too, beyond the smoke. You could reproduce the pic in colour – it never has appeared because after the other one became so famous, the colour looks sort of false. And maybe strikes a wrong note of horror flick grue – maybe papers aren't good at visual irony.

'She wasn't alone. I framed her to look like that, because it made a more striking picture, but there were others, too, children, old women, some younger ones. Her mother. No men. When I reached the spot, several victims were lying on the road, incinerated like logs in a grate in the early morning, still holding their shape, but disintegrating at the slightest poke into white, papery ash. I made several pictures of the whole massacre, but picture editors the world over went for her. Because she was a little girl. You could say she was lucky.

'I hesitated about taking the photographs at all, it seemed – it was early days in my career – indecent in the presence of the dead. But I always think of Lee Miller, who didn't flinch when she saw horror but made its picture for others to know its face too. All this has become banal, now, and getting photographs has been degraded by some of our colleagues to a slut's trade, but I still think it needs courage to look at the heaped dead at Dachau and take a light reading, and I wanted to have the same kind of steel, and the same kind of panache as Lee, who went into the wreckage with the army after the defeat and took off her cleated boots and had her first hot bath for days in Hitler's bathroom, Prinzgentenplatz 17, Munich; she's looking up with a question mark in the corner of her top lip. Do you know the photograph?'

From then on, *The Fanfare*'s campaign rolled, and in the autumn of that year Ella and Phoebe flew in an aeroplane for the first time, carrying documents identifying them and granting them entry; they were accompanied by press. They landed at the airport north of Enoch, where they were met by more journalists, and were driven to an undisclosed address in a small new town nearby. The photographer was commissioned to make a portrait of Phoebe now, and was flown to Albion and sent to meet her again at the country hotel where *The Fanfare* had billeted her. He took a simple, straight image, in which her small, oval, defiant face was blurred, almost as if seen through tears. He also photographed her back, to show the sore map of her skinned flesh.

Steve Catnach's paper continued to hide them from all rivals until the time came for Phoebe to be admitted to the Royal Bethlehem Hospital for Children, in the heart of old Enoch, where Dr Martin's private representations and the public's clamour had won Phoebe the attentions of the most skilled skin-grafting surgeons in the world. But meanwhile, waiting for the bed to become free and the team of doctors to be assembled, Ella and Phoebe learned to go to the pub round the corner from their neat little brand new red-tiled house in Market Cluer, and sit in the back in the children's room with the telly, where a fire burned whatever the weather, and a collection of darning mushrooms and pincushions decorated the cabinets. Phoebe relished the Special Kids' menu: Basket of Nuggets and Chips, with ketchup and a Coke, followed by two scoops of strawberry swirl ice cream; she would flourish a chip, dripping with gore, while she made remarks to the screen and the company. Steve Catnach began to address all his instructions to her, not to her mother, whom he felt he knew as little about now as he had when he first came across her in the office of FemMédecs du Monde. The interpreter he'd employed found Ella's speech tricky – she had an odd, unplaceable accent, he said, as if she didn't really come from Tirzah. This was not something Steve Catnach needed to explore, not when he was running a front-page campaign against the systematic extermination of the Tirzahner locals by the invaders.

Ella had no papers for herself or for her daughter, besides the ones *The Fanfare* had arranged, so he hadn't been able to ascertain her age or Phoebe's. Phoebe must have reached her early teens at the very least, he calculated, if you counted off the years of their struggle westwards. She still looked like a child, thin and fragile-boned, with that eerie jellyfish transparency of flesh. However, in the settled atmosphere of Market Cluer, she was beginning to grow, doing well at the local school and overcoming her handicaps, the teachers reported to *The Fanfare*, with courage and flair. Ella, by contrast, fretted; the enforced inactivity of life in the ribbon development that linked the old market town with the countryside's agritourism, boating and fruit farms, made her desperate.

'We must go to Enoch,' she kept telling Catnach. 'I want to work, I want Phoebe to learn – more than . . .' she waved her hand at the window and the village, and sighed. Here, the girl hung around the bus shelter outside the pub with the local youngsters who'd nothing to do but smoke and dream of dealers coming their way, until Ella appeared to drag her away to bed. But when one of Phoebe's new friends commented, the following night, 'Yer mum's really weird', Phoebe jumped on her, and then, when the girl pushed her off, she fell down on to the road, on her back. She didn't scream, but got up slowly and turned on her heels and left them, walking as ordinarily as she could while the pain blazed down her spine: they knew not to come at her again, but hung half-menacing, half-ashamed, in the chequered lozenge of light shone on to the road by the bus shelter.

'Looks like a rat when it's born,' she heard one of her friends say. 'I've seen it.'

'Newborn rat.'

'Back of arms and legs like slime – I saw her at break. She oozes.'

'Yuck,' said another. 'Brain-damaged.'

Ella argued with Catnach that they'd thrive in the capital, that they were used to cities, to noise, to activity, that Phoebe needed to be mixed with people more like her. 'Here we look different – in Enoch, we would disappear. Nobody'd notice us.'

'That's just it – we can't have you disappearing.'

On Phoebe's first visit to the hospital, Steve explained to her, she wouldn't be staying more than a night.

'The doctors have told me they're just going to take a sample of skin from you, so that they can make you a new one. They'll just put your legs to sleep, and it'll be over.'

Catnach was able to write fervently about the girl's courage. 'The surgeon lifted a small section of skin, about the size of an old penny, or, a silver milk bottle top, or, for those who don't remember such things, a slice through a hard-boiled egg,' he wrote. 'At one point during the operation, Phoebe opened her eyes and began watching. She never flinched. The ordeals she has lived through during her short life have given her amazing courage to face suffering, to accept the reality of the body.'

Having taken this piece of healthy skin from a part of her upper thighs at the front, where she had not been burned, the medical team cultured it in a Petri dish. From this portion of unimpaired, healthy, whole tissue, a scraping that looked more like the dry wing of a dead insect, the doctors began weaving a new raiment of flesh for Phoebe, a new epidermis and endodermis, as if that scrap were rather the vital cocoon of a giant silkworm whose fibres they could wind out hour after hour until they could cool and salve her rawness in its flossy filaments.

The operation took six hours, and six surgeons, working with needles and thread; they stitched the lustrous, pliant envelope of new tissue to Phoebe's body as she lay face down, making neat knots at intervals. Afterwards, Phoebe lay, swaddled, in bed, first in the hospital, then back at Market Cluer. It would take fifteen weeks of painkillers and rest and visits from the district nurse for the graft to heal; the bandages were to be changed weekly: *The Fanfare* sent a car to take Ella and Phoebe to the hospital, and Steve phoned them, and sometimes visited, to write up the girl's progress.

'Phoebe is beginning to grow into a normal healthy teenager,' he reported. 'Her mother tells me she has appetites and moods, and a streak of rebellion, but isn't that just like every other girl of her age in the world?'

She is *beginning to grow,* Ella nodded to herself. *It's true. It isn't just that she's putting on weight that could be the effect of enforced immobility and the food but I can tell it's not only that she has had her first period   it frightened us at first when we saw blood on the sheets in the morning and I looked at the bandages thinking I'd find a terrible patch with blood seeping through where the skin had torn or become infected   with the pills they give her against the pain she wouldn't feel anything if something went wrong but then I realised what it was   and I was glad   I kissed her and she let me kiss her with a kind of softness she hasn't shown before because she was glad too   though it means we have to guard now against other dangers   not yet not yet*

It seemed we had got stuck in a moment of time that would hold us for ever   that we would never be able to pull ourselves free of its hold as if it was one of these photographs they take stopping time   Phoebe is a like a monument to them but to me she should be living, changing, growing from day to day. Like an ordinary girl, the journalist is right   she is catching up now to the time that she lost her new skin is bringing her forward matching her body to her mind setting her free

When the last bandages came off, the doctors were interviewed; they beamed at their success. 'It was one of the most ambitious operations of its kind ever undertaken,' Catnach reported. '"It has been successful beyond our highest expectations," the hospital spokesman declared.'

Phoebe's new skin gleamed with the high-gloss, new-minted look of a sweet chestnut prised from its snug white casing. Her afflicted translucency now opaque, densely textured as a precious hardwood, supple with a healthy water-repellent sheen on it like teak that will turn a deck from a puddle into a watertight drum or lignum vitae that will permit clockwork to function even when saltwater is gnawing at its innards, the young girl appeared to glow. She was still chary of revealing herself, and preferred long skirts that wrapped her legs and T-shirts that dangled down over her hands. But she could not extinguish altogether

her new-made radiance. Journalists, coming to interview her, talked about her dazzling personality; instinctively, they pulled out their dark glasses as they fiddled with the buttons on their recording equipment.

'What now?' Catnach asked at the morning meeting.

'What's the progress on their documents?' asked the deputy editor.

'Slow, very slow.'

'Do you think they've a chance of remaining? Is that what they want?'

'It's tricky. I'd say that in cases like these, the barometer's falling. Public opinion, if it thinks for a moment longer than that first rush of pity, on the whole wants people to "go back where they come from", repaired, restored – and grateful.'

'Tirzah's being reconstructed. As we speak, millions of dollars of humanitarian aid are being poured into its regeneration,' the home affairs editor reminded the group, unnecessarily. 'There's no reason they shouldn't return, find their old home again, settle back. Surely that's preferable to struggling to make a new life here?'

'She wants to move to Enoch and she's very insistent that Phoebe be educated here.'

'Turning into a Tory mum, is she? Demanding access to the "Right Schools"?'

Catnach ignored this, and the fashion editor broke the awkward pause: 'Let me make a suggestion. How about I do a style job on Phoebe for a spread about the image options of young girls like her? Could be fun – the whole caboodle, Sloane to dinge, with lots of cheap high street labels and make-up and stuff everyone can buy.'

'What's dinge?' asked the property pages.

'Where've you been? Haven't you noticed who's buying up the posh houses these days? Snaggle-toothed rock stars who look like they've just crawled out of a sewer.'

Steve said, 'Please not dinge. Might look like "Before" in a "Before and After" story. After all, they might as well have crawled out of a sewer.'

'All right, we'll go a bit more upmarket – chunky ethnic jewellery and Japanese *prêt-à-porter*.'

6

Hortense to Kim; Kim to Hortense, again and again

Subject: Skipwith 673
Date: Mon, 29 June 199– 11:37:49 +0100
From: Hortense Fernly<h.fernly@natmus.ac.alb>
To: kim.mcquy<hswu@lattice.onlyconnect.com>

- -

Kim, I was out of town when you called, I wasn't 'hiding from you' as
you claimed to my colleague in Archives. You must calm down and not
get so over-wrought about this and indeed everything else. My job is to
present the National Museum's classical antiquities to the public (to
whom they belong): you are a member of that public. I am merely doing
my job. I don't share your views about history. I'm a historian, and a
pretty down to earth person and I believe that things happened and we
can find out what they were and how they came about. However,
because Education & Outreach are now priorities I have to make history
matter now, so you – your way of thinking – has some relevance to me,
even though it flies in the face of objective use of evidence. You and
people like you understand what in the past is prologue and we at the
Museum have a public responsibility to keep in touch with these issues.
This sounds preachy – and defensive – which annoys me, but I don't
know how to put it any other way.

You'll also be delighted to hear, I trust, that we have received lottery
funds for a full new exhibit; and that the director is 100 per cent behind
a complete refurbishment. No more hole in the corner displays.

Yours, HF

Subject: *Trust me*
Date: Mon, 29 June 199– 17:37:27 +0100
From: kim.mcquy<hswu@lattice.onlyconnect.com>
To: Hortense Fernly<h.fernly@natmus.ac.alb>

Hetty Hetty   don't run away from me and from the discoveries we're
making together – I should have guessed I should have known that you
were in Shiloh to bring her back – that was what you were up to wasn't
it   it gives me an uncanny feeling to think of the two of you together
miles up in the sky – but I wish you'd told me – I wish *she*'d told me –
sometimes I feel my contact's dimming not brightening   though I know
now she's so much bigger than the mask or the mummy or even the
documents: she is history yes! History now!

the hswu website is currently getting around 300-350 hits a week – the
database is growing, I'm trying for grants for someone part time maybe
fulltime to monitor and respond.

it's brilliant you'll show me the new arrangement because our
members are going to be very involved

can I come by on friday after school to see the plans – I could be with
you by 4 – *thank you* for giving me another chance

I can't wait Hetty – to see you to see her – her husk but you for real –
Kim

Subject: Plans
Date: Fri, 3 July 199– 22:48:22 +0100
From:kim.mcquy<hswu@lattice.onlyconnect.com>
To: Hortense Fernly<h.fernly@natmus.ac.alb>

Dear Hetty the plans are sad really really sad – a ghastly dungeon that'll
put everybody off – kids won't find it scary nice just sad – we must meet
to discuss getting another set drawn up – I was glad to see them but
shame you couldn't be there   Anna agrees with me though

how about a competition I thought EC rulings required open public
accesss to such things ??? (These plans are going to have to be scrapped)

I know how busy you are but please –   I'll come by on Monday after
school cheers Kim

Subject: Re: Plans
Date: Mon, 6 July 199– 09:13:45 +0100
From: Hortense Fernly<h.fernly@natmus.ac.alb>
To: kim.mcquy@hswu<lattice.onlyconnect.com>

Kim, Wait a minute. I am busy today. What do *you* do when you've
disruptive pupils in your class ?! Think of yourself in that light, and then
of me in your shoes. Perhaps that will help you to be more moderate.
And then, to use your own kind of language, chill out.

   I was away seeing my husband, if you must know. The university
where he teaches isn't a million miles from where the Leto was being
exhibited. We had a good time and a much needed rest.

   As for the plans, I'm prepared to discuss them with you, calmly. We're
in a new phase of relations with our 'customers', as the Director keeps
telling me. We've made huge strides but I know we've a long way to go.
Still, you should be glad of what you've already achieved and the
attention your wishes have been given.

   I think the main reason that I'm so interested in your relation to the
bundle, is that you're openly making use of the past in the interests of
the present.

   [I must not get involved, Hortense said to herself, as she pressed
down on the backspace delete key to remove her last sentence.]

   Hetty

Subject: Leto's return
Date: Mon, 6 July 199– 23:49:16 +0100
From: kim.mcquy<hswu@lattice.onlyconnect.com>
To: Hortense Fernly<h.fernly@natmus.ac.alb>

Hello mrs fernly – I'm attaching the stuff I'm putting out on the web
subject to your approval – of the historical bits – also my call to hswu
to lobby the museum for a better show – yours (I mean it, just the same)
Kim

303

Subject: Re: Leto's Return
Date: Wed, 8 July 199– 13.21:24 +0100
From: Hortense Fernly<h.fernly@natmus.ac.alb>
To: kim.mcquy<hswu@lattice.onlyconnect.com>

- -

Dear Kim, The meeting over the proposals yesterday postponed the final
decision over the Leto display. Everything's up in the air again, you'll be
pleased to hear. There's new room for discussion – and alternatives.

And by the way the report from the conservation lab after the show
has come in – and it's really quite exciting. That frogs story Meeks
transcribed and translated for which there was no surviving manuscript
that we could find *is* written *on the bands*, which is as I rather
guessed, after you began to ask. Best wishes, Hetty.

Subject: Re: re: Leto's return AND film!
Date: Wed, 8 July 199– 21:24:35 +0100
From: kim.mcquy<hswu@lattice.onlyconnect.com>
To: Hortense Fernly<h.fernly@natmus.ac.alb>

- -

Hetty – Excellent the proposals have been ditched   now we can start
again do something really good   as for the conservation report – I knew
it – from the very moment you said there was writing I understood what
she'd been telling me about how she inhabited this other form how she
turned herself into well – ink – don't you remember – she shifts shape
from one creature to another when she's raped and the god pursues her
until she turns on him   all legs and   tentacles and. . .squirts him Yess!

theres something else   Gramercy Poule – heard of her? – wants to see
me about a documentary she thinks she can get up and running – she'll
write a song for Leto she says and perform at the bundle's inauguration
she suggested getting away from it all to talk about it : she has a pile
on Fellmoor – she didnt say that but you know what I mean – what do
you think?

You could COME AWAY WITH ME! [now it was Kim's turn to strike
out a line.]

Term will be over soon for *two* whole months.

:-) :-) :-) :-) :-) :-)

your kim

Subject: Re: Re: Leto's return AND film!
Date: Thurs, 9 July 199– 17:29:46 +0100
From: Hortense Fernly<h.fernly@natmus.ac.alb>
To: kim.mcquy<hswu@lattice.onlyconnect.com>
- -
Dear Kim,

  Do you really have to go that far to a meeting about a film that
probably won't happen? Can't you see her here? We need to talk this
over (as well as several other things). Can you meet me at The Blue
Moon tomorrow? 5.30?
  Yours, Hetty

Subject: Blue Moon
Date: Thurs, 9 July 199– 23:16:37 +0100
From: kim.mcquy<hswu@lattice.onlyconnect.com>
To: Hortense Fernly<h.fernly@natmus.ac.alb>
- -
excellent I'll be there   kim

Freedom Days.

PART SIX

Freedom Days

I

An Interview, Cantelowes

The escalator was conveying Ella and Phoebe steeply to the surface, where the tepid light of an Enoch spring beckoned from the steel-girt porch of Cantelowes station; at a stately pace, it carried them past bright masks and gesturing bodies, some of them stuck in the eye or nose with dingy gum, two hundred feet up through a twisting wind that blew savage and hot in their faces. The plumes on the rim of the hills around Tirzah, flaring into the blackness of the curfew, leaped up again from over a decade ago behind Ella's eyes as the underground blast singed her lids, chewed at the fastenings of her jacket as if to strip her, and flattened Phoebe's long skirt against her legs. Ella gasped as she stumbled off the toothed step at the end of the flight and came to a standstill to get her bearings. It was much colder up above; the tunnels were so fuggy that passengers rode in a mute torpor, their feet in drifts of old papers, their heads into new ones, as they passed through the coiled guts of the capital.

Below, far below, the train rumbled off into the depths; Ella thought of it plunging into the darkness, snug in its runnel, leaving behind humans like warm worm casts.

They had an appointment, with the Advisory Council for Refugees and Asylum Seekers, an arm of the Bethesda Foundation. When the ticket collector inspected their tickets – the narrow turnstiles of the big central stations were yet to be installed in Cantelowes – Phoebe asked him the way by showing him the address on the letter inviting them to attend. He drew a crooked map on the paper, and carefully, mother and daughter emerged into the weekday choke and roar of Cantelowes High

Street. They turned past the dump bins of free newspapers for backpackers and travellers who'd driven six thousand miles from home in camper vans; they avoided, as they had learned to do, the sales pitch of the *Voice of the Street* vendor. But Phoebe couldn't help catching the eye of the scarecrow huddled with his cur at the entrance by the ticket machines. She twitched at the sight of his impaled eyebrow, lip, and nostril: at the sight of opened flesh she felt her old wounds again under their new, smooth camouflage.

Together, they began to descend the shallow incline of the street towards the third turning right after the police station, as the guard had indicated. Ella was carrying a bundle of things she thought might interest the tribunal – no, they weren't a tribunal, they had told her that through the interpreter, but an advisory body, there to help her. This wasn't an interrogation; this was a helping hand. To her and Phoebe. So that they could argue their case to stay here, and thrive.

In the bag, she had some mementoes to help identify her and verify the odyssey she would be telling them: a piece of shrapnel taken from Phoebe after the attack; the scrap of silver threaded scarf; a sewing kit from the Metropole with one needle left and two mother-of-pearl shirt buttons; a calling card with the crest of the Grand Hotel in Pontona and the words 'Your room has been serviced by . . .' followed by a blank where the chambermaid's name would be inscribed, and closing, 'Thank You'.

Ella made her way down the narrow and crowded pavement. Everything was in motion, even the pavements seemed to be lifting with the energy breaking through from underneath. Until now her world had been set to a slow time, but now its rhythm was picking up, so that she couldn't take in everything; the pendulum was speeding up so much that however much she told herself, Observe, pay attention, don't miss a thing, because it's always in the dead spot on the skin that the witchfinder finds you out, she couldn't keep track of everything. A fragment floated into her mind from the long time ago when she was in Cadenas: Abbess Cecily telling her and her other 'fillies': 'Keep your wits sharpened, so that your spirit stays alert, like the skins of horses trembling even when their deep flesh sleeps.'

But sights and sensations and sounds were flickering and blurring and flashing around her as she plunged through the crowd streaming this way and that in the street. She wasn't alarmed; she was used to packs.

But this feeling was different, different from the jostling, narrow streets of the Citadel, from the caravan of Feltimye, from the shanty agglomerations of Tirzah. This city was whirling, and it was catching her up into a different kind of motion, rising and spinning to its own loud but unheard tunes.

Phoebe moved more confidently, with a spring in her step, and a determined thrust of her small head and neat, square shoulders. Enoch's pace and noise appeared to refresh her, as if, her mother thought with not a little fear, her new, man-made carapace needed to vibrate to the roar of a transport lorry, like the giant now delivering frozen shrink-wrapped slabs of bread and mince on the corner they were passing. Phoebe was flourishing in this climate of grinding levers, sirens wailing and blasting, gears meshing and phones squealing, exhausts belching; she trod with light feet on the rent tarmac, the cement-tiled pavements, breathing easily as the air combusted around her, turning from fuel to ash to dust. She was growing splendid: two inches taller since the operation, with a high look from under straight brows, and a quick, clever tongue. She hadn't reacted to the idea of the fashion spreads with the enthusiasm *The Fanfare* expected.

'Do I get to keep the clothes?' she'd asked, not sulkily, but with determination.

'Oh no!' the fashion editor was shocked. 'They're samples, and we just borrow them for the shoot.' She paused. 'I might be able, I suppose, to arrange for you to keep one outfit . . .'

'Do I get some dosh?'

'Wow, you're a quick learner,' the journalist responded.

Later, to Steve Catnach, she admitted her disillusion. 'They're just in it for what they can get, aren't they? You'd think, after all we've done for her . . .'

Ella wondered about Phoebe's obstinacy.

'Aw, Mum,' said Phoebe, 'I'm jus' fed up with being gawped at.'

At the kerb of the second turning, as they waited to cross the road, Ella took in the heaps of fruits and pulses and greens set out on the stall beside her; some of them she could identify – though nothing was familiar – but in Market Cluer, the single village shop had never overflowed with so much variety and quantity. She stood amazed before the uncommon berries and globes and leaves and fronds and spurs and bunches in orange and scarlet and yellow and even blue. Now and then the stallholder flicked his hand at a solitary fly crawling wearily on a fruit; the insect immediately lumbered off, easily worsted.

Seeing Ella hanging back, undecided, he hailed her loudly, in the words of an old friend or even a lover, and the unaccustomed cheerful language of affection, which Phoebe ignored, curled through Ella like hot chocolate in cold weather. Then, on the pavement, by the barrow's wheels, Ella saw a higgledy-piggledy pile of cartons spilling browning bananas with snapped stems, plump cabbages with yellowing outer leaves, tomatoes with puckering round their stalks, and some small oranges with wrinkled rinds. "2'nds" said the sign in clumsy black letters. '50p the lot.' Later, on their way back, she decided, she'd bargain for some of this produce.

Phoebe was plucking at her sleeve. 'Let's cross, c'm'on.' She was often hostile now, Ella found, to her mother's dogged economies.

Phoebe had taken to ironing her own clothes before she went out; and was often critical of Ella's wardrobe: 'That get-up is sad,' she'd say. 'But your mother's not exactly a happy sort,' Ella once protested – it was the nearest she came to teasing this tough, newborn goblin daughter, in whom she recognised, however, something of her own sense of purpose, of her capacity to adapt to new occasions.

The cascading vegetable stand spelled affluence, plenty, surplus – such possibilities! Her heart lurched: was it possible that they would never be hungry again?

They crossed the road; by the recycling dump opposite, two men were bussing each other, dribbling cider from bottles they were waving towards their mouths. The green, black, maroon plastic bins were printed with the local borough's name in lemon yellow, with a logo showing a carpenter's square and a pair of scissors. The two men, heads down, shouting, butted each other and then fell into each other's arms against the charity clothes container; they came down in a heap on to the tangle that had spilled on to the paving stones, into the dried puddles of former brawls and the smears of passing dogs' piss and worse, and lay there quietly wound together, one with a babygro drifting across his face, the other with a six-year-old's jumpsuit twisted round his slack fist; the Strongbow bottles dripped their last drops into their newfound bedding.

One called out to Phoebe's long skirt as she went by, 'Go on, love, give us a kiss.' He rolled over and the other shouted, 'You, with a mug like a pig's bottom. Have a heart, have some respect. But she's a real beauty, aren't you darling?'

They walked on by, Phoebe haughty in contempt – though, again, Ella's fingers itched to sift the rags. Later. In Enoch, even the refuse was rich, richer by far than the rubbish tips of the foreign corps that the Tirzahners picked over.

Reaching a bus stop, where the queue was growing, Ella watched as a mother bent down to reinsert a dummy in a toddler's mouth; at her waist, between her top and the belt of her jeans, a wide smile of creamy skin appeared all of a sudden, with the plump pleat of her buttocks sliced by a black strap that slid into the crack: this strapped flesh smiled up at Ella.

Freedom, thought Ella. You can do anything here.

The young mother straightened, and Ella, her vigilance distracted by the face that belonged to the thong, was jostled by two ten-year-olds suddenly ejected from the newsagent's by the bus stop.

'See this sign,' the newsagent said. He was turbaned and bearded in suit and tie. He pointed to his window where in crooked capitals, Ella read 'NO MORE than 2 children at a time'. 'Can't you read? Don't they teach you anything at school? Why aren't you there now anyway?'

The boys hung gleefully just out of reach, dancing on their feet as if they wanted to pee.

'We don't have school, and we's goin' to report yer,' said the larger, freckled one, 'You's violent, you's laid your fuckin' 'ands on us.'

'Yeah, we're going down the social services,' said the other, 'and tell on yer. Yer abusing us – y're child abusers.' He looked thrilled with this inspiration.

The newsagent's daughter appeared by his elbow. 'I know you lot. You're not being let in here again. Let's see your pockets . . .'

But the boys were off, one of them scooting out into the road in front of the bus that had just pulled up and hurling over his shoulder at his partner, 'Chicken!', so that the other child flew out in his wake and a messenger on a motorbike skidded and slewed across the tarmac hitting the big concrete planter where something spiky was growing out of a bed of empty crisp packets and small bottles of alcopops.

Phoebe pulled at her mother's arm; sometimes, her former, scared, small girl self swam up again through the blaze of her prideful new being. She almost whimpered, but caught herself, as the rider tottered to his feet, apparently uninjured.

A woman came out of the discount shop with a folding garden chair and sat him down on it.

'Them kids,' she said.

'Oh fuck, my trainers!' Ella heard the motorcyclist wail as she and Phoebe manoeuvred past the gaggle that gathered around him. 'They're ruined.'

'There, there,' said the woman with the chair, 'They're only scuffed, they'll come up fine again if you wash them – mind, on the Delicates cycle.'

In the offices of the Centre, Ella and Phoebe sat down in orange easy chairs side by side in the waiting room, where copies of leaflets were racked: dozens of them, on communicable diseases, hereditary and genetic transmissions, help lines for drug problems, domestic violence, housing, procedures for official complaints, dietary and sanitary recommendations, language and interpreting assistance.

A woman came out to find them. 'Ella? And you must be Phoebe?' said Freddie Asman. 'Hello. I'm your interpreter – we've already spoken, I think, when you made the appointment.'

'I'll help, too,' said Phoebe.

'My daughter,' said Ella. 'She's good. She speaks very well.'

Freddie Asman had short blonde hair, a sparkling turquoise sequin between her eyebrows and loose silk trousers and tunic. 'The council's interviewer will be joining us shortly, in one of the quiet rooms. This way.' She led Ella and Phoebe up a steep flight into a small office; asked them if they'd like a cup of coffee, and went softly outside and down the corridor, her fluid trousers undulating over the plush plastic treads of her squishy shoes.

The interviewer entered, smiled at mother and daughter encouragingly, silently. He had the kind of pale eyes that look so transparent the capillaries seem to be bleeding. Placing a lawyer's yellow, ruled pad on his knees, which were sharp and thin and tightly pressed together as if in his zeal to hear their story, he leaned forward towards her.

He asked Ella, 'And how are you both doing? Did the operation go well?'

Ella said, 'The doctors made my daughter a new skin. It's miracle, I think.'

314

'They're wonderful at the Children's Hospital. Thank God it wasn't closed down. There was some threat of that, at one time. And are you comfortable, Phoebe? No problems?'

'No, no problems. It's fantastic; feels like a silk shirt.'

The interviewer looked questioning. 'Something you're *wearing*? Not part of you?'

So he was paying attention to them. Phoebe softened, and said, 'You know those stories about how you feel pain in a limb, even after it's been amputated?'

He nodded.

'So it's like I still feel my old body, like a ghost inside me, but it's not really there. You know, they gave me a colouring book in therapy at the hospital, with dresses you cut out and fitted with flaps on the figures. If you lifted my flap, you'd find the old me there still. But it doesn't mean anything now – before I couldn't do things, I was a wimp. Now . . .'

'Yes,' said Ella. 'You've changed. I'm glad, it's better, much better.' She put her hands together and inclined to the interviewer, as if to thank him.

Freddie came back, set the coffee mug in front of Ella and nodded to her warmly. 'There's a lot of traffic noise, unfortunately,' she said. 'We're hoping for a new building, but meanwhile we have to make do . . . we'll take notes at the same time, so if there's anything drowned by the usual urban chorus of sirens, we shan't have lost it altogether.'

She settled herself down, with a small, ring-bound pad. 'James, I'm all set.'

James Lowther nodded to Ella and began, with Freddie translating. 'Everything you tell us will be kept in confidence, of course. We're here to help you. To do that, it may be in your interests for us to disclose what you tell us to the relevant authorities. Do you follow? About the circumstances of your coming to this country. Your story will shed light on your reasons for wanting to remain here. As I know you know, there's huge pressure on the border authorities to keep the country sealed against . . . well, opportunists and impostors. So we do need to be able to convey to them the particular urgency of your case. The exceptional nature of your request. Clearly, many of the usual causes of alarm don't apply in your case – Phoebe was specially brought for the operation. But if you want to stay on, we have to put cogent reasons . . .

315

'Please start wherever you wish. Real life doesn't have beginnings, middles and ends, not like stories in books.'

Ella began. Freddie stopped her at intervals to translate; she was quicker at following than *The Fanfare*'s interpreter, for she was accustomed to hearing such testimony, day after day in her job at the Council, from people who'd come from a wide range of mountains, valleys, ports and villages with different accents and dialects – and languages – in the ever-widening territory of the conflict. Now and then Phoebe stepped in to correct her and adding commentary of her own, as her mother related how she had first worked in the hospital in Tirzah, but then got a job in the Hotel Metropole as a cleaner which was much better work because there were always foreigners staying there – journalists, arms dealers, medical supervisors, aid workers – and some sort of standards had to be maintained. (She showed them the needlework case.) She told them about the felling of all the trees in the streets and then in the gardens for firewood, about the famine and the rodents and the flies – the traps for foxes and squirrels that brought in food until there weren't any left, about the ceaseless shelling and the intermittent truces. About burying the dead. About Phoebe's struggles with pain ('Don't go on about it,' protested Phoebe.) She told them what they already knew.

'But you,' pressed James Lowther. 'What about you? Perhaps we had better begin at the beginning.'

They ran through a 'Data Maintenance' form, with questions about her date and place of birth, her nationality, her ethnic origins and present allegiances, her religion. To all of them, Ella responded readily, but inconclusively: 'I don't know,' she would answer, with a worried twist to her obliging smile, 'because I lost all my documents when I was too small to remember the details.'

'Don't worry, we're used to that,' said James. 'But your religion – you must know that at least.'

'For a time I was close to some nuns,' Ella began. 'And the priest of the Lazarus mission was brave and kind – that was the last time I went to church – I took shelter there some time before the end came, during a shelling I got caught in . . . I am what you call a stateless person, the officers at the border told me. Without the newspaper, without the photograph of Phoebe, we would never have managed to enter the country – me and Phoebe.'

'We've all the cuttings in our dossier,' James riffled through, showing Ella the photocopied pages in her file. 'But public interest is fickle and the newspapers run a story for just as long as they can squeeze juice out of it. No longer. We need to know what you suffered, and the threats to your survival and wellbeing if you and Phoebe are returned home – well, not home perhaps, but sent back to where you came from.

'You must understand, Ella, that there are hundreds of thousands of refugees seeking admittance to this country at the moment, and each case will be considered on its merits. We want to help you – you must help us. You must give us more to go on.'

'Mum!' Phoebe remonstrated. 'You've got to tell them.' She looked sharply at the interviewers. 'Mum was raped, you must have figured that out at least. I'm the product of war rage – me *and* my brother.' Phoebe looked rosy, fierce. 'If we go back, we're dead meat – 'cos mum's a whore – in their eyes. And I don't belong to one side nor the other. Call me a half-breed, like when a pedigree dog's been fucked by the wrong kind of mate, and they kill all the puppies. They're not worth anything and they'll bring down the value of the whole breed . . .'

Ella sucked in her breath, whispered, 'Where do you get these ideas, Phoebe?'

'I keep a look out, Mum. I see what you don't want to see.' She addressed the interviewer. 'She's always making do and getting by. And she's looking for my brother.'

Ella went on, 'After the siege, when Dr Martin said she'd help Phoebe, I had to find her, so we needed money to follow her. We went to Pontona. Then we came here to look for . . .'

'Your son?'

Ella nodded.

'You'd like to find him. Of course. I can see that,' began James. 'Do you have any idea where to begin?'

'I want to find him,' said Ella. 'But not so that he knows.'

'Aw, Mum!' cried Phoebe. 'What about him and me? What are you so afraid of?'

'Ah, Phoebe.'

So, accompanied by the rhythmic murmur of the interpreter, Ella began trying to piece their story together:

'The shantytown district in Tirzah was down by the river on the east side, where at one time there had been a busy tannery district. After the . . . bombing at Tirinčeva, the hospital did what it could for Phoebe, but they thought she would die anyway, so this was the place for us to go. Those trades – tanners and dyers and furriers – they carried a heavy stigma then, because they touch dead bodies. Besides that, tanning is a dirty business – they use cat piss and dog piss for the mordants. So those people are shunned, even more than undertakers. They blur distinctions between living and dead things. They keep hair and pelts supple and lustrous long after the bodies they covered have perished. But when Phoebe didn't die – this was the first miracle – and they found out we weren't . . . natives, and didn't belong to one side or the other, we were left there to fend for ourselves. When the war spread and began taking all the men off to fight, the women tanners continued, making boots and gun belts and holsters. As for the market in furs, well . . . some generals had girlfriends, but otherwise . . .

'The tanneries made a warren of low buildings and shelters and wharves rising haphazardly on either side of steps leading down to water, where they'd set up their buckets and vats and blocks for beating the skins. I'd seen this river shining, when I first saw Tirzah from the ridge, but once down on its bank, it was dark and dirty, and there were pitch-black corners where all you could see was firelight reflected in the black surface of the river as you . . .' she glanced over at Phoebe. 'I was often desperate, we needed the money.'

James looked uncomfortable. 'Please explain the reasons for your desperate condition, why you did these things. We know – we think we know why you had to, but we have to build the dossier on you, to argue on your behalf.'

'Phoebe was in pain all the time. She had to sleep on her front with nothing touching her back where the skin was gone. The stuff that helped her was only available in certain places and the price was always rising. I used to go to a woman, she was a nurse in the military hospital, she was able to keep back medicines for us, for people like us. It was dangerous for her, though it made her rich, too. She was good to us, though. She'd wait for me to come, even if I was late. They were often drugs dropped for humanitarian aid, which had made their way back to the army, as you know. Sometimes we who needed drugs went to her with things – with food and, when we could lay our hands on them, luxury goods. But they had to be the genuine article. She could tell, and she'd give you nothing for the fakes. But I could get a lot of Phoebe's medicine in return for anything by Louis Vuitton, for example, or for Lycra tights still in the packet or for jeans with the label in the right place, on the back pocket. With rivets.'

'Levi 501s,' whispered Freddie. 'More valuable than hard currency, we know.'

'Yes,' said Ella, barely audibly. 'I sometimes managed to pick up some things like that.'

'How?'

'At my cleaning job – at the Hotel Metropole in the mornings, before I went back to work on the river. Sometimes I'd just come straight out with it. I'd say to the guest, "Your jeans are worth a great deal here – I could convert them into food and medicine for my children." They'd look embarrassed, sometimes angry. Sometimes they'd have tears in their eyes when they handed me the trousers or the belt or whatever. But they'd often give me what I wanted.'

The interviewer peered at the revolving spools of the tape, and Freddie took the slight loss of concentration to put a question. To which Ella replied, 'Phoebe, I don't think you should stay here now.'

'Yes, Phoebe, come with me. I'll get us all some coffee.' James rose to leave the room, beckoning to a reluctant Phoebe to follow him. 'I can stay,' she protested. 'I know it every which way. All of it. I was there.'

James shook his head. 'You, a child! Come on, we all need a bit of sustenance. I'll bring back some biscuits, too.'

After they'd gone, Ella began again, quickly. 'Was it a kind of torture?' she said, echoing the last question. 'It was work, and it brought the money or the food we had to have. Taking the money at its value then, these were roughly our rates: one handjob: a tin of powdered milk.

'Taken from the front: a fair-sized pat of lard/one loaf of bread/ half a cup of sugar.

'Taken from the back: half a kilo of sausages/bacon or two loaves of bread. Really valuable.

'I could do massages, too. Just massage, if they wanted it simple. And some acts were cheap. Some of the other women preferred it – they didn't like face-to-face contact. But I . . . I needed more money. Some of the acts were new to me. I learned them in the tanneries. They came with this war. It wasn't like that – before. Ideas change, and people think of new dangers. And with new dangers come new pleasures. At first when these soldiers came, you could charge a lot for doing it that way, because they hadn't had it like that and they wanted to try it. But soon it was the cheapest tricks who went for that. They liked you on your knees. Afterwards, it was like they hadn't done it – or done it with a woman. It was cleaner, they said. And quicker. They were frightened of the dirt inside us. "I wouldn't put the tip of my umbrella there," one man said to me.

'I kept the children out of it. I was determined to,' said Ella. 'So I had to find ways of getting them looked after while I did it . . . It was often difficult to get paid. Always ask for the money upfront was the rule, but men are easier to handle afterwards. It's difficult to make someone hand something over; we were used to being forced, and there was nothing I could do, I couldn't find a protector – hah, what a word – a man who'd beat up anyone who tried it on because I had to be free to work when I wanted to – Phoebe being so, well, fragile. We always stuck together; so when things went wrong, they went wrong for all three of us.'

'You were raped. Systematically. We understand how hard this is.' Freddie nodded, encouragingly. 'How long did this go on for?'

'This is hard to say – you hear stories about girls who can sweet-talk men out of fury, but I never found that the case. A soldier will tremble all over just like any ordinary man in the grip of his passion but he'll belt you across the face and kick you in the belly if you try to stop him doing what he wants, with even a single word or a simple gesture of recoil . . .' She turned her head sideways to demonstrate. 'If you do that, you're asking to be hit from the other side, so your head will straighten. In war there are no feelings but your own: there are no other needs but the ones you have then and there. It's the fear of death that drives men mad – and women. Every man feels himself to be the only one alive, with blood and guts and the rest – the hard on comes with that fear, that threat of an end. I saw it over and over again. Even before the bombs fall on their targets, before the guns start blasting away, they've wasted everyone around besides yourself; you're the only living thing left on a planet inhabited by spectres, each and every one of us the only person becomes the last human being on earth left alive – and that's the excuse for any act, because to act is not to be dead, especially to fuck. Soldiers are always saying they're going to die and that's cause enough to have whatever they want, now. But others as well when they come to a war zone like Tirzah they catch this disease – which is the death that takes possession of you inside.

'So we were as good as dead there, all of us.

'But I kept at it, and I never let the bad days and the bad men stop me – the rapes or the violence. When I was well again I went back to the river and waited for another client. I even hoped that things would improve. After Phoebus went away . . .' she hesitated, swallowed, and continued: 'I worked more in the hotel. Phoebe helped me with the linen and the laundry, and I did massages there. The clientèle there were much less rough, and the war was winding down. Things were slower, quieter. We made do, but . . .' she paused. 'I had to get out, find a way to leave, to come and find Phoebus.'

Her daughter came in again, with James carrying the tray.

'Aw, Mum,' Phoebe put a hand on her mother's arm. Ella's eyes were glistening. 'You could've let me stay. Then you wouldn't've got upset.'

James began looking through other papers, as Freddie showed him the notes she'd made of Ella's disclosures in his absence.

'I think we can make a case that your existence in Tirzah was in every way intolerable, and that you would be returning to hostile conditions, which would not be conducive to you or Phoebe thriving . . .' James began, making a visible effort to smile. 'Let's see.' He found the document he wanted. 'Oh, good,' he continued. 'You've had a medical. You're clear. Amazing. Amazingly lucky.'

'Yes,' said Ella. 'Perhaps another miracle?' She paused.

'What happened to . . . the boy? The son you mentioned?'

'My twin,' said Phoebe. 'He's here. Somewhere.'

'Is he? Since when?'

'Since the first year of the siege.'

'And?' He shuffled through Ella's dossier. 'You didn't tell Catnach? The paper could help you trace him.'

'I don't want to find him when everybody is watching. I want it to be . . . between us. Perhaps . . .' she hesitated. 'He won't want to know.'

'So, tell me what happened? How he comes to be here?'

'Yes,' said Ella, quietly. 'He was stronger than Phoebe. He was miraculously unhurt. He is . . .' she hesitated. 'An easier character. Gives no trouble. I knew he would be taken, to somewhere better. Our life – Phoebe's and mine – was struggle. Nobody would take her, not then. So

321

I sold Phoebus. And with the money,' she continued, rapidly, full of determination, 'I bought medicine she needed.'

'Mum!' cried Phoebe. 'Don't guilt trip me like that! You didn't *sell* him – you don't sell children! You had him *adopted*. You talked about it to me – I remember. You were going bananas. There was nothing to eat, everything was crazy, and all these people were coming to Tirzah when it was really terrible there and sticking it out because they wanted to have a child so much and they couldn't. You saw a chance – for my little brother.'

She gave James a sharp, quick grin. 'So he'd do good for himself, that was the idea.'

'I was frightened for all of us, and I could do something for him . . .' Her mother put out a hand and gripped Phoebe's arm. 'Nobody else would look after you but me. He was a beautiful child – and he was a boy. Boys were really precious. Lots of girls were up for adoption, but not many boys.'

'Do you remember who helped you arrange the adoption? Anything about the family?'

'Oh yes,' said Ella, 'I was watching for the right people. They were a couple in the hotel. Professionals, from Enoch. I watched their ways for days – they were waiting for the nuns to bring them a child, but it was slow. You know you can tell a lot from things in hotel rooms. I picked them out for Phoebus. They were good people.'

'Maybe I shouldn't have told them,' said Ella to Phoebe, as they stepped back into the now drizzly street. To herself, she was thinking, They know now what I am, an infection, a criminal, a parasite, a woman who sells her own child to keep alive.

Phoebe said, 'That went very well, Mum. You were excellent.' She took her mother's arm as they renegotiated their way up Cantelowes High Street. 'I think they're going to help us.'

Oh my daughter, thought Ella, Now I'm leaning on your arm, now it's you who's tugging me out of the past.

In the Bed & Breakfast where they were lodged, two stops down the line from Cantelowes, Ella was watching television one evening. She was waiting up for Phoebe, who'd found a job waitressing in a cybercafé in return for a sort of hourly wage, plus tips; the franchise holder wasn't declaring her to his employer, and she wasn't telling *The Fanfare.*

Phoebe had told her to watch the telly, especially the news; that way she'd learn about Albion and about Enoch, and pick up the language more quickly. So Ella sat, on the edge of one of their beds with the blotchy bedspread round her, the remote in her hand, watching the screen perched at the end of an anglepoise arm up in the corner of the room.

A documentary item came on, in the chatty local bulletin that followed the national news: Ella couldn't follow exactly, but the interviewer was poking about trying to tease alight some dispute. Something about a name being changed, of a community college, or was it a school? A school for teachers. No, it was the bar, for now they were filming a sign being taken down, with a painting of a man with one eye and one arm.

'Several of the members of the governing body of the King Edward I Teacher Training College have expressed their anger that the students have changed the name of the student bar from The Trafalgar, commemorating the great victory at sea of Admiral Nelson, to the imprisoned leader of the ANC, Nelson Mandela.' A brief interview followed with one of the aggrieved governors: 'This is a very sad moment,' he was saying, 'When the history of what made this country great is set at nought by the very people who will have responsibility for teaching the next generation.'

The reporter resumed: 'We asked one of the student teachers what reasons lay behind their decision . . .' A young man appeared, jostled in among a mixed group in the bar, confidently facing the camera, defending the change.

Ella wasn't able to hear enough to decipher what he was saying in the hubbub of the packed bar. But something about his looks and quick delivery made her spring stiff-backed to attention, to get closer, to try and capture every detail of his fleeting appearance, to see the shape of his ears. But the screen was mingy, the definition blurred, the item brief.

Yet, at the first glimpse of Kim McQuy in action, Ella was possessed by a burning, raging, joyful certainty:

such a one as you is what I dreamed you'd turn into   when I think of you now

it's hard you were so small but you were a charmer not quite like this one because
you were full of laughter and you there on the screen are a little earnest   but
something about the way your head moves and your eyes   in those days Phoebe
was always fussing   you were the sunny one   but you used to take charge even
from a very young age   and so I knew I could trust you if I let you go   that
you'd escape the fate that was to be ours   the anger that drives us across the face
of the earth and never a place to come to rest   is it you or one such as
you   brought up in the ways and the language and the manners of Albion and the
safety –

'I saw someone like Phoebus on the television tonight,' Ella told her daughter when she came back, fractious from small tips from dimwit web users. 'Very like him.'

'How like him?'

'I couldn't see very well; he flashed past. But there was something that shot through me. If he was here in person, I know I'd know. I'd have an even stronger sense. But even on that screen, I felt it was him, him as I hoped he'd turn out if he became one of them, if he grew up here in Albion.'

Phoebe was sceptical. They struggled together, frequently, over this matter. Phoebe wanted to trace her twin, using official means, but her mother only wanted, she kept repeating, to know that he was flourishing, so that she could die happy.

'He looks older than you, but then he belongs to this place and to its time . . .'

'You'll always be seeing my brother, because you don't know where to look. When I've my own homepage, I'll put out a notice – something coded, so that we don't get a lot of nutters replying.'

'I trust my instincts. They got us through, till now.'

'But you're morbid,' Phoebe objected. 'I just want us three to be real again. Saved on the hard drive, not flitting about all volatile in memory.'

'That young teacher—' Ella continued later, talking into the sulphurous glow from the street lamp outside, which filled their room through the dusty and drooping curtains when they switched off the bedheads' tubes of neon. 'That's how I think Phoebus might have become – someone so at home here he can speak his own mind on the television news. It's what I wanted for him. To become someone who doesn't look backwards, but ahead. Someone who can take his own path. Time is his. Choice, too.'

'Mum, what're you tripping about now? That bloke could be anyone. My brother could be on the streets, he could be a merchant banker, he could have moved away . . . out. Fate isn't going to take you to him just like that sitting on your bottom in a B & B: life isn't a fairy tale. We're going to have to *do a search*. With documents and evidence and investigations. So go to sleep now. And stop blathering.'

2

At The Blue Moon

Kim McQuy came in through the door of The Blue Moon: he looked tired, but his quick movements made him flicker, as if a lamp was playing on his face. Hortense Fernly, waiting for him at the back of the café, blinked at the illusion. When he came near, the peculiar effect persisted. He sat down and pulled off his tie.

'I've come straight from a school meeting,' he said, rolling it up quickly and putting it in the breast pocket of a jerkin, lined with a tightly curled fleece, rather warm for the season, but a lot more stylish than she expected. His pale trousers were high-cut, sailor-fashion, making him look younger than the first time she saw him, and the determinedly smoothed and tidy haircut that had betrayed the cheap hack of a high street barber's had grown out since the last time, when she'd met him briefly in the Archives. She wondered whether he was gay: maybe his effusions were just a form of camp?

'Have you asked for something?' He was looking around for the waitress.

'You go to the counter to order. I was waiting for you.'

'There was a long, long argument about a car boot sale. Yes, we should let the playground be used, yes, it'll raise money. No, they're a fence's paradise. And back and forth it went.'

'What would you like? I'll go. You've probably had a tougher day.'

In the end they both went up to the counter; he picked out a cake from the revolving glass cabinet and carried the coffees to their table.

In spite of his sharper look, there hung around Kim McQuy some whiff of the asylum, she felt. Or perhaps not the asylum, but the stage, as if the real person was somewhere absent from the scene, and only responding with a part of himself. Of course, she told herself, this is the effect of babbling into the ether over long nights: the nerd syndrome.

These reasons for caution didn't diminish her curiosity; on the contrary, they quickened it as he sat down opposite her and let his eyes rest on her face and then look down at her hands where they were placed around the cappuccino. He had lights in his eyes, too, something almost feverish in their large pupils.

'It's good to see you there, in person,' he said. 'After so long. In the flesh.'

At the word, she flinched. Waiting for him, she'd been reading papers for a meeting the next day, or rather, pretending to read them, as in spite of her resolve not to attach any importance to this young man and his self-dramatising, she was rattled and expectant and furious with herself all at once. Sometimes in recent weeks, a patch of Kim's flesh, smoothly encased in tight, gleaming, burnished skin, would float into her consciousness crying out, as if endowed with lips and a tongue, Kiss me, kiss me hard, kiss me long, kiss me. The same skin that she now viewed sternly, noting how a disposable razor had clearly travelled rapidly over his stubble that morning for it was already well sprouted at six in the evening.

There was no reason to imagine that Kim McQuy meant the things that he wrote to her in any way that any ordinary person might take responsibility for; he was given to hyperbole, he was a manic preacher, like one of those mad reforming saints who wrote ten thousand letters to kings and queens and popes and potentates, addressing them all as 'Beloved' and covering them in effusions and protests of undying adoration so that anyone now would think the writer was aiming to jump into bed with every one of his correspondents. But things weren't the same today. Who knows the etiquette of the Internet? Intimacy at long range, whisperings from galactic distances.

Wild protestations of sincerity and exaggeration were the marks of the fanatic, Hortense knew. But, but, but. He wasn't insincere in the manner of her Museum director. It was a question of depths, of emotion. He struck her as a mixture of bad boy and head prefect, what teachers used to call 'leadership material', with all the dangers that implied; and there was just enough of a streak of the rebel in her to want to flirt with the risk Kim presented; though what that risk might be she couldn't imagine.

In her husband Daniel's absence, Hortense did not see her life as empty at all; she was always busy. But the schoolteacher from Cantelowes had opened up gaps in time she hadn't known existed, he'd rent the fabric of her daily routine, and erupted through the rent, as if on winged feet, like one of those visual devices that whisper in the ears of black figure paintings on the vases in her care – Persuasion, Fear or Grief taking possession. Or, Seduction. Whenever she began thinking about Kim's oddness, his claims to hear messages, his messianic delusions, images of him stirring up trouble melted before sudden, blazing flashes of him in some intimate connection with her: peeing in her bathroom as she watched him from her bed or taking off his socks sitting on the edge of it while she smoothed with her fingertips the hair on his chest and belly (did he have hair on his chest and belly?). She couldn't think how or why these pictures came to her. She had even considered going to the doctor's to ask for some sedative to stop the images coming on in her head – though she'd be hard put to describe what the matter was. Was she going to turn into that poor woman who kept having orgasms because some section of her brain was wired up all wrong? Or perhaps this is what happened to nuns, like those madwomen who were always administering clysters, supposedly to prevent diabolical visitations, but more likely to excite themselves to frenzy?

All she knew was that the fantasies had started, intermittently but vividly, after they had bent over Meeks's aborted *magnum opus* of translation and editing and Kim had put his index finger to his lips and tapped the middle of his mouth and said, all of a sudden, 'This is the most expressive part of a face: Leto told me it's called the "philtrum" – did you know that?' and while saying it, looked at her mouth and at the shallow indentation just above her upper lip until she felt the blood pounding to her temples and had to shuffle the fragments in front of her to defuse the shock of his focus on her mouth.

She'd inspected herself carefully that night, in the half-length mirror on her wardrobe door: what did he mean when he used all those words to her? Looking at her body, she decided that she must not mind him, not for one moment. It was all hot air: her flesh was puckered on her thighs and stomach and silvered with a craquelure that every beautician's window identified as orange peel cellulite, the curse of adipose, middle-aged, women's flesh. She was now bearded where she should have been springily tufted: the cruellest Vanitas masters were sharp-eyed and the invective of spoiled erotomaniacs like Horace wasn't that far wrong, in spite of the indignation of outraged women, diagnosing misogyny. Misogyny, thought Hortense, has its reasons. So, with her usual clever, ratiocinating mental processes, she revolved Kim McQuy's daily attentions, and held them down. But all this subduing of her fantasies hadn't succeeded in quelling her excitement, as she well knew. The morning of their meeting in The Blue Moon, she'd found herself discarding four different outfits before twisting the last failure, her beloved full-pleated skirt, into a ball and hurling it across the room, and now, now that he had come in looking startlingly kempt, she felt incredibly hot all of a sudden and needed to take off her favourite cotton lacework cardigan with tiny buttons to reveal the most boring white T-shirt of her entire range, discoloured by faulty washing on a hot cycle several years ago. Not that Kim seemed in the least bit interested in her clothes.

'Hetty, it's you,' he was now saying. 'At last.' He drew a deep breath. 'I feel it's been a century since I saw you. And so much has happened.'

She made an effort to keep to the ostensible reason for their meeting, and began briskly, as soon as the cakes arrived – a slice of orange for her, thick chocolate for Kim, who professed himself ravenous after a day with stroppy kids, exhausted by weeks of term.

'It's really on account of this tangle of paganism and Christianity, of fantasy and fact,' Hortense launched in, clutching at her role as scholar, 'that our Hereward Meeks threw in the towel. Like so many men of his time he was thrown into utter desperation by Darwin and the fossil record and the scientific revolution and the discrepancy with Revelation and the Creation etc etc, and consequently he was hell-bent on finding outside proofs for the truth of the Book: he and hundreds like him had high hopes of archaeology. But stuff like these linen bandages and papyri didn't help the cause: the material is such a mish mash of traditions, even the keenest soldier of God couldn't exactly unfurl it and march under its banner. And when he found that . . . well, the tomb was empty, the shroud shrugged off . . . that was the limit.'

'This is excellent,' said Kim. 'The cake.' He laughed. 'And what you're saying, I know. The same story, the same mystery. Only it stars a woman. That's blasphemy.' He laughed.

Hetty ignored his lightness of mood. 'Of course, some ingenious minds argued that the resemblances were there to prepare the way: Isis and baby Horus look just like the Virgin Mary and Jesus because God in his wisdom planned it like that, as a forerunner, a prototype, to smooth the path. Putting the fossils in the earth like giving Adam and Eve navels: unnecessary, but aesthetic. This material isn't like that: it's not prophetic . . .'

'Not of that faith, no,' said Kim, licking his chocolate-covered fork.

'Of other things? Maybe. You know I'm not going along with you on that score – but this material is history, too. For our time. Which is where you come in.'

Kim said: 'Can we go out somewhere else? Get a drink somewhere? I don't feel I'm getting you here – but some lady at a meeting, with a tray of coffee or tea brought in. I'd really like a beer.'

'I've got to get home.'

'Not yet.' He paused. 'We can stay here, if you really want to. Another coffee? Let me get them.'

She shook her head.

So Kim stayed put. 'Skipwith seems to me just as important to the story of the Leto Bundle coming here,' he began. 'He should figure in the display. He's easier to get across, too, than Meeks.'

'Yes, and there's a lot of visuals, too, related to him we could use. But just let me finish about Meeks.'

'Yes, teacher.'

As Hortense talked on, she was wondering, Had she mistaken the meaning of his messages? of his talk? Perhaps his crazed expressions were just so many more of his delusions, cut from the same stuff as his prophecies? He listened to her when she talked of the Leto's history, but he said he wanted to put the past behind him, but needed to show its slipperiness and unreliability. But she could hardly accept that. 'We're too much into the business of forgetting', she'd written to him. She wanted him to rely on the past. What had he replied? Something about hidden files, about the past being full of memories that have been drowned, and drowned for ever – that to have some kind of a known history is already a privilege many miss out on. What about the unstoried, untold, unremembered?

No, that wasn't fair. He'd pored through Meeks's notes on the Leto Bundle with a will: history was part of his scheme, if only to be worked to his plans, and she was central to this process, to his take on it, he'd made it clear so many times. The past meant a lot to him. But what? It was a kind of scaffold for fantasy. And what about love? Was love part of history, too? Or perhaps not love, but desire? Was Kim some new sport of nature, speaking so intimately because he'd evolved to some other phase of evolution where that kind of talk meant something altogether different?

Kim said, 'All of the Bundle is true. All of it's got to be on show.' He put his hand out towards her, lightly, to stop her flow. 'Gramercy Poule's dead keen on this film idea,' he said. 'She's paying all expenses, my travel and such – she's all worked up about HSWU – and Leto and the Bundle. She wants to write a song for it, too – and she's got a producer interested. It's just the opportunity we need. We can use it to put pressure on to make the Leto show huge – can't we?'

He wanted her to come with him, he said, to put in her contribution on the historical background, to be the one who 'knows it all'. 'You make us legit, you know. You can give chapter and verse for stuff I just hear from voices in my head or see in my mind's eye when I read through that stuff – don't look so sad. You're not sad. You're not one of those sad cynics who think the world'll never be different.'

But Hortense was shifting restlessly. She wanted to pass by all these words and ideas and wearisome work and anxieties and politics. Dimly, she wanted Kim to see his need of her differently, less instrumentally. Less *commercially*, for God's sake.

'What's she like, Gramercy Poule?' she asked. 'You know I once met her . . . manager, I think it was, in the customs shed at an airport.'

'You did?'

'Yes, and I was with the Leto, too.'

'You see, it's meant to be.'

'Is she any good – even our new director's mission for the Museum doesn't include pop promos. At least I don't believe so.'

'Don't worry. Gramercy Poule's not a head-banger. She was a big bad wild girl once upon a time – around fifteen years ago when she had her first big hit. But now she wants to do something more than be a rock star. She's conscious, not like a lot of them. I like her stuff. She was one of the first singers I liked when I was little and she was still around when I was just about to go to college. I spent too much of my grant on her records.' He laughed.

Hortense was still struggling to bring the conversation round to something personal, something that would fit with the vivid pictures that assailed her.

'She probably fancies you.'

It hurt her, to be so glaring, so awkward, inviting her own destruction.

'Naw, I want the same thing and more for HSWU – and she's sympathetic to that. National identity – we need it, she says. She must've blokes coming out of her ears. Doesn't need another one. And not me, I'm just a primary school teacher, remember.'

'She's probably insatiable – isn't that what pop music's all about?'

Kim leant over and placed his hand on her arm and squeezed it. 'Probably, but I'm not in her sights. Hetty, I've a lot of other things on my mind. Why don't you come? It'll be great. Trust me.'

3

The Fellmoor Cluster

Ella saw the notice in the post office window:

URGENTLY NEEDED! ANIMAL HELPER
Do you care about animals? Fancy you could be Saint Francis, or
Rolf Harris? Helper needed to look after (and talk with) assorted
wild creatures – birds, ducks, geese, hedgehogs, squirrels, rabbits,
ferrets, tortoises – in convalescence on nearby farm. Dogs and cats
as well.
   Ring 01837 954867 and ask for Monica.

Ella read it twice, then walked back up the street to the phone box,
where Phoebe hung around with her friends after classes, taking calls
from who knows who, and, amid the fumes of beer and piss and chips
inside the confined space, dialled the number on the card.

At Feverel Court, Monica answered; she asked, 'Have you any
experience with handling animals? Pony trekking doesn't count. We
need more than a stable lass.'

Ella answered, carefully, that yes, before she came to this country, she
was often occupied with many animals.

Monica, hearing the accent, surmised rightly, but asked anyway,
'Where you from, then?'

'Tirzah.'

'Stay there, right?'

Monica pressed the secrecy button on the phone and said to

Gramercy, 'One of the refugee cluster from the town – a woman. Asking about the job.'

'No shit,' said Gramercy.

'She won't have any references.'

'But we could have a look at her.'

'They're not meant to work. They get vouchers.'

'Monica! I thought you cared. You said I could give some money to that . . . charity that works with them.'

'Yes,' said Monica, with a laugh. 'To keep them over there.'

There were complications about Ella reaching Feverel Court, so eventually, Monica agreed to meet her in town. Monica would lay in supplies from the big, cut-price supermarket, and then give Ella a lift back to the house for the interview with Gramercy.

Ella was standing by the supermarket car park's ticket machine, as agreed. One or two others from the cluster were working the car park, offering to wash cars while their owners were inside, shopping. They complained to Ella of slow demand.

'They're frightened of us, they see us and put their yellow crook lock on and take the radios with them inside.'

'What can I say?' shrugged Ella. 'They have a point.'

The Advisory Council for Refugees and Asylum Seekers had been disappointed when they failed to help Ella and Phoebe stay in Enoch. But aspects of their experience (as Freddie tactfully put it) made the tribunal reviewing her permit of residency recommend a quiet, rural settlement. (Ella's reaction: *They think I'll go on the game.*) At the converted railway station where they were billeted, some things did go missing (toothpaste was a favourite), while others would all of a sudden appear: a TV, a child's coat, a computer with games. Their temporary accommodation lay to the west of the town, at the terminus of a branch line that had been used, till thirty years ago, to freight copper and tin worked in the mines that lay deeper within the wildernesses of Fellmoor; the fretwork wooden buildings, now freshly painted green and white by a group of volunteers, with all mod cons wired and plumbed in, the Ticket Office, Waiting Rooms, Guard's, Station Manager's and Lading Clerk's offices, the Tea Room, and the Ladies and Gents, were providing a roof over their heads to six ad hoc families, including Ella and Phoebe. The children loved it: it was now summer, and the platforms, the grassy tracks, the rickety signalling box, even an abandoned caboose on the siding turned their new home into an outdoors playground. But for the adults, the communal sleeping, eating and living, prolonged the experience of the camps from which they had come, by different routes, and tempers were touchpapers.

The local authorities had earmarked some housing of their own on the moor, where the Tirzhaners would regain their privacy as well as their liberty. They would renovate the old barracks the miners used to live in during the winter weeks, when the journey home was too dark and bleak to undertake daily. But the necessary repairs had not yet begun; the county's heritage representatives protested against the measure. It was bad enough turning the old railway station and goods yard into a refugee hostel, they declared; they could not but oppose any move to spend public money on restoring a local landmark, irreversibly changing the character of a picturesque ruin that offered a unique glimpse into a fascinating and now vanished industrial way of life and labour. A foreign ghetto, created overnight in the grim and frozen depths of Fellmoor, was doomed to turn into a sink estate, and bring endless trouble to its neighbours. How would the inhabitants live there? With no shops, no transport, no work? Far better policy would be to split them up and distribute them singly here and there, to become stitched into the social fabric.

The arguments were well received; no building went forward.

Monica saw a slight, small, tidy woman, much older than she had expected; the previous applicants had indeed been stable lasses still in their dewy passion for muck and straw and steaming flanks and soft thick lips nuzzling. Ella was dressed in a collection of clothes deemed appropriate for a country resettlement, provided in the local authorities' welcome pack: a good tailored herringbone tweed jacket, and lace-up waterproof boots. But underneath she was wearing a long, tie-dyed cheesecloth skirt; so it was apparent that she had no idea what hopeless social signals her combined hand-me-downs were making. Her face was roughened and brown as if wind-burned, but her hair, which was greying, was combed carefully into two smooth rolls and pinned, with a kind of bygone Parisian chic.

Ella got in the four-wheel drive with difficulty, the front seat was so high off the ground, and thanked Monica for picking her up.

'You could hardly have walked! It's three miles. And the bus service –
completely run down of course.'

'If you give me the work, I walk,' said Ella. 'Walking is no problem.'
She smiled, and Monica saw that she was younger than her ugly outfit
conveyed, but that half her teeth were gone.

'Oh God,' she groaned inwardly. 'Gramercy'll give her the job, even
if she's never even laid eyes on a tortoise before. Damn that Phil. Damn
him damn him. Because it'll be me that has to cope with the fall out.'

Ella did not grasp Gramercy's offered hand, until after a moment, in
which she wanted to turn and run, but knew she must not.

*is she one of the ones I robbed? she is she is that one   she looks a bit different
though so perhaps I'm confused   was that the name?   there was a singer that
week on all the posters and Pontona was all inflamed about her   Luigi told me I
should try for some souvenirs   he said she was hot and they'd fetch a good price
so I should try and work that hotel that week and so I swapped with someone
working there   fate was smiling on me because that singer she came across me in
the cupboard   she looks different with clothes on   but it's the same one   if
she knows me like I know her she will attack me for what I did that night   she
will denounce me   she will tell the people reviewing my case and seeing if I am fit
to stay here with Phoebe*

*I took things   the nightdress and the tights were best of all Luigi said he knew
people who'd die for them*

but maybe it's a trick of the mind

*maybe it's like dying   maybe I am dead now and in the other world   it
won't be full of strangers but crowded with all the people you've ever known who've
done things to you or you've done things to them   eternity will be like perfect
recall   there'll be no escape from familiarity going on and on repeating and
repeating itself   am I seeing a revenant when there's only a woman I don't know
and who doesn't know me? perhaps everything is still moving forward at random
through time and space just as usual just as it should and we are unconnected and
unknown to one another and shall remain so*

unless

Monica made a pot of coffee as Gramercy began interviewing Ella, but,
as soon as the singer encountered the older woman's mute shyness, she

found she was doing the talking, giving an account of herself, of Feverel Court, of its claims and burdens, of the animal sanctuary and Phil's departure.

'There's a wolf cub there, too, Phil liberated from some children's film that was being made down here – I didn't mention it in the ad, because I didn't want to frighten off applicants. A wolf! Do you understand?'

Ella nodded; though she was schooling her features not to betray first the panic, now the joy that recognition brings, her pupils widened, and Gramercy sensed again the tremor of some quick spirit moving beneath the basalt mask of the woman's unresponsiveness.

'It doesn't alarm you?'

Ella shook her head.

'Good. So, how did you get here?' Gramercy then asked, changing tack.

Ella opened her bag and showed the cuttings from *The Fanfare*.

'Oh my God, is that you? Is that your daughter?'

'She's very well, now. She is studying.'

Gramercy's head bobbed enthusiastically at this: 'Here?'

Ella gave the name of the college of further education in the town, and murmured, 'Computer studies.'

Gramercy felt a choking in her throat, so Monica stepped in, saying, 'Why don't we go down to the sheds, and then Ella can see for herself what the problem is?'

Ella washed up her mug in the sink, set it on the drainer, and followed them into the garden.

After Gramercy employed her, then and there, Ella hardly knew where she'd begin. The stink and the crap, the wet straw and the maggoty feeding trays and bowls, the flurry of squawks and squeals and alarum cries, the mice skittering everywhere, the putrid ceres of the birds' beaks, the rot on their claws, the bitten, torn, raw wounds, the patched and broken pens and holed and twisted chicken wire, the brimming eyes of wilting rabbits and furious squirrels, the yellow needles of the ferrets' snarl, the curled, mangy rag of the cub, made her falter at the threshold of the sheds.

On her first day of work, when Ella returned on foot in working clothes, Monica took her down again to show her the ropes; she unlatched a wooden door into a lean-to, and showed her the equipment, 'There's stuff you'll need – tools and products, disinfectants, rubber gloves, scrubbing brushes, you name it. There's stuff to worm them and delouse them but you'll have to show me to read the labels for you, I suppose. God knows what you have to do to them, and once you've got the place clean and respectable enough, we can at least call in the vet and then he can show you how to do it. But we'll be in trouble if we call him now.

'Phil didn't hold with artificial methods – he believed in nature – so things got out of hand long before he upped and left. Just tell me what more you need, and I'll have it supplied.' She gave a little laugh. 'If you can sort this lot out, and get us next year's certificate without any problems, you'll be worth more than your weight in gold.'

In a box-like kennel behind the sheds, under a tent of wire, Ella looked into scared yellow giglamps of the wolf cub, and smelled her rank fur as she stumbled clumsily towards them.

'It's not much of a life,' said Monica. 'That bastard Phil. I'd like to throttle him. Gramercy's a prize idiot sometimes. Much too soft.'

Gramercy approached Ella in the sheds one day; it was the first really bright summer's day since she'd been employed, and Ella was bringing out various feeders and dishes and troughs and water containers she'd scrubbed and scoured clean of slime; they were standing to drain and dry in the sunshine.

'Nellie?'

For Gramercy had begun calling her so, soon after she began working at Feverel. 'It feels right to me, do you mind?' she'd said. And met with no refusal.

'Yes, Madame?'

'I wish you'd stop that. Say, yes, Gramercy.'

Nellie peeled off her rubber gloves, and obeyed her employer.

Gramercy continued, 'There's something I've been wanting to ask you. I've got this ghastly insomnia and I woke up sort of twisted and now I've got a stiff neck – can you do massages?'

Nellie put a hand to her brow, and moved, out of the sun which was falling in her eyes.

'You see,' Gramercy went on, 'you remind me of someone who once gave me the most fantastic massage in the world. I've always remembered it.' She opened her hand where she was holding a piece of paper, 'I kept it, as a memento, because I always wanted to find her again.' In Gramercy's hand lay the cleaner's calling card from the Grand Hotel in Pontona: 'This room has been serviced by . . .' Then the writing, 'Rosa', followed by 'Thank you'.

'I'm not called Rosa.'

'But you did work in Pontona. Phoebe told me, she said you lived there a while, on your way here. That's why she can speak that language as well, she told me so, she's proud of it. She's right to be. Wish I had her facility.' Gramercy paused. 'I think I saw Phoebe too, with you. Is it possible?' She moved up to her employee, and tried to look into her eyes, but Nellie kept them averted.

'It was for the medicine,' she said, quietly.

'Stop that,' Gramercy came back quickly. 'I don't give a fuck about what you did. You think I've never lifted anything? I just wanted to know that it was you. I had a real sense it was, and I'm glad – I was right all along.'

'You'll tell Monica?'

'I may be an idiot, but no. It's our karma – yours and mine – *I* know who you are, and that's what I wanted, that's what I want.' Her voice went whispery and she plucked at Nellie's sleeve: 'Use the downstairs shower when you've finished here and then, please, Nell darling, give me your special treatment again!'

Phoebe had heard of the plans for the refugee cluster at the college she was attending; she'd then accessed the website where the continuing, angry debate about the refugees was reported, and found the maps where the future distribution of families seeking to stay was indicated. She led Ella up Fellmoor to see the housing. They found two facing rows of speckled granite matchbox cottages, cutting slantwise across a flank of the old mineworkings; bushes sprouted from cracks in the fabric, and a herd of tiny horses, heads down, were munching the bristling gorse, stunted oak and fern that were spreading over the exposed scars in the granite. At the approach of the two women, one mare lifted her outsized head to eye them stolidly through a tangle of matted hoary hair, but stood her ground, with the others.

There was no sign of building work; the cottages looked vacant as skulls.

'Is this really the place?' Ella asked her daughter, who was pushing through, towards one of the barred windows.

Inside, scattered tins and bottles and charred sticks and fag ends bore witness to a long season of midnight parties, bonfires and booze.

Phoebe fluttered the map she'd downloaded. 'Yeah, Mum. This is it. It's great, it's really weird. I like it. This is going to be home.'

4

At Feverel Court

' "Turks' Noses"? Is that really what you said?' Hortense was peeping inside the freezer bag that Gramercy Poule had indicated contained part of the coming dinner. Gramercy, whom she'd just met in person for the first time, was crested like a mechanical bird with sparkly clips pinning up her tie-dyed hair.

'I had this partner, Phil, who, well, he isn't around any more,' Gramercy began. But she was chary of striking a wheedling note and playing the maiden all forlorn in front of Kim. So she went on, more brightly, 'Phil's in Shiloh, in dotcom land – couldn't get any work here. Anyhow, he's a kind of sweet wise child, or a grouchy old wodewose (I once wrote a song about them – on fire). Anyhow, I'll take you both round to meet some of the animals he went around rescuing. But we'll have a cup of tea now.'

Monica was busy with the kettle, setting out rough glazed mugs on the big scrubbed table. She'd picked up Kim and Hortense from the nearest station, and they were all now grouped together at a loss what to do and where to go, in the high-ceilinged, cobalt kitchen of Feverel Court, the first room visitors usually came in by, if they skirted the front porch and used the side door. They were standing with their small overnight things on the dark blue glazed flagstones, Kim's in an old sports holdall, Hortense's in an ergonomic, strappy leather backpack piece. The terriers were whining from the other side of the door, in disgrace for crouching and snarling at Kim. 'They can always spot a townee – just don't show you're scared,' Monica explained.

'It was my mother who started us off with the mushrooms,' Gramercy was saying now to her newly arrived guests. She was gesticulating, with an echo of stagecraft. 'She and Hatters used to make omelettes with the tiddly ones like fairy umbrellas that look like nothing but give you quite a high, and when she came down here, she found lots of them. I couldn't even see them at first, but then I got my eye in.'

Was she gabbling? She had a distinct feeling she was gabbling, and so she broke off and looked over towards Kim, who was leaning back against the table, apparently listening to her intently. His gaze had a funny, strabismic way of seeming to look at you, but at the same time past you. Unsettled, she went on, addressing herself to Hortense, whom Kim had suddenly announced he was bringing.

She wasn't going to talk about any of this, though, but keep instead to the Turks' Noses – their awkward nature as a topic making them a fragile refuge for the time being from the real turbulence that was gripping her.

'Phil learned to sense 'shroom time, as he called it, and he'd get out before anyone else, and then we'd have these fantastic fricassees of lots of different sorts. He was into native foods, home-grown, organic, from the forest, from the soil: recipes using shavings from cast antlers, moss, hips, as well as fungi. If he hadn't been veggie he'd have eaten weasels. He was always finding recipes for "Hartshorn flummery" and that kind of weird stuff. I don't have his confidence. The innocuous sorts of 'shrooms imitate the toadstools, perfectly: or is it the other way round? I wouldn't want to poison anybody!' She stopped; Kim was nodding.

'Never easy to tell friend from foe,' he chanted, as if quoting. 'Or to know the lamb in wolf's clothing.'

Hortense wasn't listening carefully, but rather admiring, a little grudgingly, the mighty *raku* platters on the dark oak dresser, the carved rustic furniture, and the signature pictures on the walls – a decisive vibrating lattice of emerald and scarlet over there, a mischievous child tugging a cat's tail, near her by the window. So, when Gramercy fell silent, she was brought up with a start and realised, with some surprise, that this pop singer, with her flamboyant magenta hair raked with tines' ebb marks like the sand of a Zen garden, who was sort-of-dressed, in a wisp of puckered canary-coloured silk, who'd invited them – or was it commanded them? – to come to her country spread, and who must be at least accustomed if not impervious to public exposure and attention, had been firing her scattershot prattle at them in evident nervousness. It was because of Kim, Hortense knew. And the knowledge made her feel she was in possession of a delicious secret. She smiled encouragement to their hostess, and said, dryly, 'I'll use Kim as my cupbearer. He can taste the dish, and if he doesn't fall down dead, I'll try it.'

Gramercy gave a brief giggle.

Hortense didn't want to think of Daniel, but as she made this proprietorial joke about Kim, she felt the cold breath of betrayal pass her lips. She'd spoken to Daniel when she'd flown to Shiloh to escort the Leto Bundle back home, but it had been a quick trip, in and out, and he was a thousand miles away in the Midwest, all taken up with grading exams and preparing his end-of-the year yard sale on leaving his college accommodation. They were to be reunited anyway very soon for the whole summer, he'd pointed out, and they'd discussed for a few minutes where they might go together; they'd learned through experience that re-entry needed easing. But Hortense accumulated so many airmiles in the course of a year, they could choose almost anywhere. 'What about Lycania?' she'd proposed. 'I feel like going back there, just to soak in the atmosphere.' 'Naw,' said Daniel, who was gradually acquiring a native's intonation. 'Busman's holiday. You don't need that.'

Kim edged over to the door leading off the kitchen into the office.

'So there's your set-up,' he said with evident relief at the sight of the familiar slate-grey calyx of a nineteen-inch monitor, swimmingly pulsing greeny-blue with an Escher eyetwister for a screensaver. 'For a moment there, I panicked – perhaps we're so cut off from the world here she isn't even on-line.'

Monica laughed. 'Didn't you get any of our messages on your website, then?'

'What messages?'

She shook her head. 'We paid you several visits, suggesting that there was a striking resemblance between your Leto's lines – such as, for example, "I am the angel of the present time" and certain song lyrics written by our very own Gramercy Poule. No? You're not twigging?' She began pouring, murmuring about milk and sugar, and handing Hortense and Kim their mugs of tea.

Kim looked calmly at Monica, shook his head, and replied, 'I can't keep up, you see. It's now five hundred hits a week – I can't read them all. But we can talk about it. Of course.'

'It's water under the bridge,' said Monica. 'Or at least that's what Gramercy has decided.'

Gramercy shot Monica a confused and bitter look. 'Please don't bring that up again, ever.' She turned to her guests. 'Sit down, do.'

'I like standing,' Kim answered. 'Been sitting on the train for hours.'

But Hortense pulled out a Windsor chair and pointed to the freezer bag by the sink: a few involuted, dry brown curls were spilling from its open mouth.

'So, dinner. You were saying?'

'Turks' Noses, really easy to identify. Safe. Not like anything else and they're what's called host-specific,' Gramercy pulled a fungus out of the bag and handed it to Hortense; she took it gingerly, cupping it in the palm of her hand as if trying not to touch it and then snuffed up its savour.

She made a noise in her throat, 'Hmmm.' Gramercy didn't know her well enough to understand this as approval or disapproval but she heard Kim chuckle.

She went on, 'They only grow on dead elder trees, and there are clumps of them in the hedgerows all round here.'

'Bottled smell of damp woods, I'd say. Authentic odour of countryside.' Hortense reached across the table to coax Kim to have a sniff, but he waved away the crinkled, mummified mushroom with distaste.

'So why the name?' he asked.

Gramercy laughed, with a certain embarrassment.

'They're delicious, I promise – I make a soup. It's the Feverel high summer special, which you'd never get – not even in Enoch with all those restaurants from all over. And I wanted you to . . .' she faltered, 'have something different.'

'Isn't there another name you could use?' Kim seemed to be looking down his own nose.

'Even in Latin they're called something like *Naso turkensis*.'

'Could be a ghastly rustic joke, I suppose,' said Hortense.

'I've hardly ever been to the country before,' Kim went on. 'I'm an urban specimen, through and through. Didn't know what to expect.' But he sounded less forbidding than his words, and went over to the window. 'There's a wilderness near the school where we take the kids now and then: we show them sycamore seedlings and buddleia. Evening primrose'll go wild in scrap yards, too. But buddleia's the one. It'll take root anywhere, grow really big, out of the wall of an abandoned warehouse, out of the cracks in a garage forecourt. It doesn't seem to need anything to thrive. Not even – what was it – some particular sort of dead tree. That's being much too particular.'

Gramercy had a sudden sight of herself in the promo for their project, traipsing through urban contamination, now diminutive, now teetering skywards, singing to weeds that clung to her legs. The amplification was thrumming through her guts, her mouth was opening as wide as it would go, into that picture of a scream, till her jaw felt it might click off its hinges. She was so disconnected from the self that had acquired all this, she felt she had divided, like some single cell, and left behind her that other life form, far down in the fossil record of her existence.

She shook herself, beckoned to her new friends, 'Come on, let's go out – I'll take you round Feverel. I'll show you my home.' For an insane moment, she wanted to add, 'You can make it yours too if you like.' Since Phil had gone, she was flowing with all these longings to give to others the way she thought Kim gave, to do something good, like he did, to stop the horizon-to-horizon suffocating atmosphere of her easy-gotten gains (Phil was accusing her, in her ringing memory, of living with her head up her arse). She felt herself turning into vapour, when she wanted with all her heart and gut to become a solid rock, a hard, packed concentrate; she found herself suspended in a weak and frictionless solution, and wanted to be precipitated, by Kim's alchemical vision, into the kind of defined, crystalline structure that he inhabited, knowing what he thought about everything, planning and scheming how to achieve it.

But of course she didn't propose anything to Kim, not yet.

Kim was again wearing a suit, an off-the-peg number with a short jacket; a white shirt fitted snugly to his neck, with a perfectly dull tie. He was, Gramercy realised, the first person dressed like that ever to visit Feverel Court, if you excepted the tax inspectors who had once descended on her to find fault with her accounts. It made her want to laugh; she was touched and intrigued – by his formality, by his social difference. That sharp-tongued art historian in contrast clearly understood what to expect from a visit to the moors: Hortense was wearing well-cut dark trousers and a long slim plum-coloured cardigan, and had caught up her wavy hair with a tortoiseshell hair slide. She looked so composed, so lady-like, that random rhymes skipped into Gramercy's head, 'Thou shalt not wash dishes,/Nor yet feed the swine,/But sit on a cushion and sew a fine seam./And feed upon strawberries, sugar and cream.'

Gramercy was still babbling excitedly the while so as not to appear to be observing them: Hortense was a lot older than Kim, and conventional in a different way, in a straightforward professional manner. Yet they'd travelled down together, and, from the way they didn't seem to need to make polite conversation together, Gramercy sensed intimacy.

She quelled the suspicion; for the last three nights, waiting for him to turn up to talk about the film, she'd been seducing Kim McQuy with ever more energy and ardour – in the kitchen, in the garden, in the orangery, in the music studio, in the animal sheds, on the moor under the stars, in her bedroom, in the guest room where she was putting him for the night. Not for a long time had she so wanted to fuck someone and be fucked by him; was it his priestliness that had stirred up her hunger to this pitch, his seeming absentedness in another world, the distance his trimness put between her messy day-to-day bewilderment and his uncanny purposefulness, the odd choppy rhythms of his talk, as he alternated impassioned speeches with taciturnity?

But maybe he'd made some alliance with Hortense that would be impregnable. A worm of fear, that she wouldn't be getting what she wanted, crawled through her gut.

'Doctor Fernly?' asked Kim, with a hint of raillery. 'Coming?'

They started down the garden, leaving Monica in the kitchen looking busy with something in the larder.

'It's so excellent you both made it down here.' Gramercy bent down to fondle one of the three terriers, who'd appeared, gambolling and jumping over one another, from somewhere in the garden.

They were making their way down a path by the side of the lawn – which wasn't a lawn, but a meadow sown with wild flowers bought mail order from a nursery in the southeast that produced them specially. It was a little late in the season, but love-in-a-mist was showing its feathery crowns, and campion sewing the greenery with small pink stars. Gramercy pulled up a swathe of the long grass, shot through with spears and tassels, and twisted it into a garland.

'There', she said, putting it on her head, and, quickly winding another hank of flowers and grasses, gestured to Hortense.

Hortense shook her head. 'Not quite me, I think.'

Gramercy tossed the wreath on to Hook's bright, cocked head, and laughed as the dog threw it off, and growlingly worried at it on the ground.

They passed on to a mown path through the crooked orchard, where the old apple trees were wearing lacy sleeves of lichen. By the bench, sunk in the tall greenery, Gramercy told them: 'I sit here sometimes, to think. Try it. It's magic, you feel all kinds of presences who once were here – and still are.' She wanted Kim to respond, to talk to her about what he saw and heard.

But when he said nothing, she couldn't put up with the emptiness, so she started in again: 'I've been writing a song about one of the Feverel ghosts: Lady Agnes, stabbed by her husband for adultery – with a groom. She's cursed to walk the third Friday of every month. She walks here. She has to pick a single blade of grass in the meadow.

'I sort of get her mixed up in my mind with Emily Dickinson, wafting about in white in Amherst, writing and writing, cancelling the blankness, picking at the lines one word at a time, one dash at a time, like a rest mark, like a dot on a note. I think of them both when I'm at the piano: change a note and the whole song changes. Anyhow, Lady Agnes will never rest in peace – she can only stop when there's not a single blade of grass left to pick.'

'You could have it paved – or put in a swimming pool, if you're so worried about her.' Hortense sounded in earnest, but Gramercy knew she was being mocked. So she didn't reply directly, but suggested instead: 'Maybe Lady Agnes likes coming up for air and haunting the world. "This must be better than staying down in hell" – that's one of the lines she sings in my song.'

Kim responded for the first time, quietly: 'For this is all there is and it will have to be enough.'

'How can you say that?' Hortense came in, impatiently. 'You sound like a stoic – how can you start on about this world being the only world we can know, when half the time you're waxing strong about how there's so much more to it than that – visions, presences, ghosts talking to you. I've no idea how you square what you just said with your Leto ideas.'

Kim answered her, still quietly, spreading his hands, 'I thought you understood.'

Gramercy interrupted them; their edginess made her anxious. 'I've never *seen* Agnes Feverel. But I feel her, with my other senses. I'm like Jonty and Hook and Bonny in that way. They snarl when a storm's coming, long before you hear the thunder. They whine and paw at the door and then leap out into the drive long before anybody else knows you're coming home.' She was playing to Kim's propensities, she hoped.

'Yes,' he said, and she felt a rush of pleasure that he was rewarding her for her belief. 'In an old place like this, there are stirrings, glimpses, little leaps and eddies in the air, like trembling rings on the surface of the water from something invisible or very far away.'

They'd reached the gate in the tangle of old fruit trees and drifts of clematis and roses on the wall of the kitchen garden beyond the orchard. Gramercy opened it for them. As Hortense passed through, she said, 'I must say, I never thought, after meeting your . . . road manager . . . at the airport that day . . .'

'Yeah, TB! You met TB – that was weird.'

'I didn't imagine then that our paths would cross in this way.'

'It's karma,' replied Gramercy. 'It was meant to be.'

'Was it now?' Hortense smiled. 'It seems more like you've a good nose . . . you like success and success likes you. You see the possibilities of a situation, no?' She glanced back at Kim, who was still standing on the path in the orchard, intent on the emptiness under the trees, with his jacket now over his arm, as the July evening was muggy. 'The film suits all our purposes – Kim's political ambitions, my museum's falling figures, threatened insolvency – and your audience. The Museum director's actually complimentary, for once: this is "quality inner city outreach" which means departmental money. You can't get it for scholarship about antiquity any more, but you can get it for "relevance" "service to the community" and for – children, the younger the better. The film should go out just after the beginning of the next school year, to maximise the interaction.'

Gramercy chose not to take offence at Hortense's tone; she wanted, above all, the evening to be a success. 'This September then? Wow, that means turning it round pretty fast.'

'Yes.'

Both women stood waiting by the gate for Kim to catch up with them. As he continued to watch in the orchard, they exchanged a quick look between themselves, full of curiosity, touched by complicity, followed by a fleet shadow of rivalry.

'Kim!' Hortense called out to him. 'You're in a dream.'

'I was listening to the roar.'

'Oh that,' said Gramercy. 'The fucking motorway! Built right through a grade one preservation area. My studio's sound-proofed, but you can't tape anything outside here any more, not even the wind.'

'I thought it was a waterfall,' replied Kim. He began walking towards them. 'Shows how you hear what you expect to hear.'

Gramercy led them to the aviaries and the duck pens; the drake, sleek and tapered as if he'd been given an expensive metallic paint job, was flip-flopping up it, with his question mark crest bobbing; in the long grass around the coop the ducks had hollowed runs and were teasing him by hunkering down in them, so that he was unsure whether they were watching, and admiring, his ascent.

Gramercy's spirits lifted at the idyll of the scene. Nellie's work. Nellie was more than a treasure, Gramercy thought. From the start Nellie went straight at the filthy work, turned around the diseased chaos of Phil's legacy with her handling and her dosing, her scrubbing and sluicing; within days of starting work she'd introduced enough cleanliness and godliness that they could call in the vet again, without fear of getting had up in front of the magistrates, or being bitten by a rabid beast or catching bubonic plague. Her hands were amazing, too, the way she touched her made all her knots slip and all her tensions ease; she'd even begun sleeping better, after one of Nellie's specials – she can't overdo the asking, though, or Nellie might give her one of her Aztec mask looks. Or that daughter of hers would have words with her – Gramercy was alarmed by Phoebe's disobligingness.

Phoebe often helped out her mother, riding pillion on the canary-yellow moped that Gramercy bought Nellie after Monica baulked at picking her up in the car, and Gramercy refused to let Nellie walk there and back in all weathers.

Mother and daughter worked as if they'd been raised in a circus and had learned animals' language, even before human speech. But the numbers of animals had dwindled: Nellie and Phoebe showed little fear and less sentiment, and Gramercy felt deep gratitude that she no longer had to worry about every bird in the air and every creeping beast on the face of the earth. They no longer rescued any; Phil's dream of Feverel

Court as the ark moored on the top of Mount Ararat had been put behind her. They'd kept the terriers, of course; but otherwise, there remained the tortoise, roaming the garden, with the Cayuga duck flock, and two little owls rescued as owlets and incapable as a result of going out hunting for themselves. They'd managed to pass on the survivors among the rest, by means of ads and word-of-mouth and the vet's contacts and Phoebe's college friends: the hedgehogs returned to the wild, the ferrets were taken by a local youth who'd already been out successfully rabbiting down the lanes (Gramercy was surprised at herself for even considering this outcome, but Nellie didn't give her space to make her objections). Those rabbits that weren't so sick they had to be put down went into someone's pot. Gramercy pondered this revenge on her rival; saw herself fleetingly as the Queen in Snow White pressing her thin crimson lips together, 'Take this apple, my dear', and then smiling at the huntsman's news of the girl's demise. She'd made a mental note to write a weird song that nobody'd be able to crack but would make her, Gramercy, obtain release from that primal nightmare of Phil jerking off in the shed.

The geese were placed on a farm three miles off, much to Gramercy's relief: she'd never overcome her fear of their drumming wings and out-stretched bills and tongues. Once the vixen's trapped paw had healed, they let her go, for she wouldn't have forgotten her tricks of survival; the exotic ex-pets, the snakes and the chameleon and the spiders were despatched, by courier, to approved zoos further west in time for the school summer holidays.

The wolf cub was a problem, though. In her case, Nellie seemed attached to the animal. Eventually, she asked if she could keep her. 'For Phoebe, for company when she come back from school and I not there.'

'But it's a wild animal,' Gramercy objected.

Phoebe frowned. 'She came from a pet shop, she's been raised in captivity – she's no wilder than a guide dog.'

'But your housing – will they let you?' asked Monica.

'The local authorities know that us refugees are lonely – they're recommending pets as a way of making home from home – specially for kids, like me, who've been uprooted and known nothing except temporary shelter.'

Now, when Nellie rode to Feverel on the canary-yellow moped, the wolf was leashed to the handlebars on a long lead and galloped along on the inside of the lanes. Sometimes, when Phoebe was riding pillion, her legs dangling to the side, she crowed with delight at the lolloping of the thin-flanked grey creature whom everyone mostly took for a half-breed collie.

There wasn't much left any more for Nellie to do in that department, Monica had pointed out, except routine maintenance, and they could reduce her hours. (Monica's job was to keep an eye on the bottom line.) But Monica would also like to concentrate on managing Gramercy's business, and let go all the domestic duties that had accrued since Phil's departure. She'd had to take on housekeeping and housesitting – and night-nursing. Gramercy couldn't be left alone in this big house, even with those three nippy and wakeful dogs. Bobby Grace had come to stay, of course, but she had her own life to lead, houses to mind, and child-minding a daughter in her thirties on a long-term basis didn't appeal. So Monica proposed that Nellie should come and live at Feverel: 'You love Nellie, or you think you do,' she said, with not a little bitterness, as she didn't like the dependency she observed. She could see no other quick term solution, however, so Gramercy was trying to persuade Nellie to come and live with her; she wanted to do right by her. Nellie made her feel she was doing something about . . . the world and its problems.

'Nellie's responsible for all this—' Gramercy swept a hand over the visible order of cages and pens. 'I don't know what we'd do without her.' She began to tell Kim about the refugee cluster in the nearby town, about the animals Phil abandoned, about the massage in Pontona, about Phoebe's new skin. She was proud of having Nellie working for her, but she was careful not to play Lady Bountiful to Kim. She couldn't help hugging her magnanimity to herself, though, when she remembered how Nellie pilfered her best concert slingbacks that night. The knowledge lay between them like a low gas cloud over an exercise ground after a detonation, seeping through the air and tingeing it with tension: there was a huge question mark lingering over Nellie's status as refugee/asylum seeker. Mother and daughter still hadn't been granted full permission to stay in the country and Gramercy had offered to go to the tribunal as a character witness and sponsor.

She knew she couldn't communicate any of this intricate relationship to Kim, how sharply someone like him turned against condescension, patronage. Such imbalance of power relations was repellent to her, too, and she was struggling to trace and shape another exchange from which they could both draw benefit. But what? And she feared that if Nellie were to become her full-time housekeeper it would spoil things between them.

'Nellie's someone I really want you to meet – she came from Tirzah, like you, though where she comes from originally was somewhere else – she was already on the move when she got there.'

'I don't remember much about Tirzah,' says Kim. 'Just a few flashes of this and that – a kind of white noise in the back of my head.'

'Nellie really is the genuine article,' she appealed to Kim. 'One of our tribe—'

'Don't say "tribe" to Kim,' Hortense cut in. 'He's allergic to the word, the principle, all that it entails. It's the root of all evil.'

'You know what I mean,' Gramercy stammered, miserably. She was now beginning to hate Hortense, who seemed to be able to dip the switch on Feverel's glow and squash her giving of it – temporarily – to these guests she wanted to enfold, to claim.

Kim came in, 'I really don't feel at all like a Tirzahner, you know, and I don't know what it'd mean to be one, not now. National songs and what – those cross garters? A taste for bitter black coffee downed with a shot of applejack at breakfast and a hearty slap to my thigh? My language, my internal map, my attachments, my set of beliefs – they're here, not there. I – that is, my mind – can't ever *return* home. So, my mother abandoned me. That's no reason for to go around feeling like little Orphan Annie. I was lucky to get out. But that doesn't mean that I'm cheering Albion on the home side either. The whole point of HSWU is—' he spread his hands, 'the past is another country. Now matters now, not then.'

Hortense said, 'But you're fascinated by the past. You're obsessed, even.'

Kim came back quickly: 'Only so we can understand more. We've so many prejudices and preconceptions that history washes down on us like soil erosion. I want to build meanders and dams to prevent the mud sliding down on us and burying the present.'

At this exchange, with its ripples of tension, Gramercy rallied, laughing at one of the ducks peeping out, periscope-style, from her tunnel in the tall grass as the bird ascertained the effect of her flirtatiousness on the drake. 'You'll see Nellie in the morning. She comes in early to do the feeds. But our main problem here now,' Gramercy remarked, watching this game, 'is that the ducks will take off with wild mallards who come by on raids. *Plus ça change.*'

'I'm afraid I've got to catch the fast train,' says Hortense.

'Do you have to go? Why don't you stay a few days?'

If only Kim would agree, Gramercy would accept this prickly woman, too, for as long as he wished.

They were wandering back to the house, past the part of the kitchen garden where the wreckage of Phil's organic plot still sprouted long canes of raspberry and bolted artichokes. Feverel's front elevation came into view, for the first time. The long light of a midsummer evening turned its stone buttery, its buff and russet tiles soft as fledgling feathers, the roses and creepers and trees taking the house's bathed rose body in their arms.

Hortense couldn't help herself. She exclaimed at the perfection of the scene.

For his part, Kim couldn't believe Gramercy was living in such a vast place – and on her own. He had an odd impulse to bring his mother Minta here, to the country, to see this mansion. After his father's third stroke finally killed him, Kim watched his mother deteriorate daily as she mourned; he'd come back from school to find her unkempt, vacant and starving, and they'd sit together watching the telly with a tray before she fell asleep on the sofa. At first he couldn't undress her; it seemed indecent. But then it seemed more indecent not to, so he'd begun washing her and lifting her to bed until the social services recommended transfer to Close Care housing where she now sat, day by day, vacantly watching the crows that flapped down on the parking lots outside her window to claw and peck at blowing packets of pork scratchings. Like a phantom at the window in a picture of a haunted grange, she stared out of the still neat house of her body, and did not know who Kim was any longer.

He must get on with selling his parents' semi, he was thinking as he took in the view of Feverel. He must tidy away all Gerald's belongings and find himself somewhere of his own to live. But he was too busy, and he hadn't any idea where he might look, where he could afford to live within reach of his work. Where indeed he might feel at home.

'It wasn't the plan,' Gramercy responded, making an effort to control her voice. 'That's why I'm moving into new work, going into films, producing stuff that's not just mine. Bringing people like you to Feverel, using it as a base to brainstorm, to seed new ideas, to make something, to bring life to this place. It deserves it.'

Dinner reached the table late; it was half past nine before the casserole of soup, smelling of damp mulch, was lifted off the stove. Kim had already consumed a bowlful of black olives, and half a sunflower-seed-and-honey loaf, for he was used to eating at six-thirty or seven, as soon as he got back to his childhood home after work. He didn't care for the rubbery mushrooms, they reminded him of surgical gloves. But many more dishes were on their way, he noticed with relief, though no smell of roasting meat, he also noted, with disappointment.

The man from Channel Y who was putting up the money for Gramercy's film project had driven down to Feverel, and arrived around nine. His linen clothes wafted plumply against his much-lunched body, and, when Kim shook his hand, it was moist from holding the wheel.

This commissioning editor, introduced by Gramercy simply as Taffy, roared with delight as he kissed her, 'My stellar friend!' he shouted, then clasped Kim's hand in a strenuous shake and flushed with boisterous high spirits as he met first Hortense, then Monica, all the while deploring at staccato speed and at the top of his voice the condition of the roads, the multitudes of cones, the heavy goods vehicles that might as well be freight trains and run on tracks, the hay carts and combine harvesters and the flocks of dim sheep that prevented him arriving several precious minutes before for this meeting that was a pure tonic after what he'd endured at work that day in town.

He lifted their mood, with his noisiness; his guffaws at Gramercy's soup, his excitement about their joint project, his mock-furious laments at the money he'd stumped up already without anything to show for it.

'What one'll do for a better world! Sing, girl, c'm'on! I want to hear this Leto stuff!' he cried, and Gramercy felt the colour rise to her temples.

'Maybe she'll play you the tape, later,' said Monica, adding to the blaze of coloured vessels on the table and standing bottles beside them. 'Red wine, white, cider. And liquid vitamins – for Gramercy,' she added, positioning a flask of something orangey-crimson near the hostess, who was smoking a joint made with a herbal tobacco that smelled like Guy Fawkes Night. Gramercy had been preparing food with the fervour of one who never ate herself but found satisfaction in seeing others feed; picky, mostly off her food, and quick to feel queasy, she exulted in watching others cram themselves at her kitchen table.

Taffy was a trencherman; Hortense, too, had heaped her plate with approving sounds and was accepting Taffy's offer to refill her glass.

'So, where're we at with this idea?' began Taffy. Hortense started in, laying out the plans for the Leto's reinstallation (she'd brought with her photocopies of architects' drawings, publicity material, print-outs of computer realisations); Kim joined in, speaking softly, in his grave public persona, to deliver his start-of-history speech, which Taffy challenged, but good-humouredly, like an affable teacher goading a student to express himself more vigorously, to tighten his position.

'That's great, great,' he muttered, as Kim launched into tough tolerance, double identity, the present time when all post-this and post-that perspectives must end. There was to be no more belatedness, no more looking back.

Taffy listened on, with effusive interest. After Kim had first begun to be interviewed and featured and discussed in the media, the commissioning editor had taken the extent and degree of attention to the schoolteacher as insincere and opportunistic, a kind of hostility inverted, a symptom of host embarrassment or reverse racism. But he now realised that Kim had become more than a token marginal, or an object of curiosity. He'd become bankable – perhaps.

But they were having difficulty keeping strictly to the topic, for the wine was launching Gramercy's guests adrift on a winking, dancing, whitewater current into which they leapt, now going where it took them, now forging upstream, flying in the face of its force. Some well-worn landmarks guided the conversation's passage: the globalised economy, telly chefs, ways of giving up smoking (gum? patches? laser treatment? hypnosis?), the forthcoming alignment of the sun, the moon and the seven planets, and the incontrovertibly predicted end-of-the-world that would follow. They passed on to new plagues, catastrophes and autoimmune diseases, remote control medical diagnosis and treatment by computer menus. Taffy: 'Click on the icon that best describes your condition? Do you have flashing lights behind your eyes? Your turn!'

(To Hortense) Hortense: 'Do your piercings ooze?' Kim considered, then offered: 'How about those moles? How much time in your life have you spent sunbathing?' Monica: 'Does your heart ever skip a beat?' Gramercy: 'Do you feel inadequate?' And Taffy roared in response: 'Select one of the following options: Viagra! Prozac! St John's Wort! Garlic!'

Glasses brimmed over, plates emptied, smoke rose around the five of them as the dusk in the midsummer garden deepened, leaving the mica glint of a lopsided moon through the window.

The talk began to break up between them. Gramercy wanted to know what Kim thought about altruism in nature: 'Nellie says that animals start pining if you leave them alone, and that was one of the problems with Phil's arrangements. Overcrowding *and* loneliness, at the same time. If you put a donkey in a field on its own, it'll pine. But it only needs a duck to keep it company, and they both perk up. So it's a kind of mutual aid.' When she leant across the table and put a hand on Kim's arm, almost imploring him to crack the secrets of survival for her, Hortense realised how profoundly irritated she'd been ever since they'd arrived in this flaky singer's ridiculous pile, and even more so now that she'd been drinking.

She drained her glass, again. She hadn't wanted to come; Kim had made her, and now she was trapped here, and Gramercy's little girl eyes seemed to have grown larger in her face and to be dripping dew on Kim. Abruptly, Hortense stood up.

Monica got to her feet too, and showed Hortense the downstairs bootroom with the Victorian patterned enamel water closet with a royal coat of arms, Sanitation Engineers by Appointment. The wine fizzed out of her, and she felt lightened when she returned to the strewn table, where Monica was now placing baskets of fruit, a cheese board, a huge bowl of salad.

'Not more food!' said Hortense, but took her place again, resignedly. 'Altruism isn't incompatible with the selfish gene,' Taffy was saying. 'The thinking is that it can serve your best interests to do unto others as you would be done by.'

'But that's exactly what's broken down,' Kim put in. 'That economy of reciprocity and care. Remember the story about the kid whose father tells him, "Trust me, trust me, I'll catch you"? The kid doesn't want to jump into his father's arms. He stands there, scared his father'll drop him. But Dad insists. Dad promises, Dad gives his word, the word of a father that he'll catch the boy. So the boy jumps.

'And Dad doesn't open his arms and break his fall. He just lets his son crash to the ground. "There," he says to the lad who's lying there moaning, "That'll learn yer. That's the real lesson a father has to teach his son. Never trust anyone."

'That's what's happened to us, since – ten, fifteen years – since I was little. That's what we're up against.'

'But how do we switch into reverse?' Gramercy was plaintive.

'We don't go back,' Kim replied. He was flushed and spoke quickly. 'We go forward, we start again. Evolution? We're going to have to make one of those blips happen that suddenly fast forwards the universe into a higher phase of consciousness.'

Taffy picked up the theme: 'Did you hear the story about the little old Jewish clockmaker living in X – who gets taunted by schoolboys every day when they come down the lane past his house? And manages to stop them . . . ?'

Gramercy began humming in an undertone to the company, 'Tell me another one Not just any other one Tell me a better one, do.'

'Ah yes,' said Monica. 'I've heard this one – I think – go on.'

'It's an Isaac Bashevis Singer story – if you know it, you tell it!'

'No, no – I'm making the coffee.'

'Go on. I'm always talking too much – too loud.' Taffy gave out a great gust of self-delight and passed the storytelling on to Monica, who began, 'Okay. It goes like this – interrupt if I get it wrong!

'The boys go past the clockmaker's house every afternoon after school and they call him names and throw stuff. I shan't repeat it, you all know the kind of thing. He comes out and thanks them, very politely and gravely—' Monica put down the cafetière in her hand and acted out the courtesy – 'and he offers them a silver coin, with his profound thanks. So they can't believe their luck and they rush away hooting with delight.

'The next afternoon, the same thing – and so it goes on.'

Taffy couldn't help himself, but roared out, 'But after a few days, the crafty bugger begins doling out a bit less, then a bit less and a bit less . . .'

Monica chuckled, waved him on, and Taffy accepted her cue: 'They look at the money, and they feel dissed, don't they? "Wot's this then," they say. "Why aren't yer paying us like yer used to?"'

'And he says, "Because that's the limit of what I'm prepared to pay now."

'And so it goes. Every time after that, he just gives them a little bit less again, until one day, they look at his old pennies in disgust and throw the money back at him, shouting, "If yer think we're going to come and do it for this lousy sum, you've another think coming. Mister!" '

Gramercy exclaimed, 'Oh, wicked!'

Monica, passing round coffee, was chuckling to herself.

Kim was thoughtful. 'Hmm. Carrot and stick,' he said. 'Don't like it. There's got to be another way.' His head flicked to one side in dissent: like a robin, Gramercy thought. I wasn't right, his movements aren't like clockwork. He has this way of appearing to skip a frame, but it's bird-like, not mechanical.

Hortense noted, not for the first time, that Kim was completely humourless, and leant towards him. 'Kim,' she coaxed. 'You're among friends. You don't have to shoulder the world's ills here.'

Kim's face twisted with puzzlement, but he didn't answer, as Taffy surged on: 'Survival of the canniest. But what's canniest? Do you lot know the Prisoner's Dilemma? It's a game, invented by scientists – neo-Darwinists, evolutionary biologists, that little lot. It's designed to test the limits of self-interest, to put a spin on arguments about survival of the fittest, about natural selection favouring the strong and randy or the unscrupulous and criminal types. It's about knocking the selfish gene on the head. C'm'on, let's play!'

There was a flurry of sighs and appeals; but Taffy plunged on: 'You've been arrested,' he looked at Hortense. 'And you have too.' He pointed at Gramercy. 'For something you did together. I'm your jailer, sweeties, your interrogator, your judge, all in one, and I tell Hortense that if she talks, and gives evidence against Gramercy, she'll walk free and Gramercy'll get ten years. But only if Gramercy doesn't make the same choice.' He paused. 'I also tell you that if you both sing dumb, there won't be enough evidence, and I'll be able only to get you both sentenced to two years.'

A hubbub followed; they were pressing him to go over it again.

Monica said, 'It must be in their interest to betray each other. It's the only rational choice.'

'At first,' Taffy crowed, 'that's the obvious solution. But remember, Gramercy has to make a different choice.'

358

'I know!' said Hortense, 'The jailer double-crosses them both, and they both get ten years.'

Taffy laughed. 'No, no. The game doesn't work like that!'

'Right.' Kim was excited. 'There's a lot on the web about this. It's a zero-sum game. If they stop and work out a strategy between them – and think ahead – then betrayal turns out not to be the best option, after all. Isn't that it?'

Hortense asked, 'They're allowed to talk to each other?'

'In some versions.'

Taffy added, to Kim: 'I don't think there is an "it" – it's open-ended, endless.'

Gramercy offered, slowly, her solution: 'They make a pact, and then they both do less time.'

Taffy, more softly, continued: 'It does seem to be the case that if you play it many times, even with computers who have no consciousness and no fellow feelings, then cooperation – not defecting – is ultimately always the best decision.'

'I wish you'd bring those computers to speak to my colleagues,' Hortense said. 'With this Leto project – they'd all cheerfully disembowel me, if the director wasn't behind it.'

Kim continued, carefully: 'Here's another thing I want you to think about. There're these bats – in equatorial jungle. Vampire bats.' He looked at Hortense and she saw that he was making an effort to lighten up.

'Mmm,' cooed Gramercy, putting out the tip of her tongue to lick her upper lip.

'They all need a nice long drink of blood every three days at least. But the supply's unsteady, and some of the bats are weakened by hunger and can't go out hunting. Sometimes, it's hard to find the right prey – this species is particular. You don't just drink any blood.' Kim lifted his glass of red wine, eyed it, and drank.

Gramercy clutched herself, half-mewing her pleasure at this new side of Kim. 'Grue*some*.'

'The older bats are dab hands at locating food sources – they strike lucky nine times out of ten. But the youngsters keep failing to satisfy their cravings and they often need help . . .'

Taffy gave Gramercy a bluff look: 'Sounds familiar.'

'So the successful vampires,' Kim went on, 'drink more than they need and come back, all full up. They regurgitate the surplus to feed others – *selected* others.'

A stir of mixed delight and revulsion greeted these words, and Monica began passing the coffee cups – to Kim and to Taffy; Gramercy was pouring water straight from the kettle on to sachets of fruit and spice for the others. Taffy lit a cigar, puffed a blowtorch of smoke and flame, and waved another in front of Kim, who took it.

'Better than a nice deep drink of blood?' laughed Taffy.

General murmurs coaxed Kim to go on. 'So who gets to be fed? Some of the bats try and cheat, and pretend they're all weak and feeble so as not to have to give away any of their private feast. But ze colony haf a vay of detecting zeese deviants . . . These bats go in for grooming one another – and they concentrate especially on the tummy area. They can tell from a bat's belly how much it's imbibed. And they don't let it get away with any dog-in-the-mangerish behaviour. They know who's been generous and who hasn't, and that makes a big difference later, when it's the hoarders' turn to be hungry.'

'I get it!' Gramercy put out a hand to give Kim five – but he didn't meet her gesture, so her hand fell on his arm, which she found herself stroking instead. 'Tit for tat!'

'Yeah. But the real point,' Kim continued, 'is that the bats *remember*: this data about who owes what to who has made their brains bigger and more efficient. They're survivors because they're clever as a group, not because each of them is out there on its own, taking what it can get for itself. And the ones who share survive more than the ones who don't – so those genes get bred in and the selfish genes bred out . . . it's another spin on the prisoners' dilemma—' he gave a short laugh. 'I think I've visited the same website as Taffy!'

'I produced the bloody film that's got everyone interested in this stuff. Didn't I bloody well see it a hundred times! It won the something or other award, didn't it?' He was flushed with bonhomie. But he gave Kim a sharp look, and challenged him, 'But how do you get to be a member of the colony in the first place? Come off it, you've got to face it – it's blood, it's tribe, it's kin.'

'They're *bats*,' retorted Kim. 'We've gone and evolved bigger 'n' better brains, haven't we? So we get to *choose* who we want to be kin.'

Hortense was weary of all this talk, far from subjects she knew something about; she was longing for quiet and solitude and beginning to think that she'd soon go to the calm bedroom she'd been given for the night, but then she found, to her fury, that she was reluctant to leave Kim drinking at the table, grafted to the company – to Gramercy.

Meanwhile Taffy was striking back at Kim, 'Utopians! I don't know which is worse, liking your own kind for their own sake, or having to cast about for like-minded folks.'

Kim muttered, 'Not if you don't belong anywhere.'

In response, Taffy shouted: 'What's your solution for all those who don't see it your way? No blood for *your* breakfast!' His mood was still genial, though he was shaking his heavy head.

Hortense managed to get to her feet, and announce that she was going up. She looked over to Monica, who nodded back, kindly.

'I'll set the alarm, don't worry. And I'll run you to the station in time for your train.'

'Please stay,' wooed Gramercy. 'We haven't hardly begun.'

'I've got to be at work,' Hortense was starchy. 'Some of us don't have school holidays.'

'Aw, Hetty,' Kim smiled up at her. 'We haven't even heard the tape yet.'

Taffy supported this, warmly: 'Come on, sweetie, we've come for this. This wining and dining's great, but let's hear it from you, girl!'

'I want to go out, to the garden,' protested Gramercy. 'Look at the moon!'

But Monica took charge and patted her on the shoulder, and fortified her, and they trooped off to her music studio, with its twenty-four track recording console, its looped webs of cable and tassels of plugs, keyboards, and litter of beaten metal percussion pieces, rain-sticks, tamla finger drums, stringed instruments from around the world. They settled themselves down here and there in the room to listen, Hortense included, resignedly.

Gramercy's fey fluting voice floated out around them; she'd doubled herself in a new version of 'Angel of the Present', singing a descant over a rendition of 'Jerusalem' which she intoned so slowly and so dejectedly that it sounded flat, vacant, terminally sad; it croaked along under her anthem.

'I wanted it to sound like those funerals in the steppes—' she began to explain. 'The female mourners round the corpse – keening.'

361

'I thought we were going to hear new stuff,' Taffy objected, after a silence.

'That is new,' Monica rejoined.

'A new *arrangement*, yes. But, where's the Leto stuff?'

Monica came back quickly, 'You know very well Gramercy's not going to let people hear something until it's perfect – she's an artist.'

'There's a lot of new ideas floating about,' said Gramercy, 'But nothing's really finished enough to put out.'

But they pressed her, hard, and Taffy looked so bearish that eventually she let herself be begged. On the demo, so far, her thin voice implored and railed; she'd searched out cadences from home-grown chapel services and marching music and even brass bands, which she'd drawn out with angry irony beneath passages taken from private lamentations in Tirzah and other elsewheres, from the wordless, grieving lullabies of mountain women over the female baby nobody prizes, from the prescribed ululations of professional mourners at the deaths of patriarchs. They sat, trying to pick out the words: in 'Chronologies', Gramercy waveringly tracked the life of 'a woman you could know', giving dates and events of world significance in a digitalised voice, 'like those telephone menu messages', beneath a chronology of ordinary birth and marriage and struggle and illness and old age.

'This is good stuff,' beamed Taffy. 'I can see you now, drifting through some derelict cityscape, where there's nought but trashed fridges and a few weeds – singing, looking like a dream . . .'

'I think we've seen that. We want something much more . . . *extreme*.' Gramercy was glowing hot from the effect of listening to herself through their ears; she wanted to hear Kim's response to her new songs, so that she could tell him that he could use them, gladly, as he had before.

Taffy, still strewing film ideas this way and that, led them back to the wine and the fruit on the kitchen table. 'We'll film over the summer, edit late-August and have it ready for a prime slot in the autumn schedules. I think I can fix that – if the Museum can come in with the necessary . . .'

Drowsily, Hortense approved this: 'We've got the Leto unveiling in the schedules for late September – that'll give the schools time to prepare. Kim's bringing his class but we want lots more – from teeny tots to teenagers, those are the director's orders. A unifying symbol for fragmented times. Your bunch are a mixed lot, aren't they? How many languages?'

'It changes year to year,' Kim answered. 'But last year I had – I don't know – thirty-two in the class and about fifteen different languages – some I'd never even known existed. But kids learn quickly. It's teaching the mothers who never leave the flats, except to go to the health centre or the supermarket – that's the problem.'

'What a life.' And this time, Hortense did manage to say goodnight, and left the room all heavy-limbed, like a long lap swimmer stepping out of a pool.

Monica followed soon after, and it began to look to Gramercy as if Taffy and Kim were set to talk all night, so she announced that she was going to bed too. Taffy jumped up to hug her, overwhelming her. 'Gram girl, you're such a star!' Kim smiled a goodnight, with his head to one side. She gave them both a careless-seeming wave, though she was feeling anything but.

As she left, she heard Taffy push the bottle over the table to Kim, with the order, 'Now, let's hear it from you. You're the one with the story, the man of mystery with the secret powers. Just tell it to me, as if you didn't know who I was. Give it to me straight, like it's the first time I've heard it. I need to know where all this loot's going to . . .'

5

A Midsummer Night

Hortense hadn't travelled to the country to hear a flipping pop singer pretend to save the world, she'd made space in her life to be with Kim, space beyond her ordinary world, well out of reach of her familiar surroundings, so that it could seem as if the act weren't taking place at all. She'd arrived at understanding what Kim made her feel. Not love, not even lust, but freedom, as if she'd come out as gay and was picking partners – different partners – across all the usual boundaries of colour and caste and money and age and custom and the other regulatory norms by which she lived – and most of the people she knew likewise. Kim's peculiar fervour was her own deep secret, and she liked the idea of it best when she was attending to the most formulaic aspects of her life: during her weekly phone call to her mother-in-law, or wrestling with a Museum colleague about the latest data maintenance questionnaire ('How many members of the public have you spoken to?' 'Do they mean, "How do I get to the Bog Man?" Or "Where's that Homeless Mummy?" Or don't directions count?'). Through all such tiresome, trivial, recurring, and also comfortingly predictable routines of her existence, she fondled, deep inside her, Kim's strange, exalted claims on her . . . She opened his messages with growing anticipation, only to close them instantly when the bold letters sprang up, announcing that yes, there was another e-mail from him. She'd consign it quickly to a separate, encrypted file, where she would read it later, in hiding, when her colleagues had gone.

But what did all this work on the Bundle mean? Or rather, mean to him? She understood less now than she had at first. The past was to be swept away. Yet there he was, digging deeper. It was a kind of scaffold for his fantasies: he'd once shown her, on her computer at work, a programme you could access through one of the default settings.

'You double-click on these options – look,' he'd said. Leaning over her shoulder and opening a spread sheet: he first pointed at one icon, then put in another command, then when that menu appeared, another. The screen flipped, spun and resolved itself into the pitted surface of some celestial body, over which she found herself skimming in a small spiky spacecraft.

'And there you have it: you're in the driver's seat and you're now heading out of our galaxy. Careful!'

She held on to the mouse for dear life, trying to keep the vehicle steady over the pocked crust of a star.

'What is this?' she'd laughed.

'Some nerdy idea to bring a little fun to the deskbound life.' Kim had put his hand over hers to steer the careering machine. 'No magic involved, swear to God, Miss. It lies just underneath the surface – you just have to know the steps to take to find it. It's a bit like the past, you see? Whose memories are being remembered, what story's being told? Under one, there's always another.'

He was clearly barking mad, and she was an idiot to think that she could deviate so far from her day-to-day existence: she'd never even mentioned to Daniel that she was meeting Gramercy Poule – the idea of trying to explain such a deviation from her routine to her conscientious husband defeated her.

In the attic bedroom, she burrowed further down under the duvet, but the absence of Kim, whom she had been expecting at least to knock on her door before . . . she wouldn't spell that out to herself . . . To her fury, she was wideawake, on the spike of waiting, wondering, wanting. She tried to curl up into a tighter ball, but still sleeplessness had her in its white grip. And now she was thirsty. The red wine had parched her till her limbs seemed to catch and scratch at the bedclothes and her eyeballs and nostrils were scuffed and rough inside her skull. If she went to the kitchen, Kim and Taffy might still be there, Aguecheek and Belch, carousing, sprawling, and she long-faced, reproving, erect, a spoilsport Malvolio.

Two-thirty a.m. She'd pin up her hair again, and have a look outside.

How was it that the whole bloody world seemed to be having sex all the time, and she wasn't in a position even to worry about getting AIDS?

She couldn't go down, not as she was, with no make-up and bare feet; but if she did, she wouldn't appear to be coming on at him ... She began to need badly to see if anybody was still about; she wanted to know which way they were jumping, before she knew what was left for her. Her dilemma presented itself to her, even in her unsettled state of exhausted, fading inebriation, with a strange coldness: should she let this opportunity slip, when Gramercy Poule probably came straight out with her desires, no inhibition, singing them loud and clear, Girls just want to have fun, Don't you tell me nothing, Daddy. I wanna be me. Making snarling faces and pulling tongues, and giving details about their underwear to the papers.

She was the older woman, hah. He must have been waiting for her to take the initiative. She should have known, acted on her own account, made it clear. Outreach, it was her job, after all.

The photograph from the brochure of the sea view from the hotel where she was due to meet Daniel, soon, rose up before her; she found herself cringing from the idea of being there with her amiable, hard-working husband, trying to make love.

There was nobody in the kitchen. The thirst that had seemed to rage now faded; the kitchen seemed cavernous and desolate. Still, she reminded herself of her first needs, and went to the fridge; it was soothing, the pool of blue light, the draught from the bottle.

'Hetty?' Kim was calling to her, softly. 'Come and see this.'

He was sitting in front of the monitor, in the office.

She went halfway to the door. 'I was thirsty.'

'I'm so glad you're awake. Why did you leave us?'

She hovered. 'More messages from the beyond?'

'Look!'

'I'm tired.'

'Not too tired to look at this.' He pointed the cursor, clicked and the images expanded, changed, spiralled and swirled upwards, plasma spreading in purpleised aureoles, heat-coded pillars of cloud, pixillated sheaves of stars. Kim went on, eyes on the screen, 'That's beauty, that's the real thing – and it's all out there. This is state-of-the-art image definition. God I wish I could fall through the screen and disappear – spontaneous combustion back into the galaxy.'

'Isn't that what you do anyway?'

'We're stardust – look.' He paused, took his eyes away from the screen. 'Doctor Fernly, I've wanted to be alone with you all night.'

Hortense involuntarily put a hand to her throat as if he'd clutched it. 'Oh, don't start that again,' she said, 'You know it's absurd.'

'Why is it absurd?'

'Because . . . I'm a woman with a full life, a husband, a job I like that keeps me busy.'

'And that means you won't come to bed with me?'

She was struggling to meet the moment she'd never been able to envisage with any clarity: so his wild words on her e-mail weren't simply the currency of some kind of out-of-body state, like saints enraptured before their visions, having their souls ravished and spouting the metaphors of the Song of Songs. He was coming closer now and seemed to be vibrating as he took her by the shoulders. She felt a lick of fear rise inside her.

'Hetty, be soft—'

She was trying to look at him, but something was preventing her, pinioning her from another, scared, muddled place inside her. She wasn't made of the stuff of adventure; he might hurt her – she saw him mauling her, spread over her, and stifling her; what if he was dirty underneath that neat, tight exterior? What if he battered her? Then there was afterwards, too. What happened afterwards?

He was coaxing her, with his face very near hers. 'Not just to me. Be kind to yourself.'

All the conflict of first hoping, then planning, then finding the situation slipping out of her control, then finding him so coolly playing with the computer, as if he knew she'd come down for him, then the fear coursing so wilful and turbulent, exploded in hot gusts inside her; she didn't know the codes of courtship, she wanted to be wooed, not expected. So she found herself storming at him, 'What the hell do you mean? It's not enough you've set yourself up as some sort of fucking messiah for the human race, you think you're god's gift to womankind too, you think *I* need *you*?'

'I didn't say that. But I just think sex makes me happy, Hetty, and it might do the same for you.'

'What?' Hortense was enraged. 'Sex? Happiness? What the hell do you mean? If you think you're talking to me in the language I understand, you've bloody well got another think coming.'

*

Upstairs again, she certainly couldn't sleep now; she was struggling with the realisation that she'd made a false move, that she'd somehow defected from the pact they had – whatever it was. Her anger began to look unwarranted, overbearing. Then she regretted her regret; how foolish it had been of her to be so incapable of rational decision-making that she'd lost her temper.

Uncomfortably, she lies there, thinking how she'll scrape away this encounter to reveal another one underneath it, how she and Kim'll replay this bungled sequence through another set of variations, how tomorrow, or the day after, they'll be allies again, still conjoined by the enigmas of the past, not pulled apart under the strain of choosing between the bifurcating paths of the turbulent present.

Gramercy's bedroom was upstairs, but sometimes, she'd move her duvet and her pillow (and the dogs) to the cushioned *bergère* she loved in the orangery, because then she could look at the sky through the glass roof. She liked being close to the old vine inside with its pebble-hard grapes, and to the trees in motion outside in the shadowed garden, breathing out deeply, long exhalations of cool oxygen. Their nocturnal vitality encouraged hers, restfully.

She'd get a recording of the vampire bats, she was thinking as she lay there; and she'd slow it down till its frequency became audible to human ears, then use it in a song, though she wouldn't tell anyone where the music came from – except maybe Kim. He'd given her the idea, after all. In the morning they'd all be leaving – Monica was taking them to the station, or maybe Taffy would be driving them later to Enoch. But even so, at this rate, she wasn't going to be up and about to see them off.

She wondered what time it was, for she'd like to ring Bobby Grace, to talk. She'd roll a joint and tell her mum all that was happening. But what was happening?

Nellie didn't want to come and live at Feverel, she knew, because of that queer daughter of hers. The plan to renovate the cottages on the moor was still blocked, and Nellie and Phoebe had been moved from the railway station buildings to a flat on an estate on the edge of the town. Gramercy hadn't seen it, but she could imagine it. Yet Phoebe packed so much power in that tiny body, it was hard even to begin to try and persuade her; there was something goblin-like, preternatural about the tight, strong set of her shoulders. She looked pristine, but you felt if you glanced away and then back again, you might catch her crumpled and wrinkled, like a dry apple under that integument they'd crafted to cover her. Did Kim have that peculiar quality too, at times? Of looking split off from himself, as if underneath his eyes and mouth and skin there was silicon or mica or chitin or krypton, eerie, shiny, radioactive?

But Nellie declared she couldn't be parted from Phoebe, not while she was still studying; when Gramercy invited them both to stay with her, to try it for only a week in the holidays, Phoebe stamped on the proposal, outright.

In Gramercy's mind's eye, Phoebe was hanging upside down from a rafter while Nellie was giving her little sips of blood from her mouth.

Maybe Phoebe would take off, to Enoch, in that stroppy way of hers, and then Nellie would be left on her own and then she could come to live at Feverel and start feeding Gramercy with bloody kisses from her lips, too.

But tonight, she was a prisoner of circumstances; no means presented itself to make any comforting relation with the things she wanted – so self-pity reared up and gripped her as she lay there in her lovely orangery with the chandelier drops of the bunches of grapes above her. She stroked one of her hot-pelted dogs, who was lying by her feet like a hound on a tomb effigy; the bitch's eager, kind responsiveness cheered her. She'd go out, into the garden, and find the setting moon, for she couldn't see it up in the sky any longer.

She found the window lock keys and let herself out of the orangery, snapping her fingers softly to the dogs to follow. When the moon reappeared between a gap low in the trees, it was a smoky orange and lying on its back in drifts of cloud; it was a barque in someone's system, Gramercy remembered, ferrying souls. The flaring sun of yesterday – or was it tomorrow's? – which was shining on the other side of the world was caught in the floating ribbons of clouds through which the moon glided; under just such a volatile summer moon the garden was stirring with the industry of unseen things, with a scurry and skittering, with the composting and distillery of underground hunters and hoarders, airborne flitters and darters. Gramercy felt afraid of their invisible business, but pulled irresistibly towards the thought of them beneath her, around her; a little owl's distant hoo-hoo sounded reassuringly human by contrast to the white fluttering of moths, the sprinkle of nocturnal gnats, the bony mandibles chewing.

Hook was bristling, then gave a bark. Bonny joined in, then Jonty, who always followed his two siblings but never initiated anything, added to the alarums. She hushed them; she had a moment of excited hope, that Agnes Feverel would rise up and speak to her. But this hope was quickly followed by fear's usual thrilling clutch, that an intruder would materialise in the star shadows and pounce on her, or that bats, folding and unfolding in the trees, would dip the pipette of their fangs into her.

Above, the trunks of trees inclined towards one another in confidential conversations of leaves and branches. They seemed to join hands like the crowds of fans reaching up to her on stage; only the trees' dark arms were giants' limbs, and their roots were pushing far far down below, forking through the glinting schist of Fellmoor on which Feverel stood. Such a thin layer of soil, every garden hand she'd ever tried to keep complained. Shale a foot under the surface, too hard for flowers not used to resistance, but turning to mud under the driving force of the water-seeking roots of the trees, cracking it and crumbling it to get at what they needed. It made her dizzy to think how the root system ran as deep below as the topmost crowns swayed above her: the earth was swinging open like a silent strongroom door to admit her to its damp, interior ventricles, where the busiest of all the living things were combining and recombining to keep the cycle of growth continuing.

She was lying down now, in the meadow, too heavy in her head to stay on her feet, and her surroundings were gradually turning light, while still remaining monochrome, as if a divine photographer were dipping the night in a developing tray and pulling out its wet and shining images printed in a dozen pulsing velvet tones. The grass was prickly on her cheek and cold, but its touch refreshed her and the earth gave her moorings; she could feel her anchor line tugging fathoms down where the crown of the trees, mirrored in the roots, dipped and soughed like weed on the ocean bottom.

She felt him approach her then, or rather come upon her, and the dogs snarled and crouched back to tuck themselves into her corners. Her heart bucked inside her and knocked loudly: so loudly she couldn't hear him or the trees or the nocturnal busyness of all things underground.

'It's only me,' Kim would whisper, but penetratingly enough to carry. 'I came out to look at the sky. You can't see it in Enoch, not like this. There, it's dirty mustard from the lights.'

'I know,' Gramercy would whisper back. She'd be stepping out, across the wet turf underfoot: 'Remember, I'm a city girl, born and bred.'

She was trying to still her blood so she could make sense, and she managed to scramble to her feet; that skunk she'd smoked was powerful stuff, she knew, as she felt the deck of the earth heave and skew again.

She managed to stay upright to wait for him to reach her, and had to call the dogs to heel; they were whining at the flickering darks and lights out there on the lawn.

'I couldn't sleep, my head was so full of things,' Kim would be saying quietly. 'I'm on a kind of endless rush – and I thought, Why not go out? So I came out – and I frightened you.'

'I wasn't asleep.'

He'd then fall silent with her, in contemplation of the end of the night, and then, she'd add something about the film, how she was going to stir people up ... and he would say, perhaps, 'I don't think I'll leave tomorrow. I want to think about things.'

'Oh,' Gramercy would let out a cry she couldn't help; and with express clumsiness, she'd reach out to throw her arms around his neck. To her surprise, she'd feel his tight body pliant to hers, returning the gesture that she'd made in the spirit of a child who's been at long last promised a longed-for treat by a stern parent, but with the tip of a pointed tongue slipping past her lips, altering its course and its nature.

In her fantasies, she'd been the active one; she'd imagined that he would want this or that and she would meet his desires so quickly she'd appear to be anticipating them, even leading them. But now that she felt his warmth steal through her, that part of her that held the traces of motion and gesture, of caress and kiss, flew out through the holes of her ears and the tips of her fingers with the breath of her body. Leaves rustled in her hair and tendrils trailed from her hands and wreathed her ankles and from their entangled mouths flowed roses and berries as he pressed his fingers into her cleft limbs; she twisted to unwrap herself and comb out the knots that were binding her will, but every flexion wound her closer to him, every step tightened the stems that were shooting round her legs, her arms, her torso.

'Who are you, Kim?' she'd ask him, but her voice would come out like the wind in the topmost branches, as she'd give herself up, night-blind, efflorescing, to his warm and slithering coils.

Ella has been to the duck coop, to rake out the straw, and she's bringing up in a shallow straw basket three lumpy, thick-shelled, pale green-blue eggs, to leave in the kitchen. It's early, and the sun hasn't yet burned up the dew on the ground or the mist rising as it begins to evaporate. On her way across the meadow, she spots a pair of Gramercy's shoes, lying on their sides one step in front of the other, as if Gramercy had stepped out of them in mid-stride. Ella doesn't pick them up, as Monica will be up and about soon; Ella does not want to trigger any recognition in her mind: restoring one pair might revive memories of that earlier loss.

Then she sees one of the Indian silk cushions from the orangery, tossed to one side, so this she does pick up, balancing the basket of eggs on it, and comes through the side door.

Hortense is sitting at the table, having an orange juice; Monica is brewing coffee and examining the train timetable; Kim is cutting some bread near the toaster, and asking Hortense if she'd like a piece of toast. She nods, in response, and then groans.

Ella hears the murmur about headaches and pills and rehydration. But she isn't listening to it. Though she's standing upright, the floor seems to tilt and fall away, as on board ship in a high wind. There he was, at last, a little taller than her, but more compact and well-knit than Phoebe, with his pointed ears; grown-up. He's lived in step with the time here, she thinks, he hasn't dropped through rents in the proper continuum of one day after the next.

Monica exclaims, 'Nellie, it's you! Put them in the larder.' To Kim and Hortense, she announces, 'Here she is, our treasure, as Gram was saying yesterday, that is if you remember anything of what transpired . . .' She chuckles. 'Nellie's the one from Tirzah via . . . well, various other points east of here.'

Kim looks tranquilly through his tiredness at the small, weathered, stringy woman with the eggs on the cushion in front of her, and asks her, with a kind of politician's courtesy, 'I was adopted – and you, what happened to you?' Very steadily, controlling the pricking tears filling her eyes behind her large new glasses, Ella answers Kim with a summary of her story, about the siege and Dr Martin, about Phoebe and the operation. She ends. 'Can *you* remember anything?' She tries a few words, but Kim shakes his head. 'I remember a boat, and confusion, artillery fire, smoke. Someone playing a penny whistle. Sometimes, something seems to tug at me, especially when I'm talking to . . . when I'm researching the Bundle.' He looks across at Hortense, but she is keeping herself turned away from him. 'I feel something, but then it fades, I think I'm seeing a face I know, and then I find I don't remember a thing.'

Monica takes the cushion from Ella, and they exchange a look and a shake of the head. Ella recognises that Monica is worried about Gramercy's restless walking at night, about her general state of mind, but she can't think about that now.

'Can you stay here?' Kim bends sympathetically towards Nellie; he's acting the defence counsel, with her interests at heart; she is the kind of person, he recognises, that HSWU is all about. 'Have you been given papers?'

Ella wants to reach out and touch his hair, to find the spirals of his crowns and follow the rim of his ears with her fingers to feel for the kink, to lift his shirt to see his smoothness, to sing to him something that might sink deep into that stratum of his cortical being that, years and years ago, might have been seeded by her.

In some stories, she knows, mothers know their lost children through some prickling of the flesh; but there are others she's also heard, when they need tokens, identifying features, parchments and certificates – the right papers.

Monica interposes, with a cough, 'The application's dragging on and on, but I think we'll get there in the end. Won't we, Nellie?' She smiles grimly. 'Nellie has a wonderful daughter too, who's by now so completely part of the environment that she couldn't possibly belong anywhere else. And I think that'll make a very strong case for giving them both permits to stay. But God, does it take grinding away, day after day, year after year – and it really winds me up that someone like Nellie is meant to be able to cope with all the fucking stuff . . . this document in triplicate, small print to make you go stark staring mad.'

'When HSWU is really up and running,' Kim said, 'when there's somebody in the office, not just me, the website will take you through all that – step by step, in twenty, thirty languages . . .'

Monica glances over at the clock on the wall above the stove: 'But we must go, if we're to catch that train and get you back in time for whatever it is you have to be there for – pity, Gramercy'll be disappointed. You'll have to come back!'

They're nodding; Kim is picking up Hortense's bag, and smiling into her grey face protectively, as they begin to pass through the door.

'Why's your name "Kim"?' Ella asks. 'It isn't a name from Tirzah.'

Kim smiles at her. 'It was on a button on my clothes, when I was . . . handed over to my Mum. Funny, I know. I thought it might be some kind of Tirzahner brand name – like being called "Lacoste" or "Oshkosh" . . . Still, I quite like it.' He pauses, then adds, 'I found it in the Bundle, too – made my skin prickle. There it meant something like "Good, Holy Memory"—' He looks at Hetty, who mutters, on automatic, 'It must have been a charm of some kind.' Then Kim glances back at the woman, Gramercy's help, the Tirzahner refugee. She looks like many of the HSWU followers, especially in the way her eyes cling to him; it's an expression he knows. It's recognition – that he can help; it's made up of inextinguishable hope; it's the look in certain faces that gives him belief that what he does is necessary.

At the threshold, he turns back to Ella, 'Good luck. I hope it all works out. We'll talk properly – I'll be back.' He nods, to himself, to the absent Gramercy, to Monica.

Ella watches him and sits down at the table, something she doesn't usually do. Her head is light and her eyes are focusing strangely. The past is pouring through her vision, obscuring the dresser and the sink and the stove and the windows of morning in the kitchen at Feverel.

Kim – K-I-M – Kalē Ierē Mnemosynē – O, Memory, Lovely and Holy . . . we used to scratch the letters into buttons for good luck . . . did I still have one of those buttons then? It's all so long ago and the button wasn't one of the tokens by which I expected to find you again   my glossy boy   as long as it is you   if it is you   it must be you and yes you are thriving   you are at home here   as I always hoped   as I dreamed

374

6

In the Playground

It was the beginning of term, and a mild, blue September, still attached to summer's kite strings, bathed the school, transfiguring the Cantelowes wasteland; in the playground, children were showing one another talismans they'd found and telling one another secrets they'd discovered or invented and made their own over the holidays; Kim was in the staff room, having a coffee with his colleagues, conscientiously putting his coins into the biscuit collecting box and generally trying to ensure with modesty and amiability that his recent moments of fame in the papers and on the telly should provoke minimum resentment and suspicion and hostility among them.

The head teacher, Kate Daiges, had telephoned him for a talk the week before term started; she'd asked him to guarantee that this new, public phase of his political activism would not interfere with his participation in the school. Kim was electric with hope, with plans, with possibilities, and he radiated confidence down the line: he was passionately committed to his job at Cantelowes, he declared; young children in just such a part of Enoch were the central motive of his life and work.

'But all this stuff about visions – it makes some of us very uncomfortable. It's one thing to campaign for greater justice and equality, to speak up for community, but . . . come off it, Kim.'

'You wouldn't tell the kids that Joan of Arc was lying, would you? Or that the Bible's full of fantasies? It's part of human nature and history to experience revelations. I'm not setting myself up as a saint – you know that. It's no different from you waking up one day with an absolute, clear sense that something has to be done and can't be done in any other way . . . Call it instinct, a sixth sense, the unconscious. To me, it's a vision.'

'So you keep saying, I know. I've read your interview. Your interviews. But I have to tell you I'm going to be watching closely your input in the classroom. I don't want one thing getting mixed up with another. I don't want the kids upset – or their parents – by religious fervour of some new order. And I don't want absenteeism. Or excuses.'

'I'm not denominational, I'm not sectarian. The whole point of HSWU is to combat all that.'

'Mmm. I know that's what you say.'

So Kim had yet to convince his head that the kids of Cantelowes would benefit from taking part in the film, featuring in the vanguard of the Museum celebrations for the Leto Bundle's unveiling and recording the chorus backing to Gramercy's Leto anthem – but he was confident. Hortense would be writing to Kate Daiges in her best official civil servant mode. No head of a run-down inner city primary could hold out for long, he felt, against such opportunities.

Happiness is a funny word, he thought, as he asked the children in his class to make a list of three things that had made them happy over the holidays.

Food – of various kinds. Outings – to the sea, to a film. Animals. My gerbil. My hamster. People. My Nan.

He made suggestions: What about colours, he said. Think of a colour that lifted you up. Yellow of sunflowers. Orange of satsumas. Cherry coke pink. Frosted mint of Mum's toenails.

What about doing things? Did any of you make anything? Help your Nans cook? Draw what you made. Pat-a-cake pat-a-cake. Write me a story about what you did.

Were there any surprises? Any secrets? Such things make for happiness.

(Also for unhappiness, but we shan't talk about that today.)

What about a song you like? Can you sing one to me? Do you girls still like that boy band Nixzone? (Titters, groans.) What about the Natural Selections? (A girl band, clearly down the tubes from the expressions of disgust round the low tables.)

You like who? Oh, I'll have to have a listen to them.

To himself, he was saying, Happiness: haply I think on thee. Hapless in the jaws of fate. Can one be hapful? Happenstance is chance, accident, Lady Luck's territory: not quite fate, because random through and through, whereas fate is driven by unseen forces, has a will and a purpose behind it, the knowing laughter up the sleeve of the old gods. But happenstance shows its direct links to happiness: it's the country of perhaps. Destiny forecloses options: the one who's cursed can never escape, he shall meet his father at the crossroads, marry his mother and put out his eyes. But the country of maybe lets things happen, it's that messy corner in time where you turn back on the journey because you think you left the immersion on and so you escape the multiple pile-up on the motorway or miss the plane that goes down in a ball of fire. Happily, I wasn't there when the chariot with the angry patriarch reached the crossroads, happily I got stuck in the tunnel during a bomb scare and I wasn't on that flight after all.

Happily: you are fortune's child.

Haply I think on thee, Kim murmured again, and he looked out of the window, to avert his bright face from the children.

It had been a happy summer for him; the happiest he could remember. Six hundred hits a week on the HSWU website now, and a part-timer funded by Gramercy. She was keen to employ someone full-time, at Feverel, to answer the queries – she wanted Phoebe. That way, she'd secure Nellie. But Phoebe was wary and had only agreed to temp for a while. Kim also urged Gramercy to respect Phoebe's objections to taking up the work full-time: 'She doesn't want you to overwhelm them – it's simple. She wants her independence. Don't suffocate her! I want to go on teaching, too, you see. I don't want to be sucked in to . . .'

Gramercy did not have to listen. She'd heard this before.

Then Hetty, who was miserably spending the summer with her husband, first two weeks' holiday up north on the islands, then back in Enoch, at the Museum, was writing Kim e-mails full of awkward officialese between tackling the Leto manuscripts. A full monograph was to follow the first background booklet. But it would take years: she was commissioning new translations, finding editors to collate the results, to trace the relations between one document and another.

A year ago, he would not have recognised himself as he had become. Before Minta moved to the Close Care home, he'd stay in, he'd tell himself, to watch out for her, but once he was all on his own in the house, he'd begun to build the website at night and he hadn't gone out much. But now, HSWU's profile was growing strongly: politicians of every stripe were making enquiries, many of them with startling unctuousness. The opposition was bringing it up, too; there were taunts to the website as well. They showed people were sitting up and taking notice. He wasn't to be dismissed easily any more. All those features about Kim that had fazed people and provoked jibes ('Change water into beer, come on.' Or, 'Here's a bit of soap!') were now part of his 'charisma'. He was 'sombre', he was 'mysterious'. Besides, he was enjoying Hetty's rivalry with Gramercy: she now wanted him to know how much better she grasped the meaning of his mission than that rock star.

At break after lunch, some of the bigger girls were doing their French skipping, in and out of the elastic to a rapid patter. Many of the lines were new this season, and so Kim stood and listened, while a gaggle of kids bounced around him, plucking at him for his attention and crying foul against one another:

> 'Milkman milkman do your duty
> Here comes Mrs Macaroony
> She can do the pam-pam
> She can do the splits
> But most of all she'll kiss, kiss, kiss.'

A new boy that term, eight years old, small for his age, was watching them as they skipped; he stood entranced, eyes shining, his fists in his cheeks. The dinner ladies who helped out during breaks after clearing away and doing the dishes, tried to coax the quiet and frightened little fellow to join a mixed game of He, but he shook his head, and retreated further, in silence. Kim knew that little-boy yearning to belong, especially to a group of bursting, noisy, self-assured girls, for whom words and rhymes and jokes were so much knicker elastic, a tribe from whom tongue-locked boys like Simi would always be exiled.

They were chanting:

> 'My boyfriend gave me an apple
> My boyfriend gave me a pear
> My boyfriend gave me a kiss on the lips
> And then threw me down the stair.'

Thwang, schlwink, thwang, schwlink, went the skipping elastic; in and out the first girl jumped, her quick feet crisscrossing, but then she stumbled and was caught in the traces, so it became another's turn, who dashed into the mesh, as the others crowed and bounced up and down, their eyes dancing with the mischievous delight of it. They were glad to be back at school, teachers and pupils alike: the summer holidays had been long.

When the sequence of events was reconstructed later, Sally, one of the dinner ladies, remembered seeing a man in a car with a mobile phone, parked outside the Girls' gate on the zigzag lines, and feeling then impatience and contempt: 'Men behaving badly, again', she'd said to herself. But she didn't take action then – it was the first day of term, the general mood was excited, but trusting. Later, she pictured the man clearly: he was sitting in some kind of customised, metallic green vehicle, with the window buzzed down, and when he finished making his calls, he turned up some techno dance stuff and jounced to it as he smoked, his eyes screwed up against the light so that she couldn't see his features then, even though he was parked on the pavement side so that he could survey the playground through the barred gap between the walls. He didn't look like one of the dirty mac brigade, more showbiz, more like a TV presenter pretending to be hard, with a baseball cap on back to front. The Girls' gate of the playground was closed, but not bolted.

When he got out of the car, he looked gigantic, because it was a low-slung number which he swung himself up from, and because he was the only man, with the exception of Kim, and he was bearing down through the lines and loops of children and their female minders in the playground; besides, he was inflated by a huge, vivid magenta puffer jacket, in spite of the weather, and it bore fluorescent yellow stripes across the shoulders and on the upper arms and wrists; he looked, Sally said later, like a gigantic hazard sign on the march in some frightening cartoon ad.

One of the children who gave her version of events on television (before the social services clamped down on journalists approaching pupils about the incident) said that she saw him marching in like the bad brothers of the BFG – the fleshlumpchewer and the babyguzzler, and that she was scared: he was coming back, she said, 'Because he's still hungry 'cos he didn't get anything to eat last time.'

Sally asked the man, 'Can I help?'

'Yeah,' he said, 'looking for him.' He pointed across the yard, and began making straight across it, over the hopscotch markings, through the clusters of children. They were still dancing up and down, singing,

'I gave him back his apple
I gave him back his pear
I gave him back his kiss on the lips
And threw him down the stair.'

As he passed by her, Sally noticed, she said later, that he was younger and smaller than the impression given by the swollen mass of his jacket, that he looked pasty and sort of stretched and tired round the eyes. But it was the roughness of his tone and the purposeful gliding of his eyes towards one of the kids that made her realise here was real trouble.

'Hey!' she called out. 'Where you going?' But he went on, regardless, past another troop squealing as they jumped up and down round one child in the middle. As soon as Simi saw the man coming, the child ran to the far corner of the playground, and huddled against the wall, his face buried in the brickwork, his arms cradling his head. So Sally then shouted to Kim, and to Eva, the two teachers supervising that break. Kim heard her over the sound of the children's skipping songs and the hubbub around him in the centre of the playground where the games were heated; he saw the quiet new boy cower against the wall, and he swivelled to see the man, with his face splotched with anger, gain on his prey.

It all happened so quickly, as everyone was to say afterwards, that most of the kids didn't see it at all, and it wasn't clear if the man in the puffer jacket sauntered or strode or ran to snatch Simi where he was crouching and whimpering against the wall. He seemed to leap, long-leggedly, moving through the ranks of playing children without let or hindrance to pick up the boy and crush his head against his chest in the crook of his left arm and lift him off his feet and drag him away. Simi put up no fight, but seemed to expect his assailant, and play dead, as if total submission might ward off the coming blows, his dangling legs limp, his face squeezed in the bulging folds of the man's jacket.

Kim felt something seize him, first cold, then hot; he could feel how the world tossed sickeningly as you were grabbed and hoisted and jolted upside down; he tasted, as searing as battery acid on the tongue, the child's fear of beatings ahead; it was as present to him as if he were Simi, and so, dipping into speed, he ran across the ground to accost the child's abductor.

The game of He was still whirling round the playground, one boy bumping into the man and the child he was hauling off.

'Sorry,' said the boy, and then stopped, seeing what was happening.

'You're caught!' called another player in triumph, laying a hand on him and speeding off. There were squeals and whoops, the rings of running boys and girls looping over the ground.

The skipping game, too, was carrying on.

> 'I know a little Dutch girl
> Called Eye Shoe Shemima
> And all the boys in the football team
> Go Eye Shoe Shemima
> How is your mother?
> All right.
> Died in the fish shop
> Last night
> What did she die of?
> Raw fish.
> How did she die?
> Like this.'

Down flopped the child on the playground floor, playing dead.

When Kim tried to block the man's path and pull Simi out of his grip, the man pushed him aside with a blow to his shoulder. So Kim ran instead to the gates and bolted them, and was standing in between them, ready to bar the man's way, whether he made for the Boys' or the Girls' as his exit.

'Let go of that child immediately.' Kate Daiges, small and ferocious in authority, confronted Simi's abductor. 'Or I'll call the police.'

'He's coming home with me, and he knows what for.' The man's eyes were funny, said the head afterwards, blank with dot pupils, and when his cap fell off, which happened later, during the struggle with Kim, his head had been shaved in a checked pattern that made him look mangy. Sally was behind Kate Daiges, screaming.

Kate Daiges squared up to him. 'You're not taking Simi anywhere not until you've told me what you think you're doing. This is a primary school, and until you explain who you are and give me an account of your business here, and your relation to this child, I consider you are trespassing.' She was very controlled, though her heart was jack-hammering inside her. It was the start of the scholastic year, she would explain later, so she didn't know much yet about the family; she only remembered her interview with the parents because the man was there and had a job. He was a telecommunications engineer, who'd moved into the estate recently from somewhere up north. They were anxious for their youngest child, who they said was shy, and they'd clearly dressed carefully for the meeting with his future head teacher.

The man said to her, 'His brother knows what my business is.'

Then Sally saw his right arm move, and the hunter's knife, with a thick curved blade. He was holding it to the boy's head, under his chin.

'Get out of the way.'

'Don't hurt him!' cried Kate Daiges. She paused, spoke quietly, slowly. 'Please give me that, now.' They were all at the Girls' gate in a tangle; they were determined to stop him, although they realised, afterwards, as everyone kept telling them, that it would have been best to call the police and then let them deal with the matter; they shouldn't have intervened; none of them should have played the hero, not Kate, not Kim. But as it was, in that struggle to prevent Simi's capture, Kim tackled his assailant, seizing him by the arm wielding the knife, and throwing his own weight back on his heels. There wasn't any way of grabbing the boy, everybody agreed later, and so Kim must have thought, they worked it out, that he could pull the knife away from the boy's neck and force the man to drop him. But Kim's slight build met the bigger man's bulk as he lunged to get past them with his quarry and out into the street to his car – that green souped-up saloon that was later found abandoned after his getaway – and in the collision, the hunter's knife twisted. It entered Kim's lower abdomen, the doctors reported, at an acute angle and plunged in up to the hilt, slicing a mortal wound into his liver.

Simi hit the ground, and so at first, when his abductor had sprinted off, leaving him behind, with blood spurting from his nose, and his eyes and mouth round Os of terror, the head and the others paid attention to the fallen boy and to the kids who were clustered around by now, some of them crying and shrieking and wetting themselves and some of them giggling. It was essential to bring order to the situation; when the police arrived, in their bawling cars with their yammering lights, the children grew demented with excitement, and in all this commotion, Kim was slumped on all fours head down like a deaf-and-dumb animal trying to graze the tarmac. The head was issuing instructions to end the break and get the children calmly back in the classrooms, Sally was opening the First Aid box she'd fetched and was staunching Simi's nosebleed; when the paramedics arrived, one of them spotted Kim, who was trying to get up. But getting up from all fours and standing up straight was proving far harder than he expected.

At first there was no pain; the blade slipped through so sharply that Kim only gasped at the impact. But in the ambulance they gave him a shot of something because the agony was coming on. There were so many questions he wanted to put, about the new boy Simi and Simi's family, and why what happened happened; there were several urgent messages he wanted to send about it so that they – Hetty and Gramercy – should both hear the news from him, not from anyone else; there was the pressing business of the Bundle and the celebrations and the HSWU – what would happen to it all without his hand on the mouse, at the cursor? But Kim was alone in the screaming vehicle except for the paramedics, who were applying things to him, dangling bladders with cords inserted into his arm, and a diver's mask to his face, and he found his tongue was too swollen in his mouth to speak. The middle part of his vision was fiery black, the edges flaring sulphurous; he'd like to lift the big blot in the centre like a flap or a door and look behind it, for something lay buried under similar noise and darkness, something that pointed another kind of blade into his gut. But the memory of what was once lost to him and never found – if that's what it was – was spooling free, falling off the edges of his mind, into that crammed, vital, populous ether all around, where fibre optics trembled and swayed like sea anemones as they strained to capture the floating knowledge of what was to be, what was to come: the phantom shapes were gliding into the future, and their slipstream was lifting him away.

7

'History Starts With Us'

Hortense was bicycling home from the Museum as she did in fine weather, and she didn't notice the headlines of the evening paper; she only bought it when she travelled home by tube in the winter. Daniel met her at the front door; his fall semester had not started and he had not yet left Enoch. He put a hand on her arm and sat her down; he had heard the news on the radio. He was upset for her, he knew it would be a terrible shock and a blow, and he made her a cup of tea and held her arm. Because she seemed composed enough to be left alone, he went out to buy the evening paper, and then they watched the television news together, and again later, and the following morning.

He said, sympathetically, 'It's the sort of thing that happens where I teach. Not here, you'd never expect it over here.'

'Maybe such things are catching,' said Hetty. She was grateful to Daniel that she could grieve without him asking questions.

During the immediate aftermath of the murder at Cantelowes Primary, the evil of the abductor and murderer concentrated an outraged public's attention. The fizzing, potassium-carbon mix of children's sanctuary, laddish predator and cold-blooded killer, broad daylight, hunting knife, baseball cap, souped-up car, blaring music, excited explosions of fury: against television (violence of), government employment policies (young men with nothing to do), pop culture influences (violence of), video nasties, video games and couch potatoes (young men with nothing to do), weapon licensing laws (young men with nothing else to do), feminism and single mothers (young men with nothing to do and no one to fuck) and pop music of every kind, but

384

especially techno dance bands (young men doing something wrong, and taking drugs with it).

Because so many witnessed the incident and before, and were certain they could pick him out at two hundred yards in any identity parade, because he was caught full face by the CCTV camera over the Girls' gate, because he'd dropped his baseball cap in the struggle and there was follicle fluff caught in the rim from which the laboratories could construct his DNA profile, because his fingerprints were all over the virulent green saloon, which was unmistakably seen here, there, until it was found abandoned the following week in a side street to the south of the city, police and detectives issued numerous confident bulletins that soon, the killer would be traced. But his motive continued to elude enquiries, and he himself to escape pursuit.

Hetty rang Gramercy from the Museum the next day; she desperately needed to speak to someone with whom she didn't have to pretend mere professional acquaintance with Kim. Now that Kim was dead, they were able to talk of him, together, when before they had handled each other carefully on his score. Now Gramercy would ask Hetty, 'And did you go to bed with him?' and Hetty would say, 'No,' looking back at her, to which Gramercy responded, 'No, no, it wasn't like that.' Neither woman believed the other, though both were relieved. The question hovered; it was a connection between them, for they had shared a longing for something Kim had brought to them.

They talked about the reasons, or rather the non-reasons for his death.

'This journo thinks it's all due to racist feuds, that makes sense, doesn't it?' cried Gramercy. For the man in the puffer jacket was presumed to have arisen from the city's eastern marshes, like a chemical whiff out of estuarian contaminated mud. They followed the possibilities:

Did that reference to 'his brother' reveal a local vendetta about respect and disrespect?

Was this brother sleeping with the killer's sister? With his mother? With his wife?

Investigations yielded no clues: Simi's brother was fifteen, it turned out. 'That boy – he's like a St Bernard puppy, all gangling limbs and huge feet he doesn't know where to put . . .'

'Not exactly a heart-throb, is he?' said Hetty, agreeing with Gramercy, for Simi's 'brother' simply didn't fit the picture of a precocious, super-cool, testosterone-enriched teenage gangsta who might go around dishonouring estuarian menfolk by giving their women a good time.

'His parents are the kind who want him to do his homework,' added Gramercy. 'That's what this paper says, and he even has extra music lessons at weekends with one of the ten thousand fucking lottery-funded brass bands.'

'You never can tell, I suppose,' said Hetty, 'but it makes no sense.'

So, was it an underworld rite of passage? A male dare, an initiation test to show how hard the killer was, how he had a right to be One of Us? It seemed such extreme risk-taking, to march out in front of everyone and try and kidnap a child just like that.

Or was it some drug baron's bungled foray into protection racketeering in Cantelowes?

Or was he a paedophile who'd conceived a passion for the child?

Or was it a mistake? Not just Kim's death, but Simi's attempted abduction as well? Some writers thought so. Was Simi the right target at all? The little boy couldn't say how he knew the man. Or even that he knew him. The interviews with the child were conducted carefully, as he was in a profound state of shock, and barely able to speak. 'I saw him coming for me, like I's 'fraid of always,' was all he could give them to go on. But raiders from a dozen cult video films could instil such a fear –

That it was Kim McQuy, the founder of HSWU, who'd died didn't focus media interest in the way the two women expected; or at least not to begin with, and then not for what seemed a long time. Splutters of indignation erupted at first at a schoolteacher's tragic murder, but HSWU was cursorily mentioned, as if Kim's activism almost marred the picture of his fortuitous martyrdom, as if it was inappropriate that the victim should have been a campaigner well known to the police. And nobody seemed to notice, Hetty pointed out, that Kim was a young man too, who warranted rather more attention than his killer and his killer's kind. 'You'd think they'd pay attention to the fact that here we have a hard-working, public-minded, completely vocational young man who's probably around the same age as this thug they're spending all their time on drivelling on about, and they don't seem to have an idea in their head how to write about him. About Kim. They just paint this mimsy picture of him, a boring goodie slaughtered by the oh so much more fascinating forces of darkness.'

But Gramercy decided the muteness around Kim's campaign was part of the conspiracy; that he'd been the victim of a skilful and deliberate plot to put him out of the way. 'He was *assassinated*, Hetty. I see it all now: someone didn't want him around stirring up trouble with his ideas about the new mongrelised non-native state. It could be many people, many different interests behind it. Take a look at those websites urging on hatreds against anyone who speaks up for . . . Listen to this one I found last night: "This is the site you need if you want to publish names and addresses and photographs of the scum that's polluting our streets, our countryside, our homes . . ." Then it goes on, you won't believe this: "Send a trophy – an ear, a hand, any part of the enemy you deal with – to this Box Number and we'll send you a reward."

'It figures, Hetty, doesn't it? The creator of a message that disrupts the fucking fixed, bigoted, complacent status quo is suddenly knifed in broad daylight. Yeah, Kim had made enemies and they were all the right enemies to have. And they're not going to have their way.'

Kim's death could not be left to do nothing, that was her furious resolve at the loss of him. His death was going to mean something, because he meant something; she would fling herself, with all the force of her media clout and her contacts, with the seduction of her frayed, urgent, hoarse whispering and keenings, into making him live on.

August Farrell, the poet, sent a letter to every member of the workshop in cultural identities, including Gramercy; she rang him back straightaway.

'It's not good,' he said. 'The barrier of silence, the lack of explanation.' Then Rob Chowdury called her; Sanjit May had called him.

Hetty said, 'Conspiracy theories – don't go that way.' But she was staunchly behind the new resolve not to let Kim's murder pass unnoticed and unavenged.

'Even if it was a fucking mistake,' Gramercy hissed at Hetty down the telephone from Fellmoor, 'there's got to be a pattern, a meaning. We're going to find it, we're going to make it come out.'

August added, 'Let's make a noise, come on, let's do it. Let's see some justice done. I'm angry now. I didn't much like Kim when he was alive – too squeaky clean for me. But this is . . . this is *horrible*.' He was writing to Noakes, he added. Through HSWU's website, they could muster an e-campaign. Some stories start with a death, not to be cynical about it.

387

Nations sometimes start with a death. Many world religions start with a death. But some deaths inaugurate nothing, they only blot out the brightness of hope, of possibility. That's the usual outcome.

At first this seemed to be the case with Kim: that alive, he had captured attention from many quarters, for a moment here and there. But dead, he'd joined the superfluity of those whose lives mean next to nothing.

'I wonder,' Hetty replied, when Gramercy reported the conversations she was having with Rob, with August; even Sanjit, his rancid take withal, was coming on side. Shareen Ghopil telephoned; she too was indignant, upset, wanted to lend her support: could she become a patron of HSWU? 'We've got to transform this tragedy: it's foul, it's cruel, but maybe, like mud where the lotus grows, it can bear fruit.' She paused. 'I should say rather, like the plane tree, which grows so well in the brickdust and clay here.'

And Hetty thought of the cults of fallen heroes, of dying gods in their mothers' laps, of the founding blood of martyrs: the brutal logic of sacrifice. Would the plot never stop repeating? Would it ever be possible to start again, as Kim had wanted, and delete the old files of history? 'It is ghastly,' she said, quietly, 'and I wish with all my heart that it weren't so. But Kim is dead, and maybe that makes it his story now.'

There were further delays to the installation of the Leto Bundle in its new setting, but HSWU's campaign that the Museum make a very strong statement when the new plans were published won support, to Hetty's surprise, from many of her colleagues, keepers of various collections that had been considered exotic in the past, but were the natural patrimony of groups now rooted in the country. Kim's legacy helped resist the calls to repatriate such treasures to their homelands; there were now larger numbers of some communities in Albion than there were in the territories their ancestors had inhabited far away and long ago.

Hortense was preparing two publications: the booklet, which she was writing, was to appear to coincide with the planned procession of school kids from all over the inner city. Cantelowes Primary was to lead it (after Kim's death, Kate Daiges quickly became a powerful voice in the movement for his recognition). This booklet would be included in a school pack filled with supporting materials, with maps, reproductions of manuscript from the mummy bands, a make-your-own-papyrus kit and various study sheets about the historical background: 'Goods & Services', 'Power & Authority', 'Pleasures and Penalties' and so forth. The annotated catalogue, edited by Hortense, with articles by several other scholars, was planned for the following year. It would be followed, if one of the big remunerative foundations gave a grant, by full facsimiles and translations of the contents of Skipwith. This was a long-term project, but the signs were hopeful.

Gramercy released her anthem, written for Kim, 'History Starts With Us', as a single the Christmas after he died. The song's melody was folksy, with a simple sequence of a repeated phrase that rose to a plangent diminished seventh that made it sound half-ecstatic, half-elegiac – Gramercy was surprised at herself, and worried that it was schmaltzy and commercial, especially when it started selling like no other recording she'd made since her first hit when was nineteen years old. She began working furiously, and an extended version soon followed on a full CD of the same name, with a twenty-four-track backing including wooden flutes and rain-sticks, a tabla solo from a guest musician and other syncretic touches. It won her a nomination on the shortlist for the most prestigious prize in contemporary music, rock and classical.

The forty-five-minute documentary programme about the Leto Bundle was cancelled by the television channel that had promised an arts slot the day of the unveiling, but Taffy did not at all lose heart. 'This issue's building. I can feel it. It's not going to go away now, and we can do better. This is *good* for us. We'll switch from the dead art & archaeology slot to prime time. We're no longer culture, we're news.' The material would be re-edited to tell the powerful story of Kim's tragic short life and high ambitions, as part of the news channel's hard-hitting investigation into the capital's lawlessness, the authorities' loss of grip, and the turbulent undercurrents of hostility that were claiming more and more innocent lives. Kim McQuy, Cantelowes schoolteacher, knifed in the playground by a thug: he was the symbol now. His fate packed so much more value than a sheaf of old manuscripts and a few scattered objects.

8

The Harvest Fair

Phoebe pitched her tent at the fair next to the reconditioned Victorian merry-go-round, where vermilion and gold goats and dogs and horses rose and fell on their barley sugar poles to the whirling music. Over the low entrance she hung a sign, 'Phoebe's Face Painting – £1.00', and then propped up a board with a selection of designs, from spiders' webs to the logos on kids' favourite trainers. On her other side, the stall was selling soil-testing equipment ('Test for contamination!' 'Organic farming at your fingertips!').

The sky was racing with high cumulus; with shining scalloped edges the clouds shadowed the dark heavy haunch of the Nine Maidens behind the school sports field where the Fellmoor Harvest Fair was being held. But it was mild and fine, the lateness of the year indicated only by the length and wetness of the grass and the copper shadows of the bracken and the drift of crimson and lemon leaves from the hawthorns and crab apples in the hedgerows. So Phoebe set out her palette and brushes on the trestle outside the tent; against it she stood up a third, more decorative notice which called out to passing adult revellers:

> map your inner feng shui:
> find the place you feel at home
> image the self you know but lost
> make a chart of your very soul.

Written in spiky letters, blocked out in black ink, the sign gave out a message of a unique, intimate, ancient method of commingling and communication; meanwhile, behind the tent, stood the generator Phoebe was sharing with the merry-go-round; it spluttered along, a ramshackle contraption necessary to sustain her therapeutic enterprise, for Phoebe's inner mapping was hooked up to a reconditioned computer and grinding old printer given her by one of the agencies that had originally helped settle the cluster in Fellmoor.

The tent was an idea Phoebe had come up with for weekends over the summer before she left to take up the place she'd been given at a specialist science college. It gave her a way of following the fairs and camping with her new boyfriend; he was working with a music theatre youth group, the Penny Whistles. But it was also bringing in extra, which she needed to keep towards her move to Enoch that autumn. With her exam predictions, she'd managed to persuade the authorities to delay her repatriation.

So Phoebe was moving away from Fellmoor, where she'd made her home for a longer time than anywhere previously, apart from Tirzah.

Her hair these days was waxed and burnished into curls flat against her head in the latest style, and she had a tiny sapphire crescent between her brows, and was applying the same in stencil to her fingernails, which were varnished in frosted silver. Some children began to come up; they approached cautiously.

'She's fine with kids,' said Phoebe, putting out a hand, with fingers spread to dry, to indicate Lucy, who was lying across the tent flap entrance, her eyes opened, with yellow flares lighting, and her nose twitching. 'She knows when I need protection,' she added, laughing. 'She won't attack *you*.'

The kids shuffled together towards the board where Phoebe had posted the snapshots of faces she'd painted over the summer.

'So, what's it to be?' she called out. 'Butterfly wings or tiger stripes or flower fairy? If that's too soft, what about a witch's wart on your nose ...' she tapped one of the little girls on hers. 'And horns on your forehead? Or I can square you up in football colours ...' But the children were as captivated by Phoebe herself as by her range of patterns, and they were stuck gazing at her as she sat in the autumn sunshine, giving off that faintly radioactive luminescence that hadn't faded altogether since she was given her new skin.

She dipped the little brush back into its sparkling bottle and waved her fingers in the air to dry the nails, in a small mist of acetone fumes, while calling to her small customers that she'd still be a few minutes, but that she'd be open for business soon, and to have their money ready.

By the rostrum in the centre of the field, the Penny Whistles band was striking up, on fiddle and banjo, pipes and tambourine; she could see her new boyfriend, Timmo, in a saucepan helmet over his thick ropes of hair talking to his mate Bolan, the fiddle player. Timmo's costume of tin trays caught the light and flashed – a signal to her. He was laughing and rolling a cigarette, and she could feel, even at a distance, the way the tip of his tongue passed across the paper; she shivered happily at the thought of it. Then he was off, bashing away at the Turk across the field, dinning into his enemy's dustbin lid shield and shouting the lines at the top of his voice, not even trying to choke back his laughter as the band scraped and strummed and banged to keep up the good work of Albion and St George. A third player sprang into the acting area, in red tights, flourishing a garden fork in one hand and a frying pan in the other:

'I am Beelzebub,' he shouted, 'Lord of the flies!'

'Your teeth are black as charcoal,' shouted Timmo, the champion of the civilised world. 'Your breath smells like the devil's arsehole.' But then, as a swipe landed hard, he cried out, 'Steady! 'Ere! Have a care with that,' at the excessive enthusiasm of the attack. Then he obligingly toppled down and lay stretched out on the field.

> '"Where's a maiden pure of heart," came the call.
> "To kiss the gallant knight who's slain
> By the foul fiend's wicked art
> And raise him to his feet again?"'

'Your cue, Gramercy,' nudged TB. They had just arrived.

Gramercy was dressed up, but not for that role. She was to give away the prizes in the raffle. Monica's urging, after Hilda in the post office suggested it to Monica one morning when they'd met in the queue between the revolving pic 'n' mix Candyman sweet drum and the rack of guides to Mystery, Magic and Myth on the Moor. Gramercy had said yes; she was pleased the villagers saw her as one of them. They wanted a local celeb; she was striking out in her new role as a committed campaigner, so she was happy to appear. Or, rather not unhappy to try public speaking, in this new context for her cause, her home patch. So that morning Gramercy and Monica had chosen an unstructured acid lime linen suit, and a hat – or so the designer called it, though it consisted of one curl of some tropical feather pinned to a cherry pink hairband.

TB said, 'You look every inch the lady of the manor.'

Monica groaned, 'That's not what's intended, at all. The message is, Seriously Grown-up Now, but not Posh.'

'But,' said TB, 'that's what the lady of the manor looks like these days.'

'"Send the Fair Sabra to my aid",' cried the prone knight-at-arms.

'Phoebe! Phoebe!' joshed the crowd around him, the Devil and the Turk, who were still stabbing and thrusting with their wooden weapons.

'Can't you see I'm busy?' Phoebe protested, as someone came over to pull her into the play to resurrect the dying hero with a kiss. There was a murmur of laughter as Phoebe was pulled over and bent down reluctantly; she brushed the corpse with her lips on his forehead.

'A real kiss,' cried the crowd. '*That* won't wake him up!'

Phoebe wriggled away from the arms pushing her back towards the dead champion of civilisation and Albion where he lay prostrated, with a beer mug in one hand and the saucepan on his head, but they insisted. Phoebe said, firmly, 'No tongue, Timmo,' as she knelt down and placed her mouth on his; his limbs jerked and he leapt up like Frankenstein's creature galvanised. A full measure was poured into his tankard. He raised it to her: 'The Fair Princess Sabra!' he called out, and downed the drink; for all his swaggering, he was looking at her shyly, wonderingly, as she turned with a laugh and a shake of her gleaming head to go back to the tent and avoid Gramercy; besides, she was there to make some money and the punters were lining up.

A customer for inner feng shui mapping came over from the soil tester's stall. 'So what's this you're up to here then?' he enquired, tapping the sign.

'Two quid and I'll make you a complete map of your inner psyche. A "chromograph". A picture in full colour of your inner personality . . . it's ancient science. Really strong. Try it.'

Inside the tent, a string of fairy lights sparkled, and the computer monitor glowed subaqueously. It felt like a sea cave, secret and intimate, and she started on her patter to the soft pulse of a tape of wooden flutes and gongs from a distant rainforest.

*

'You've got this twin inside you,' Phoebe began, conspiratorially. 'And when you were born you were together, you were one, but then, soon after, you lost contact – you were split, you forgot each other.'

Half-dubious, half-excited, the soil tester smiled, 'Yeah, I've always felt something like that. How d'you know?'

Sometimes one of her subjects would interrupt her, with a torrent of detail about all the premonitions and sensations of déjà vu that he or she'd experienced, and Phoebe would nod, and say, 'Yes, that's the sign of the other you that knows stuff the first you doesn't.'

'I thought that story of the lost twin', the soil tester went on, 'was about love – about looking for your lost half all your life until you're at last reconciled – twin souls, soul mates.'

'Yeah,' Phoebe answered. 'It's usually told as a love story. But I think it's more than that . . .'

'More!'

'Yeah, more! Love isn't everything, you know. Leastways, not that kind of love.'

'So what do I do?'

'You find your twin inside – the real you that's gone missing. Here, sit down, that's right, in front of me.'

Phoebe settled herself at the keyboard of her computer.

'Now I ask you some simple questions and when you answer, you get to pick a colour from one of the colour wheels there. Then I feed your choice into the computer.

'When you think of the house where you were a child, what colour do you see?'

'Blue, deep blue . . .'

'Which blue – choose—' She pointed to the colours on the screen. He chose, 'Ultramarine.'

'That's good!'

'Now, think of the food you liked best when you were a child – what colour comes up?'

'I don't know—'

'Spin, then. Choose one of the dials and spin – there!' She'd made colour wheels from paint swatches she'd coaxed out of the local DIY shop.

Eventually, 'a unique chromograph of the inner you' whirred from the printer.

'"The inner you,"' she read, '"is a tall, lean, dark and sensitive extrovert, capable of giving a great deal to others . . . fond of travelling, mushrooms and dogs . . ."'

'But I'm a cat person.'

'Maybe you're not, deep down.'

'It's rubbish!'

'I'm working on it.'

'What a laugh.' He took the printout, shaking his head.

In the course of the afternoon, Phoebe painted a clown, a pirate, an endangered species of bat, a yeti, a marquise, a seal, a zebra and the colours of the Premier League's top football team. She issued about half the permutations of inner yous she'd so far programmed into her machine; and the jam jar of coins was nearly full for the third time (she put the notes away).

Phoebe heard Gramercy start speaking; her voice came in fits and starts across the field, through the rackety music from the merry-go-round: she was thanking a list of benefactors, praising the organisers.

She'll have to practise if she's going into politics, thought Phoebe. She should stick to singing.

'. . . I'm more used to writing songs,' Gramercy began, as if on cue 'but I've got something I want to say to you, now.

'I came here from Enoch, as you all know, but I feel, if you'll let me say this, part of the scenery. And I love it here. People are doing things here the way they've done them since forever. But they're – we're – also doing different things: I write world music, folk rock, whatever you call it, it's made from sounds from all over the planet. Patrick in there—' Gramercy tossed her head towards the Crafts Tent, '– we were just talking about his dulcimers and his zithers. He's bringing you sounds and the instruments that played them from far away and long ago. But they're here, now, and they're different when they're played by us, for us, in this time that's ours.

'We're none of us the real thing, we're all of us mixed up and we have to take form here there and everywhere, we have to question the past in order to make ourselves a new future. That's what my friend Kim used to argue . . .'

The crowd was moving around, buying ice creams and chocolate flakes from Donato's purring van, and India Pale Ale and Fellmoor draught beer from the Bar Tent, children were lolling on the grass under their parents' legs, or sizing up the form of the ferrets in their cages for the ferret races down drainpipes laid out in a pen. There was a murmur or two as Gramercy's voice came and went over the PA system rigged up in the field, but mostly the inattention was good-natured. Back in the tent with another customer for inner mapping, Phoebe could no longer catch the words clearly.

'What I'm trying to say,' Gramercy went on, 'is there's no ethnicity that's clean. Nowhere, and certainly not in this country.' She took a breath. 'You remember the refugee cluster in the town? They were deported, mostly. Back to the hell many of them had fled. Some stayed. Some hang around waiting for the tribunals to decide.' Phoebe would not be pleased if she singled her out, so she left it vague. 'The national policy's all over the place, causing deep damage to people – some of them children – who deserve better.

'I want to ask you to help me do something about it . . .' She could see on the dais beside her the chairman of the Festival Committee looking anxious beneath her summery smiles.

She looked at her notes, scattered on the paper like a sketch for a song, and rushed on, 'In the north, yellow butterflies started turning black and grey in the last century, to match the industrial pollution. Nature knows about change. And we do, too. There's even a herd of ostriches in the next village now – you all know that! Look at the things you're wearing: they've come from everywhere. But we haven't lost connection to tradition. We're still recognisable, to ourselves and to others. Tradition's in play with the present and with the future and with things faraway from us as well as near. And you can't have everything moving globally – goods, information, music – without people moving too.

'You can see the process in the garden plants that were on sale in the tent (All Sold Out now!): they've been thinned out from overflowing beds, swelled by all the wet summers we've been having. They're going to circulate, cross-pollinate, settle elsewhere. There are oriental yellow poppies in our hedgerows – and Himalayan balsam along our streams.

And then there's buddleia – the butterfly tree – which will seed and put down roots – anywhere.'

And Gramercy remembered Kim, looking at the shrub flourishing on urban wasteland.

'All this is just to say to you – thank you for welcoming me to your festival and asking me to speak. If you're interested in joining my campaign – we've brought the literature. Just come up and talk to me – or to Monica.'

But the festival crowd wanted to meet Gramercy more than take her HSWU leaflets; still, she felt better. She'd spoken, rather than sung, in public, about what she felt, what concerned her, and it made her feel loyal and connected, through Kim and his legacy, to something vital.

After she'd met a few of the audience, and signed a CD and a tape or two, she looked around for Phoebe.

In the tent Phoebe could hear the festival prizes being announced by a bass-voiced member of the Fair Committee as Gramercy picked the tickets out of a hat: 'A ride with the local firemen after a guided tour of the station – No. 23. Anyone have No. 23? ... A basket of organic vegetables – a free perm or tinting courtesy of Big Hair in the county capital – a £10 voucher for the local supermarket – a bottle of wine – a pot of homemade blackberry jam courtesy of Jenny Dimples' Café—'

As the event wound down, Phoebe began tidying up inside the tent, boxing up the equipment. She must find the money for a colour printer, she was thinking. But it was the cost of the cartridges that was the real problem. As she came out of the tent, her arms full of gear, Gramercy was standing a little way off, looking at the sign for inner mapping with TB beside her. He left with a low wave as soon as Phoebe appeared.

'Phoebe, it's been ages,' Gramercy came towards her over the grass, crookedly, on account of her hobbling shoes. She peered under her feather through the flap. 'This looks good.'

'Here!' said Phoebe, calling to Lucy who'd risen to her feet and was pushing her nose up between Gramercy's knees.

Gramercy gave a nervous laugh, and gestured the wolf away. 'Haven't you heard anything?'

Phoebe scowled; then pushed her chin out. 'I knew you were going to ask me, everyone keeps asking me. No, I haven't seen or heard anything from Mum. And I don't expect to.'

'I thought she'd get in touch with you. That she might call or something.' Gramercy paused, and sighed. 'I went to the hearing. I went twice, Phoebe. I did my best.'

'I know what you did. I'm aware of it. But after that Kim fellow died, Mum was so cut up, she was bonkers. She is bonkers. She said if it wasn't my brother, she was going off looking for him. Now I was doing all right. That's all I know,' Phoebe paused. 'She always loved him best, you see. It's simple.'

'Don't talk like that.'

'I know what she did for me, of course I do.'

'Don't get all edgy now. I wasn't saying anything.'

'No? Huh. You think I should've been able to hold her back.'

'No I don't. You're her daughter, not her keeper. But how, how's it possible for somebody just to disappear like that?'

'Happens all the time,' said Phoebe. She paused, hooked her thumbs into the belt of her jeans. 'I know you helped. I know what you made happen. But nobody could help her. She's no use, that's what they think, you see.'

'You really don't know where she is? You don't have to tell me. I just want to know she's okay. No pressure. I'm not coming after her.'

'Mum pestered me to find out about Kim – she was dead certain he was – well, my twin. But I never got the right feeling about him. And Phoebus is my mirror, you know.' She fingered the whorl of hair behind her right ear. 'It was Mum's fantasy, that he was doing so fabulously and everything was working out, that she'd done the right thing by us.' She paused. 'Mum wanted me to get the autopsy report.' Phoebe pulled her thumbs from her belt and pulled down the waistband. 'He'd have had no navel, see. Like me.

'It took me a while, but even the autopsy stuff wasn't clear – said, knife wound in area of navel, penetration six inches, pierced the liver, cause of death – that doesn't tell you if he had a navel or not.

'Anyhow, I found lots of sites where you can look for your relatives – and I gave some of the stuff to Mum. Though I told her that it's really up to Phoebus to look for us, and maybe he doesn't want to.' She paused and looked straight at Gramercy. 'I wish I'd met Kim at least one time – I saw him on the telly once or twice. But in person, I'd have known, twins always know. It was terrible to start with, after we were separated and I still feel strange now – but I've felt cut off from him for years.' Her bright head rose sharply. 'Yess! Mum will find him. That's what'll happen. And they'll come back here and find us – me and . . .'

'I knew Kim,' said Gramercy. 'He was my friend. He was special, I know it's a cliché. He was my soulmate. Nellie was wrong to see his death as a failure – it was horrible, of course it was. But in so many ways it gave HSWU what we needed. You think that's cynical. But Kim himself would be really pleased at what's happening. Not that he's become a hero. But that his death's waking people up to issues that they hadn't wanted to face before. I wish you'd join us, Bebe—' she faltered at the old, pet name she'd heard Nellie use sometimes, and her eyes filled. 'The movement's doing really well: we've got an office, a database, hundreds of members mobilising protest in the key areas, and the government's changing its tune. Kim's the necessary hero. I wish it wasn't so. I wish he was alive, but he's the founding martyr, as Hetty puts it. The new history. Starting with him.'

Phoebe softened a little, at Gramercy's evident emotion. 'Sometimes I wake up in the night,' she began, 'or I turn around in the street because I'm hearing Mum's voice again. Sometimes I see her in big landscapes, against huge skies, forging her way ahead, purposefully – keeping going, the way she always did. She's indestructible.'

Gramercy shivered, and shook her head. 'No. Nobody's indestructible.'

'I thought there was time – time for everything for all of us,' Gramercy went on quietly. 'There seemed to be so much ahead of Kim—' She broke off. 'God, was I angry, was I fucking angry, I was, when your Mum just took off and didn't explain. Didn't even leave a note. When I'd just paid those socking bills for hundreds of pounds for her fucking teeth to be fixed and – never mind.'

'I think it was because she couldn't face you to say goodbye. She felt she was letting you down. She was always on about not wanting to let you down.'

Gramercy shook her head again.

'So what's all this, then?' she asked, keeping her dark glasses on as she ducked into the tent, so Phoebe couldn't see her screwing up her eyes.

It was quiet and dark and underwatery green inside and smelled of trampled grass. She was in the country, this was the heart of the country, the heartland, the depths, the core of the land, dark, high Fellmoor:

people doing things the way they'd done them since for ever, and the past was still a safe place, to which everyone belonged.

She followed through the shadows of her dark lenses the small silvery phantom Phoebe presented as she settled herself in front of the monitor. Gramercy took £2 out of her bead purse; Phoebe didn't look over-enthusiastic, but she didn't baulk completely.

'Go ahead, Bebe darling, tell my fortune,' said Gramercy Poule. 'Can't be worse than what's been happening so far.'

9

Threnody

*you aren't really dead now   you can't be   it can't be   not that   not all
my plans all my hopes come to this after the struggle   when I thought I'd found
you a safe place in Enoch with a family who would bring you up to fit in
Phoebe says I'm dreaming that I don't have to feel like this she says she would
know if you were you   she says she has no sense of your being the one I loved
so   from the beginning I thought I could hold you in my dreams and keep you
safe there   if my thoughts kept concentrated on wishing you well I could weave a
shining indestructible web that would hold you like a cradle first   then a safety
net when you grew   I was paying out a line between you and me in my thoughts
all the time we weren't together you were there at the end of its silk   and you
weren't struggling   but dancing*

*the important point was to be vigilant on your behalf   it was vigilance that
made me give you away   vigilance on Phoebe's account   and on yours   and
the trick of the vigilance was to imagine what might happen   and forestall it*

but this raider in the playground I never thought of that

*now I look back and some of the bitter times are turning sweet   in memory
you used to remind me sometimes of your father   that could hurt   but now
even that doesn't give me pain but a kind of longing again   to fold time
back   to have all of it again   but different*

*they say we are the strays of history and we lick our master's hand because we
don't know better   maybe   but what I feel I feel and I only know the love I
felt even when I was cast off   that is the lot of my past   the story I
lived   and if life was a book I could write it another way   but that isn't
possible with a life   if it's wretched it's still the only one I have   you are its*

core   even if I am a fool and a slave   and can't grasp the full condition of being free

but was it you in my lap when we were abandoned among the tombs? was it you Lycia picked up in her velvet mouth and carried away to the cliffs to safety   from the rushcutters that day? my thoughts could work changes then   I could dream a man into a frog   then

you played with Phoebe on board the Shearwater and the sailors nicknamed you Sunshine for obvious reasons   you sang with Teal on the road to Tirzah   even the first months on Tirzah's streets strike my mind now as happy   you were light and strength to me

or was it you?   but but   you became serious in Enoch   if it was you   Enoch dimmed you

maybe Phoebe is right

but she never was with the one called Kim   she never saw you in the flesh the way I did

she doesn't want you to be you   because she still says we're going to find you   she doesn't want me to have a reason to weep   she wants me to stop grieving   it gets on her nerves

I get on her nerves

I could believe her I can believe her I will believe her

I will look for you again   you must be somewhere here   one day one of the faces will be you again

you will be well   all will be well   we shall be well

EPILOGUE

The ID card portrait, which had been taken for Ella's permit of sojourn, was sent by Gramercy to the *Voice of the Streets*, and appeared in due course on the back page dedicated each week to Missing Persons. Freddie, operating a Polaroid camera in the offices of the Advisory Council, had taken the picture after their representations had first won right of appeal against the decision to deport Ella and Phoebe, and it had been found, with the documents of her whole dossier on the case, on the bus that was carrying Ella to Enoch for a final hearing.

In the picture, her face looked clenched; there was a blaze of something furious in the eyes that seemed madness in that context, beside half a dozen lost souls' blurred family snaps, but may have been the result of a failure of the red-eye switch on the camera.

The notice read:

'Ella Outis, known to her family and friends as "Nellie", has not been seen since September 199– when she left Fellmoor on the coach to travel to Enoch; she had an appointment with a lawyer who was accompanying her to the central tribunal of refugees and asylum seekers for a final hearing. She never arrived for the appointment.

'Ella/Nellie arrived in this country eight years ago from Tirzah; she can speak well in English, and knows several other languages. She was in some distress when she disappeared, so her friends and all those who know her are very anxious. They have attempted to reach her by every means, and there have been unconfirmed sightings of her sleeping rough in different parts of the city. The authorities want her to know that every care and consideration will be shown her and that she does not need worry about facing penalties if she makes herself known again. Her health and safety are their foremost concerns.

'Ella/Nellie is in her early forties, five foot three inches tall, with dark eyes, and mid-length dark hair with some grey in it. She may be wearing glasses.

'If you have seen her, or have information about her state of mind or her whereabouts, please call the Missing Persons National Helpline on the number below. All calls will be treated in strict confidence.'

CHRONOLOGY

Lycania

400–350 BCE Cult site of Leto founded

250–275 CE Tomb carved with bas-relief

c. 325–350 CE 'The Letoniast Version' (papyri in the hand of the Circumflex Scribe)

425–475 CE Cartonnage or face mask made for tomb occupant; linen bands inscribed

620 CE Necropolis buried by landslide

Cadenas-la-Jolie

700 – CE Disputes over territory between Ophiri, Lazuli and others

998 Fortified outpost founded by St Cyriacus; conflict between Ophiri and Lazuli persists

1135 Birth of Cunmar on northern littoral

1165 The Great Siege of Cadenas; definitive victory of Ophiri; Cunmar becomes Vice-Procurator in Cadenas

1175 Ser Matteo and Cunmar make a pact; Leto, aged five, given as pledge

1178 Leto sent to Convent of the Swaddling Bands

1181 Leto returns to the Keep

1184 Leto's wedding; birth of twins – Phoebe and Phoebus; Cunmar deposed and Chrysaor takes over rule of Cadenas; restores Lazuli power

c. 1190 Anon., *Annals of the Convent of the Holy Swaddling Bands*

c. 1200 *Chronicle of Barnabas;* depositions for the *Petitio in Causam Sanctitatis Laetitiae* drawn up to present to Congregation of Rites

c. 1350 The 'Cunmar Romance'

HMS Shearwater

1839–41 Sir Giles Skipwith's excavations in Lycania; transportation of the 'Leto Bundle' to Enoch, deposited in the Royal Museum of Albion

c. 1850 Hereward Meeks, Keeper of Near Eastern Antiquities (1858–76) begins transcribing and cataloguing Misc. Mss. deposited by Sir Giles Skipwith

1859 *Adventures of a Ship-Boy, etc.* published

Tirzah and Albion

1956 Hortense Fernly born

1960 Gerald McQuy marries Araminta St Clair

1963 Gramercy Poule born

1970–75 Civil war in Tirzah

1971 Leto and the twins arrive in Tirzah

c. 1972 McQuys adopt Kim

1975 End of siege and fall of Tirzah; Dr Séverine Martin's promise

1982 Gramercy's hit single 'People Like You'; first album in the charts, 'Freedom Days'

1987 Kim McQuy founds HSWU ('History Starts With Us'); *The Fanfare* brings Phoebe to Enoch for operation

199– Kim McQuy begins job at Cantelowes Primary; demonstrations at National Museum of Albion; Gramercy Poule tours with her band; Hortense Fernly travels, accompanying the Bundle . . .

ACKNOWLEDGEMENTS

I owe more than I can express here to loved ones, to friends and colleagues, and my gratitude goes to all of you, who have opened avenues, offered suggestions, sparked ideas and argument, shown interest, offered encouragement. Above all, Carmen Callil made it possible to begin this novel in the first place; Irène Andreae saw me through to its close. Talking with Nick Groom has been a continuous stimulus, a resource, and a pleasure. Conrad Shawcross has inspired me and inspires me in every way throughout. My thanks, always, to them for everything they do. Alison Samuel, my editor, read different incarnations of the novel with acuity, helpfully tempered by enthusiasm and sympathy; Gill Coleridge has sustained me unfailingly with her considerateness and generosity; Lucy Luck's spirited optimism gave me heart. I would also like to thank Trinity College, Cambridge, for precious time granted to me in 1998 as a Visiting Fellow Commoner. I've drawn on many writers and many sources; but I would like to acknowledge in particular Sophie Cragg for performing playground songs; the late Dom Sylvester Houédard for his translation of Basho; Suniti Namjoshi for that press clipping about a frog massacre; and Roy Kotansky for his unique work deciphering magical gems and amulets.

The author gratefully acknowledges the kind permission of Farrar, Straus & Giroux to quote on page 243 from Elizabeth Bishop, 'The Map', *Complete Poems 1927–1979* (1984).